**Praise for *New York Times* bestselling author
Heather Graham**

"An incredible storyteller."

—*Los Angeles Daily News*

"Graham stands at the top of the romantic
suspense category."

—*Publishers Weekly*

"Graham is a master at world building and her
latest is a thrilling, dark, and deadly tale of
romantic suspense."

—*Booklist*, starred review, on *Haunted Destiny*

**Praise for *New York Times* bestselling author
B.J. Daniels**

"B.J. Daniels is a sharpshooter; her books hit the
target every time."

—#1 *New York Times* bestselling author
Linda Lael Miller

"B.J. Daniels spins an eerie tale with an
appealing, determined heroine in her gothic
When Twilight Comes."

—*RT Book Reviews*

New York Times and *USA TODAY* bestselling author **Heather Graham** has written more than a hundred novels. She's a winner of Romance Writers of America's Lifetime Achievement Award, an International Thriller Writers Silver Bullet Award and, in 2016, the ThrillerMaster award from International Thriller Writers. She is an active member of International Thriller Writers and Mystery Writers of America, and is the founder of The Slush Pile Players, an author band and theatrical group. An avid scuba diver, ballroom dancer and mother of five, she still enjoys her South Florida home, but also loves to travel.

For more information, check out her website, theoriginalheathergraham.com, or find Heather on Facebook.

B.J. Daniels is a *New York Times* and *USA TODAY* bestselling author. She wrote her first book after a career as an award-winning newspaper journalist and author of thirty-seven published short stories. She lives in Montana with her husband, Parker, and three springer spaniels. When not writing, she quilts, boats and plays tennis. Contact her at bjdaniels.com, on Facebook or on Twitter, @bjdanielsauthor.

New York Times **Bestselling Author**

HEATHER GRAHAM

THE PRESENCE

HARLEQUIN® BESTSELLING AUTHOR COLLECTION

ISBN-13: 978-1-335-83471-3

The Presence

Recycling programs for this product may not exist in your area.

This edition published by arrangement with Harlequin Books S.A.

For questions and comments about the quality of this book, please contact us at CustomerService@Harlequin.com.

® and TM are trademarks of Harlequin Enterprises Limited or its corporate affiliates. Trademarks indicated with ® are registered in the United States Patent and Trademark Office, the Canadian Intellectual Property Office and in other countries.

Printed in U.S.A.

CONTENTS

THE PRESENCE

Heather Graham

For Rich Devin, Lance Taubald, Leslie and Leland Burbank, Connie Perry, Jo Carol, Peggy McMillan, Sharon Spiak, Sue-Ellen Wellfonder, Kathryn Falk and Rubin, with much love—and to great memories of streams and castles in Scotland.

Prologue

Nightmares

The scream rose and echoed in the night with a blood-curdling resonance that only the truly young, and truly terrified, could create.

Her parents ran into the room, called by instinct to battle whatever force had brought about such absolute horror in their beloved child.

Yet there was nothing. Nothing but their nine-year-old, standing on the bed, arms locked at her side, fingers curled into fists with a terrible rigidity, as if she had suddenly become an old woman. She was screaming, the sound coming again and again, high, screeching, tearing, like the sound of fingernails dragged down the length of a blackboard.

Both parents looked desperately around the room, then their eyes met.

"Sweetheart, sweetheart!"

Her mother came for her unnoticed and tried to take the girl into her arms, but she was inflexible. The father came forward, calling her name, taking her and then shaking her. Once again, she gave no notice.

Then she went down. She simply crumpled into a heap in the center of the bed. Again the parents looked at one another, then the mother rushed forward, sweeping the girl into her arms, cradling her to her breast. "Sweetie, please, please…!"

Blue eyes, the color of a soft summer sky, opened to hers. They were filled with angelic innocence. The child's head was haloed by her wealth of white-blond hair, and she smiled sleepily at the sight of her mother's face, as if nothing had happened, as if the bone-jarring sounds had never come from her lips.

"Did you have a nightmare?" her mother asked anxiously.

Then a troubled frown knit her brow. "No!" she whispered, and the sky-blue eyes darkened, the fragile little body began to shake.

The mother looked at her husband, shaking her head. "We've got to call the doctor."

"It's two in the morning. She's had a nightmare."

"We need to call someone."

"No," her father said firmly. "We need to tuck her back into bed and discuss it in the morning."

"But—"

"If we call the doctor, we'll be referred to the emergency room. And if we go to the emergency room, we'll sit there for hours, and they'll tell us to take her to a shrink in the morning."

"Donald!"

"It's true, Ellen, and you know it."

Ellen looked down. Her daughter was staring at her with huge eyes, shaking now.

"The police!" she whispered.

"The police?" Ellen asked.

"I saw him, Mommy. I saw what that awful man did to the lady."

"What lady, darling?"

"She was on the street, stopping cars. She had big red hair and a short silver skirt. The man stopped for her in a red car with no top, like Uncle Ted's. She got in with him and he drove and then…and then…"

Donald walked across the room and took hold of his daughter's shoulders. "Stop this! You're lying. You haven't been out of this room!"

Ellen shoved her husband away. "Stop it! She's terrified as it is."

"And she wants us to call the police? Our only child will wind up on the front page of the papers, and if they don't catch this psycho murdering women, he'll come after her! No, Ellen."

"Maybe they can catch him," Ellen suggested softly.

"You have to forget it!" Donald said sternly to his daughter.

She nodded gravely, then shook her head. "I have to tell it!" she whispered.

Ellen seldom argued with Donald. But tonight she had picked her battle.

"When this happens…you have to let her talk."

"No police!" Donald insisted.

"I'll call Adam."

"That shyster!"

"He's no shyster and you know it."

Donald's eyes slid from his wife's to those of his

daughter, which were awash in misery and a fear she shouldn't have to know. "Call the man," he said.

He was very old; that was Toni's first opinion of Adam Harrison. His face was long, his body was thin, and his hair was snow-white. But his eyes were the kindest, most knowing, she had seen in her nine years on earth.

He came to the bedside, took her hand, clasped it firmly between his own and smiled slowly. She had been shaking, but his gentle hold eased the trembling from her, just as it warmed her. He was very special. He understood that she had seen what she had seen without ever leaving the house. And she knew, of course, that it was ridiculous. Such things didn't happen. But it had happened.

She hated it. Loathed it. And she understood her father's concern. It was a very bad thing. People would make fun of her—or they would want to use her ability for their own purposes.

"So, tell me about it," Adam said to her, after he had explained that he was an old friend of her mother's family.

"I saw it," she whispered, and the shaking began again.

"Tell me what you saw."

"There was a woman on the street, trying to get cars to stop. One stopped. She leaned into it, and she started to talk to the man about money. Then she went with him. She got into the car. It was red."

"It was a convertible?"

"Like Uncle Ted's car."

"Right," he said, squeezing her hand again.

Her voice became a monotone. She repeated some

of the conversation between the man and woman word for word. Perspiration broke out on her body as she felt the woman's growing sense of fear. She couldn't breathe as she described the knife. She was drenched with sweat at the end, and cold. So cold. He talked to her and assured her.

Then the police arrived, called by neighbors who were awakened by her screams.

The two officers flanked her bed and started firing questions at her, demanding to know what she had seen—or what had been done to her.

Despite the terror, she felt all right because of Adam. But then huge tears formed in her eyes. "Nothing, nothing! I saw nothing!"

Adam rose, his voice firm and filled with such authority that even the men with their guns and badges listened to him. They left the room. Adam winked at her and went with the men, telling her that he would talk to them.

A month later, the police came back to the house. She could hear her father angrily telling them that they had to leave her alone. But despite his argument, she found herself facing a police officer who kept asking her terrible questions. He described horrific things, his voice growing rougher and rougher. Somewhere in there, she closed off. She couldn't bear to hear him anymore.

She woke up in the hospital. Her mother was by her side, tears in her eyes. She was radiant with happiness when Toni blinked and looked at her.

Her father was there, too. He kissed Toni on the forehead, then, choking, left the room. An older man in the back stepped up to her.

"You're going to move," he told her cheerfully. "Out to the country. The police will never come again."

"The police?"

"Yes, don't you remember?"

She shook her head. "I'm sorry… I'm really sorry. I don't know who you are."

He arched a fuzzy white brow, staring at her. "I'm Adam. Adam Harrison. You really don't remember me?"

She studied him gravely and shook her head. She was lying, but he just smiled, and his smile was warm and comforting.

"Just remember my name. And if you ever need me, call me. If you dream again, or have a nightmare."

"I don't have nightmares," she told him.

"If you dream…"

"Oh, I'm certain I don't have dreams. I don't let myself have dreams. Some people can do that, you know."

His smile deepened. "Yes, actually, I do know. Well, Miss Antoinette Fraser, it has been an incredible pleasure to see you, and to see you looking so well. If you ever just want to say hello, remember my name."

She gripped his hand suddenly. "I will always remember your name," she told him.

"If you ever need me, I'll be there," he promised.

He brushed a kiss on her forehead, and then he was gone. Just a whisper of his aftershave remained.

Soon her memory faded and the whole thing became vague, not real. There was just a remnant in her mind, no more than that whisper of aftershave when someone was really, truly gone.

Chapter 1

"Imagine, if you will, the great laird of the castle! The MacNiall himself, famed and infamous, a figure to draw both fear and awe. Ahead of his time, he stood nearly six foot three, hair as black as pitch, eyes the silver gray of steel, capable of glinting like the devil's own. Some say those orbs burned with the very fires of hell. His arms were knotted with muscle from the wielding of his sword, his ax, whatever weapon fell his way in the midst of battle. It was said that he could take down a dozen men in the opening moments of a fray. Passionate for king and country, he would fight any man who spoke to wrong either. Passionate in love, his anger could rage just as deeply against a woman, if he felt himself betrayed.

"Imagine, then, being his beloved, his bride, his wife, burdened with the most treacherous of advisors, men determined to find a way to bring down a man so great in

battle, to further their own aims. Imagine her knowing
that she had been betrayed, maligned, and that her laird
husband was returning from the blood of the battlefield…
intent upon a greater revenge. There…there! He would
come to the great doors that gave entry to the hall."

Toni stood at the railing of the second-floor balcony,
pointing to the massive double doors, high on sheer
exhilaration. A crowd of awed tourists were gathered
below her in the great hall entry, staring up at her.

This was really too good, far more than they had imagined they could accomplish when she and the others had
set their wild dream about procuring a run-down castle
and creating a very special entertainment complex out
of it. So far, David and Kevin had rallied their crowd
magnificently by playing a pair of hapless minstrels in
the reign of James IV, when the current structure had
been built upon the Norman bastion begun by thirteenth-
century kings. Ryan and Gina had done a fantastic job
playing the daughter of the laird and the stable boy with
whom she had fallen tragically in love during the reign
of Mary, Queen of Scots. Thayer—the wild card in their
sextet—had proved himself more than capable of por-
traying a laird accused of witchcraft in the time of James
VI. And they had all run around as kitchen wenches or
servants for one another.

Beyond a doubt, the crowd was into the show. Below,
they waited. So Toni continued.

"Alas, it was right here, as I stand now, where, tragically, Annalise met with her husband, that great man
of inestimable prowess and, unfortunately, jealousy and
rage. Believing the stories regarding his beautiful wife,
he curled his fingers around her throat, squeezing the
life from her before tossing her callously down the stair-
case in a fit of uncontrollable wrath. Since he was the

great laird of the castle, his servants helped him dispose of the body, and Laird MacNiall went on to fight another day. He was, however, to receive his own just rewards. Though he had bested many, and countless troops had been slaughtered beneath his leadership, Cromwell was to seize the man at last. He received the ultimate punishment: being castrated, disemboweled, decapitated, dismembered and dispersed. His pieces were then gathered by his descendants, and he now lies buried deep within the crypt of these very stone walls! Ah, yes, his mortal remains are buried here. But it's said that his soul wanders, not just around the castle itself, but through the surrounding hills and braes, and he is known to haunt the forest just beyond the ruins of the old town wall."

Her words were met with a collective "Ooh!" that was most encouraging. Toni flashed a smile to Gina, hovering in a room off the second-floor landing, watching. Any minute now, Ryan would come riding into the main hall.

"They say he roams his lands still, hunting for his wife, anxious to see her face, filled with love and lust… and a fury seizes him each time he would hold her in all her spectral beauty!"

She glanced at Gina, frowning. Ryan should have made his appearance by now.

Gina looked at her and shrugged, then lifted her hands, indicating that Toni should finish up, however she could manage.

"That night the great laird of the castle came bursting through his doorway!"

As if on cue, a fantastic flash of lightning suddenly tore through the darkness, followed by a massive roar of thunder.

The doors burst open…and a man appeared.

Toni inhaled on a sharp breath of disbelief. It wasn't Ryan. The man was on the biggest black stallion Toni had ever seen. She thought that the prancing animal might breathe fire at any instant.

And the rider… He was damp from the rain, but his hair appeared to be as black as pitch. And though he was atop the giant horse, he appeared massive himself. If his eyes had glowed like the devil's just then, she didn't think that she could have been any more surprised. He was the great Laird Bruce MacNiall, the warrior in mantle and kilt, just as she had described him.

Again lightning flashed and thunder rolled and roared.

Toni let out a startled scream, and a collective squawking rose from the audience.

Perfect! Toni thought. It was time to announce that the laird had come home, in all his glory—and wrath. But for once in her life, words failed her. Like the others, she was mesmerized, watching, afraid to breathe, thinking she must have conjured a ghost.

He dismounted from the stallion with such ease that anyone there with a question would still be in the dark as to what a Scotsman wore beneath his kilt. He looked around the great hall with dark, narrowed eyes and a jaw of concrete.

"Who is running this charade?" he demanded harshly.

The spellbound crowd still seemed to believe it was all part of an act.

David, down with the crowd, jumped to life. "The lady at the top of the stairs!" he informed the stranger, pointing up to Toni. Then he did his best to vacate the place as quickly as possible. "And there we are, at the end of the show. Ladies, gentlemen, thank you for your attention!" he said.

The crowd burst into applause, staring at the newcomer as they did so.

The stranger's scowl deepened.

"Thank you again," David said. "And now let's adjourn into the kitchen, where we'll have the promised tea and scones!"

As Toni watched the crowd disappear, she heard Gina whispering frantically to her. "What is it? What the hell...?" She stepped from the bedroom, moving out on the landing. "Is it Ryan? What on earth has he done now?"

"It's not Ryan," Toni murmured beneath her breath. Kevin had followed David and the crowd into the kitchen, but not before looking up the stairs and glaring at her, lifting his hands in a "what the hell...?" motion himself. Thayer must have gone out to help Ryan, since it appeared that Toni and Gina were alone with the irate stranger, who was now slowly striding his way up the stairs.

"Oh, God!" Gina breathed. "You said you made him up!"

"I did!"

"Then who or what is walking up the stairs? Never mind—I can tell you. It's one very angry man."

He was angry? Suddenly Toni, who had been so stunned and awed herself, was angry, as well. Who the hell was he, charging in on them? They had a lease option on the castle, and whatever he might be, Great Britain had laws, and he surely had no right here.

"Hello," she said, determinedly putting ice and strength into her voice. "Can I help you?"

"Can you help me? Aye, that you can!" he snapped.

Now that he was close, she could see that his eyes were gray, a dark stormy gray, right now. "Who in the hell are you people and what in God's name do you think you're doing here?" If his eyes were a storm, his voice was the thunder that cracked through it. He was a Scotsman, definitely—it was clear from the burr of his words— but his clean, crisp enunciation suggested that he had traveled, as well, and spent a great deal of time in other places.

"Who are we?" she said, frowning. "Who are you?"

"Bruce MacNiall, owner of this castle."

"The MacNialls are all dead," she told him.

"Since I am a MacNiall, I beg to differ."

Behind her, Gina groaned. "Oh, Lord! It sounds as if there's been some terrible mistake."

"There's been no mistake," Toni said softly to Gina. "There can't be!" To the stranger who had arrived in perfect theatrical form, she said, "We have a rental agreement, a lease-purchase agreement, as a matter of fact."

"Whatever you have is not legal," he said crisply.

"We honestly believe that it is." Gina stepped forward, smiling ruefully and trying the polite approach. Gina was petite, with a wealth of lustrous brown hair, and green eyes that surveyed the world with intelligence and an easy courtesy. Her forte was public relations. "This," she continued politely, "is Antoinette Fraser. Toni. I'm Gina Browne. Honestly, sir, we've gone through all the right steps and paid a handsome sum for the right to be here. We're registered and have a license as tour guides. I can't begin to imagine why you've suddenly burst in here tonight. The people in the village, including the constable, know that we're here. If there was a problem, why are you appearing only now?"

"I have been traveling. The constable didn't throw you out because he hadn't had a chance to talk to me, and find out if, for some reason, I had decided to rent the place. I just arrived back in the village this evening, and learned that my home was being turned into the Pete Rose Circus!"

"Oh! Really!" Gina sucked in air.

Toni looked at her, smiling grimly. Gina looked stricken, and certainly she felt the depth of the insult herself. "I quite enjoy the Pete Rose Circus," she said. Arms crossed over her chest, she turned back to the stranger. "Look, we're truly baffled by your sudden appearance, especially since we didn't know that you existed and because we do have legal forms. Perhaps people here keep their own counsel, but surely someone might have mentioned you to us! And…we walked right in here, without even having to acquire keys—we found a set on a hook by the door. Perhaps you're out of town too frequently, Mr. MacNiall."

"It's Laird MacNiall," he said, his tone dry. "And I could hardly expect to come home and find—"

"Aha!"

The roar of the word sounded along with a new clatter of hoofbeats, cutting off Laird MacNiall. Ryan Browne had at last arrived, sword drawn, risen in his stirrups. He realized almost immediately that the room was emptied of people and filled with a huge black horse. He reined in swiftly, his eyes following the steps until they fell upon the upper landing, and he stared at the three of them.

"The great laird returns to his castle?" he said weakly. "Where he finds…?"

The black stallion let out a wicked-sounding snicker. Ryan's horse, their handsome roan named Wallace, shied. "Another great laird with a bigger horse! Okay… This great laird is leaving," he said quickly, getting the gelding under control. "But I'll be back," he promised.

He turned and left, the roan clattering its way out of the castle.

"I really will have the lot of you arrested," Bruce MacNiall said. It was more like a growl than a spoken comment. "How dare you burst in here, mocking Scottish history? Americans!"

"Excuse me, I think that we've explained all this. We have a lease, a legal document," Toni said. "And we're not mocking Scottish history, we're here because we love it."

"Listen to me one more time, you addled woman! I own the place, and it has never been for sale or lease!"

It simply couldn't be, yet his irritated aggression was so vehement that Toni found herself suddenly afraid that something could be really wrong. Gina looked stunned, and equally worried.

Toni stepped up to the plate, ready to do battle. "You're wrong," she informed the man claiming to be the living MacNiall. "We have an agreement."

"The hell you do!"

"We should have you arrested, since you're doing your best to destroy the tour," Toni told him, aware that she was taking a slight step back despite her words. "And you've certainly no right to call me an addled woman. We have papers that prove we have leased the place. Now you say that *you* own it! It was filthy and in horrid disrepair. It was obvious that no one had given the least care to this place in years. We've been through here repairing electrical connections, replacing wires, plastering and painting—just to keep the place from falling apart completely. The first day, David and Kevin shored up the front wall. We've worked our asses off to make it livable."

"I told you, I've been out of the country."

"All of your life?" she said sharply. "Because if not, you should be ashamed. This place is incredible. If I had owned it since birth, I'd have never let it come to this!"

"My castle is not your concern," he said icily.

"But it is, because for the next year—at the least— it's *our* castle," she said tightly.

"No, it is not," he said. "I own the place and I did *not* lease it!"

Toni was forced to feel another moment's unease. There was definite conviction in his voice.

"I can see that you've put time and work into the place," he told Gina. "For that, I'm sorry. But the place is not now, nor ever will be, for rent. I would have stopped you, but as I said, I've been out of the country."

"Well, that's just amazing," Toni said, stepping in before Gina could reply. "In this day and age, one would have thought that someone in this little village might have known where you were and called you, or at least said something about you when we were buying the paint and materials!"

"Right!" Gina said.

At that moment Ryan came striding back into the great hall. Being Ryan, however, he paused. "Great horse!" he said, staring at the stallion. "What a beautiful animal."

Bruce MacNiall started back down the stairs. "He's a mix of long and careful breeding."

"Draft horse…look at the muscle and the size! And there's Arab in the history somewhere. He's almost got the legs of an American Thoroughbred," Ryan said.

Bruce MacNiall kept walking down, talking to Ryan

as easily as if they were friends meeting at a horse show. "Good eye," he commented. "The mare was a cross between an American Thoroughbred and one of our own stallions. He is something. He's got the strength of a Belgian, the grace of an Arab and the dignity of a Thoroughbred."

"Majestic," Ryan agreed.

Toni and Gina stared at one another, then followed MacNiall's path down the stairs. The men were both standing at the stallion's head, admiring the length of his neck and the wide set of his very large eyes.

"Excuse me, but we have a problem here," Toni reminded them.

"Yeah, what's up?" Ryan said. He flashed a smile. "Has Toni's invention come to life? I'm Ryan, by the way. Ryan Browne. Gina's husband."

"Pleasure, but I'm afraid that I've been very much alive and well for quite some time," MacNiall said, staring at Toni. She seemed to be the one capable of really drawing his wrath.

Ryan cast his brown gaze toward Toni worriedly. "Didn't the rental company tell us that the family had died out?"

"They did," Toni said.

"They lied," MacNiall informed them. He stared straight at Toni. "Either that or you're lying." His words didn't seem to include the others, only her. "And you are all trespassing. Which you should know, because it's obvious that you've gotten hold of family history *and* local lore and rumor."

"I did not lie!" she protested indignantly.

"Well then, you 'imagined' an incredible facsimile of the truth," he said.

She shook her head. "I knew that a family named

MacNiall had owned the place, but that was it. Bruce is a common enough Scottish name. Since we have been working our butts off here, we didn't really get a chance to question the community on the past!"

"Six-three, pitch-black hair, gray eyes…like the devil's own," Gina murmured, staring at the man, then looking at Toni.

"I swear, I made it all up!" Toni said irritably.

"We do have documents," Ryan said.

Toni bit her lip. Ryan's approach might work better than her own.

"All right, look, maybe you have some kind of documents—an agreement, a lease, whatever. The point is—" he paused to stare at Toni "—no matter what you have, I'm afraid that you've been taken in. Unfortunately, it does seem to be something that happens to Americans now and then. They believe in the almighty Internet, and don't really research what they're doing. This is Europe."

He was beyond irritating. Toni looked at Gina. "Imagine that. This is Europe."

"You've been taken, and that's that," MacNiall said flatly to her. "In American? Screwed, Miss Fraser."

Toni stared at the man without blinking, feeling her facial muscles grow tense. "Gina, perhaps you could show the nice man our documents."

"Oh, yes! Of course!" Gina turned and went flying down the hallway.

MacNiall shook his head, looking at her.

"We put so much into this—years of saving!" Ryan said with dismay.

MacNiall wasn't budging. "I'm sorry," he said flatly.

"Everything," Ryan murmured.

"Wait a minute, we have to find out the truth here.

There's no reason we should vacate simply on this man's say-so," Toni stated. "He's claiming that we have no right to be here, but how do we know that he really has a right to be here?" The man had called her a liar. She stared straight at him and smiled sweetly. "There are a lot of penniless gentry running around Europe, as we all know. Maybe *Laird* MacNiall is unaware that government powers have taken control of the property because of nonpayment of taxes or the like?" she suggested.

For a moment, she could well imagine the man strangling her in truth. He did, however, control his temper. His eyes scorned her to the core as he said, "I assure you, that is not the case."

Gina came running back down the hallway, their lease agreement and licenses in hand.

"Look, Mr. MacNiall… *Laird* MacNiall."

Papers fluttered. They all started scooping them up, including MacNiall.

MacNiall righted and studied the documents, shaking his head. "I grant you, they look good. And your licenses and permits appear to be in order. You simply haven't any right to this place because you were taken in by fraud. I'm very sorry about that, but—"

"Bruce?" A sudden shout came from down the stairs. "Everything all right?"

The new voice came from the entryway. Toni saw that the village law had arrived in the form of Constable Jonathan Tavish. They'd met briefly in town. He was a pleasant man in his early thirties, with sandy hair and a beautiful voice. His *R*'s rolled almost hypnotically when he spoke. Though he hadn't mentioned that there was a living descendant of the once great lairds, he had seemed to view their arrival and their plans with worry and skepticism.

Her heart began to sink, and yet, inside, a voice was insisting, *No! This just can't be!*

"Everything is just fine, Jon," Bruce said, eyes coolly set upon Toni once again. "But perhaps you could assure these *nice* people that I am indeed the owner of the property."

"The Laird MacNiall," Tavish told them solemnly. "Owns the castle, half the village and the good Laird above us all knows just what else."

Toni stared at the man incredulously. Now her heart seemed to thump straight downward into the pit of her stomach. The stunned confusion remained, and once again her temper soared.

Toni suddenly found herself furious with the constable. How could the man have let them all do this without saying a word if there might have been a problem? "Constable Tavish, if this is all true, sir, you might have informed us that there was a living MacNiall who rightfully owned the property and wasn't known to rent it out!" Toni said, trying very hard to keep her voice level.

The constable looked at her, grimacing ruefully. "If I've added to your confusion and distress, lass, I am, indeed, sorry. You never suggested to me that you weren't aware that Laird MacNiall existed. And until I saw Bruce, I couldn't be certain that he hadn't rented the property…though I definitely found it a surprise that he might have done so," Tavish said.

A crack of lightning showed them that Tavish had not come alone. Behind him was Eban Douglas, a man who had introduced himself as the jack-of-all-trades for the place. They'd explained that they'd put just about everything they had into the rent on the castle and for the repair materials. He'd seemed very pleased, but then again, he always seemed pleased. He was a small, wizened man with tufts of white hair on his skeletal face. Gina referred to him as Igor, and was convinced that he might have made a fortune in life performing as Riff-Raff for the *Rocky Horror Picture Show.*

He'd actually talked to them a great deal. At times, he'd appeared to help. And never once—in any way, shape or form—had he mentioned that there was a Laird MacNiall who still owned the place.

Despite that—and his rather creepy appearance—he had certainly seemed decent enough. Toni had seen him working about the grounds and had assumed that he was paid by the agency that had rented the castle to them.

A shopkeeper in town had told them that he lived in a little carriage house just beyond the hill in back, a piece of landscape created by the fact that the moat that had surrounded the castle no longer existed.

"You, Eban!" Toni said. "Why didn't *you* tell us about Laird MacNiall?" she demanded.

"Y'didna ask," Eban told her, then grimaced. "I didna know myself—perhap His Lairdship had decided such folks as yerselves might ha been good fer the old place." He shrugged. "After all, y'were doin' a fine job of set-tin' 'er ta rights, that y'were!"

"Well, thank you for that acknowledgment, at least! I think we've been really good for it," Toni said, feel-ing her jaw clench.

"Ah, then, back to the buses!"

David, who had apparently been charming the guests in the massive kitchen, came bursting back into the hall-way, the large group of tourists behind him.

"Now, now!" David said as his group began to splin-ter. "The buses are waiting!" But he had lost control, and their guests began to mingle before leaving, stop-ping by Toni, Gina, Ryan and Bruce. The four of them, including Bruce MacNiall, received glowing compliments for their performances.

"Oh, it was great!" a woman named Milly—from Chicago, if Toni remembered correctly—cooed to Bruce MacNiall. "I mean, it was all just so wonderful. And then you on this magnificent beast here—pure magic! Thank you so very much. I'll never, ever, forget this trip to Scotland. What a dream fulfilled it has been!"

"Thank you, dear," Kevin said, quickly sweeping up behind her to draw her away.

"I loved it!" Milly said.

"Buses are waiting!" Kevin said cheerfully. "Mustn't hold them up!"

"Really!" Milly called to Bruce MacNiall as she was ushered out.

He had the grace to slightly incline his head to her. "I'm delighted that you're enjoying Scotland," he said.

The crowd moved on, passing by the constable and Eban, the tourists chatting and boisterous as they moved out to the courtyard, ready to board their buses.

Thayer, however, was now in the room.

"My cousin! He is a Scotsman!" Toni said. Her words sounded defensive, as though, because Thayer was a Scot, they couldn't possibly be in a mess here.

"A Scotsman, or an American of Scottish descent?" MacNiall queried.

"Glasgow, born and bred," Thayer said, frowning. He stepped forward, offering a hand. "Thayer Fraser, sir. I've overheard just a bit of this. And I'm *really* sorry regarding this and my own confusion. We may well be at your mercy. Toni did the paperwork from the States after finding this rental through the Internet. The agreements went through a rental agency, a corporation. But we had a lawyer—and I saw the ads for the place myself, down in Glasgow."

MacNiall shook his head. Toni once more felt a fierce irritation. Again, the men's club was meeting, and she and Gina were entirely ostracized. MacNiall was decent enough about horses, and give him a fellow Scotsman and he could almost resemble polite.

"There's definitely a problem, I'm afraid."

"Aye, but they been good, Bruce, really good a fixen 'er up!" Eban announced suddenly.

"We really have put a lot of hard work into it," Ryan said.

Apparently the tourists had been loaded back onto their buses. David and Kevin came back into the hall. For a moment, they were all a tableau, at an impasse. David moved up awkwardly. "Laird MacNiall?" he murmured. "David Fulton, and my friend, Kevin Hart. We're only beginning to understand the gist of what went wrong, but, honestly, no group could have put more toil and loving effort into making improvements here. If you'll take some time and look around, you'll see what very real elbow grease has gone into our stay here."

Then, to Toni's amazement, Bruce MacNiall uttered an oath beneath his breath, and made what to him must have been a very generous statement. "All right. It's Friday night. Jon is here with us and can validate who I am, but the legal offices are in town and they won't be open again until Monday morning. Until then, I believe you'll have to stay."

"We'll have to stay because we paid a great deal of money to be here, and we have legal documentation," Toni said stubbornly.

Gina jabbed her with an elbow to the ribs. She winced, realizing that maybe she was pushing it. But she wasn't going to blindly believe this man, or even the local-yokel constable, when she had brought the agreement to an attorney, and he had read over the deal.

"We do have an attorney!" she murmured.

"Solicitor," Thayer murmured to her softly. "We have *solicitors* here."

"I get the feeling he knows what an attorney is," Toni murmured back softly.

Jonathan Tavish cleared his throat. "Ladies and gentlemen, I'm truly sorry now that I didn't try to stop you. As I said, I didn't know for certain that Bruce hadn't decided to rent out the old ancestral place. But I am afraid that someone knew about the castle—and how much Bruce traveled—and took you for a soaking." He cleared his throat and looked at Bruce with an uncomfortable shrug.

"Should I take those papers now? Not much I can do on this till Monday, though. Law enforcement spends the weekends goin' after the dangerous fellows running around out there, I'm afraid. All the law offices are closed."

"We'll keep the papers until Monday," Toni said. Gina stared at her, but the papers were all that they had. She wasn't letting them out of their own keeping.

"Fine," Tavish said. "When you come in Monday, bring all your papers." He cleared his throat. "If you say that everything is in order for the night, Bruce, I'll be going."

Bruce MacNiall inclined his head toward the constable, as if he weren't just the laird here, but world royalty. "Thanks, Jon," he said. "Come Monday morning, we'll get these papers they're talking about into the hands of the proper authorities. Hopefully they'll be able to track down the frauds who soaked them for their money."

"Hopefully," Jonathan Tavish agreed. He gave a smile that seemed to offer some sympathy to the group. "Don't feel too badly. Won't be the first time Americans have been taken in. And it won't be the last. We'll see what we can do."

"Thank you," Thayer said.

Jonathan Tavish gave them all a nod.

"Good night!" Gina called cheerfully.

"And thank you," Kevin added.

"I'll be movin' along, too, then, lest y'be needin' me," Eban Douglas said, looking at Bruce MacNiall.

"I think I can manage, Eban," MacNiall said.

Eban turned and left. He didn't have a hunched back, nor did he limp, but he somehow gave the appearance of both.

"Do you, uh, stay here when you're in town?" Ryan asked politely.

The answer was a little slow. An ironic smile seemed to twitch MacNiall's lips. "With the ancestral home filled with unbelievers? Indeed."

"Want me to see to the horse? I did some work in the stables. He isn't usually there, is he?" Ryan asked. "I only ask because the stables were in serious disrepair, and this fellow is so obviously well tended."

"He was boarded in my absence."

"How long were you gone? Twenty years?" Toni muttered.

Once again Gina jabbed her fiercely in the ribs.

"I'll take him out, bed him down," Ryan offered.

Toni wanted to knock him in the head for the offer, but she knew that he wasn't being subservient. Ryan simply loved horses. And she had to admit that the animal was magnificent.

"Sure," MacNiall said. "Thanks. His name is Shaunessy."

"Shaunessy?" Toni couldn't quite help herself. "Not Thor, Thunder or King?" Gina's third strike against her rib cage nearly caused her to cry out. She winced. "Shaunessy," she said. "Great name."

Ryan came to lead the horse out. "I'll give you a hand!" Kevin offered quickly, and they departed.

"There's tea!" David said suddenly into the awkward silence. "And scones. Great little scones."

"Wow, tea! I'd love tea!" Gina said. "You'd love tea, too, Toni!" Gina grabbed Toni's hand. "And we'd love for Laird MacNiall to join us so we can explain about how and why we rented the place...talk about all the work we've done here, and find out about Laird Mac-Niall, while we're at it?" She looked at him hopefully.

"Since you've been so kind to let us stay while we get to the bottom of this, would you be willing to join us, Lord MacNiall?" Thayer asked.

"Thanks. I had a long flight in today, a lot of business and a long drive, only to find out that the castle had been...inhabited," MacNiall said. "I'll just retire for the night, if you don't mind. Please feel free to enjoy your tea, however. And the hospitality. Until Monday."

"Until Monday?" Toni said, and her reward was a final jab from Gina. This time she protested, staring at Gina. "Ow!"

"Good night!" Gina said, "And thank you."

"Your papers," MacNiall said, handing them back to Gina.

"Thank you," Gina said again. "And thank you for... for letting us stay until Monday. Until this is all straightened out. I don't know where we'd go, especially at this hour."

He inclined his head. "I sympathize with your situation," he said. "Good night, then." He took one long last look at Toni and turned away.

Toni opened her mouth, about to speak, but Gina clamped a hand over her mouth, desperately whispering, "Just say, 'Good night, Laird MacNiall!'"

MacNiall looked back, all six feet three inches of him. His eyes now appeared to be more of a true blue, and as sharp as a summer's sky. Something strange ripped through Toni. She was caught, frozen. She felt as if she knew him, knew the way that he looked at her.

Had known him before.

And would know him again.

A tremor ran down her spine. Ice. Fire. *She had invented him!*

He was just a man, she told herself—irritating, superior and angry that they were in his house.

Not true. If his hair were a little longer, his clothing a bit different, just a bit different...

"Good night," he said.

The ice and fire, and a feeling of foreboding so intense she trembled, became too much, far too intense. She turned herself and hurried down the stairs. Ran.

Yet a voice whispered to her all the while.

You can't run away. You can't run away.

And something even softer, an afterthought.

Not this time...

Interlude

When Cromwell Reigned

From his vantage point, MacNiall could see them, arrayed in all their glittering splendor. The man for whom they fought, the ever self-righteous Cromwell, might preach the simplicity and purity one should seek in life, but when he had his troops arrayed, he saw to it that no matter what their uniform, they appeared in rank, and their weapons shone, as did their shields.

As it always seemed to be with his enemy, they were unaware of how a fight in the Highlands might best be fought. They were coming in their formations. Rank and file. Stop, load, aim, fire. March forward. Stop, load, aim, fire…

Cromwell's troops depended on their superior numbers. And like all leaders before him, Cromwell was ready to sacrifice his fighting man. All in the name of God and the Godliness of their land—or so the great man preached.

MacNiall had his own God, as did the men with whom he fought. For some, it was simply the God that the English did not face. For others, it had to do with pride, for their God ruled the Scottish and Presbyterian church, and had naught to do with an Englishman who would sever the head of his own king.

Others fought because it was their land. Chieftains and clansmen, men who would not be ruled by such a foreigner, men who seldom bowed down to any authority other than their own. Their land was hard and rugged. When the Romans had come, they had built walls to protect their own and to keep out the savages they barely recognized as human. In the many centuries since, the basic heart of the land had changed little. Now, they had another cause—the return of the young Stuart heir and their hatred for their enemy.

And just as they had centuries before, they would fight, using their land as one of their greatest weapons.

MacNiall granted Cromwell one thing—he was a military man. And he was no fool. He had called upon the Irish and the Welsh, who had learned so very well the art of archery. He had called upon men who knew about cannons and the devastating results of gunpowder, shot and ball, when put to the proper use. All these things he knew, and he felt a great superiority in his numbers, in his weapons.

But still, he did not know the Highlands, nor the soul of the Highland men he faced. And today he should have known the tactics the Highlander would use more so than ever. For MacNiall had heard that these troops were being led by a man who had been one of their own, a Scotsman from the base of the savage lands himself.

Grayson Davis—turncoat, one who had railed

against Cromwell. Yet one who had been offered great rewards—the lands of those he could best and destroy.

Like Cromwell, Davis was convinced that he had the power, the numbers and the right. So MacNiall counted on the fact that he would underestimate his enemy—the savages from the north, ill equipped, unkempt, many today in woolen rags, painted as their ancestors, the Picts, fighting for their land and their freedom.

Rank and file, marching. Slow and steady, coming ever forward. They reached the stream.

"Now?" whispered MacLeod at his side.

"A minute more," replied MacNiall calmly.

When the enemy was upon the bridge, MacNiall raised a hand. MacLeod passed on the signal.

Their marksman nodded, as quiet, calm and grim as his leaders, and took aim.

His shot was true.

The bridge burst apart in a mighty explosion, sending fire and sparks skyrocketing, pieces of plank and board and man spiraling toward the sky, only to land again in the midst of confusion and terror, bloodshed and death. For they had waited. They had learned patience, and the bridge had been filled.

Lord God, MacNiall thought, almost wearily. By now their enemies should have learned that the death and destruction of human beings, flesh and blood, was terrible.

"Now?" said MacLeod again, shouting this time to be heard over the roar from below.

"Now," MacNiall said calmly.

Another signal was given, and a hail of arrows arched over hill and dale, falling with a fury upon the mass of regrouping humanity below.

"And now!" roared MacNiall, standing in his stirrups, commanding his men.

The men, flanking those few in view, rose from behind the rocks of their blessed Highlands. They let out their fierce battle cries—learned, perhaps, from the berserker Norsemen who had once come upon them—and moved down from rock and cliff, terrible in their insanity, men who had far too often fought with nothing but their bare hands and wits to keep what was theirs, to earn the freedom that was a way of life.

Clansmen. They were born with an ethic; they fought for one another as they fought for themselves. They were a breed apart.

MacNiall was a part of that breed. As such, he must always ride with his men, and face the blades of his enemy first. He must, like his fellows, cry out his rage at this intrusion, and risk life, blood and limb in the hand-to-hand fight.

Riding down the hillside, he charged the enemy from the seat of his mount, hacking at those who slashed into the backs of his foot soldiers, and fending off those who would come upon him en masse. He fought, all but blindly at times, years of bloodshed having given him instincts that warned him when a blade or an ax was at his back. And when he was pulled from his mount, he fought on foot until he regained his saddle and crushed forward again.

In the end, it was a rout. Many of Cromwell's great troops simply ran to the Lowlands, where the people were as varied in their beliefs as they were in their backgrounds. Others did not lay down their arms quickly enough, and were swept beneath the storm of cries and rage of MacNiall's Highlanders. The stream ran red. Dead men littered the beauty of the landscape.

When it was over, MacNiall received the hails of his men, and rode to the base of the hill where they had collected the remnants of the remaining army. There he was surprised to see that among the captured, his men had taken Grayson Davis—the man who had betrayed them, one of Cromwell's greatest leaders, sworn to break the back of the wild Highland resistance. Grayson Davis, who hailed from the village that bordered MacNiall's own, had seen the fall of the monarchy and traded in his loyalty and ethics for the riches that might be acquired from the deaths of other men.

The man was wounded. Blood had all but completely darkened the glitter of the chest armor he wore. His face was streaked with grimy sweat.

"MacNiall! Call off your dogs!" Davis roared to him.

"He loses his head!" roared Angus, the head of the Moray clan fighting there that day.

"Aye, well, and he should be executed as a traitor, as the lot of us would be," MacNiall said without rancor. They all knew their punishment if they were taken alive. "Still, for now he will be our captive, and we will try him in a court of his peers."

"What court of jesters would that be? You should bargain with Lord Cromwell, use my life and perhaps save our own, for one day you will be slain or caught!" Davis told him furiously. And yet, no matter his brave words, there was fear in his eyes. There must be, for he stood in the midst of such hatred that the most courageous of men would falter.

"If you're found guilty, we'll but take your head, Davis," MacNiall said. "We find no pleasure in the torture your kind would inflict upon us."

Davis let out a sound of disgust. It was true, on both sides, the things done by man to his fellow man were surely horrendous in the eyes of God—any god.

"There will be a trial. All men must answer to their

choices," MacNiall said, and his words were actually sorrowful. "Take him," he told Angus quietly.

Davis wrenched free from the hold of his captors and turned on MacNiall. "The great Laird MacNiall, creating havoc and travesty in the name of a misbegotten king! All hail the man on the battlefield! Yet what man rules in the great MacNiall's bedchamber? Did you think that you could leave your home to take to the hills, and that the woman you left behind would not consider the fact that one day *you will fall?* Aye, MacNiall, all men must deal with their choices! And yours has made you a cuckold!"

A sickness gripped him, hard, in the pit of his stomach. A blow, like none that could be delivered by a sword or bullet or battle-ax. He started to move his horse forward.

Grayson Davis began to laugh. "Ah, there, the great man! The terror of the Highlands. The Bloody MacNiall! She wasn't a victim of rape, MacNiall. Just of my sword. A different sword."

Grayson Davis's laughter became silent as Angus brought the end of a poleax swinging hard against his head. The man fell flat, not dead—for he would stand trial—but certainly when he woke his head would be splitting.

Angus looked up at MacNiall.

"He's a liar," Angus said. "A bloody liar! Yer wife loves ye, man. No lass is more honored among us. None more lovely. Or loyal."

MacNiall nodded, giving away none of the emotion that tore through him so savagely. For there were but two passions in his life—his love for king and country…and for his wife. Lithe, golden, beautiful, sensual, brave, eyes like the sea, the sky, ever direct upon his own, filled with laughter, excitement, gravity and love.

Annalise.

Annalise...who had begged him to set down his arms. To rectify his war with Cromwell. Who had warned him that...there could be but a very tragic ending to it all.

Chapter 2

Gina caught up with Toni at the bottom of the stairs.

"What are you doing?" she asked in dismay.

"What am I doing?" Toni echoed. Now that she was away from him, from the way that he looked at her, the trembling had stopped. The strange moment was gone. He was just a man. Tall, wired, muscled, imposing—and irate that they were in what he claimed to be his property.

"Gina!" she said, determined that they would not be groveling idiots, no matter what the situation turned out to be. "Do you hear yourself? You're thanking him for throwing us out on Monday, after all this!"

"Shh!"

Gina pulled her along, anxious that Laird MacNiall not hear any more of her comments. They moved from the great hall, through a vast dining area and then through another door to the kitchen, a large area where a huge hearth with antique accoutrements still occupied most of the north wall.

There were concessions to the present, however, including the modern stove, freezer, refrigerator and microwave. The huge island counter in the center of the room, set beneath hanging pots and pans, was surely original, and at one time had certainly hosted huge sides of venison, boar and beef. Now cleaned and scrubbed, it was a dining table with a multitude of chairs around it.

The fact that MacNiall hadn't joined them had opened the floodgates of emotion. Thayer, Gina and Kevin all accosted Toni immediately.

"How the hell did this happen?" Kevin demanded.

"We all saw the agreements! And signed them," Toni reminded them. She looked around. These were her friends, her very best friends. Gina and Ryan, whom she'd met three years ago while at college. And David Fulton! Tall, dark and handsome, with the deepest dimples and warmest smile in both hemispheres, David had been Toni's friend in college. Brokenhearted by the loss of a lover, he'd quickly rallied when he and Toni had gone to a concert with Gina and Ryan, and he had met Kevin—who had immediately fit in.

Toni had been the loner in their group, but in a strange way that had changed when they had come to Scotland together six months ago. They had visited a castle bought by some of its clan members, who had then opened the house to visitors for whatever money they could bring in, thus affording to restore the place. And their wild scheme had hatched. If others had done it, why couldn't they? It was possible if they pooled their resources.

And that was where Thayer had come into the picture to complete their group of six. Thayer was her cousin, a Fraser. A distant cousin, Toni assumed, since their respective grandfathers had been cousins, which made Thayer…exactly what, she wasn't sure. He was certainly intelligent and attractive, but he was something even more important to their enterprise—an authentic Scot. Not only was he fluent in Gaelic, he understood the customs and the nuances of doing business in the small community. He acted as their interpreter—in more ways than one.

Her friends and her kin stared at her, almost accusingly. She stared straight back.

"Think about it! Maybe he doesn't have a right to be here. We just don't really know, do we?"

"Well, not positively," David murmured, but he spoke without conviction.

That MacNiall might be in the wrong, and they were the ones with the right to the place, was a nice hope. Unfortunately, none of them really seemed to believe it. Toni didn't even believe it herself.

"The constable said that MacNiall owned the place," Thayer reminded her wearily.

"So? Constable Tavish is a local. He has loyalties to an old family name. We really don't know the truth. Our lawyer may be American, but he still knows the law. We need to get more serious legal advice, and get it fast."

"Legal advice from the States may not help us now," Kevin reminded her.

"Thayer?" Toni said.

He shrugged, shaking his head. "I saw the ads for the place in Glasgow, and I saw the same thing on the Internet that you did. And yes, I read the rental agreements, just as we all did. Gina, can I see the papers?" he asked.

Gina set them down before him.

"Even *Laird* MacNiall said that they look real or proper or…whatever!" Toni murmured.

"Yeah, they look legal," Ryan said bitterly. "Tons of small print."

"We actually rented from Uxbridge Corporation," Thayer murmured. "We're going to have to trace it down. When you sent the euro-check, Toni, was there an exact address?"

She groaned, sinking into one of the chairs.

"What? What is that groan for?" Ryan demanded.

"The address was a post office box in Edinburgh," she admitted.

"Okay!" Kevin said, reaching over to squeeze her hand and give her some support. "That will give the police a trail to follow, at least."

"It will help the police," David said softly, offering Toni a half smile despite his words. "But I'm not real sure what it will do for us."

"Toni, why didn't you want the constable to take the papers tonight?" Gina asked, frowning. "Wouldn't it have been better for him to have gotten started on this as quickly as possible?"

"Those papers are all we have," Toni said. "What if I'm right and this man has lost his family castle yet still has illusions of grandeur in his head? If the constable is his loyal subject, our papers could disappear."

"She has a point," David said.

"She has a point, but this fellow isn't broke. You can't be broke and own a horse like that," Ryan told them.

"Sorry, but it looks like we'll have to suck up to this guy if we want to make it through the weekend," Thayer said.

"Maybe he borrowed the horse," Toni said.

"Oh, honey, come on. You're just getting desperate here," David said softly.

"Well, hell, it is desperate!" Toni said.

"Everything we've saved has gone into this!" Gina breathed, sinking into a chair, as well.

"Maybe we can arrange a new rental agreement," Toni said.

"With what?" Thayer asked. "We put a fortune into this. Unless one of you won a lottery before you left the States...?"

"No. But I still say we have to have some rights!" Toni insisted.

"The sad thing is," Kevin told her, "unfortunately, people who have been screwed don't generally have a right to anything. They're just..."

"Screwed," David said.

Toni shook her head, rising. She felt a pounding headache coming on. "I'm going to go to bed. Tomorrow afternoon, I'm calling the lawyer in the States. He can give us some advice, at the very least." She started toward the door, then turned back. "I am sorry, so very sorry. At best, this is really a mess."

"Amazing," Gina said suddenly.

"What?" Toni demanded.

"That he looks just like your MacNiall—the one in your phony family history. I mean...it's incredible that you could invent a man who existed down to the last detail."

"No, not to the last detail. The MacNiall I invented died centuries ago," Toni said bitterly.

"Yeah, but apparently, there was one of those, too," Gina said.

"Look, I don't believe it, either!" Toni said.

"Toni," Kevin said softly.

"Yes?"

"We don't blame you just because you were the one who found it on the Internet and got us all going. We all—every one of us—read the agreements."

She hesitated. They were staring at her sorrowfully. And despite the denial, she felt a certain amount of blame. Sure, they'd all wanted to do this, all been excited. But she'd pushed it. She'd been the one to do the actual work. But what had there been to question?

She bit her lip, feeling a little resentful and a lot guilty. If this really was totally messed up, to herself, at least, she would be the fall guy.

"Thanks," she said.

"Get some rest. We'll all get some rest. When we're not so tired and surprised, we'll be much better at sucking up!" Kevin said cheerfully.

Toni nodded, gave him a weak smile and departed.

In the great hall, she paused. They had been so happy here. This place had truly been a dream. And they had been like kids, so excited.

She hurried up the stairs to the upper landing. There were rooms on the third floor, as well, but the main chambers were here. Servants had once slept above. Her group had chosen rooms in the huge U that braced around the front entry to the main keep of the castle. Hers was to the far right and she had assumed that it had once been the master's chamber. It was large, with both arrow slits and a turret with a balcony that looked out over the countryside. After claiming the room she had discovered that it also had the most modern bath, and that the rug and draperies were the cleanest in the castle. Still, she remembered uneasily that her room also contained the huge wardrobe that had been locked tight—something to explore at a later time.

As she walked to the room, she felt a growing wariness. She hesitated, her hand on the antique knob, then pushed the door open.

There was a naked man in her bedroom. Nearly naked, at any rate.

A fire was beginning to burn nicely in the hearth. The dampness was already receding. A reading light blazed softly near the huge wing-backed chair before the fire.

The chair was occupied. Bruce MacNiall was seated, already showered, his hair wet, smooth and inky-black, his form covered in nothing but a terry towel wrapped around his waist. He was reading, of all things, the *New York Times*.

"Yes?" he said, looking up but not setting the paper aside. "Don't you knock in the States?"

"Not when I'm entering my own room."

"Oh?"

"I've been living in here," she informed him.

"But it's not your own room, is it?" he queried.

"So…this was your room," she murmured.

"*Is* mine."

Suck up! They had all warned her. But she was tired—and aggravated.

"If you're the one in the right," she reminded him, regretting her words at once.

"I do assure you that I am," he said solemnly.

"At this particular moment, I don't really have any legal proof that you're telling the truth, so I'm not entirely convinced that it is your room, that you have the right to claim it from me," she said. "You'll note my things at the dressing table. They do look like mine, unless you customarily wear women's perfume, mascara and lipstick."

He stared at her politely, and maybe a bit amazed.

"My wardrobe, you'll notice," he pointed out. "Since you're ever so observant, I'm sure you noted that when you came in and made yourself so thoroughly at home, you had no place to actually hang clothing since the wardrobe was locked."

He had won from the beginning and she knew it. She didn't know why she was still arguing. She loved this room, though, and she was settled into it.

Maybe she was just incapable of giving up a fight, or accepting the fact that they could have been taken, that their dreams had been dashed.

"My suitcases," she said, pointing to the side of the bed.

He set the paper aside and rose suddenly. She prayed the towel wouldn't slip.

"Would you like me to help you gather your things?" he asked politely.

There was something about the man that irritated her to such an extent that she couldn't keep her mouth closed—or prevent herself from behaving with sheer stupidity.

"No. I'd be happy to help you relocate, though."

"You really do have…what is it the Americans say? Balls," he told her.

She flushed.

"I'm not relocating," he said flatly.

"Unless you have the deed to this place right here and now," she said sweetly, "neither am I."

He stared at her a long moment, and she found herself flushing.

"Do you think I keep my important papers under a mattress or something?" he queried. "My documents are in a bank vault." He shrugged, then took his seat before the fire once again, retrieving his paper. "If you're stay-ing in here, do your best to keep quiet, will you? I have a hell of a headache coming on."

"You *are* the headache!" she murmured beneath her breath.

He had heard her. Once again, his eyes met hers. "I believe that you're supposed to be *sucking up* to me, Miss Fraser. I am trying to be patient and understand-ing. I've even offered a helping hand."

"Sorry," she said swiftly, though she couldn't help adding a soft, "I think!"

But she had lost and she knew it. Now she just had to accept it. She entered the room, slamming the door behind her. After gathering up what she could hold of her toiletries, she headed back to the hall.

"Next door down is the bride's chamber for this room. It's very nice," he told her absently, studying his paper again.

"I've seen it. I got down on my hands and knees and scrubbed in there—just as I did in here."

"Yes, very nice, actually," he told her. "Good job. As I said before, I can help you move your things."

"Wouldn't want you to have to get dressed," she said.

"I don't have to get dressed, actually. Just go through the bathroom."

"These two rooms share that bath?" she murmured. She felt like an idiot. She knew that. She'd also cleaned the bathroom!

"This is a castle, with some modernization—not the Hilton," he said. "Most of the rooms share a bath. Since you've been living here, surely you know that."

She only knew at that moment that she wished she had chosen a room on the other side of the U.

He rose and grabbed one of her suitcases. "Through

here," he said, walking down the little hallway to the bath, and through it.

The next room was one of the nicer ones, not as large as the one she had vacated, but there was a fireplace, naturally—*it was a castle, not the Hilton*—and a wonderful curving draped window. "Widow's walk out there," he pointed out. "You'll love it, I'm sure."

"Naturally, I've seen it," she snapped.

"Right. You cleaned that, too."

"Yes, we did."

"Lovely."

He deposited her suitcase on the floor.

It was fine, it was lovely. But...*it attached to his room.* How did she know that the man wasn't...*weird?* What if, in the middle of the night, he came through the connecting doorway? No, there were other vacant rooms. She should choose one of them.

He must have read her mind, for a small smile of grim amusement—and a touch of disdain—suddenly played upon his features. "Rest assured, you can lock your side of the bathroom door."

"I should hope so," she murmured.

"Really? Seems I'm the one who should be concerned about locking doors. Have no fear, Miss Fraser. There's really not a great deal for you to worry about. From me, at any rate."

His look assured her that he found her less appealing than a cobra. For some reason, that was disconcerting.

Because the *bastard looked good in a towel?* she mocked herself. More than that, he had assurance and self-confidence. Sharp, intelligent eyes, well-sculpted, masculine, handsome features. And his other assets were well sculpted, too.

"I'll keep my door locked, too," he assured her.

"You do that," she said sweetly.

He turned and walked back through the connecting bath. The towel, amazingly, remained just as it had been tied.

Toni shut the door in his wake. She leaned against it, wondering how such a brilliant night could have possibly ended in such disaster. And how she had not only invented a historical figure who had actually existed, but one with a seriously formidable, modern-day descendant who was here, in the living—near naked—flesh?

Fear trickled down her spine, but she ignored it. It was very late now, and she was determined to get organized and get some sleep. And that was that.

She looked around, trying to forget the man on the other side of the door and keep herself from being cowed by him in any way. Surveying her surroundings, she decided it was more than just a fine room. Really. It was a *better* room.

She moved away from the door, telling herself that she liked it just fine, that she was going to move right in—even if it did prove to be just for the next few nights.

So determined, she went about arranging her toiletries and unpacking some of her belongings. But despite her resolve to settle in and get some sleep, she was restless and disturbed. First, this really was one total mess. She couldn't believe that they had been taken by some kind of a shyster. But worse, it bothered her that his family history, which she thought she'd made up, had turned out to be true.

Finished with hanging a number of her garments, she gathered up her toothbrush, toothpaste and flannel nightgown and headed for the bathroom. She hesitated at the door, then decided that for whatever length of time she'd still be in the castle, she had to take showers. She gritted her teeth, knocked tentatively and heard nothing. She went in. The shower-tub combination was to her left, and a large vanity with double sinks to her right. The last time anyone had redone the bathroom had been many years ago, but it was still decent with artistic little bird faucets and a commode and bath and shower wall that had surely been state-of-the-art at the time.

The doors to the master's chamber and the bride's room were directly opposite one another. She stared at the door to the other room for several seconds, then walked over to it and tapped on it.

"Yes?"

She opened the door and peeked in. He was still in his towel, deeply engrossed in the paper, and he had a fire going. The entire room seemed much warmer than hers.

A little resentment filled her until she remembered that there was a fireplace in her new room. She could build her own fire.

"I was going to use the shower. I just wanted to make sure that you didn't need it." *And that you don't intend to barge into the bathroom.*

She had a sudden, absurd image of him riding the great black stallion into the tiny bathroom.

He arched an ebony brow. "My apparel would seem to show that I've already bathed," he said.

"Right. Well, I'll unlock the door from this side when I'm done."

"Yes, please do," he said, and looked back at the newspaper.

She couldn't resist. "The *Times,* huh? You apparently like American newspapers better than American people."

"I usually like Americans very much," he said. There was the slightest accent on the second word he spoke.

She closed the connecting door and locked it, swearing beneath her breath. The situation was bad enough. If there had to be a living MacNiall, why couldn't he have been eighty, white haired and kind!

Fighting her irritation, she stripped and stepped into the shower. The hot water didn't last very long; she was probably the last one getting to it that night.

Still swearing beneath her breath, she stepped out, towel-dried quickly and slipped into a flannel gown. In her room, she debated the idea of attempting a fire. She'd had one herself in the other room, but David and Kevin had built it for her. Despite her Chicago homeland, she'd never built a fire.

Using the long matches from the mantel, she tried lighting the logs in the hearth. But nothing happened. Some kind of kindling was needed. Perhaps a piece of newspaper or something. Looking around the room, she saw nothing to use.

Lightning suddenly flared beyond the gauzy drapes that covered the door to the widow's walk. It was an actual balcony, she thought, not a little turret area, as was found in the master's chambers.

Immediately after, thunder cracked. The wooden door that led outward to the old stone area swung in with a loud bang as the wind blew it open with a vengeance. She hopped up and hurried over to the door. It was a nasty night, not the kind she had imagined here!

She closed the door with an effort and bolted it. Staring through the slender openings of the arrow slits, she saw another flash of lightning. She should count her blessings that they hadn't been thrown out that night.

She gave up on the fire and curled into the canopied bed, then hopped up again. The only light switch for the room was apparently right next to the bathroom.

With it out, she was plunged into a darkness so deep it was unnerving. Shaking her head, she opened the bathroom door, turned the light on, hesitated, then left the door on her side of the room ajar—she would have killed herself trying to get into bed in the pure ink that had filled the room.

Was she being an idiot? No, this fellow truly had no interest in her. Maybe she should be insulted, she thought wryly. At five-nine, with deep blue eyes and light hair that had deepened over the years to a dark blond, she was usually considered to be attractive. But apparently not to the ogre in the next room.

Bruce MacNiall. She *must* have heard the name somewhere.

Lying in the great bed, she shivered as she hadn't shivered in years.

No! It was not some kind of precognition coming back to her. She had stopped all that years ago, closed her mind, because she had willed that it would be so!

Still…

She tossed and turned, wishing that there was a television in the room. Or a fire. Watching the flames would have been nice.

Her mind kept racing, denying that this could be happening when they had tried so hard to do things right. There had to be a mistake. There had to be something to do!

How had she come up with the name Bruce MacNiall?

At last, she drifted to sleep.

* * *

Bruce had just lain down when he heard the ear-piercing scream. Instinct brought him bolt-awake, leaping from the bed. A second's disorientation was quickly gone as he heard a second cry of terror.

It was coming from the next room.

He raced through the connecting bathroom to see his uninvited guest sitting up in the bed, pointing in front of her, a look of terror on her face.

"Miss Fraser... Toni! What is it?"

He realized only then that she wasn't really awake. Racing to her, he took her by the shoulders and gave her a gentle shake. Her reaction stunned him. She jerked from his hold and leaped with an incredibly lithe and agile motion to her feet and stared down at him.

She was a rather amazing sight, mane of gold hair caught in the pale light, shimmering like a halo around her delicate, refined features. Her eyes were the size of saucers, and in the soft-colored flannel gown, she might have been a misplaced Ophelia.

Something hard inside him wondered just what new act she was up to now. Something else felt a moment's softness. The terror in her eyes seemed real. For the first time she seemed vulnerable.

"Toni," he said firmly, stretching out his arms to catch her around the middle and lift her down. "Toni! Wake up!"

She stared at him blankly.

"Toni!"

With a jolt, she blinked and stared straight at him.

He thought she was going to scream again. Instead, she blinked once more and quickly stepped back, eyeing him up and down. Luckily he had donned a long pair of men's cotton pajama pants.

"I think you were dreaming," he said.

She frowned, flushed and bit her lower lip. "I screamed?"

"Like an alley cat," he informed her. He stepped back himself. In this pale light, in this strange moment, he suddenly realized just how arresting a woman she was. Not just beautiful, but fascinating. Eyes so intensely blue, bone structure so perfect and refined, her mouth so generous. Her features seemed carefully drawn, as if they had been defined by an artist. And despite the vivid color of her hair and her eyes, there was a darkness about them, as well.

"I woke you," she murmured. "My deepest apologies."

"I wasn't actually sleeping, but I am surprised you didn't wake the entire castle. Or maybe you did," he added. He couldn't refrain from a dry smile. "Maybe they're creeping down the hall now, afraid to come in and find out what's happening." He left her and walked to the door, opened it and looked out. Then he shrugged. "Well, castle walls have been known to keep the sounds of the tortured from traveling too far."

She still stood there, tall, elegant, strangely aloof. He found that he was annoyed to be so concerned. She seemed to be the head of this wretched gang that had the gall to "invent" history and entertain others with their perception of the past. "Are you all right?" he asked her.

"I just… I'm fine. And I'm truly sorry." Her words were sincere. Her eyes were still too wide. And she seemed to be afraid of something.

Him? No. Something in her nightmare?

Bruce hesitated. Leave! he told himself. He didn't want them here. Lord, with everything else going on…

She shivered as she stood there. That was his undoing.

"The wretched room is freezing. Why didn't you build yourself a fire?" he demanded.

"I..."

The uncertainty seemed so unlike her. She'd been a tigress, arguing with him before. Impatiently he strode to the fireplace, dug behind the poker stand for kindling, laid it over the logs and struck a match. Hunkered down, he took hold of the poker to press it deeper into the pile of wood. He wondered if that had been a mistake, if she was going to think that he'd turn and take the poker to her.

But she was still standing, just as he had left her. To his sincere dismay, he felt a swift stir of arousal. The flannel should have hung around her like a tent, but it was sheer enough for the light to play with form and shadow. And there was that hair...long, lustrous, blond, curling around her shoulders and breasts.

"A drink. You need a drink," he told her. Hell, he needed one.

She lifted a hand suddenly, obviously regaining some of her composure. "Sorry, I don't have any."

"Thankfully you didn't jimmy the wardrobe," he told her. "I'll be right back."

He went back through the bathroom and opened the wardrobe, found the brandy and poured two glasses from the left-hand shelf. Returning to the bride's room, he found that she had taken a seat in one of the old upholstered chairs in front of the fireplace.

He handed her a glass. She accepted it, her blue eyes speculatively on him. "Thanks," she told him.

"They say it will cure what ails you," he told her, lifting his glass. "Cheers."

"Cheers," she returned. A little shiver snaked through her as she took a long swallow. "Thanks," she said again.

He set his glass on the mantel, hunkered down and adjusted the logs again. A nice warmth was emanating from the blaze now.

He stood, collected his glass again and took the chair by her side.

"So…do you want to talk about it?"

A twisted smile curled her lips. She looked at him. "Sure. It was you."

"Me! I swear, I never left that room," he protested.

"I know. It was very strange. It was as if I had wakened and…there you were. Only, it wasn't really you. It was you—as you might have been—in historical costume. It was very, very real. Absolutely vivid."

"So I was just standing there, in historical costume? Well, I can see where that might be a bit unsettling, but those screams… It sounded as if the devil himself had arrived."

She flushed slightly.

"You were in more than costume."

"Oh?"

"Were it a picture, the caption might have read, 'Speak softly and carry a very big and bloody sword,'" she said.

"Ah. So I was about to lop off your head. Sorry, I may be irritated and rude, but I do stop short at head-lopping," he told her, then turned, getting comfortable in the chair. "Don't you think you might have gotten a bit carried away with your historical fiction?"

"I have to admit, I've scared myself a bit," she murmured. "I made up a Bruce MacNiall, only to find out that he exists. Well, in the here and now, that is."

Bruce shook his head, wary now. "You must have known some of the local history."

"No, not really. We hadn't ever been to this area when we decided to attempt this venture," she assured him.

It sounded as if she was telling the truth. And yet…

He swirled the brandy in his glass, studying the color. Then he looked at her again. She couldn't be telling the truth.

"There was a Bruce MacNiall who fought with the Cavaliers. He opposed the armies Cromwell led and beat them mercilessly many times. At first, he even survived Cromwell's reign. But he and some other Scottish lairds kept at it, wanting to bring Charles II back from Europe and see him crowned king. He was eventually caught when one of the lairds supposedly on his side turned coat. That man was killed by MacNiall's comrades, but unfortunately MacNiall rode into a trap and was caught himself. He had defied the reigning power, which was Cromwell. You know the penalty for that. He received every barbarity of the day that was reserved for traitors."

She turned to him, blue eyes enormous. Then she closed them and leaned back, looking ashen.

"Hey, sorry. It's history. I didn't get the sense that you had a weak stomach."

She shook her head. "I don't," she said flatly, and he realized that the particular history he was giving her was more disturbing to her than it was to him.

She looked at him. "He didn't murder his wife in a fit of jealousy, did he?"

Bruce shrugged, watching her closely. "No one knows. There was some rumor that she kept company with a certain Cromwellian soldier—whether true or a pure invention, I don't know—and that she disappeared from the castle. It's historical fact that MacNiall was castrated, disemboweled, hanged, beheaded and generally chopped to pieces. But as to his wife, no one knows for certain. She disappeared from history, right when he was caught. He was trapped in the forest. And executed there, after a mock trial. At the time he died, he had a teenage son running with Charles II in France. Very soon after MacNiall's execution, Cromwell died, and the people, very weary of being good, were anxious to ask him back to take the throne. Charles proved to be a very entertaining king, and a truly interesting man. He might have dallied with dozens of mistresses, but he steadfastly refused to consider a divorce from his wife. So after him, his brother became king, and that was another disaster for history to record."

"It's…horrible!" Toni said.

He smiled grimly. "From what I hear, you didn't mind fleecing the public with such a horrible story."

"But it wasn't true when I told it!" she protested.

He waved a hand in the air impatiently. "Say you're telling me the truth—"

"Are you accusing me of lying?" she demanded indignantly. The anger was back in her eyes.

"I don't know you, do I?" he asked politely. "But even if you think you're telling the truth, it's quite possible that you heard the story somewhere else. Because you made it up to a tee."

She waved a hand in the air. "The land belonged to the MacNialls. And if there is anyone famous in Scottish history, it's Robert the Bruce. Bruce. A very common name here!"

"Aye, that's true. But you went a step further."

"How?"

He stared at her. She was either the finest actress in the world, or she really didn't know.

"MacNiall's wife," he said slowly, watching her every reaction.

"You just said that history didn't know about her!"

"Aye, that's true enough."

"Then...?"

"Her name," Bruce said softly.

"Lady MacNiall. That would be fairly obvious!" she said disdainfully.

"No, Toni. Her first name. Her given name. Annalise."

Chapter 3

Could anyone act so well, or even lie with such aplomb?

"What?" Her eyes were saucers, and her color was as close to pure white as he had ever seen on a human being.

"Annalise. Our famous—or infamous—Bruce Mac-Niall was indeed married to an Annalise."

She shook her head. "I swear to you, I had no idea! It has to be…chance. Coincidence. Okay, the most absurd coincidence imaginable, but… I honestly have never heard this story before. Stories like it, sure—your ancestor wasn't the only man to meet such a fate."

He wondered if she was trying to convince him or herself.

"Aye, that's true enough," he said. She was an audacious interloper in his home, he reminded himself. And yet… At this particular moment, he couldn't add to her distress. She needed some color back. Hell, she could pass out on him at any moment. She could be such a little demon, as self-righteous as Cromwell himself. But right now, she was simply far too vulnerable, and that vulnerability was calling out to whatever noble and protective virtues he might possess.

"Yes, it's true!" she said, desperately clinging to his words. "I've been to Edinburgh. I've seen the tomb built for Montrose, who was a Cavalier and who sided with the king, finally meeting his end in such a manner. And there were others…but I had no idea there was really a MacNiall! Or," she added, wincing, "an Annalise. Look!" She sat up straight, finding her backbone again, and stared at him with sudden hostility. "We did not come here to mock your precious history or your family. I am telling you, I did not know about your MacNiall or that he might have even existed!"

"Well, he did," he said flatly, and stared at the flames, anger filling him again. He loved this place. Granted, he hadn't given it much attention lately. Though he'd always intended to do so, there was always something else that needed to be done first. And now, with everything that had been going on…

"Don't you understand?" she demanded. "There's never been anything the least disrespectful in what we wanted to do. Every one of us came here and simply fell in love with the country. Unfortunately none of us is independently wealthy. Gina, however, is a marketing genius. She decided that she could take all of our talents and market them. That way, we could acquire a castle, work hard and give some of the magic to the public."

"Stupid idea," he murmured hotly, looking at the fire again.

"It's not a stupid idea!" she protested. "You saw how the people came."

"The locals will never enjoy such a spectacle."

"Maybe not, but the shows aren't intended for the locals. They will help the economy all around, don't you see that? People who come to the castle for the history, the splendor or even the spectacle will spend money in other places. It will be good for local stores, for restaurants... for everyone around."

"I don't agree," he said, fighting the rise of his temper again.

"Then you're a fool."

"Oh, really?"

"Indeed, a blind fool!" She turned toward him, no longer ashen, passion in her voice, fire in her eyes. "You saw those people when they left here! They were thrilled. And they loved Scotland. Don't you want people to love your country?"

"Not a mockery of it," he told her.

"I told you, we're not mocking it!" She shook her head, growing aggravated. "Others give tours of the closes and graveyards in Edinburgh. People are fascinated. We like to think that we've come far from doing horrible things to one another, even under the pretext of law. We're not saying that the Scots were especially brutal, we're explaining that it was just a different time!"

"Voyeurs!" he said roughly, waving a hand in the air. "And that's Edinburgh. A big city. We're talking about a small village here."

"It's hard these days to buy a castle in the middle of town," she said sarcastically.

"Many people don't want to be reminded of mayhem and murder," he said.

She let out a sigh of exasperation. "Don't you ever do anything for fun?" she asked him. "Have you ever seen a movie? A play? Gone to the opera?"

He looked at the fire again. "The point is, this is a small, remote village. It could be a dangerous place for tourists to wander."

"Dangerous!" she said dismissively.

He felt tension welling in him.

"There are forests, crags and bogs. Hillsides. Crannies and cairns. Places where the footing is treacherous at best," he said. "Places that are remote, dark and, aye, believe me, dangerous." His own argument sounded weak even to him.

Maybe he was a fool for being so suspicious, wary... when he need not be. But the lasses were gone, were they not?

Gone. Two of them. Found dead. Here.

"What are you talking about?" she demanded.

He had no intention of trying to explain what had happened, or why he was so concerned. Even Jonathan Tavish thought it was a problem for others, for big-city authorities. After all, the women had not disappeared from here. They had just been found here.

"Antoinette *Fraser*," he said suddenly, determined to change the subject. "So...your father was Scottish, or Scottish-American?"

"He was half, but born here. His dad married during the war. On his side, my grandmother was French. My mother was Irish."

"Was?"

"I lost her my first year of college."

"I'm sorry."

"Thanks."

"And your father?"

"I lost him, too," she said softly. "A few years ago. His heart gave out. I think that he missed my mother, actually."

"I'm sorry again."

"Thanks." She hesitated, then asked, "If you are the laird, then…?"

"Indeed, my parents went together. An automobile accident in London."

"I'm sorry," she murmured.

"Thank you," he acknowledged. "It was over a decade ago, now."

"You still miss people," she said.

"Indeed, you do." He didn't want the two of them growing morose together, so he brought a small smile to his lips. "Still…" he murmured.

"What?"

"You couldn't have bought a castle in Ireland, eh?"

She halfway smiled, but her eyes flashed. He realized that he had been breathing in her scent. She really was a stunning woman. Brilliant as an angel one second, claws extended, blue fire in her eyes the next.

She shouldn't be here.

He looked at his brandy glass again and swirled the liquid. "The truth of the matter is, I didn't rent this castle to anyone. I do own it, and you are trespassing." He added the last very quietly, and swallowed more of his brandy. The warmth was delicious.

She was quiet for a moment, then said, "I'll admit to having the sinking feeling that we were taken by a British scam artist."

"Might have been an American. They are here, you know, in vast numbers."

Ah, yes, that goaded her temper again. Was he doing it on purpose? Enjoying the rise of her breasts, the flash in her eyes? Wondering what it would be like to suddenly strike a bargain for total peace, draw her in front of the fire and find some real truth in those generous, sensual lips?

"If something was pulled off, it was done by someone over here," she said vehemently.

He realized that he was actually enjoying watching her trying to control her temper.

"You've got to understand! We've sunk a fortune into this!" she told him.

"Aye, that I do believe. I've seen the work."

She frowned, staring at him. "How do you know exactly what I made up?" she demanded. "You didn't ride in until...well, it was almost as if you'd ridden in on cue!"

"I'd meant to stop it before it started," he told her. "Eban had heard you rehearsing, and though he was pleased with all the work being done, he wasn't pleased to hear the family slandered."

"But you said the story I made up was true!"

"I never said that Bruce MacNiall strangled his wife."

"She did disappear."

"She disappeared from the pages of history."

Lightning suddenly filled the sky again, followed with rocketing speed by thunder that caused the castle to shake. Startled, Toni let out a little scream, jumping to her feet. Seeing him, she flushed, lost her balance in her attempt to regain her seat quickly and toppled over—directly into his lap.

Long elegant fingers fell against his bare chest. The silky soft sweep of her hair caressed him. Warm and very solid, her scent, that of lavender soap and femininity, caused an instant physical reaction in him that he prayed wasn't evident through the sheer fabric of his pajama pants.

"Oh, God! I am so sorry!" she swore, struggling to

get up. Trying to brace against his knee, she missed. Her flush deepened to something of a painful crimson, and her apologies came out in a garbled stream.

"It's all right!" he expelled, plucking her up, setting her on her feet and remaining vertical himself. "It's very late. If you're sure that you're fine..."

"Yes, yes, I'm fine," she said, looking toward the window. He had the strange feeling that she was expecting to see someone there. Or that she was afraid that she would.

"You know, I'm not exactly tired, but I can see that you are. Go to sleep. I'll get the newspaper and study the pages here, in this chair. That way, if you have a nightmare about me being in your room, you won't panic, because you'll know that I'm here," he said.

"I'm a big girl. Really," she told him.

"I'd rather read the paper than fall asleep to another scream," he told her.

"It's all right," she said, tossing back a length of hair. "I don't want you to feel that we're any more of a burden than you already do."

"So go to sleep," he said.

"I won't scream again, really."

"I'm going for the paper," he told her.

When he returned, she was still standing there uncertainly. There was a conflict of emotions in the deep blue of her eyes. She obviously wanted to tell him to jump in a lake, but she was doubting her own rights. For her own sake, and that of her friends, she didn't want him as angry again as he had been when he had first arrived.

Yet...he sensed a strange touch of fear in her, as though she really didn't want to dream again. That she would prefer a living, flesh-and-blood stranger in her room to being alone in it with her dreams.

"Look, I'm serious!" he said. "Go to bed, get some sleep. I'll be here."

"You're going to sleep in the chair all night?"

"Frankly, there's not a lot of night left. When the dawn breaks, I'll head over to my own bed. If you wake up then, it will be light so you won't panic. It always works that way."

"How do you know?" she demanded suspiciously.

"Because people never panic in the daylight. You know, the light of day. Reason and sanity. They go together."

She stared at him uncertainly, then headed for the canopied bed.

"This isn't fair to you," she said, turning her back to him.

"Go to sleep."

She crawled on top of the bed and pulled the covers around her.

He shook out the paper and took a seat before the fire. But though he tried to read, he couldn't pay attention.

He glanced over to the bed. So much for her having difficulties sleeping. Her eyes were closed. She was on her side, facing his way. An angel at rest. Ivory features so artistically sculpted. Full, dark lips, parted just slightly. Arms embracing a pillow.

Oh, to be that pillow!

She had to be a shyster, he told himself angrily. No matter how innocent or vulnerable she appeared, she couldn't have just made up his history, not down to the name Annalise. He had to take care around her, despite the fact that she could twist something deep inside of him. Or maybe because of that.

Annalise.

Impatiently he tried to read again, but then he gave

up, folded the paper and simply watched her sleep, doing his best to stretch his length out comfortably in the chair.

After a while, he dozed.

Then...he awakened with a violent start.

He didn't scream; he made no noise. But his dream had been no less the terrible.

He had seen her...facedown, hair flowing in the bubbling water of the little brook in the forest. Facedown... as he had found the murdered girl.

He reached for his brandy glass and swallowed the pinch of deep amber remaining within it. He gave himself a fierce shake. Looking to the window, he saw that the dawn was breaking at last. Silently he rose. One more brandy and maybe he could get a few hours of sleep. One more brandy...and he might quell the tension that was ripping up his insides.

He walked to the door of the dividing bath and then paused. He returned to the bedside.

She slept, an angel still. That spill of hair...

It might have been any hair.

He hardened his jaw and swore softly, decrying his own nonsense. It was fucking dawn. He needed to get some sleep.

Thayer Fraser shivered as he walked along the path, heading down toward the stream, valley and forest. "A nice brisk walk in the lovely morning air!" he said, speaking aloud. "Actually, that would be fucking cold morning air!" he added. His voice sounded strange in the silence of the very early morning as it echoed off the stone walls of the run-down castle. Eerie, even.

At the base of the hill, he turned back. Most folks outside the country didn't know that there were still many such places as this castle—smaller castles, family homesteads, not the great walled almost-cities-within-cities such as the fortified castles at Edinburgh and Stirling. They could be found, and some of them poor, indeed, much smaller than many a manor house. And naturally, in a far sadder state of being.

He stared up at the stone bastion, beautiful against the sky this morning. There was not a drop of rain in sight, not a single cloud. Ah, yes! This was the stuff of postcards, coffee-table books and calendars, the kind of thing American tourists just had to capture in a million and five digital pictures!

So far—though they all claimed to be in the bad times together, just as they were in the good—they were all secretly blaming Toni. For she had been the one to find the property on the Internet. She had been the one to write to the post box. And she had been the one to receive the agreement, bring it to her lawyer and then pass it on to all of them.

So, yes…they were blaming Toni. But pretty soon they'd be looking at him.

After all, he was Scottish, born and bred. He'd seen the advertisements in Glasgow, and had told Toni that it looked fitting for their purpose.

"Shite!" he muttered aloud.

He looked to the forest. Hell, he'd actually never known what they called the damned place. They should understand that. Most Americans had never seen their own Grand Canyon. Why should he be supposed to know about every nook and cranny of Scotland?

Hopefully they would continue blaming Toni, his American cousin. His kin. With her wonder and exuberance, she had convinced them that they could do it. He could remember first meeting her, how pleased she had been to meet a Fraser, an actual—if slightly distant—

member of her father's family. He'd been bowled over by her. Indeed, he'd found her gorgeous, stimulating, though she'd rather quickly squelched any thoughts of more than a brother-sister relationship between them.

It wasn't as if he didn't have enough blokes for friends in Glasgow, but she and her American group had been a breath of fresh air. In Glasgow, it was too easy to get into the old work by day, live for the pub at night mentality. The Americans had nothing on the Scots when it came to alcoholism and drug addiction. The working class was the working class, and therein lay the pub, the delights of escape, drugs—wine, women and song.

And though Toni might not want a hot roll in the old hay with him, she trusted him. Liked him. Relied on him.

He smiled grimly. Oh, aye! Americans, God bless them, just loved to look back to the old homeland. Give them an accent and they were putty.

He stared at the forest again, a sense of deep unease stirring in him. He never had known the damned name of the place, and that was a fact.

The forest was still as dark as a witch's teat in the glory of dawn. Dense, deep, remote. And he realized that he was just standing there, staring into it. Time had passed, and he hadn't moved. He'd been mesmerized.

It was an effort to draw himself away, to shake the sudden fear that seized him. It was almost as if he had to physically tear himself away from the darkness, as if the trees had reached out, gripped him...and held him tight.

"Fooking ass!" he railed against himself as he turned and hurried back to the castle.

Jonathan Tavish sat at his breakfast table, morosely stirring the sugar in his tea.

His home might be old by some standards—built

around 1910—and it might have a certain thatched-roof, quaint charm. But it sure as hell wasn't any castle.

Through the window, he could see the MacNiall holding, just as he had seen it all of his life. A dilapidated pile of stone, he told himself.

But it wasn't. It was the castle, no matter what else. It was Bruce MacNiall's holding, because he was the MacNiall, and in this little neck of the world, that would always mean something, no matter how far the world moved along.

Bruce had been his friend for years.

"Wonder if he knows what I've felt all these years?" Jonathan asked out loud. "You're a decent chap, Laird MacNiall, that y'are! Slainte, my friend. To your health. Always."

He smiled slightly. Aye, he could have told the Americans easily enough that there was a Bruce MacNiall. Then again, why the hell should he have done so? Bruce had never seen it necessary to explain his absences from the village, or suggest that Jonathan keep an eye on things or, heaven forbid, ask his old chum to keep him informed when he was away. And that was often. Bruce spent time in Edinburgh, confiding often enough with Robert, his old friend from the service, delving into matters though he'd been out of it all long enough himself. Of course, with the events of the last year or so…

Then there were his "interests" in the States. Kept an apartment there, he did. Well, money made money, and that was a fact.

Hell, who had known when he would return this time. It was all legitimate that he hadn't said a word to the new folk about there being a real Bruce. And those folk had, amusingly enough, done real work at the place. Bruce sure hadn't kept up the place. In fact, there were times when it seemed that he hated the castle and the great forest surrounding it, even the village itself.

That, of course, had to do with Maggie...

"Well, old boy," he said aloud softly, "at least you had her once. She loved you, she did. She was my friend, but she loved you."

Maggie had been gone a very long time. There was no sense thinking about those days anymore.

Impatiently Jonathan stood, bringing along his tea as he walked to the window. There it was, the castle on the hill. Bruce's castle. Bruce was the MacNiall. The bloody MacNiall. *Laird* MacNiall.

"To you, you bloody bastard! These are not the old days, my friend. I am not a subject, a serf, a servant. I'm the law here, the bloody law."

He stared at the castle and the forest, the sun shining on the former, a shadow of green darkness enveloping the latter.

"The bloody law!"

A crooked grin split his lips.

"Y'may be the MacNiall, the bloody great MacNiall, but I am the law. I have that power. And when it's necessary for the law to come down, well...friend or nae, I will be that power!"

Chapter 4

"What are we going to do about *tonight?*" Gina asked Toni.

They were alone in the kitchen. Gina had been the first up. Ever the consummate businesswoman, she had apparently been worrying about the tour they had planned for Saturday night since waking up. In fact, she might not even have slept.

Toni was still feeling fairly haggard herself. When she woke, she had found the chair empty and the dividing doors shut. She'd tapped lightly at the bathroom door, but there had been no answer. She had entered, locked the other side, gotten ready and unlocked it. She hadn't heard a sound and assumed that he was at last sleeping. The night seemed a blur to her now.

Even the absolute terror that had awakened her seemed to have faded. And yet…something lingered. A very deep unease.

"Toni, what on earth are we going to do?" Gina repeated.

"Maybe he'll just let us have our group in," she said.

Gina folded her hands in front of her on the kitchen table, looking at Toni. "We could have had our butts out on the street last night. You have to quit aggravating the guy."

"Wait just a minute! I was actually in the right last night. How did we know—until the constable came—that he really was who he said he was."

"You have to quit being so hostile to him," Gina insisted.

"I talked to him again last night. And I wasn't hostile," Toni told Gina.

Gina instantly froze. "You…talked to him again?" She sounded wary and very worried.

"I told you, I wasn't hostile!"

David, looking admirably suave in a silk robe, walked into the kitchen. "Did I hear that Toni was talking to our host again?" He, too, sounded very worried.

"Hey, you guys! This isn't fair. When he came bursting in like Thor on a cloud of thunder, I assumed we were perfectly in the right," Toni said, exasperated. "And we were. We did everything right."

"Well," David said, opening the refrigerator, "for being right, we're looking awfully wrong. We have tourists coming in tonight. What are we going to do?"

"What else? I'm going to get on the phone and cancel," Gina said. She laid her head on the table and groaned. "Where am I going to get the money for refunds?"

David smoothed back his freshly washed dark hair and shut the refrigerator. "Wow, we sure have made this home. Do you think it's still all right if I delve into the refrigerator?"

"Yes, I'm sure," Toni said. "It is our food in there. There wasn't a thing in the place when we arrived, except for a few tea bags!"

"Hey, I know. I'm going to whip up a really good breakfast. Think Laird MacNiall will like that? You know, Toni, you're going to have to be careful when making things up from now on. This guy turned out to be real, and you have his ancestor being a murderer! From now on, invent characters that are noble and good."

"Hey, Othello was noble, and he killed his wife," Toni said.

"That breakfast doesn't sound like a bad idea," Gina said.

"We should make Toni cook," David said.

"No!" Kevin protested, standing in the kitchen doorway. "We'll definitely get kicked out if we do that." He grinned, taking the sting out of his words, and surveyed the kitchen. "Imagine this place if we had a few more funds! I'd love to see baker's rows of copper pots and pans and utensils."

"It's not our place anymore," Gina reminded him.

"Soft yellow paint would bring in the sunlight," David mused.

"How the hell can you be so cheerful this morning?" Gina asked him.

"I'm eternally and annoyingly cheerful, you all know that," Kevin said. "Things will work out. Hey, whoever made the coffee did a full pot, right?" he asked, moving to the counter.

David closed the refrigerator door and leaned against it, looking at Kevin. "Think that Scottish lairds like eggs Benedict?"

"Shouldn't we do something with salmon?" Kevin countered.

"Good point," David agreed.

"I'm glad you two can worry about breakfast," Gina murmured. "What are we going to do?"

"We're going to sit down like the good friends we are and figure a way out of this," David said flatly. "Where's your husband, Gina?"

She shook her head. "He wasn't in the room. He's out somewhere…walking, playing in the stables, Lord knows."

Thayer came walking into the kitchen, bearing the newspaper from Stirling, the nearest major city. He set it on the table, offering them all a grimace. "Good morning, we can at least hope."

"Maybe, but only if we start over with the coffee. Gina, did you make this?" Kevin asked, tasting the brew. "What did you use, local mud?"

"It's strong, that's all," Gina protested.

"So, what do we do?" Thayer asked.

"We'll wait for Ryan and then figure out what we can do. Of course, we have until Monday before we need to worry about where we'll sleep!" Gina sighed. "I should call the travel agency in Stirling and start canceling the arrangements for tonight."

"Sixty people at twenty-five a pop—pounds sterling," Thayer said woefully. "My place in Glasgow is small, but if we buy a few pillows we'll be fine."

"We all quit our jobs," Kevin reminded him.

"And we can get new ones," David said.

"There has to be some recourse here," Toni said.

"Toni has been talking to Laird MacNiall again," Gina warned, trying to keep emotion from her voice.

"I wasn't fighting with him!" Toni protested.

"Well, you didn't exactly offer him warm and cuddly Southern hospitality," David reminded her.

"I'm not Southern!"

"You could have faked it," Kevin said.

"Actually, you are from the south—the south side of D.C.," David offered.

She glared at him. "Look, I had a conversation with him, and he wasn't miserable at all," Toni said.

David gasped suddenly and walked around to her, looking down into her eyes. He squeezed her shoulders. "You didn't... I mean, Toni, we're in trouble here, but you don't have to...you don't have to offer *that* kind of hospitality, no matter how dire things are looking!"

"David!" she snapped, feeling a flush rise over her cheeks. "I didn't, and I wouldn't! How the hell long have you known me?"

Gina giggled suddenly. "Hey, I don't know. In the looks department, he's really all right."

"What she really means is," Kevin teased, "if it weren't for Ryan, *she'd* do him in a flash."

Gina leveled a searing gaze at him. "The breakfast better be damned good."

"Look!" Toni said. "I talked to him but I didn't sleep with him. He was in my room, but..."

"What?" David demanded, drawing out the chair at her side and looking at her, his dark eyes very serious.

"It seems that I was in his room, so I moved into the next one," she told him. "We had to talk and we were both cordial, okay?" she said.

"You just talked to him...without..."

"Being bitchy?" Kevin asked bluntly.

"Dammit! I was polite."

"Okay, okay!" David said.

That was it. She was offering no further explanations

of how she might have gotten into a *cordial* conversation with the laird. "And now I'm thinking that if we ask really politely, maybe he'd let us do tonight's performance so that we can recoup some of our losses."

"She's got a good idea there," Thayer said.

"Omelettes!" Kevin said suddenly. "Salmon and bacon on the side. So who gets to ask Laird MacNiall if we can do the tour tonight?"

"Toni," David said, suddenly determined. "She has to ask him. She's the one who's talked to him."

"Toni? Oh, I don't know about that," Thayer protested. He looked across the table as she glared at him. "Sorry! But you seem to have a hair-trigger temper with the guy. It's kind of like sending in a tigress to ask largesse of a lion!"

Toni groaned. "I don't have a hair-trigger temper. Ever. He was very aggravating last night, and I thought that I was defending us."

"You were," David assured her.

"All right," Gina said. "Toni, you ask him."

"Ask him what?"

They all jolted around. Bruce MacNiall was standing in the kitchen doorway with Ryan. This morning, he was in jeans and a denim shirt. Apparently, he hadn't been sleeping. His ebony hair was slightly windblown and damp.

"I've got to get dressed," David said. "Excuse me."

"I might have left the water running," Thayer murmured. "I'll be right back."

"Got to plan the menu!" Kevin said, hurrying for the door. "Mr. MacNiall... Laird MacNiall, we're going to cook a great...uh...brunch. In thanks for your hospitality, whether intended or not."

Ryan, staring at all of them as if they'd lost their

senses, came striding in, heading for Gina and Toni. "The countryside! My God, I thought I'd taken a few good rides, but you should see the sweeping hills! There is nothing like seeing this place through Bruce's eyes!" Ryan loved both horses and free spaces. His work the last several years as a medieval knight at the Magician's Court right outside Baltimore had seldom allowed him a chance to spend time with his beloved animals that wasn't part of training in closed-in spaces. He must have been happy.

"Why don't you tell me about it upstairs, sweetheart?" Gina said, rising.

"Why upstairs?" Ryan demanded.

"Toni wants to talk to Laird MacNiall," Gina said. She rose, caught hold of his shirtsleeve and dragged him along with her, smiling awkwardly as she passed Bruce MacNiall.

Toni was left alone at the table. Bruce was aware that his arrival had caused an exodus, and he was evidently somewhat amused. Especially since it had been so very far from subtle.

"They're afraid of me?" he queried.

Toni inhaled. "Well, it seems that we're all realizing that you do actually own this place and that we have been taken."

"Good," he said, striding toward the counter.

Toni winced. "The coffee is a bit…"

He'd already poured a cup and sipped it.

"Like mud. It will do for the moment," MacNiall said. He turned and leaned against the counter, looking at her. "What are you supposed to ask me?"

"Well…"

"Well?"

He might be in jeans and tailored denim, leaning

against a counter with a coffee cup, but she could well imagine him in something like a throne room, taking petitions from his vassals.

She stared at him a minute, determined that she wasn't going to be so intimidated. They weren't living in the feudal ages, after all.

"We had booked a large tour group for tonight. We don't want to have to cancel."

"What?" His question was beyond sharp. It was a growl.

Maybe she shouldn't have been quite so blunt. He had slept in a chair in her room last night, but that hadn't made them bosom buddies.

"Look," she said impatiently, wondering what it was about him that goaded her own temper so severely. "You know that we're really in a mess here. And if you take a good look around, you'll have to admit that you owe us."

"I owe you?" The words were polite, but it was quite evident that he found the mere idea totally ludicrous.

So they were right! she thought with a wince. She was quick to become defensive and then offensive with the laird. But she had gone this far with a brash determination. There was little to do other than play it out.

"Yes," she said with conviction. "We've worked on walls, done masonry, fixed electric wiring…scrubbed on our hands and knees! Quite frankly, we're more deserving of such a place—at least *we've* put love and spit and polish into it. How you could own such an exquisite piece of history and…let it go like this, I can't begin to imagine."

She could see the outrage and incredulity slipping into his eyes. Though he didn't move, every muscle in his body seemed to tense, making his shoulders even broader.

Inwardly she winced. Great, she thought. So much for playing it out!

She was supposed to be talking him into allowing them to operate their tour, not offending and angering him.

"So now you're an expert on maintaining a Scottish castle," he said.

She stared into her cup. A sudden and vivid recollection of falling into his lap came to mind. Her fingers against his flesh, pressing into his...lap. The easy way he rose and simply deposited her down...

Last night his behavior had been courteous—and kind. She realized then that she was attracted to him, and somewhat afraid of him, as well. And her hostility toward him had everything to do with her inner defense mechanism.

Ryan suddenly burst back into the kitchen. Toni was certain that he hadn't been far away, that he'd been listening in.

"Toni isn't explaining this very well," Ryan said, turning toward her with a fierce frown. "We really did do a lot, and not just cosmetic work. We did some structural work, as well. Honestly—"

"Yes," Bruce said, staring at Toni.

Her heart quickened.

"Pardon?" Ryan said.

"Miss Fraser wasn't particularly eloquent in her plea, but I do see that you've done a lot of labor here. And I quite understand that you're in a bad position. Your group can come. Apparently you're going to need the money." He poured his coffee down the drain and exited the kitchen.

Ryan stared at Toni in amazement. Then he bounded

toward her, drawing her from the chair, grinning like a madman. "Yes! Yes!"

Gina came in behind her husband. They hugged one another, dancing around the kitchen.

In a moment Thayer was back in, and then David and Kevin. They were so pleased, Toni wondered if they realized that they hadn't gained anything but a single night. And though it would keep them from sleeping on Thayer's Glasgow apartment floor for the next week, it would far from recoup their investment.

"We're going to cook up the best breakfast in the world," David said.

"We might want to start by brewing a new pot of coffee," Toni told them, and she couldn't help a grimace toward Gina. "Laird MacNiall just dumped yours down the sink."

"Really!" Gina said.

"So your coffee sucks!" Ryan said cheerfully, kissing her cheek. "You're still as cute as a button."

"Get out of here, the lot of you," Kevin said. "Shoo! We have to cook."

Toni rose to leave, and as she did so, she glanced at the paper Thayer had left on the table when he'd first come in. The headlines blazed at her: Edinburgh Woman Still Missing. Police Fear Foul Play.

"Wait! Not you, Toni," David said.

She looked over at him. "What do you mean, not me? You all insult my cooking!"

"But you're the best washer, chopper and assistant we've ever had," Kevin told her sweetly. "And then there's the table. We should set it really nicely."

"Wait, I get to wash, chop and be chef's grunt?"

David set his arm around her shoulders, flashing her a smile, his dark eyes alive and merry. "Think of it as historical role-playing. Everyone wants to be the queen, but you have to have a few serfs running around."

"Serf you!" she muttered.

"The others will have to clean up," he reminded her.

"All right, there's a deal," Toni agreed. She walked over to the table and picked up the newspaper, sliding it under the counter so that she could go back for it later.

"Laird MacNiall?"

Bruce had been at his desk—where, he had to admit, the lack of dust was a welcome situation—when the tap sounded at his door. Bidding the arrival enter, he looked up to see that David Fulton was at his door.

"Aye, come in," Bruce told him.

Fulton was a striking fellow, dark and lean. His affection for Kevin was evident in his warmth, but he also seemed to carry a deep sense of concern for the rest of his friends, as did they all.

Bruce was surprised to discover he somewhat envied the repartee in the group. The gay couple, the married couple, Toni Fraser—and even her Scots cousin. They were a diverse group, but the closeness between them was admirable. Riding with Ryan that morning, he had gotten most of the scoop on the group, how they had met, and how they had first begun the enterprise as a wild scheme, then determined that they could make it real.

"We're really grateful to you," David said. "Anyway, we like to think that we've prepared a feast fit for a king—or a lord, at the very least. Would you be so good as to join us?"

Bruce set down his pencil, surveyed the fellow and realized his stomach was growling. He inclined his head. "Great. I'll be right down."

He waited for David to leave, then opened his top drawer and set the sheets he'd been working on within it, along with the daily news.

He didn't close the drawer, but studied the headline and the article again, deeply disturbed. The phrase *all leads exhausted* seemed to jump out at him.

Jonathan Tavish was fine enough as a local constable, but he hated giving up any of his local power, and he just didn't have the expertise to deal with the situation that seemed to grow more dire on a daily basis.

Down in Stirling, Glasgow and, now, Edinburgh, they believed that the girls were seized off the streets of the main cities, then killed in other locations and finally—with the first two, at least—left in the forest of Tillingham because it was so lush and dense that discovery could take years.

Bruce's question was this: Were there others, sad lives lost and unreported, decaying in the woods, their disappearance unnoted? And now another.

Stirling, Glasgow and Edinburgh. The killer was striking all over, yet in Scotland, the distances were certainly not major. The first three abductions had taken place in large cities. But if he had found it easy enough to seize women off busy streets, would he grow bolder and seek out quieter locations?

He drummed his fingers on the desk. Thus far, the local populace had not felt the first whiff of panic. But thus far, the girls reported as "missing" had not been what the locals would consider "good" girls. Not that the people here were cold or uncaring; it was quite the opposite. But since the victims had been known to work the streets and to have fallen into the world of drugs, the average man and woman here did not worry.

It was sad, indeed, tragic. Hearts bled. But women

who fell into the ways of sin and addiction left themselves open to such tragedy.

But MacNiall didn't feel that way. There was a killer on the loose. And no matter what the state of his victim's lives, he had to be stopped.

And he had the power to stop him? MacNiall mocked himself.

He had come home—as far as Edinburgh, at least—when Robert called and told him that there had been no leads on the case and he was just about at wits' end. Then, just two days after arriving in Edinburgh, Robert had told him of a new missing persons report.

The strange thing was, he'd felt an urge to return even before he'd gotten the phone call. Actually, he'd wanted to ignore the haunting sense that he'd needed to be here. But after speaking to Robert, he'd taken the first flight out of New York.

So here he was. Yet, really, why? There were fine men on the case, and he wasn't an official anymore.

But they needed…something. Hell, they needed to realize what they were up against.

Bruce was afraid that all available manpower would not be put on the case until the killer upped his anger or his psychosis, or until the "wrong" victim was killed.

By then, God alone knew what the body count could be.

He pressed his fingers against his temples, remembering the other reason he was actually anxious to have the group gone—his dream. How could he explain having such a strange dream?

Then again, maybe it wasn't so strange. After all, he had found the first body. That vision would never leave his mind.

And now maybe it was natural to meet a woman,

find her irritating beyond measure and then sexy as all hell... And then fear for her.

Annoyed with himself, he snapped the drawer shut and rose to join his uninvited guests in the kitchen.

The setting was a wonder to behold. Toni was certain that Bruce MacNiall thought as much, because he paused in the doorway. And for once, he certainly wasn't angry. He gave that slight arch to his brow and curl to his lip that demonstrated amusement, then he wandered in and took the seat left for him at the head of the table.

Everyone was there, seated and looking at him. "I'm sorry. I didn't realize that I'd kept the rest of you waiting," he said pleasantly, taking the napkin that had been arranged into an elegant bird shape from his plate.

"Almost hate to use this," Bruce said, looking around the table.

"Please, they're nothing to fold," Kevin said. "I've worked in a number of restaurants. That's the fate of most theater majors. Actually, though, I'm a set designer."

"So Ryan told me," Bruce said.

"We each have special and unique talents," Gina said.

"I've heard a few," Bruce said.

"That's right, you were out riding with our Ryan," Thayer said, clapping his hand on Ryan's back. "He's our master of horse and arms! There's not an animal out there our boy can't ride."

"Yes, Ryan is quite skilled," Bruce agreed.

David lifted a hand. "Costumes," he said.

"Yes, and he juggles," Kevin said. "He's really a fantastic actor, as well, but we are the technical whizzes."

"And they're both so humble and modest," Toni said sweetly.

"Sorry, modesty never gets us the job," Kevin reminded her.

"Touché," she agreed.

"And you? What were you doing in Glasgow?" Bruce asked Thayer.

"Piano bar," Thayer said ruefully.

"I'm marketing and promotions, and whatever else is needed," Gina said. "The jill-of-all-theatrical-trades, but my major was actually on the business side."

"Ah." Bruce stared at Toni then, waiting.

"Writer," Toni said, certain that he thought her one hell of a storyteller all right.

"Now you see," Kevin said. "Her imagination is legendary."

"So it seems," Bruce mused, staring at her.

"Our Toni is far too modest. She wrote a one-woman show on Varina Davis—she was the one and only first lady of the Confederacy—and spent six months performing it for sold-out audiences in Washington, D.C., and then Richmond. She writes, acts, directs, sews and is a regular vixen with a paintbrush. Naturally, we do whatever is needed."

"Like scrubbing floors," David said.

"And cleaning latrines," Thayer added.

"Sewing, wiring, flats, paints…we've done it all," Toni told him.

"And what part of the States are you from?" MacNiall asked them, looking around at the group again.

"I'm from Iowa, originally," Gina said. "Toni's from the D.C. area, David's a native New Yorker, Ryan is from Kentucky and Kevin's from Philadelphia."

"We went to college together," Toni murmured.

"NYU," David offered.

"Most of us went to college together. Toni, Ryan,

David and I went to college together," Gina corrected softly. "Then, when Ryan got his job with the Magician's Castle, I moved to Baltimore. Toni moved nearer to D.C., but we stayed close. When she wanted to mount her Queen Varina show, I spent time down there to help her, David did her costume and set. We met Kevin about that time, almost two years ago, and then we finally met Thayer and dragged him in on the scheme the last time we were in Scotland."

"And that was…?"

"Just about six months ago, right?" Ryan said, looking for agreement from the others. "We were at a castle owned by the Menzies family. Clan members had bought it, done some renovations and then opened it for tours."

"Ah," MacNiall murmured, still watching them. Toni wondered what he was thinking. He looked at Thayer. "You were in Glasgow and you just got roped in?"

"I had tried to meet Thayer when we were here just before that. We've vacationed in Scotland at least four times since college," Toni informed him. "But every time I was in the country, Thayer had a job somewhere else. When we finally met…"

"It was as if you'd known one another all your lives?" Bruce MacNiall suggested dryly.

"Actually, yes," Thayer said.

"I see."

"I wasn't roped into anything," Thayer said, offering Toni a small smile. "Their idea was a good one."

"Aye, it might have been," Bruce MacNiall conceded, surprising Toni. "What I saw was wonderfully dramatic."

"You know, we've got a problem tonight," Ryan said. Toni realized that he was looking at her. "Yes?"

"I really had trouble going from costume to costume, and then doing the whole horse in the great hall thing last night. Of course, it worked, because—" he stared at Bruce and smiled weakly "—because Bruce showed up, but otherwise you'll have to stall more."

"She can't stall. The timing was great. Suspenseful. We'll lose them if she has to pad what is a perfect speech!" Gina protested.

"You want Bruce MacNiall to ride into the great hall as he did last night?" Bruce asked. "I can do that for you again. Is that it?"

They were staring at him incredulously.

"You would do that?" Gina said.

"Hey, you're here, and I already think I'm insane myself. Why the hell not?" he returned.

"There's a little more to it, as written," Gina said.

"Oh?" Bruce queried.

David grinned. "You're supposed to dismount, walk up the stairs and strangle Toni."

"Ah." Bruce stared at Toni again, a smile teasing at his lips. "I think I can handle that."

"You only pretend to strangle her, you know," Thayer interjected.

"And that might be a lot harder!" Kevin said, winking at Toni.

She wasn't particularly amused. "I don't really see how we can ask *Laird* MacNiall to join in with us. He's already doing us such a tremendous favor," she said very sweetly.

"I don't mind at all," Bruce MacNiall said, rising. "This was a feast, ladies and gentlemen. If you'll excuse me, though, I'd like to get into the village before your evening events."

They watched as he left.

"Well, there you go. The chap isn't really half bad after all," Thayer said. "We'll have to keep an eye on him, though, when he's up there strangling Toni, eh?"

To Toni, his accent seemed to accentuate a real danger for some reason. But the others were laughing, so it was probably just in her mind.

"Ryan, you've just been shoved out of your big moment," David said.

"Hey, that's okay. It's worth it just to watch that horse of his come racing in and stop on a dime," Ryan said. He grinned, glancing across the table. "I will miss getting to strangle Toni, though."

"Ha, ha," she said and rose, stretching. "Well, let's see…under the artistic direction of Mr. David Fulton and Mr. Kevin Hart, I did the washing, chopping and table adornment. Ryan, you can rue your lost opportunity to strangle me while you wash the dishes with your lovely wife and Thayer."

"Me? But I got to shovel out major horse shite already today!"

"Hey, horses are your thing, and you're the expert. As for KP, we're all in on it. So! Ta-ta, cheerio and all that! I'm off!" And with a smile, she made her exit.

Bruce entered Jonathan Tavish's office after a brief tap against the doorframe. Jonathan looked up and arched a brow. "Bruce, I thought you'd be guarding the family jewels, what with that houseful in the old estate."

"Hardly an estate, and totally a crumbling castle," Bruce said, taking a seat. "Actually, the more I walk around the place, the more amazed I am. They've taken care of a ton of minor things that I've put off for years."

"It's tough when you're keeping up with too much," Jonathan agreed. He grinned. "Now, if you were just among the local peasant law-keepers, you'd be here year-round, pluggin' up holes at any given time. So…it seems you're not quite as angry as you were when you first learned about your guests?"

Bruce angled his head slightly as he surveyed his friend. They were close in age, had known each other since childhood. They shared a passion for this little neck of the world, though they didn't always agree about how it should be run. Bruce was the local gentry, as it were, and Jonathan was the local law. But because Jonathan was local, and had always been local, he seemed to maintain a chip on his shoulder where Bruce was concerned.

One day, maybe, Jonathan would run for the position of provost. As such, he could implement more of his own ideas. Thus far, though, he seemed to like being constable.

"I've cooled down some, yes," Bruce said. "Since no one threw them out in my absence, I thought another few days couldn't hurt too much."

"Ah," Jonathan teased. "It was the blonde, eh? What a beauty—and what absolute hell on wheels!"

"She does have a way about her," Bruce agreed. "But this isn't the first time I've heard about this happening."

"Your castle being taken over?" Jonathan said, puzzled.

Bruce shook his head. "This sort of thing in general. People going through what they think are private enterprises or legitimate rental agencies and winding up in a similar circumstance. I really want to find out what happened in this situation."

"Like you said, it happens too often."

"Yes, but *this* time it happened to be *my* castle that was taken over."

"Come Monday, you can let those folks see all your records. They can bring their documents down, and we'll get someone on it right away. Unfortunately, sometimes—especially in this age of the Internet—people can clean up their trails." He lifted his hands. "I might have gotten started on it already, but they didn't want to hand over the documents."

"It's all they've got to prove anything."

"Great. They don't trust the law."

"Well," Bruce said, offering a certain sympathy. "They don't trust me, either."

"Ah, there we are! In the same boat, as they say."

"Right. But actually, that's not why I'm here," Bruce said.

"Oh?"

Bruce tossed the newspaper on Jonathan's desk.

"Oh, that."

"Aye, oh, that!"

Jonathan shook his head. "Bruce, they're not local girls disappearing."

"But in the last year, two bodies have been found in the forest."

"If you haven't noticed, it's a big forest," Jonathan reminded him.

"Have you had men out searching?" Bruce demanded.

"This girl just disappeared," Jonathan reminded him. "But yes, I've had men out searching."

"Right. The last two girls who disappeared wound up in our forest. We should be looking for this latest lass. I'm willing to bet my bottom dollar that's where she's going to be."

"Careful with that kind of prophecy, Bruce," Jonathan warned, sitting back. "People will begin to think you know more about these disappearances and murders than you should. They do keep occurring when you're actually in residence." He raised a hand instantly. "And that doesn't mean a damned thing. I'm your friend and I know you. I'm just telling you what someone else might think."

"Bloody hell!" Bruce cursed, his tone hard. Jonathan's suggestion was an outrage, and he was both startled and angry.

"Sorry, Bruce, I didn't mean anything by that. It's just that you're getting obsessive. I understand, of course. But you're not what you were, Bruce. Time has gone on. Just because you struck it lucky once in Edinburgh doesn't make you an expert."

Bruce prayed for patience. "I'm not claiming to be an expert. But murdered women being discovered in Tillingham Forest does bother, seriously. And it should bother the hell out of you."

"I know my business, Bruce."

"I'm not suggesting that you don't."

"How can I stop a madman from kidnapping women in other cities? If you haven't noticed, we've miles of dark roads around here, not to mention that whole companies of fightin' men used to use that forest as a refuge! And again, this girl has just been reported as missing. She's an Irish lass, might have just taken the ferry home."

Bruce rose. "If she isn't found in a few days' time, I'll arrange for a party myself to search the forest."

"Bruce, mind that MacNiall temper of yours, please, for the love of God!" Jonathan said. "I told you, we've taken a look in the forest. We'll go back and search with greater effort if she isn't found in the next few days."

"Good." Bruce rose and started for the door.

"Hey!" Jonathan called after him.

"Aye?" Bruce said, pausing.

"Did you close down your haunted castle tour for this evening?" Jonathan asked.

"Actually, no. I'm joining it," Bruce said.

"You're joining it?" Jonathan said, astonished. "You've never acted in your life!"

"Well, that's not really true, is it? We all act every day of our lives, don't we?" Bruce asked him lightly.

"Ach! Go figure!" Jonathan said, shaking his head. "It's the blonde."

"It's the fact that they are in a rather sorry predicament," Bruce said. "And they did do a damn good job repairing a few of the walls. See you on Monday."

He exited the office, leaving the newspaper on Jonathan's desk. He knew what the front page carried—a picture.

She was young, with wide eyes and long, soft brown hair. She had originally hailed from Belfast, Northern Ireland. Apparently, she'd intended to head for London. But she'd never made it that far, discovering drugs and prostitution somewhere along the way instead. She'd gotten as far as Edinburgh, and been officially reported as missing when a haphazard group of "friends" realized that they hadn't seen her in several days.

News could die quickly, unless it was really sensational. The missing persons report on the first girl had run in the local papers and then been forgotten. Until Bruce had discovered her body in the forest while out riding, facedown, decomposed to a macabre degree.

He'd missed the notice about the second disappearance. But there had been no missing the fact of where the body had been found—Tillingham Forest. Eban had found the second victim there, months later.

Prostitutes. Drug addicts. The lost and the lonely. They'd needed help, not strangulation.

He sat in his car for a minute, staring out the windshield. He was parked right in the center of town, where a fountain sat in the middle of a roundabout. Atop the fountain was the proud statue of a Cavalier. There was no plaque stating his name, or the dates of his birth or death, or extolling his deeds. But the locals all knew who the statue portrayed—the original Bruce MacNiall. And tonight, he'd play his ancestor.

A sudden irritation seared through him. "You'd think they'd give you the benefit of the doubt, old boy. But let time go by and now you're a hero—suspected of killing the love of his life!"

There really was no proof that Bruce MacNiall had killed Annalise, but it made for a good story. And just as some historians saw the Stuart champion as a great hero, others saw him as a fool willing to risk the lives of far too many in his own pursuit for glory.

The idea of Bruce MacNiall having killed his wife didn't sit well with him. And still, he had said that he'd play the part. Life sure had it ironies.

"Well, old fellow!" He muttered, "I've never heard it proved that you did any such thing, but it's entertainment these days, eh?"

He threw the car into gear and started toward the castle on its tor.

Entertainment! Was someone killing prostitutes for fun?

He drove by the forest and slowed the car to a crawl. He knew that to find anything within it, they'd have to delve deep into the woods and the streams.

His heart ached for the girl. He knew she was already there, decaying in the woods. And he had known it as a certainty last night, when he had dreamed about seeing a body floating facedown.

Except…in his dream, it had been the body of Toni Fraser.

Chapter 5

"Hey! What are you doing out here?"

Toni turned to see that David had come out to the stables. She was a little surprised. David liked horses well enough, but usually when they came to him or happened to be where he was. Ryan was the expert rider in their crew.

She had been stroking the gorgeous black nose of Bruce MacNiall's huge Shaunessy. The animal was mammoth and, she was certain, an amazing power when ridden. He was also well mannered and seemed to enjoy affection. Amazingly, he seemed to have nothing against Ryan's gelding—at least, not so far as sharing the same living quarters.

"I was just out exploring," Toni told David, "and thought I'd come down here. I love that fellow Ryan bought—he's a great horse for the money. But this guy—" she indicated Bruce MacNiall's huge black "—he's really

something. Of course, I still love our horse best, but...
he is gorgeous."

"Yes. And imposing, just like his master."

"The great Bruce MacNiall, who happened to ride in
after we put our blood, sweat and tears into his place!"
Toni commented.

David grinned. "That's *Laird* MacNiall to you, so I
understand," he teased.

She waved a hand in the air.

"Well, the situation is pretty sad," he murmured. He
strode across the stables then, coming to her side. He
searched her eyes. "You okay, kid?"

"Well, as okay as any of us," she told him.

David gave Shaunessy a stroke on his velvet forehead.
"Don't feel that you are to blame, no matter what happens. We all rushed into this. And if it seems that we're
giving you a hard time, it's mainly teasing—or the fact
that it's human nature to want to blame someone else!"

She touched David's face, then gave him a hug.
They'd met her first year in college, painting sets for a
university production of *Aida*. They'd been best friends
ever since. She loved him like a brother.

"Okay, so we came here...only to find out that we've
been duped. But seriously, it's not all that bad. We put
a lot of sweat and elbow grease into it, but blood and
tears? That's a bit dramatic."

"All right, maybe I am being a bit dramatic. You
would have thought that the damned constable would
have said something to us, though."

"Apparently he believed that the great laird had
rented the place," David said. "MacNiall's been out of
town. I guess no one knew where to reach him to find
out what was up."

"Don't they use cell phones in this country?" Toni murmured.

"I've gone away without feeling the need to tell anyone where I was going. And I definitely don't give my cell number to everyone," David said.

"Well, whatever, it was convenient," Toni murmured. "However you want to look at it, we've put an awful lot into the place. The sad thing is, I don't think any of us needs to wait till Monday to accept the fact that we've been screwed royally."

"Yeah, but MacNiall's being pretty decent now. Hell, he's not just letting us bring in our tour group tonight, he's going to take part in what's going on."

"Right," Toni murmured.

"So…?" David's dark eyes were questioning.

She grinned, knowing the look that he was giving her very well. "So…?"

"Come on, kid. Come sit on a haystack and tell Uncle David all about it. Hey, this may be the only time in your life when you're invited to a haystack for purely platonic reasons."

She laughed and allowed him to lead her to a pile of hay, which David pushed around a bit to create a formation that was almost like a prickly love seat. It was actually rather comfortable.

"It's almost like a shrink's office, huh?" David said.

"I wouldn't know," she told him. "I haven't seen a shrink—yet."

"But something is bothering you, and I think it goes beyond being in the middle of financial disaster."

She shook her head. "David, the thing is, I really thought that I made up my story about Bruce MacNiall's ancestor."

He lifted a hand, shaking his head at her. "All right,

so you made up something real. Dr. David will work on it. Hmm, let's see. Six months ago, we were here doing an extensive tour. In Edinburgh, we saw that really beautiful marble tomb built in honor of Montrose—monster to some, brilliant hero to others. We knew that the castle we were renting had been a MacNiall holding. And Bruce is a pretty common name. I don't think there's anything unusual about all this falling into place."

"Except that I learned a little more about the man— and his wife—from the current Bruce MacNiall," Toni said.

"He strangled his wife?"

"No—at least, it's not known that he did. She disappeared from history—that's how Bruce described it."

"Hmm," David said as he chewed on hay. "Sadly, my dear, many husbands have done in their wives. And many women have disappeared. Things don't really change, no matter where you go. We've got our problems in the States, big-time. There was even an article in the paper about women disappearing around here, too."

"Well, the good thing is, if Lady MacNiall disappeared, she did so centuries ago," Toni said, but she felt uneasy. She had seen the headlines herself.

"There you go."

"The bad thing is, her name was Annalise."

David stared at her, arching a brow high. "No kidding?"

"According to Bruce."

"You know, Toni, maybe you did hear this story somewhere along the way in life and just don't remember," he suggested.

She was silent.

"Hey, it's all right. Really. And apparently this guy doesn't have a Lady MacNiall, so there will be no skeletons in the closet, right. He really is something, though, huh?"

"Yes." Toni was surprised to feel herself coloring a little.

David smiled, finding another blade of hay to gnaw. "There were lots of sparks flying when you two were arguing last night."

"I'm known to send off sparks now and then."

"Usually only when you're defending friends or the downtrodden!" David said with a laugh. Then he looked at her seriously. "You aren't still raving mad about this guy, and we all think that he's right—despite the fact that we don't want to. So…something else is bothering you."

It was a simple statement from a man who knew her far too well.

She glanced his way, hesitated, then said, "I had the most awful nightmare last night. And I screamed bloody murder. That's why he and I wound up talking."

"Okay…" David said slowly. "Talking to him upset you?"

"No. The nightmare upset me."

"You remember it?"

"Yes, it was terrifying. But the strange thing is that Bruce—or his ancestor—was the nightmare."

David arched a brow so she continued. "He was just…there. It was as if I had opened my eyes and seen him, huge, in full battle regalia, standing at the foot of my bed. And he was dressed like a Cavalier. He looked like our Bruce, except that his hair was longer and kilted, he had something like half-armor on, there was a sheath of some kind at his ankle with a knife and he was carrying a sword."

"And standing at the foot of your bed?"

"Yes."

"All right, let's analyze this. Why was he so terrifying?"

She stared at him. "He was at the foot of my bed!"

"And that's all?"

"Well, what if you woke up and found a ghost at the foot of your bed?"

"I'd wake Kevin, and knowing Kevin, he'd be all excited and try to talk to the fellow."

She knew that he was trying to tease her, to make her feel better. But she knew more.

"He was carrying a sword," she said.

"Well, if you dreamed about a Cavalier who fought many battles, naturally he'd be carrying a sword."

"It was dripping blood."

"Toni, you were a theater major who has written a number of plays. You're imaginative. I'd expect no less from you than a dream in living color with complete attention to detail."

"You don't understand, because I've never even talked to you about this, but…" She hesitated, staring at him. She saw nothing in his eyes but the deep concern of a very good friend. "Years ago, as a child, I… dreamed things."

"All children dream."

She looked across the stables. "No. I dreamed things that had happened, really bad things. Murders. The police would come to my house and grill me about what I had seen. I could describe people, sometimes. And could generally tell them exactly what had happened."

"Did they ever catch anyone because of these dreams of yours?" David asked, his tone grave.

"I believe so."

"Then, you were doing something good, Toni."

"Maybe," she murmured. "But I couldn't live with it. And my poor parents! How they fought over it. Anyway, there came a point where I really couldn't stand it anymore. I blacked out, or something, and wound up in the hospital."

"And your folks didn't take you to a shrink?" he asked incredulously.

Toni shook her head. "There was a man, a friend of my mom's. He was wonderful. He seemed to understand exactly what I was going through. When the cops got too persistent, he came in, gentle and quiet, and calmed me down. When I woke up in the hospital, he was there. He seemed to know that my little mind was on overload. I told him that I didn't dream, that dreaming was bad."

"And then?"

"We moved. And I made it stop."

"You *made* it stop?" David said.

She nodded. "You don't know what it was like. My parents were torn apart. The dreams were horrendous. David, I could *see* murders—as they happened, after they happened, just before they happened. Then there were those people who found out about it who weren't with the police. They behaved as if I had leprosy. You can't imagine."

"Yes, actually, that part I can," David murmured. He picked up her hand. "Toni, I don't think you should worry, not just yet, anyway. Seriously, I'm not insisting that everything in the world has a logical explanation, but we're in Scotland, and we did learn about a very similar history to the one you invented. As for seeing an ancient Scotsman in your bedroom in full fighting regalia, well, let me tell you, when the modern-day Bruce MacNiall came riding in during your presentation, that was pretty darned memorable."

"You think I'm being silly?" she asked him.

"I think that you shouldn't worry too much," he told her. He squeezed her hand. "Bruce MacNiall is still what you might want to call a variable. But don't forget that you are surrounded by friends here, friends who love you very much. It's going to be fine. Trust me. Besides, what can you do?"

"Nothing, I guess."

"What happened to the man?"

"What man?"

"The man who came to talk to you. The one who apparently controlled things and made you feel better."

"Oh, Adam."

"Adam…?"

"Harrison," she said.

"Is he still alive?"

"Oh, yes. Well, at least he was two years ago. He came to see my show when I was doing Varina Davis in D.C." She smiled. "He didn't look as if he'd aged a day. He was still and straight and dignified, soft-spoken…very nice."

"Seeing him didn't awaken anything?" David asked.

"No, seeing him was lovely. He asked me how I'd been, applauded the play and was just as nice as could be. He even gave me his card again and reminded me to call him if I ever needed him."

"Well, there you go!" David said, as if having someone's card solved everything. "If anything too weird happens, you call the fellow. Hey, he's not an attorney, or maybe an American ambassador, is he?"

She shook her head.

"What does he do? Or is he retired?"

"He owns a company. Harrison Investigations."

"Investigations. There you go. He can investigate the scam artist who got us into this!"

"I don't think it's those kinds of investigations."

"Ah! You mean he's one of those guys who goes into haunted houses with weird cameras and tape recorders and stuff like that?"

She nodded, finding that she had to grin. "Um. I think that's exactly what he does."

"You don't think that a ghost screwed us all via the Internet, do you?"

Toni had to laugh. "No!"

"Well, then, let's wait and see. Hey, want to take a walk? It's gorgeous around here. Gina was saying that she wanted to go barefoot in one of the trickling streams just below our little hillock here."

"I think it's going to rain."

"Then getting our feet wet won't matter," David said.

She rose, turning back to draw him up. "Sure. Let's go."

She started to drag him along, but he pulled her back, giving her a hug again. "Hey, I'm here if you need me. Always."

She stepped back, eyes twinkling, and sighed. "You love me, you're here when I need you and you're absolutely gorgeous. Why on earth couldn't you have been heterosexual?"

"God knows," he said. "But I do love you."

"I love you, too."

"Anyway, let's get the other guys and go for that walk."

"You're on."

When they returned to the castle, they found the others in the hall, ready to head out.

Thayer was standing by the main doors, where a drawbridge—long gone now, as long gone as the moat—had once led to the portico entry. He appeared reflective.

"What's the matter?" Toni asked him.

He shook his head. "I was just thinking—we really were idiots."

"Why do you say that?" Toni asked, suddenly feeling guilty again.

"We didn't question anything. After we signed the agreements, we just accepted the fact that we would get here and get in. And we did, of course, because the door was open. The keys were hanging there, right inside, as soon as we came in! The door locks with a slide bolt, so we've been sliding it at night. Apparently, Laird Mac-Niall doesn't lock the place up when he's around. What do you think that means?"

"That the castle is a small one, which wasn't on any tour maps or advertised about at all until we got here. And that, in a village such as Tillingham, there's no need to lock your doors," Toni suggested.

Thayer shrugged. "I guess. I'm still feeling like an idiot."

"Ditto," Toni assured him.

"We ready?" Ryan asked, coming to the door.

"Aye," Thayer assured him. "So where are we going?"

"Just down the hill and into the woods a bit. Gina wants to romp in a brook." Ryan looked up. "I think it's going to rain."

"Probably," Thayer agreed cheerfully.

Kevin, coming to join them, said, "We'll probably catch the fricking flu. Do we really have to do this today?"

"If we're out on our arses come Monday, we might not get the opportunity again," Thayer reminded him.

"True," Kevin agreed. "All right, let's go frolic in a bubbling little brook."

Gina came through the door. "It will be fun. Trust me."

So they headed out. It was cool but not cold, which made the walk very pleasant. And the overcast sky was fascinating, painting the landscape around them in beautiful dark shades of green and mauve.

On distant hills, they could see an abundance of sheep. Climbing atop crags were also scattered groupings of the long-haired cattle that Toni had seen more frequently in the far north of the country. Apparently, they were popular in this area, too. Between the cattle, sheep, wildflowers, sloping hills, crags and cairns, the scenery around them was breathtaking.

"This place is really gorgeous," Toni commented.

"It is—and we would have been a real boon for its economy," Ryan said.

"Oh, yeah? There could have been a buildup of fast-food restaurants and Motel 8s all along the way," Thayer said.

"Right! Like Scotland doesn't depend on tourism!" Ryan argued.

"The world goes round on tourism, I guess," Thayer acknowledged.

"We've got a long walk back once it pours!" Kevin shouted down toward Gina, who was ahead of him along the path. She shot him the bird, and he laughed.

At the base of the hill, the canopy of trees began. The color was lighter, there, at the base, and oddly inviting. They followed Gina as she dashed into the woods. A minute later, she shouted out with delight, "There, look, how charming!"

A little curve in a brook jutted out into a dapple of light that made it through the branches overhead. Though the water was a bit dark under the threatening skies, the sound of it rushing over pebbles and stones was light and airy, and the shelter of the neighboring trees made it look like a little piece of heaven. The whole scene was charming.

Gina started hopping along in her haste to remove her socks and shoes and keep moving at the same time.

Toni found herself staring at the trees. Deeper in, beyond the immediate area of the brook, the forest was dark. The green canopy made it appear like a dark den that beckoned and yet, somehow, warned of evil. Staring into the verdant growth, suddenly she felt herself shiver as an uneasy feeling assailed her.

It was as if the trees were breathing. As if the entire shroud of dark green were a living being, an entity unto itself, something that crouched and waited, watching...

"Toni, what are you waiting for? It's great, sumptuous, wonderful, cool..." Gina said, her enthusiasm high.

Shaking off her unease, Toni rolled up her jeans and started to travel carefully out into the middle of the rushing water.

"Ouch! Hey, we didn't think about the rocks under bare feet thing when we agreed to do this!" David shouted, following her example.

"Ouch, indeed!" Kevin cried. He hurried past David, but then hit a sharp rock, lost his balance and crashed into Toni.

Outraged and off balance, Toni went down. "Kevin!"

They were both on their butts, soaked in a foot of water. Kevin started to apologize, but then he stared at her and burst out laughing.

"Oh, you think this is funny! Get him, guys."

At Toni's prompting, the rest of them piled on. And in a matter of minutes, the six of them were drenched, bedraggled and laughing hysterically.

At last, gasping for breath, mud from head to toe,

Toni struggled to get up—and realized suddenly that they'd all fallen silent.

She tried to smooth back her muddy hair, and blink away the water and muck that was blinding her. Then she saw. Once again, the great laird of the manor had returned.

Bruce MacNiall was there, bareback on his great black, Shaunessy. He was watching them as if they were, indeed, part of a theater of the absurd. And there was the oddest expression on his face. Tension, anger? Toni wasn't sure. He looked like a thundercloud himself.

She thought that, for a moment, he stared beyond them, deeper into the forest, from...*from the place where the eyes seemed to watch, from where the sense of breathing and evil seemed to emanate.*

His eyes fell upon the group again.

With...relief? Toni wondered.

And when he spoke, his tone was pleasant enough.

"Having a good time?" he called pleasantly.

"Yeah!" Ryan said. He truly looked like an over-grown child. "It's great—wonderful. The water feels terrific."

"A little cold," Gina said. She sounded nervous, as if they had been caught doing something they shouldn't have.

"We're having a wonderful time," Toni said, staring at Bruce. Surely, once in a while, he let down that stern guard and simply had fun. "Really, you just need to have a bit of a sense of humor to be down here."

"Great," MacNiall called to them from the height of his stallion's back. He smiled. "Glad you're having a good time. You might want to watch out for the leeches, though."

They were dead still, like a tableau.

Then Kevin shrieked, *"Leeches?"*

Toni didn't think that she had ever moved so quickly. The same might be said for the others as they scrambled over one another to get out of the stream as quickly as possible. She knocked into Kevin. Ryan tripped over his own wife. Toni reached down to Gina, and in his haste to do the same, Ryan knocked Toni back down. Thayer caught hold of Toni, David helped both Ryan and Gina, and Kevin was on his own. Finally, after a scene straight from the Three Stooges, the six of them made it out of the water and to the shore. And there they began to hop up and down, checking what parts of one another they could actually see.

Gina, screaming, banged at her thigh. "There's one on me! Get it! Get it!"

They ran around behind her, staring her up and down.

"There's nothing there," Toni said.

"There is!"

"No, honestly, there's nothing there. Look, let's just get back to the castle—and the showers!" Toni said. She, too, was feeling things all over.

Twenty minutes later, after a fierce pounding of hot water, Toni was sure that she had none of the little buggers on her. Wrapped in her terry robe, she emerged into her room, ready to find clean, warm clothing.

What she found instead was Bruce MacNiall, in her room, getting the fire going. Hunched down by the hearth, he coaxed kindling and logs to flame. In the light, his hair was sleek, blue-black in its darkness. As he moved, she was aware of the breadth of his shoulders and, oddly, a sense of the power within them. It was almost as if he, too, like his long-dead ancestor, had hefted the great weight of a sword or battle-ax to gain such a strength.

She swallowed, feeling a strange quickening. It was one thing to acknowledge that he was an imposing, exceptionally attractive man. It was quite another to feel… such a strange affinity with him. She needed him out of the room—now.

"Hmm," she murmured, crossing her arms over her chest, leaning against the wall and forcing a pleasant tone to her voice. "Interesting. I could have sworn that I had to vacate the room on the other side of the bath since that one was *yours*." At the end, her tone had risen. She couldn't help it; she was unnerved by his appearance. It might be his castle, and he might have fallen asleep in her chair, but still…he had no right to be in here.

"Sorry," he said coolly. "I certainly didn't mean to be intrusive. I had hoped to get this going and be out before you were finished." There seemed to be a slight smile on his face. She immediately felt even more defensive. "I thought you might want some warmth. It's chilly out there, and the rain has begun. Interesting day for a lark in the water."

"Sorry. The concept of wading through the rushing water was a bit too much for us to resist."

"*Wading* through the rushing water? That was more like a mass, a Holy-Roller baptism!"

"Yes, yes, I know. We got a bit carried away," she said. "We're silly Americans, being fools playing in the brook or the brae or whatever the hell it is. You'll have to forgive us. We were just having fun. I have heard that the Scots are just a bit dour, so you probably wouldn't understand."

"Seeing as how I lack a sense of humor, you mean," he murmured.

"Well, we're very close friends. And maybe such a thing wouldn't exactly be *your* cup of tea, but I would hope that you could appreciate a little silliness. Call it an American sense of humor."

Dark lashes swept over his eyes and his grin deepened as he gave the fire a last prod. Then he rose and headed for the door to the hall. But as he passed her, he paused.

"Yes, of course, an American sense of humor. Surely I can appreciate that. And I hope that you can appreciate a Scottish sense of humor."

"What do you mean by that?" she demanded, very aware of the size and scope of the man, and the smile that lent a certain charm to his face.

"Well, there are no leeches in that brook," he said lightly, and exited the room before she could reply.

Chapter 6

Toni stood next to Gina on the upper landing while David played his role as the kitchen maid below. They grinned at one another as they heard the laughter.

"This was such a good idea," Gina murmured.

"Right. If only we really had a lease option on the castle," Toni replied.

"Under the circumstances, Bruce has been really above and beyond," Gina said.

"Oh?"

"This afternoon I showed him our papers again. He inspected them closely, then said that they certainly looked as if they were in order. He was very sympathetic. He even called his insurance company. Though he's willing to help us, he didn't particularly want to get sued."

"I thought we had insurance," Toni said.

"We did. It covered us and damage, but apparently

I didn't read the fine print well enough. We also need a special clause to cover anyone who might get hurt. And we really should have more signs and warnings out. Anyway, he's taking care of it."

"All that, for just tonight?" Toni murmured.

"I'm getting the feeling that he might let us go on awhile," Gina said. "Long enough to make some money, anyway."

"I guess we'll see," Toni murmured.

"David is about to introduce you," Gina murmured. "He was a bit strange about this afternoon, though, don't you think. I mean, about our foray into the brook."

"There are no leeches," Toni murmured back.

"Oh, he told us that," Gina said. "But I don't think it was actually the idea of us in the brook that disturbed him so much. It was the fact that we were in the forest. At lunch he was adamant about us staying out of the forest."

Toni felt a little shiver snake through her. She could remember how the forest had made her feel. As if it were alive. As if there were eyes. Watching.

"You're up!" Gina said.

Toni walked out to the landing in the white gown and began to talk about the great Bruce MacNiall, passionate in his defense of king and country. "There were those who called him a hero, and those who called him a monster. Be that as it may, he never wavered in his loyalty, or in his passion. In the end, the great Bruce, like Shakespeare's Othello, would find his undoing in his passion and in his heart. For years, he bested Cromwell's forces. For years, as he rode the countryside and fought, he loved his wife, Annalise. Yet, while he strayed far from home, rumors reached him of her infidelity. He returned, her betrayal like a blade that dug into his heart greater than the wounds inflicted by any real sword."

That night, there was no mighty bolt of lightning, no massive crack of thunder. Yet, Bruce MacNiall arrived on the great black in a stunning burst of speed and noise and perfection. He was not dressed as he had been the night before, but rather in period breeches, with a leather chest guard, his family colors apparent in the great length of tartan swept around his shoulders and pinned there with a silver brooch. A typical Scots knife was in a sheaf at his calf. His sword belt was buckled to his hip and swung with pure theatricality as he dismounted from Shaunessy.

The sight of him caused that strange quickening sensation in her again. He indeed appeared fierce.

Tonight—maybe because he'd had that talk about insurance with Gina—Ryan was there to take the great black the minute the man dismounted.

There was a roar of pleasure and then applause from the crowd as he came to the floor and looked up the stairs.

Toni still had no idea what he actually did for a living, but he could have been an actor. He ignored the crowd so completely, all those people might not have existed at all. When his eyes fell upon her, her own breath caught. And when he started up the stairs, more imposing than ever in his historical attire, she found herself taking a step back.

"Annalise!"

There was a hiss at the end of the word that sent shivers down her spine.

"Even upon the field of battle, word of your treachery comes to me!" he bellowed.

The crowd was dead silent as he took the steps slowly and fluidly.

She tried to remind herself that she was acting. "Nae, you're wrong, you're deceived!" she cried out. And as he neared her, she continued, the argument in her voice certainly sounding very real. "Would you doubt me so easily, m'laird? All these long days, weeks, months! I do naught but wait…for your return."

"Lies fall prettily from your lips!" he informed her, moving closer.

"Never! I do not lie! I swear it!"

"Annalise…!"

Again, the hiss at the end of the name. And then, he was there.

"Wife! Beloved wife!" he said, reaching out for her, crushing her into his arms. His fingers trailed into the length of her hair. "Wife!" he cried out again.

His face was buried against her throat. And when he whispered, "How am I doing?" he caught her completely off guard. She realized her own terrible tension, and the way that the bulwark of his chest felt against her own. There was something so incredibly electric and vital about him. She had become a victim of her own fantasy, caught up in the strength of his hold, the rich scent of his aftershave and the whisper of his breath against her neck.

"Uh…great!" she managed to whisper back.

"Beloved, betrayer!" he exclaimed then in a sudden fury, shoving her from him.

"Nae!" she shrieked, feeling a real unease for a moment.

Then his hands were around her throat, his fingers so long that he could wind them around her neck without putting the least pressure on her.

"Sweet Jesu, how could you betray me so?" His cry was full of passion and pathos.

Everyone below was dead silent, feeling the laird's pain and yet horrified at what he was about to do.

He shook her.

Toni grasped his hands, pleading, gasping. "Nae, nae, I have done naught but love you, naught but…love you."

He supported her as she slowly sank to her knees before him.

In another piece of perfect theater, he held her still. His face came closer to hers.

"Annalise…"

His lips touched hers, just briefly.

"Before God! I cannot bear it!"

Again he pretended to shake her as his fingers tightened around her neck. Toni was stunned by the entire show herself. She managed to die in a pile of white silk at his feet. And then there was silence from below again. Real silence.

Bruce MacNiall knew how to work a crowd. He rose to his full height, gripped the banister and looked down at the silent people gaping up at him.

"Can't really throw her down the stairway, folks, she might get hurt!"

There was a burst of laughter and then the thunder of applause. The tourists were thrilled.

David, Kevin and Thayer, down among them, were still gaping. Then David came to his senses.

"Tea and scones, ladies and gentlemen. If you'll follow me to the laird's ancient kitchen, we'll have a bit of a repast!"

Still on the floor, Toni knew she should be delighted that they were doing so very well—even if their host had stolen the show.

As the crowd filed out, she heard them exclaiming about what a great experience it had been, how real, how it was almost as if they could touch the past.

"Are you getting up, Toni?"

He was hovering over her, a hand extended. She accepted it, coming to her feet.

Gina came running out from the hallway, practically crashing into Bruce. "You were incredible! Magnificent. My lord, just phenomenal!"

"Thank you." He inclined his head, accepting the compliment.

"We didn't even rehearse anything," she continued with awe.

"Well, walking up the stairs and pretending to strangle someone is really not so hard," Bruce said with a shrug.

"But you came up with lines! Hey, my own heart was beating, and I know the story. Well, Toni's story…anyway, it was just amazing."

"Toni?" Bruce inquired politely. "Was everything all right with you?"

She didn't get to answer.

David, apparently having escaped tea-and-scone duty, came running up the stairs. Excitedly taking hold of Toni, he gave her a hug, then told Bruce, "Wow! You had me shaking in my boots down there. I almost ran up here to tell you that you couldn't really do it! What a fabulous laird you make!"

"He is a laird," Toni reminded him. Meeting Bruce's eyes, gray as slate, unfathomable, she added, "And I don't think the concept of strangling any of us is a big stretch." She offered him a rueful smile, thinking her words a joke. Yet, for a moment, as he stared back at her, she felt anger emitting from him.

"The concept of strangling anyone should not come easy to any man," he said. "Well, madam manager," he said, addressing Gina, "did last evening help?"

"Oh, certainly... Of course, we'd need to work this a long time to begin to recoup our investment, but you have saved us—really!" Gina told him. "I know that you're a busy man, and that we certainly can't count on you every night, but is there a possibility that..." She paused, unsure of her words, then plunged right in. "I'm rambling here. Actually, what I'm doing is begging. Bruce, would you consider giving us a little run? We had nothing booked tomorrow or Monday, but our people in Stirling and Edinburgh were taking reservations for the rest of the week."

Bruce was dead still. Then he sighed.

"I would love to accommodate you, really, I would."

"Then do!" Gina pleaded prettily.

Bruce shook his head. "There's a situation going on here," he said. "I really think it would be safer if you all weren't here."

"What situation?" Ryan asked, joining them.

"There's a serial killer in Scotland, or so they believe," Bruce said.

Gina shook her head. "Yes, I read in the paper that a couple of girls had disappeared, and that their bodies had been discovered later in the woods. But I'm not sure I understand what that has to do with us and our performances."

"I agree with Gina," Toni said, looking at Bruce. "This is very serious, of course, but it's not as if we're a hotel and it's our guests who are becoming victims."

Bruce's slate eyes fixed on her.

"I think there's a bit of this story you're all missing," Bruce said.

"And what's that?" Gina asked.

"There's another girl missing right now," he said.

"But she wasn't from here, right?" Toni said. "I've seen the newspapers. He's attacking prostitutes, right?"

Bruce sighed. "You aren't understanding my point. There's a serial murderer at work. He's been taking his time, and he's been careful enough that, once the victims have been found, the police have gotten almost nothing from clues left on the remains to help them capture the man. And yes, he's been attacking prostitutes, but there's no guarantee this man won't change his choice of victim. Besides, even if you two young ladies are not in personal danger, don't you think it's rather in bad taste to stage this event when women have so recently been murdered?" he demanded.

"Were they strangled?" Ryan asked.

Bruce shook his head impatiently. "They don't know. The bodies were in such a severe state of decomposition when they were found that the medical examiners couldn't pin down the cause of death."

They stood awkwardly on the stairway. Voices began to rise from below.

"You and your friend could have been minstrels, you were adorable," a young woman was telling Kevin as he led the group back through the great hall to exit the main doors.

"Aw, shucks!" Kevin said. "Thanks!"

David turned to hurry down the stairs and help.

"We've got to go bid them all good-night," Gina murmured. "Even if it is our last performance, we should play it out properly." She linked arms with Toni and they started down, followed by the others.

A tall, elderly fellow walked up to Toni. He spoke with an English accent, from somewhere far to the south. "Young lady, we were laughing away, enjoying it tremendously. But when you died! My poor heart just broke."

"Well, thank you."

A younger man stepped up. "Pete and me were about to race up the stairs and save you!" he told her, indicating his friend.

Pete, a blond fellow about the same age, grinned. "Yeah, but the concept of an encounter with the Bruce kind of quelled the idea," he said, causing a rise of laughter among the entire group now traipsing out.

"How could you, man?" the first fellow said, looking over Toni's head.

She was startled when Bruce set an arm around her. "Ah, well, the lass was not doing as she ought, and I'm afraid that back then…well, that particular Bruce was known to be loyal to a fault, good to those who supported him, lethal to those who betrayed him."

"Is the story real?" Pete asked.

"Laird Bruce MacNiall was real," Bruce assured him. "As to the disposal of his wife, no one knows. She simply fell from the pages of history, so anything about her is just local lore. Poor Bruce did meet a sad end. Since his Annalise perished tonight, we didn't include the part about him castrated, hanged until half-dead, disemboweled and beheaded."

"Ugh!" someone said from the crowd.

"Luckily, that was several hundred years ago," Bruce said.

"Luckily!" the older man said. "Honey, I couldn't strangle you, no matter what you did!"

"Thank you," Toni told him.

"I think poor Annalise was innocent. I mean, why cheat on a fellow like that?" a young woman said with awe, smiling at Bruce. A little too wistfully, Toni thought, surprised by her own annoyance. "So…does the great Laird MacNiall sweep up his wife and carry her off to the master's chambers?"

A quick no came to Toni's throat. But as she'd noted earlier, Bruce knew how to play to a crowd.

"Of course," he said simply. And turning, he swept Toni off her feet as effortlessly as if she were a rag doll and started for the stairs.

Gripping his shoulders, Toni quickly queried in a whisper, "What are you doing?" Her words were a little desperate.

His eyes were lighter, amused, as they met hers. "Trying to get them all out of here. Say good-night, my love."

He turned at that, clearing his throat loudly. "A little privacy in the castle, please!"

His words were followed by laughter—and an exit.

On the landing, Bruce set Toni down perfunctorily and turned, immediately retracing his steps. Their guests were out the doors. Kevin remained in the hall.

"There's still food in the kitchen?" Bruce asked.

"Yes, certainly. And we can whip up anything you want, really quickly," Kevin assured him.

"Great, I'm starving. Get the group together when the buses are gone. We'll discuss the morning, and where we go from here."

Toni bit back her sense of extreme aggravation and followed him down the stairs to the kitchen. The "great laird" was apparently not in the mood for something as simple as scones, and quite capable of taking care of himself. He headed straight for the refrigerator, grabbing all kinds of sandwich makings, while the others jumped around to wash lettuce and slice tomatoes. The circumstances were very bad, Toni admitted, but she hated the fact that they were so obliged to Bruce MacNiall.

"So, Bruce, what do you think?" Gina asked anxiously.

"I think that you went through a lot of work, and that it looks like your papers—license, permits—are in order. And now the insurance has been dealt with…" He shrugged.

"If you have to leave again, I swear, we will be so good to this place!" Ryan said. "And you won't have to stable Shaunessy anywhere else. You know that I'd just about lie down and die for that horse."

"So?" Gina persisted.

Toni was surprised when Bruce stared at her. He seemed reflective and worried.

"We began a conversation on the stairs. Women have been killed." He directed his gaze upon Thayer. "You must have known about it."

Thayer made a choking sound. "Well, yes, but…" He lifted his hands. "Sadly, these things happen often enough. People don't stop living because of it. We've had much worse situations, every country has. I never saw it as something that really concerned our efforts here."

Bruce shook his head, looking downward for a minute.

Gina said, "Bruce, people in the village don't seem to be concerned…for their own safety, I mean."

"No, I guess they don't," he murmured.

Ryan cleared his throat. "Terrible things have happened in almost every major city, and naturally, they can happen in the countryside, as well. Please…we'd never let ourselves be victimized." He winced, realizing that they *had* been victimized. "Gina and Toni are too smart to set themselves up for a dangerous situation. We're always together."

"The women have disappeared from the *big* cities," Thayer reminded quietly.

Bruce looked hard at Thayer. "So they have."

"Please! We're adults, and we're less naive than before," Toni added. "We'll be careful. Please, give us a chance?"

They were all staring at the man. Again he shrugged. "Let me say a tentative yes, we can give it a go. For the next few weeks, at least. There are problems that will arise. Aye, there's the fact that your 'guests' are usually from far away, and I don't know how the local population is going to take to this. The story Toni invented is too damned close to truth. There are those who think that I have an ancestor out there, running around in the forest, possibly capable of doing ill will. There are the other, very real problems—the situation at present. But we'll see. First thing Monday, we will go to the courthouse. I'll prove my ownership, and we'll get Jonathan going on finding out just who is behind the scam that took you people in."

"We would gratefully appreciate it!" Gina said.

He shrugged. "I do admit, you've done a lot for the place."

"Thank you," Thayer said, looking at him curiously. "I don't mean to be rude, but...but when we got here, the place didn't look very...lived in," he murmured.

Bruce looked at Thayer. "You are from Glasgow, right?"

"Aye, that I am."

"As the crow flies, not so far," Bruce said.

"Not so far, yet Glasgow is a world unto itself. Edinburgh, too, as a matter of fact. It may be a wee country, Laird MacNiall, but we both know that it's still very regional."

Bruce nodded. "Regional, aye. I'm just surprised that you didn't know that there was a real Bruce MacNiall."

Thayer grinned ruefully. "Maybe I owe you an apology, then. But, I'm sorry to admit, I've never been to more than half my country. I made it to the Orkney Islands last year for the first time, though I've never been to the Isle of Skye."

"I see," Bruce murmured.

"Hey, I've never been to California," Kevin said.

"And I've never been to—Utah," David offered.

"Who can cover a whole country?" Ryan asked cheerfully.

"Ah," Bruce murmured. "It's just that news regarding the killings certainly reached the major newspapers. Murder may be something that happens everywhere, but in Scotland, such crimes do bear note."

Thayer appeared a bit tense, as if he'd been accused of lying.

"I knew about the murders. Everyone has seen something about them in the paper," Thayer said, looking confused.

"But you didn't notice any specific references?"

"I don't know what you're talking about," Thayer said.

"References to the area?" Toni asked.

Bruce ignored her. "Thayer?"

"I swear, if there was mention regarding this place in the newspapers or on the telly, I didn't see it," Thayer said. "I live and work in Glasgow, and as you must know, with our size and certain factors, we do have our own crime rate."

"I'm aware of the city. I've actually been there," Bruce said.

Toni was oddly uncomfortable, feeling, as Thayer apparently did, that he was somehow under attack. "In the old U.S.A., most farm boys have been to the big city. Doesn't mean all the city folk have made it out to the farm," she said lightly.

Bruce's eyes shot to hers. "I see. So we're yokels out here, are we, Toni?"

"It's small, that's all I'm saying," she told him with exasperation.

"Perhaps we should talk about this in the morning," Gina said softly. "Tempers seem to be rising a bit."

"My temper isn't rising," Toni said, staring at Bruce. "It's just that Thayer is my cousin, and I understand completely how he might not have heard of the great and almighty Bruce MacNiall."

"Toni!" David warned.

"No, really! Bruce, please, listen to me. I'm grateful that you're being magnanimous. But if we're going to make this work, you need to trust us."

After a moment Bruce turned to Thayer. "I'm not accusing you of anything, Fraser. I'm just curious, that's all. Naturally," he said, addressing Gina, "we will have to have some kind of contract written up, but we can work that out at another time." He set his sandwich on a plate and turned to leave. They watched him in silence. At the kitchen door, he turned back. "One last thing. Stay out of the forest. That's a must." He stared at Toni. For a moment, it seemed that he was speaking only to her.

She felt almost as if they were touching. Her heart hammered, her breathing quickened. Kinetic energy seared between them, and she wanted to reach out and shake the man.

After he left, they remained in stunned silence for a minute, and Toni felt something deflate in her.

"I don't know about this," she said. "Every time I start to think he might be decent, he turns back into an ass."

"Toni, it's just you!" David said.

"He was on to Thayer!" Toni said.

"Hey, kinswoman," Thayer said lightly, "it's all right. This is Scotland. I can see where he was coming from. Aye, he got m'dander up! But it's all right. There was no revolution here, you know. There's still royalty, nobility, peerage, the whole bit. They tend to think they should be known, though, as you've seen, old piles of stone like this one tend to be all about. The bloke probably can't quite admit that this isn't exactly Stirling or Edinburgh castle!" Thayer shrugged. "We're at the base of the Highlands, you know. The Lowlanders and the Highlanders have always been a bit off. I'm fine with it all. Hey, I am a Scotsman. I should have seen to it that I knew more about the place, eh?" He walked to Toni, smiling ruefully, and gave her a kiss on the cheek. "My fierce little American! I'm all right on my own, honestly."

She nodded, liking him very much then.

Thayer's small dimples showed and his green eyes were light. With his fingers he shoved back a lock of sandy hair and said again, "Toni, I'm all right, honestly."

"Well, there you have it!" David announced. "It's late."

"Yes, if the lot of you will just get out of the kitchen, David and I will whip it all clean in a matter of minutes," Kevin said. "We can make more sense of things in the morning."

"No, we'll stay and help," Toni murmured.

"No, you will not!" David protested. "You'll make it take longer."

"You'll start breaking dishes," Ryan said.

"I will not!" Toni protested.

David came by her side, hugging her. "Toni, you're in bitch mode," he said softly.

"I am not!" she protested vehemently. Then she looked around, they were all staring at her. "I am not," she said stubbornly, but far more softly.

"It's him," Thayer said.

"You're right, it's him," she agreed, thinking that, naturally, Thayer was on her side. Then she realized that he hadn't meant the words quite the way that she had taken them, because the others were suddenly grinning.

"You noted it, too?" Ryan said to Thayer.

"The sparks that are always flying?" Kevin suggested.

"Chemistry in the air," David said.

"Oh, no!" Toni protested.

"I'd do him in a flash," Kevin said, "if I weren't taken."

"And if he weren't reeking heterosexuality," David said pragmatically.

"Trust me—" Toni began.

"Oh, Toni! Quit being so blind!" Gina advised. "Every time the two of you talk, I'm waiting for one of you to lunge at the other and grapple on the floor!"

"I give up," Toni said, very aggravated and tense.

"You are free, white and female," David reminded her.

"Hey, might be good for her," Ryan commented.

"Look how calm and sweet Gina always is! And she can thank me for that!"

"Okay, I've had it—I'm out of here!" Toni said.

To her complete irritation, they all laughed as she departed.

Upstairs, she showered and was just crawling in for the night when she heard a tapping on her connecting door. She thought about calling out, but didn't. Instead, she rose, walked across the room and opened the door.

Bruce was there, in his bathrobe, his hair slick and black, slate eyes enigmatic. "If you're not all right, just call out," he told her quietly.

"If I'm not all right?" she murmured.

"If dreams plague you. Nightmares," he said.

She met his eyes. There was concern in them, and she was amazed at the sudden sense of *knowing* him that leaped into her heart. *Wanting him,* she thought.

He touched her face, his thumb moving gently over her cheek, rounding down around her chin. "You know," he mused softly, "it is just a matter of time."

"Excuse me?" Her words were breathless. She should have just moved away to begin with. His touch was somehow extremely intimate. She felt as if her flesh was crying out to be touched by him. All of it. The length of him beckoned—his hands, the size of him, cast of his features, texture of his skin, even the slate of his eyes.

"A matter of time," he repeated.

"Until…?" she managed with a smile.

"Well, until you jump me, of course."

"Until I jump you?" she demanded, some sense of indignity coming to the fore. "Laird MacNiall, I'm afraid that you do have a rather inflated opinion of yourself!"

He was still amused. He leaned closer to her and said softly, "I won't be stopping you, you know, lass."

Then he turned and quietly closed the door between them.

Toni kicked it.

"Call if you need me," he said.

She made a point of locking the door.

But later that night, the dream came again. She was sound asleep, or so she thought. Then she opened her eyes, and he was there. At the foot of her bed. In full war regalia, with his sword at his side. Dripping blood.

And she began to scream.

The first scream cut through Bruce's subconscious like a razor. He bolted up, seeking the danger for a millisecond, then he burst from his bed and hurtled through the bath.

She had the door locked.

He hesitated for a moment, listening. Then, once again, he heard her scream. Swearing, he hurried back in his room and dug in the cuff-link drawer of the wardrobe for the skeleton key. Seconds later, he had the door open.

She was sitting up in bed, staring, her blond hair streaming out over the lilac print of her flannel gown. Her eyes were open, dead-set on something in front of her, something that he couldn't see but which was so very real to her.

Another scream ripped from her.

There was something achingly vulnerable, young and fragile about her at that moment. The fine construction of her features seemed more delicate, the wheaten beauty of her hair more sheer. She looked for all the world like an otherworld Ophelia.

And, like the mad Ophelia, if he didn't move, she would not be reprieved.

He started for the bed, then halted, because suddenly she was moving, no longer simply staring and screaming, but shrinking back. As if something—someone— were after her.

He flew across the room, calling her name.

"Toni, Toni!"

Falling upon the bed, he caught her by the shoulders. She was stiff and cold, as if she were nearly dead herself. She didn't acknowledge him, but neither did she look through him. She looked around him.

"Toni!" He gave her a shake, drawing her to him, determined to transfer some of his own warmth into her form. "Toni, wake up, it's a dream, a nightmare." He stroked her head, his fingers cradling the shape of her skull. "Toni!"

At last, he felt her resistance. She pulled away from him, her eyes wide and confused in the night. She said his name, but with a strange hesitance and uncertainty.

"Bruce?"

"Aye, it's me."

She still looked so wide-eyed, not so much terrified as...confused.

"In the flesh," he added, trying to speak lightly. He was very nearly in little but the flesh, and was glad he'd gone to sleep in boxers.

"Bruce?"

One of her hands fell against his chest. The fingers were still chilled, but the brush against him seemed to evoke a flash of fire. He caught that hand, held it between his own, rubbed it, tried to warm it.

"Aye, kid, you're having something of a poor time getting sleep in here, eh?" he asked her.

She flushed, then looked at him sheepishly again. "It's rather ironic, really. I make up a fellow, only to find out that he existed, and now he keeps appearing at the foot of my bed, with his sword dripping blood." She hesitated. "Do you think he's trying to warn me to get the hell out of your castle?"

They faced one another on the bed then, not touching, but very close. He couldn't help the small smile that came to his lips. "Nae," he said softly, purposely allowing the Scots burr into his voice. "Nae, fcr 'tis said that Bruce were a man what loved a damselle, and wouldna hae it that one should suffer at his door."

He was glad of his speech, for she smiled, as well, and it seemed that the terror and confusion had at last lost their grip upon her. "How did Lady MacNiall feel about that? If she was running around with some local fellow, it might have been out of revenge for all the lasses he kept giving, er, sanctuary? At his castle?"

"They were different days," hc told her lightly.

"Oh?"

"Well, there were a few instances in Scottish history that certainly wouldn't be the least politically correct these days. Take Robert the Bruce. His poor wife was captured by the English and held prisoner for years, just for being his wife. He loved her dearly—honestly, he did—but there were a number of children born in those days that bore the king's protection. So…while she was locked up for being his wife, he was still prey to manly temptation."

"So Bruce MacNiall cheated like crazy, then killed his poor wife?" Toni said, wrinkling her nose.

"You made that part up. No one knows what happened to his wife," Bruce reminded her.

"I made the whole thing up!" she reminded him with a soft groan.

He pulled her against him again, stroking her hair. "It's a castle, you invented a bloody warrior, he happens to have existed."

She leaned against him, apparently content to be there. Her hair was a velvet tease against the nakedness of his chest, the scent of her a strange and riveting intoxication in the night. She could speak with such determination, quell with a look, move with grace and dignity... by day. But at night, she was like a brush of pure silk, sweet smelling, lustrous, supple and...vulnerable. Tonight she was vulnerable.

"It's more than that," she whispered.

"What more could it be?" he asked gently.

She shook her head. He threaded his fingers into her hair, gently tugging back, anxious to see her eyes. Huge, bluer than the midnight sea, they met his. Little triggers of electricity seemed to tease both his muscles and his flesh. Something akin to pure agony clamped down upon his groin. He gritted his teeth, determined not to let her see the rise of pure carnal instinct and natural humanity.

"I... You don't understand. I'm afraid. Never mind..." she murmured.

"What is it? You can tell me, honestly," he assured her.

"Ah...so that you could mock an American further?"

"Americans are lovely people," he told her, smiling. "Most, anyway, right?"

"Toni, if there's something wrong, you can tell me. I swear, I will not bring it beyond the walls of this room," he vowed levelly.

She shivered suddenly, then moved, as if pretending that she had not done so. She set her hands upon his shoulders. "You know, you're rather a lovely man yourself—but only in the dead of night."

"Ach, I'm really lovely as hell by day, as well. You're just not noticing," he informed her.

Another shiver, almost imperceptible, ran down her spine. She moved closer, resting her head against his shoulder and throat. "I have noticed," she informed him. Then she looked up. "You know that question you asked earlier?" she whispered.

Ah, and that whisper brushed his cheek, and soft and light as it was, it beckoned to an even greater desire inside, one that shrieked and cried out, in bone and sinew and blood.

"About jumping me?" he inquired.

"Yes, I would be referring to that one."

The flannel of her nightgown suddenly seemed to hug her breasts with pure temptation, concealing, too clearly giving away structure, firmness, rise...

Her voice was meant to be casual, almost haphazard, but it was tremulous.

He caught hold of her chin.

"I won't sleep with you because you're frightened," he told her.

"I wouldn't dream of sleeping with any man for that reason!" she told him.

"It's all right. I won't sleep with you, but I won't leave you," he told her, stretching out on the bed, drawing her against his shoulder. "If my ancestor comes anywhere near, you can always try arguing him to death. You've come quite close with me, you know."

She thumped on his chest with a finger.

"I am not that bad. And I am not a bitch."

"Ah...so, your friends even know you want to jump me," he said.

She started to push away from him in a sudden, indignant fury.

"Get some sleep!" he told her, drawing her down again, smoothing her hair as she rested her cheek against his face.

It was absurd. He'd known her so very short a time. She hadn't been so much as a figment in his mind just two days ago. And now...

He breathed in her scent and felt her softness, the warmth in his arms. *It was almost like forever.* He also felt the insane drumming in his groin. Lord, he wanted her. But...not because she woke screaming in the night, having seen *his* ancestor at the foot of her bed.

"Sleep," he murmured again.

Later, when she breathed easily against him, her every breath adding torture against his awakened flesh, it was himself he mocked.

"You are an ass!" he whispered aloud.

When daylight came, he left her once again.

Interlude

The bodies had been taken to a mass funeral pyre. It hadn't been out of a sense of brutality; they were sorry that many a good soldier with a different loyalty could not be returned to his family, could not receive honors and a proper burial. But they knew that, with so much death, flies and maggots would come in droves and the blood would taint the water and the earth. Sickness would soon follow.

The air was ripe. There was nothing so horrible as the smell of burning flesh, but there simply was no choice.

MacNiall's own men were seeing to their wounded, their own dead and their dying.

But victory had been achieved, and even among the wounded, aye, and the dying, there was a sense of justice and purpose. They had prevailed. Whiskey and beer were flowing freely—the wounded needed it, the victors craved it. Still, in the midst of jubilation, the troops knew discipline, and they celebrated in close-knit ranks.

From somewhere within the many pockets of men came the plaintive notes of a bagpipe. Despite victory, Bruce MacNiall could find no pleasure or solace that night. Secure that his scouts remained on the lookout, that the wounded had been gathered and that the ranks would not break, he went to Angus at last.

"Ye are in charge, man. I'll be gone but a day or two."

Angus shook his head. "Ye canna be runnin' off half-cocked, man. Not on the word of a liar who would see y'be the one hanged!"

"I have to go."

"Nae, y'do not!" Angus protested. "She waits, as she has always waited. She loves ye, man!"

"Aye, and that be so, she is in danger herself. I must see to her welfare. She canna stay at the castle longer. Thus far, they've ignored it. Too far from any place that counts! Fer many years, I've been the enemy, they've not taken their vengeance ta the homes. Now, with the words Grayson Davis has spoken, I canna be sure!"

"Ye canna go! I've a fear deep in me heart. Ye canna do this, Bruce."

"I must do this. As I must breathe," he said simply.

He set his arms around Angus, giving him a fierce hug. "Y're in charge, man. They'd be no other ta know the heart and soul of the men. Keep them safe, keep yerself from harm, Angus!"

He had led his great black warhorse to the copse to speak with Angus, his right-hand man, his fiercest warrior, his dearest friend. He stepped away then and mounted, swinging easily upon the giant stallion. Then he looked down at Angus.

"Ye canna do this!" Angus begged again.

"I can, and I must," Bruce said. "I wish to God that I dinna feel so urgent a need!"

Before he could swing the stallion around, Ian Mac-Allistair came hurrying through to the copse.

"Laird MacNiall!"

The fellow appeared stricken.

"Aye, man, what?"

"Three of the prisoners…have escaped."

"Now how in bluidy hell did that happen?" Angus began in a fury.

"Which men?"

"The Smithson brothers, and Lord Davis. Grayson Davis."

"He was half-dead already!" Angus roared.

"Ah, but half-dead isn't dead," Bruce said.

"How?" Angus roared again, fear in his thunder.

"They were shackled together," MacAllistair said, shaking his head. "MacIver and others watched them, but the fires were burning, the smell, the bluidy smell, and the smoke! When the wind shifted, they were gone, the lot of them!"

Angus turned to Bruce. "See there, man! Ye canna go."

"Nae, Angus, more than ever, I must! God go with ye, lads. Heal the wounded. I'll be back in a few days' time!"

He could wait no longer. From their rocky tor, the castle was a day's ride.

And so he began. Usually he scorned what major roads there were, but this time he rode the night and the darkness bold as brass. By day, he was forced to pause, forced to realize that he would kill his noble mount. And when the light came, once again, he forced himself to care. He was a wanted man, a marked man. A dead man, if his enemies were to see him.

And still, he pushed and pushed. He knew the back ways as no other man could. He could ride them more recklessly, and with his heart ruling his head, he did so.

At first, he prayed to come upon Grayson Davis. There would have been no mercy then.

He thanked God that the man was wounded, and on foot. He could not have reached the castle before him.

Rain hampered him, then cleared. By nightfall, he was nearly home.

Near midnight, the moon rose. It was full and glowing when he reached the last valley and looked up—at the castle.

Beneath the moon, the old stone seemed to glow. There was light, fires that burned to warm those within. All was well, he tried to assure himself. All was well.

The bridge over the moat was up. His men, bless them! They did intend guard against unlikely attack. They kept his vigil for him. By day, all here went about their business, good subjects of the Lord Cromwell's reign. But night, they were ever watchful, protecting their lady, as befitted her, and their absent laird. He had long ago told his tenants that no working man was to suffer for his allegiance to a distant, running king. They obeyed the laws, Cromwell's laws. And Cromwell kept care, ruling with a stern but judicial hand, ever wary that the Scots were a fierce lot, ready to rise and turn at any moment. Aye, they'd been beaten, those who honored the king. But they could rise again in mass, and that the governing powers did not want.

In the moonlight, he breathed a sigh. Pray God, it was all right. And pray God that Davis was a liar.

He spurred his horse. Shouting, he rode the distance

to the castle, rising them upon the hill to the moat. The lookouts were at their station, and recognized their laird. With a great cranking sound, the bridge was lowered. He thundered over it. A groom came forward to take his horse; men gathered around. He assured them of his welfare and told them of the victory. Then he begged away, for he would see his lady. The men understood.

He burst through the front doors and stood in his great hall.

"Annalise! Annalise!" he shouted.

She was there already, standing at the top of the stairs, having heard the drawbridge, he was certain, and...hoping.

She had come running from the master chamber in a gown of white. It flowed about her in elegant swirls. Her delicate features were pale—had she been frightened that it was someone else? Her fingers, long and delicate, were at her throat. Blond hair like the sun at its highest point cascaded around her shoulders, swept down the length of her back.

Eyes bluer than blue were enormous in her face as she looked down at him.

"Annalise!"

He began to take the stairs, two by two. But...there was something wrong, something very, very wrong. He saw it in the way she looked.

And a fury gripped him, deep and terrible.

"Annalise!"

He had her by the shoulders, longing to enwrap her, to kiss the fullness of her lips, bury himself in her, seize her up, sweep her to their chambers...

"Tell me, before God, that Davis is a liar!" he demanded.

"My laird!" Trembling, her voice a whisper, she

fell, shaking, to her knees. "My laird! My dear, dear Bruce…"

He lifted her chin, looking into her eyes.

"Before God, Bruce!" she whispered.

Chapter 7

Toni awoke early; Bruce was gone. She lay quietly for several moments, wondering if he had merely returned to his own room.

She didn't think so. Oddly, she was certain that he had left the castle.

Looking at her wristwatch, she saw that it was just eight. Though she wished she had slept longer, she was antsy and anxious to be up. With a groan, she rose and headed into the shower. She hesitated at the connecting door, then tapped lightly and pressed it open. As she had sensed, Bruce wasn't there.

She showered and dressed, then decided on a cup of coffee. But going down the stairs, she realized that she was resentful. The castle was silent; the others were all managing to sleep.

In the kitchen, she put on a large pot of coffee, thinking that she'd leave it for whoever stumbled down next.

The coffee had barely brewed when she heard a thunderous banging that made her jump a mile. She realized instantly that it was only the front door. Apparently the laird of the castle had remembered to lock the door when he left.

She hurried to the door and threw it open. The constable, looking quite nice and casual in jeans and knit sweater, was standing there. "Morning, Miss Fraser. Is Bruce around?"

She shook her head. "I don't think so."

Jonathan Tavish sighed. "His car isn't about, but after the drive up, I thought I should give it a try."

"Can I help you with anything?" she asked.

He shook his head and frowned slightly, looking concerned. "Everything is all right, eh?"

"Fine, thank you. It's going well. Bruce has actually been very decent."

He remained at the door. She hesitated.

"I just made coffee. Would you like some?"

"Actually, that would be wonderful."

"Come in, please."

He followed her to the kitchen and took a seat at the table. Just then David came in, yawning, scratching cheeks with a sign of morning shadow. He stopped short, seeing the constable.

"Ah, morning!" he said.

"Good morning," Jonathan said.

David stared at Toni. "Is…there anything wrong?"

"No, the constable was just looking for Bruce, but he's…" She shrugged. "He's off somewhere."

"Ah." David grinned. "Well, Constable, excuse my appearance."

"Call me Jonathan, please, and I'm the one interruptin' here."

Toni set out the coffee, sugar and cream. "I'll grab some scones," David told her.

"Thanks," she murmured. Actually, the last thing she wanted this morning was a guest for breakfast.

"Well, Jonathan," David said, stirring his own coffee, "it seems we will be around for a bit."

"Aye?" Jonathan seemed surprised.

"Our host has agreed to let us make up some of what we've spent," Toni explained.

"Ah," Jonathan murmured. "Well, then, that's fine."

"Good morning!" Gina called cheerfully, strolling into the kitchen, dressed in a robe, as well. She, too, stopped short at the sight of Jonathan. "Hi! Is...anything wrong?"

Jonathan smiled, shaking his head. "No, not at all."

"He stopped by to see Bruce," David explained this time.

"Who isn't here," Toni added.

"Ah, I see."

"Well, I've just heard you'll be around a bit," Jonathan said.

"Yes, isn't it great!" Gina said cheerfully. "Bruce has been wonderful, really. Not just tolerating us, but helping us!"

"I admit to being surprised," Jonathan said. "But then, as you're aware, he comes and goes as he pleases, sometimes on a whim." He shook his head ruefully. "Indeed, when I saw you all about town, I was surprised that he'd rented out the castle, but I honestly couldn't have said that he hadn't done so. Strange situation, though, eh? And a bit of a frightening one. In this day and age of computers and machines, some awful things can happen. We had a young woman a few years back who was in dire trouble, indeed. Someone stole her passport, and with it, her identity. Before it was all straight-ened out, she was wanted for a bank robbery in Cannes!"

"Identity theft!" David said, nodding sagely. "I won-der if…if that's what happened!"

"We'll get to the bottom of it," Jonathan assured them.

"I hope!" Gina said. She smiled. "Bruce really has been great. All he's asked is that we make sure to stay out of the forest. He's so concerned about what's been going on in Scotland—the women disappearing and being murdered," she murmured. "I'm afraid that, in the States, we're far too accustomed to such horrible things happening. When it's not right in your own back-yard, well…"

Jonathan was staring at them strangely, looking a little ashen.

"What is it?" Toni asked.

"He asked you to stay out of the forest, did he now?"

"Yes. Why, is there something bad in the woods?" David asked.

"I'd have thought that y'd 'ave known," he said softly.

"Known what?" Gina demanded.

"You see, the bodies of the murdered lasses were found in Tillingham Forest." He grimaced. "Not quite the backyard, but…close enough," he ended softly.

Toni, Gina and David stared at one another. "Both bodies?" murmured Gina.

"Indeed."

"But the girls weren't from here," Toni said.

"No, they were not. And…well, they were a different sort than yourselves," he assured her. "Still, not a bad idea to stay out of the forest, as Bruce said."

"I'll stay out of it all right," Gina said.

Jonathan still looked uncomfortable.

"There's something more," Toni said, her tone determined as she watched him.

"Well, I can see why it makes Bruce so uncomfortable. Y'see, it was he that found one of the poor lasses."

Hell, it was bloody early, Thayer thought. Eleven o'clock. Well, bloody early for him to start drinking, anyway.

Fuck it. He'd already been awake for hours. He'd left himself right after he'd seen Bruce pull away from the castle, and that had been hours ago now. Early? No, plenty late enough.

"Aye, give me a pint, luv," he said to the barmaid. He'd come for the Sunday roast, or so he had thought. But he wasn't hungry, he'd discovered, once he'd chosen the Silver Crow, a dark, somewhat aging pub in Stirling. Most pubs in Stirling were aging, he determined with wry humor. But then…this one was struggling, he thought. It was very dark within, the floors needed to be swept and the tables all carried a thin layer of grease. And there was but the one harried barmaid, and a number of locals, demanding better service.

There was much about Stirling to be admired. It was a beautiful city, with progressive people and an air of the present. And the huge castle welcomed visitors from all over. Fairly recent improvements had made the place quite charming, in truth. Mannequins in period costume, all going about their period business, displayed some of history's darkest moments along with some of the finest.

"We were damned bloody, bloody bastards, through it all!" he muttered.

"Pardon?" the barmaid said.

"Nothing, luv, just talking to myself."

He smiled. At least the barmaid was attractive. She was in a little black halter shirt, and wore black shorts, as well. The way they hugged her rear end didn't leave much to the imagination. And what they did was mighty graphic.

Maybe that's how this place was surviving. Dingy lighting and dirty floors were okay if a bloke could have himself that kind of a view.

He looked around. The tables were mostly empty; the bar was full. Aye, folks around here came for the view.

His stomach growled. He'd taken off that morning without a bite to eat, aware that the great laird of the castle had vacated it early, as well. Hell, it seemed the man needed to escape his own place. But then again, it appeared he'd escaped it often enough in the past. Thayer looked at his hands. Raw. They'd put work into it, all right. He hadn't realized how much work there'd be when he agreed to their mad scheme. But the piano bars of Glasgow hadn't been quite a dream fulfilled. He'd had a few pounds and, under his circumstances, given his *habits,* thought why the hell not. There had been so many very interesting directions in which to take the idea.

"Think I'll have me a wee bite to eat," he told the barmaid.

She flashed him a smile. She was young, and still had a kind of innocence about her—despite the shorts.

"Good. The roast is not so bad, really, sir," she said.

Sir. He liked that.

He took a seat in the back, unnoticed by the rest of the clientele. A few moments later, the barmaid came over. She smiled at him again. Why, bless her, she was flirting. She kept flashing him something of a blush and something of an invitation as she laid out silver, a napkin, salt and pepper. He mused over his own assets. He wasn't bad-looking, really. He even had a look of his American cousin about him, since his hair was a tawny color—full and rich and all there, thank you very much! His features were not badly assembled, and he had some decent height, too, though he'd often rued the fact that his shoulders were never really going to fill out—not like those on Ryan or the great Bruce.

Pity that he had so many of the same characteristics as Toni. The night he'd met her—she with all her unbound enthusiasm to have actually found a family member!— he'd been smitten. Those deep blue eyes were something else entirely on Toni. She'd been electric, with her slim, natural elegance and her total vitality. She'd made him quicken all over. But he'd realized soon enough that she'd wanted a cousin. What he'd wanted, what he'd needed… The barmaid's shorts came to mind again.

Maybe that was why Toni's scheme had looked so good. He'd thought time spent with her might change the way she saw him. It hadn't changed anything for him. He'd been fascinated by her more every moment they shared. She had talent and a passion. She could dig into hard work, just as she could wane rapturously about a dream. When her hair brushed his fingers, when she gave him her smile, eyes brightening…

But then, there had been MacNiall. Even as Toni faced off with the fellow, any fool could see that the sparks were about to ignite.

Fuck MacNiall. Thinking about him was damned irritating.

Sometimes Thayer hated being British, and he loathed being Scottish. Many centuries had gone by, yet too often they were considered something of a lesser country by their neighbor—good old England! Wars, and the fact that they shared an island and pacts, be damned. Underneath, it was still there. They still groveled so over any old bloke with a title before his name!

"Your roast, sir." The pretty little barmaid was back. She hovered after she put the plate down.

Not bad. Not bad at all. It was those shorts…

"I'm Thayer," he told her. "What's your name?"

"Katherine," she said. "Katie, to me pals."

"Katie, then, nice to meet you."

She glanced back at the bar. Another girl had joined the workforce there. She was older, tougher looking, someone who'd worked pubs for a few years, no doubt.

"I'm on break," Katie said.

He angled his head, smiling. "So, can you join me, luv?"

Her smiled deepened. She'd been waiting for the invitation. Ah, so his shoulders weren't what they might have been, but he seldom had trouble with women.

She took the seat opposite him. "What brings you to Stirling?"

"I'm looking for a bit of excitement."

"In Stirling?"

He shrugged. "It was close enough."

"You're out in one of the villages, eh? Sounds like you come from Glasgow."

"That I do," he told her. He took a bite of his roast. It was good.

"And you, Katie? You're from Stirling?"

She shook her head. "Orkney."

He arched a brow. "Talk about a need for excitement! So, have you found any in Stirling?"

"I've only been here a few days." She leaned closer. "And the bloke what owns this place…what a jerk! I think I'll do better heading for Edinburgh, or Glasgow. They say there's some life going on there, at least."

"Katie, life is where we find it. All along the road."

She smiled and proved to be more of an aggressive little vixen than he had imagined. "Think that you could show me some life along that road?" she queried.

He hadn't realized that her hands were beneath the table until he felt her fingers squeezing his knee.

He placed his fork down, crossed his arms over his chest and surveyed her with definite interest and amusement. "Katie, lass, you can't begin to imagine what I can show you along the road."

"I'd love to see," she said.

He smiled, leaning back in his chair. "Maybe we could meet later."

There was a breath of excitement in her voice. "Maybe we could!" She rose quickly. "I'm off at two. So I shouldn't be seen sitting here with you…if we're going to get together later."

"Good thought," he told her gravely. "Very good thought."

"Meet me down by the graveyard?"

"Perfect," he told her.

Jonathan's information regarding Bruce had been accepted as it had been offered, Toni thought—as a good sound reason for them to stay out of the forest, and as a darned good reason for him to feel very uneasy about the situation.

Toni was certain that David had told Kevin, and that Gina had let Ryan know. Thayer wasn't around, so he was the only one who didn't yet know.

The bodies had been found here. And Bruce had discovered one of the dead girls. Now they were all left a little uneasy, she thought. And she couldn't help wondering if they should just cut their losses and leave.

She was scrounging in the refrigerator, looking for something cold to drink, when Gina came into the kitchen.

"Don't get any food!" Gina ordered.

Toni closed the refrigerator and looked at her. "Actually, I wasn't, but why not?"

"Because we should go on a picnic."

"A picnic? Where?" she asked Gina carefully.

"Don't worry. I'm not going to drag anyone into the forest. I'm not sure where to go, but we'll find a meadow somewhere. With sheep."

"And sheep poop!" David added cheerfully, coming on in behind Gina and taking a seat with them at the kitchen table. He grinned at Toni. "I've already told her, Kevin and I are in."

"I guess it's just us," Gina added. "Bruce is gone, and Thayer took off this morning."

Toni looked at both of them quizzically. "You're not upset?"

"Upset?" David said, looking at Gina, frowning.

"About the bodies having been dumped in these woods, and about Bruce having made the discovery of one of them," Toni said.

David shook his head. "As long as you and Gina don't…pick up the trade and go running around in the forest, no. I'm sorry, of course. And I understand now why Bruce is so weird about it. But no, I'm not upset."

"We just need to be cautious," Gina added. "Women usually need to be smart about what they're doing."

Toni nodded. "Um. Good."

"Are you upset?" Gina asked.

"No!"

"Are you coming on our picnic?"

Toni was quiet for a minute. "Mind if I beg out of it myself?"

"Why?" Gina asked, sounding a bit hurt.

"I'll leave it as a romantic outing for two couples," Toni said.

"Hey, it's never like that," David protested. "We're all friends."

"But I'm still the odd man out when we're down to five."

"We've been five lots! Last trip to Scotland, we were five. And the year before that," Gina reminded her.

"You guys are all great. I didn't mean that I felt like the odd man—or woman—out when I'm with you. It's just that you should go alone. Besides, I want to go wander around the village a little," Toni said.

Gina sighed and looked at David. "I guess it's just the four of us, then. And the sheep."

He rolled his eyes at Toni. "Very romantic."

"You'll love it," she told him. "I know you guys—you'll pack real plates and glasses, you'll sip champagne on a hillcrest, looking out over gorgeous hills and dales, and you'll have a great time."

"I still don't understand why you don't want to go. We've been in the village," Gina reminded her.

"Yes, but every time we've been in, it's been with a mission, buying things, getting to know the local hardware store. I'm going to explore like a tourist. They've a centuries-old church and an ancient graveyard… And you know me, I like to dawdle. You guys just get bored," Toni told her.

"She wants to be an isolationist," David said.

"You know you hate old churches and musty grave-yards," Toni reminded him.

"I always go to them."

"Of course, you do. And then I feel guilty when I dawdle too long," Toni said.

"The sheep are going to miss you," he said.

"And I'll miss them, minus the sheep poop, of course," Toni said.

Toni had planned on taking her time getting ready, but she discovered, to her dismay, that she found being alone in the castle somewhat unsettling—especially after Jonathan's revelations that morning. Grabbing her handbag, she ran down the stairs, anxious to get out.

One of their rental cars, a minivan, was parked out by the stables. Thayer must have taken the little BMW, she determined. But the van would be fine. Any vehicle would be fine.

She quickened her steps, surprised that she was in such a hurry to reach it. Yet, as she neared the car, she stood stock-still.

A scratching sound was coming from the stables.

Of course, there are horses in it, idiot! she told herself.

But it didn't sound like the kind of noise a horse would make.

She hesitated, caught between the stable doors and the car. *What would make that kind of a noise? Someone stealing the horses?*

She stood for a moment in indecision. If someone was stealing the horses, and she tried to stop them, she might well get hurt. No, the smart thing to do would be to get the hell out, go to town and get Constable Tavish to come back with her.

But as she stood there, the noise stopped suddenly.

She'd been seen. Absurdly frightened by such a small thing, she started to hurry toward the car.

"Ah, Miss Fraser!"

She froze, then turned. Eban Douglas was standing in the shadowy doorway of the stables. The wizened little man was wearing his customary grin. An eerie grin, she decided.

"Eban!" she said, trying to sound cheerful. She didn't know why, but today, his presence made her uneasy.

"Seein' to the lads, I be," he said, indicating the stables.

"Yes, thank you!" Toni said cheerfully.

"The rooone…he's lookin' a bit weathered."

"Excuse me?" Toni said, then realized that he was saying "the roan."

"Oh, well, Ryan will look in on him later," she said.

"Y'don't want to give the boy a look yerself, miss?"

Go into the dark stables with only Eban around for miles? Not in a thousand years!

"Um… I'm afraid I wouldn't know if he was ailing or not, Eban. Ryan is the one who knows about horses. If you think he's really ill, though, we could call a vet?"

"I'd not feel right, mum, callin' in the doc withoot one of ye seein' to the boy."

"Eban, trust me, you have my permission to do so," she said. She felt as if he was pressuring her. *Pressuring her to go into the dark of the stables.* If he didn't look so strange, would she have thought anything of it?

Yes! Because women had been murdered around here. Their bodies had been found in the forest. And like it or not, this little man was weird!

Bruce MacNiall and Jonathan had done a fair job of scaring them all, she thought. Still, she wasn't going into the stables.

"Eban, I'm asking you to please call the vet out. And thank you so very much. I've got to get going."

Whatever it was that unnerved her, she was hard put *not* to run to the car. With a forced smile and a friendly wave, she hurried her footsteps.

Old habits died hard. She raced for the left-hand door, then felt like a fool, remembering that she was in Great Britain.

She grimaced foolishly as he watched her, and walked around to the right door.

"Mind ye, keep yer eye on the roads!" Eban called to her.

"Yes, I will, thanks!"

In the car, she switched on the ignition and started down the rocky driveway. Angry with herself, she stopped the car near the point in the forest where they had gone into the canopy to find the stream and wade in the water.

Her hands were shaking.

She put the car into Park, telling herself that she was being ridiculous. So much for priding herself on the fact that she didn't have a prejudiced bone in her body! Eban had frightened her—because he had such a strange look.

Then again, she didn't really know Eban. He was just…around. *Caretaking.* He'd helped them out several times when they'd been working. They'd seen him…and they hadn't seen him. Yet, when they hadn't seen him, he still must have been around, watching them.

She took a breath, ready to put the car back into gear, really beginning to feel a bit ridiculous.

Eban worked for Bruce MacNiall, keeping an eye on the castle. It would have been his job to report to Mac-Niall, they just hadn't known it.

Then something caused her to look toward the forest.

Bruce was there, on his huge black horse, right at the point where they had entered to reach the stream. She shaded her eyes from the morning sun, trying to get a better look at him. He was waving to her, beckoning, and he looked impatient.

"What?" she murmured aloud. "He insists we stay out of the forest, and there he is, waving me into it!"

And then, there had been Jonathan's words that morning...

Frowning, she got out of the car, wishing that she'd remembered her sunglasses. He waved again. The great black turned and went down the path.

"What the hell...?" she muttered aloud.

He'd disappeared down the trail, expecting her to follow.

"All right. Great!" she said. Maybe it was safe to go into the forest as long as she was with him. But he'd found one of the two bodies dumped in the forest! she reminded herself.

"I'm only going so far!" she said, and realized that she was still talking to herself. But even as she approached the first canopy of trees, she felt again the strange hesitance she had felt the day before. And she had been with a crowd of people then! And that was before she knew about the bodies!

This was insane. She shouldn't trust him. And yet... she did. Somewhere in her heart, she'd felt a deep unease regarding Bruce. But even as she'd felt it, something in her soul had rebelled.

And now, for some reason, she was compelled to follow him.

As soon as she came into the field of trees, she was blinded again, having gone from surprisingly bright sunlight to a dark expanse of green.

"Bruce!" she called out, irritated. "I am not coming any farther—"

He had dismounted and was in front of her again.

"Bruce, dammit!" she told him.

Come, please.

She thought he said the words softly, yet she questioned her own sanity because she wasn't certain that they had been real words.

She thought about just turning and running, but for the life of her right then, she couldn't do it. Nothing had changed. She had to follow. She was drawn.

"Stop, then, wait up for me!" she said, her words angry. She was starting to feel like an idiotic teenager in a bad B horror movie, who's in the very spot where the maniacal killer always strikes.

But that was insane. Bruce was right in front of her. Sanity be damned. Instinct assured her that he'd never hurt her.

She didn't want to rely on instinct; she didn't want to dream. She never, ever wanted to admit that she hadn't shut down the visions that had haunted her with such vivid brutality...

"Bruce! Damn you, wait!"

But he wasn't waiting. And she couldn't turn back.

She started to hurry, walking quickly to catch up, stumbling slightly as she reached the soft, rocky embankment of the brook. She stubbed a toe and stopped, swearing. She rubbed her foot, really angry then, ready to tell him to go right to hell. Yet, when she looked up, he was nowhere to be seen.

And she had come much farther into the forest than she had imagined.

The trees seemed to be surrounding her, massive, so deeply green, in an eerie darkness. And there was a sudden hush all around her. No birds chirped, no insects buzzed.

It was as if the world was waiting.

"Bruce!" Her voice wavered, shocking in the stillness.

And then...

She had followed the trickle of the brook, but not even that sound seemed to be able to pierce the stillness. Ahead of her, water dashed and jumped over little rocks and fallen branches. She tried to remember playing in the water with her friends, how they had soaked one another, how they had laughed. She tried, desperately, to keep that vision in her mind.

But she could not.

She saw the large, downed branches, the blanket of green that was oddly out of place on the water. It was out of place. It was a piece of the forest, yes, but...set as if by human hands.

No! A voice inside her shrieked out.

Fear gripped her. The silence remained, as if all the forest, trees, bushes, fish, fowl, insects and even the air itself stood still and waited. And watched.

She knew, long before she actually found the strength to propel herself forward, what she would find. She knew, yet she didn't want to know. Then a calm settled over her and the blind fear abated.

She walked purposely, steadfastly forward and lifted the branch. It was heavy, heavier than she had expected. She dragged it but inches.

A scream formed in her throat, but it never left her lips.

Bones. She had found bones.

Chapter 8

"Ah, a hill full of long grass and flowers, a delightful breeze and bubbly! What more could one ask?" Kevin said, leaning back on the blanket.

Ryan sipped his champagne, wishing that he could feel as relaxed as the others seemed to be.

"A beer, maybe. A Bud. Cold," Ryan said.

"Aren't we grouchy," David said.

Ryan shrugged and rose, stretching. "I wish Toni had come with us," he murmured.

"Well, of course, I wish she'd come, too," Gina said. "But...why?"

"I don't know. I guess I'm worried about her. Rambling around in that castle alone...and going to the village alone," Ryan said. "Who knows what she's up to? Maybe she's asking too many questions...irritating people."

Kevin laughed aloud. "Oh, my God, Ryan! You're

making it sound like the Village of the Damned, or something of the like!"

He turned and looked at them. "Maybe it is."

"Oh, Ryan! I thought you loved it here," Gina said.

"I do."

"Then…?" David demanded.

Ryan shook his head. A restlessness was sitting upon him. He gazed at Gina. She knew him, knew his moods, and she didn't look happy. She touched his arm. "We're out for a picnic with friends now, Ryan," she said.

"Right."

"And everything is going well—as well as can be hoped, under the circumstances," David reminded him.

"Yeah, great! A tall guy on a fantastic, huge horse rides in and we discover we've been gypped out of our life savings. Then we find out that this same guy has found the body of a murder victim in the woods. And now Toni is alone at the castle. What if MacNiall returns before we do? We don't really know a whole hell of a lot about him," Ryan finished.

"He's the laird," David said.

"Yeah? And Countess Bathory sliced up virgins and bathed in their blood," Ryan said.

Gina was staring at him hard. Warning him? he wondered.

"The laird has been damned decent," David said.

"What? Do you think he'd chop us up in his own castle?" Ryan said.

"Oh, Ryan, stop! Please," Gina begged.

"I like the guy, honestly like him," David said. "And, Ryan, you've been riding with him, have talked horses with him. You seemed to be his biggest fan."

"Yeah, that's true. He came on like a warrior lord of old that first night, but, hey, we were in his castle. And he's damned good with horses. Sure, I like him," Ryan said. "Respect him," he added thoughtfully.

"Me, too. He demands a certain respect, but he's been damned decent to us," Kevin agreed. "Look, he probably wasn't even in the country when those girls disappeared."

Gina shivered violently. "Maybe he wasn't, but…"

"But what?" Kevin demanded.

"Nothing," Gina said. "Nothing, really."

"I know what you were going to say," David said, staring at Gina. "*We* were in the country, probably, during the time of…well, at least two of the disappearances."

"What the hell does that mean?" Ryan demanded.

"It means I'm damned glad that we stick together," David said. "That we watch out for Gina and Toni."

"Well, it probably helps that we're not streetwalkers," Gina said pragmatically.

"True," David agreed.

"Hey, can we get back to the beauty of the day, the champagne and all that?" Kevin demanded.

Ryan was still tense, but he joined Gina on the blanket, sat back, closed his eyes and let his wife work the knots out of the muscles in his shoulders.

Toni could see the skull protruding from mud and rock, and bits of flesh, she thought, blackened by the soil. There was also a length of hair and pieces of cloth, all but glued or fused with the bone, or plastered to it by the mire, the very dark muck that formed on the banks of the little brook or stream.

Get away! a voice of self-survival cried in her head. *Scream, just start screaming, and run as fast as you can!*

And still, she didn't scream. There was no need to

look farther. Whoever this victim had been, she had been here some time. There was certainly no need to feel for a pulse, to attempt to drag her from the water. None at all.

Get away! the voice repeated.

Yes! Now!

She thought that she would run then, able to scream and shriek at last, in the darkness of the eerie forest. But she didn't. Instead, she stayed, trying to ingrain every detail of the moment in her mind. It might be important.

The water was no more than two feet deep here, and the skeleton was lodged against a large rock. Until she had moved it, the huge branch had all but hidden the corpse. People could have walked right by without seeing it, for a very long time. How long had it been there? Had the rains carried it from elsewhere, or caused the earth to shift so that they were dug up after a long period of time?

She turned then at last, slowly. Running could cause her to trip on the underbrush and hurt herself. She was deep into the wood, having followed the brook quite far in her attempt to catch up with Bruce. But she didn't think she'd get lost. All she had to do was follow the water.

She didn't dare think about fear. Fear could cause panic. If there was one thing she didn't want, it was to fall, sprain an ankle and remain in the forest as darkness fell.

She'd been shouting before, convinced that Bruce was ahead of her; now she was silent, careful in her footsteps.

She still felt…watched. Yet, strangely, that sense didn't create a rise of…terror. The trees would not come to life, branches like arms, and suck her into themselves. She was simply being watched as she left.

That woman had been hidden long before they'd come to Tillingham.

She kept her eyes looking forward, afraid of what she might see gazing out at her from the green darkness.

Straight ahead! Look straight ahead. Walk, don't run. Steady, steady, follow the brook, get out!

And at last…she did, emerging in the same area where she had entered.

She half expected her car to be gone, but it wasn't. And as she crawled into it, she realized just how frightened she'd been. Other bodies had been found in Tillingham Forest. Had she just stumbled upon the first of the killer's victims, perhaps? A woman never reported as missing? Someone lost to society, and then life?

Fear began to seep through her then, a very real fear. This was a killing ground. Yes, women were abducted from other places. But they were brought here.

Did that mean the killer knew this area very well? Knew that disposing of a body here meant that chances of discovery were small, or that this type of environment would play such havoc with a body that no clues would ever be left?

Her hands were shaking as she gripped the steering wheel, trying to decide what to do. It would be quickest to go back to the castle and call until she got someone on the line.

But Eban was at the castle! She felt a surge of hysteria at the thought of the man. Could he have done something like this?

He never seemed to leave. And if he did, she didn't think he ever went far.

But what if, when no one knew, he silently took a car

and drove off, drove out to the big cities, where no one knew him. Where women who worked the streets for their income were accustomed to servicing men who were sometimes less than attractive?

Suddenly remembering that her cell phone was in her purse, she turned to scramble for it, only to hear a tapping at the driver's window.

Startled, she turned.

It was Eban. Face pressed far too close to the window. Macabre through the glass.

Fear, blind and, perhaps, unreasoning, let loose within her system and she let out a scream at last. She tried to twist her keys in the ignition, but they weren't there! Staring at the man, she fumbled on the seat for them. He backed away, looking puzzled.

She found the keys. After three tries, she got them into the ignition.

When she floored the gas pedal, he literally hopped away.

Without looking back, she sped all the way into the village.

Detective Inspector Robert Chamberlain was thirty-five, tall and wiry, with dark hair already showing signs of serious silver—brought on by his work, he had long ago told Bruce.

They had known one another forever, having met in the service. For a while they had worked for the Lothian and Borders Police in Edinburgh together, until Bruce had left and Robert had moved on. Throughout the years, they had remained friends. A year ago, when Bruce had found the body in the woods, he had been appalled by the lack of technique displayed by Jonathan and his men upon their arrival at the scene. Granted, they had never dealt with such a situation before. But since they hadn't, the proper steps to take would have been to alert the authorities with more expertise. Despite the fact that Bruce had long ago left the police force, Robert often discussed cases with him. On occasion, he had been able to trigger the right hint, clue or information to help Robert solve a case. And both were now deeply concerned about the disappearing girls and the murders.

Robert sat with Bruce in a pub in Edinburgh close to the Greyfriars churchyard where the famous Bobby—the terrier who came to his master's grave to sit vigil for a decade—now lay buried alongside the man to whom he had been so loyal. Robert looked particularly glum.

"Jonathan has told me that he's had men out," Robert said, referring to the Tillingham constable. "They've combed the woods, but not discovered a body." He ran his fingers through his graying hair. "'Tis difficult. So far, we've a woman missing for about a week, we think. In fact, she might well have disappeared just after you reached Edinburgh. I knew I needed you back here. And I'm grateful that you came."

Bruce shrugged. "I was restless. Needed to come anyway," he told Robert. "And, as it happens, it was a good thing I did return."

Robert nodded. "With Annie we're just guessing. We don't really know when she disappeared, because none of her 'friends' kept tabs on her." He pushed the file on the table between them toward Bruce. "Annie O'Hara. Northern Irish, came over from Belfast about five years ago. No known employment—legal employment, that is. She's been arrested three times in those years. Drug abuser, but not the haggard-looking desperate kind as yet. She was picked up twice working the Royal Mile, and both times she was released—you know how that goes. Anyway, one of her friends realized that she was gone after five days or so and reported her missing, but she had no idea how or when Annie disappeared." He shrugged. "Who knows? She might have headed on back to Ireland, but since Helen MacDougal disappeared in like fashion a year ago, and was found by you, and then Mary Granger, just six months ago, and found by that fellow, Eban, in the forest, as well, I think there's a real possibility that Annie'll be found, too, and sadly, found deceased."

"In the forest," Bruce murmured bitterly.

Robert shrugged. "Maybe not. Maybe the killer will find a new place to dispose of the bodies."

"Why would he bother? Jonathan Tavish isn't too concerned. He doesn't consider it his problem at all— because the women have disappeared from Glasgow, Stirling and now Edinburgh."

"Well, he has a point in that the killer has to be operating out of the big cities."

"We don't actually have a 'red light' district in the village," Bruce said. He was irritated with Jonathan, though. His old friend seemed to be more suspicious of his activities than worried about the fact that a real psychopath was on the loose, and probably growing more dangerous with each passing day. He'd run into him in the village, just before leaving. Apparently Jonathan had been looking for him, wanting to know if he'd lost his wallet recently, if there was any possibility that he might be a victim of "identity theft." Actually, he had to admit that Jonathan might have a point there. How else could he explain how his castle had wound up listed as being for rent. According to Jonathan, there was no Web site for the castle, and, thus far, the legitimate ones he had checked had never had a listing for the place.

Even seeking out the case of fraud, though, Bruce would have far more faith in Robert's knowledge—and, naturally, the fraud department of a major force—than he would in Jonathan. He understood Jonathan's resentment, but it didn't change the fact that Tillingham was small, and major crime was not a frequent event there.

"No. Of course, this is far more serious than Tavish is willing to admit," Robert said. "I don't blame him for not using all his local funds to mount an inch-by-inch combing of Tillingham Forest, not when we've got a disappearance with no guarantee that any foul play happened to this woman."

Bruce sat back, shaking his head. "The killer will return with his victim's remains to Tillingham. If we'd found just the one girl, then it might have been merely a convenient place for him to dispose of the body. But a second corpse discovered? He's using Tillingham as his personal refuse property, and he's going to keep at it. I even think there may be a 'why' behind it."

Robert shook his head. "Now, Bruce, y'are taking this far too personally. Tillingham is lush and deep. We've not got a thing on the killer yet because of the advanced stage of decomposition of the bodies by the time they were found. We don't have hair, fibers, semen, anything. There's nothing personal about the fact that the bloke is hiding his heinous crimes there. It simply puts him in the classification of an organized killer, a fellow who thinks it out and knows how best to keep himself from being discovered."

"I suppose I do take discarded bodies in what is very nearly my backyard personally," Bruce agreed. "It means one of two very bad things. Either we have an organized psychotic on a methodical killing jaunt dumping bodies once he's had his jollies, or someone in that area knows that it's the perfect dumping site and is traveling farther from home for his victims."

"You should have stayed with the force, Bruce," Robert told him, shaking his head. "You were good. We'd have never gotten the Highland Hills killers without you, you know. It was uncanny, the way you could read the fellow's mind."

"Behavioral science," Bruce said, waving a hand in the air. He didn't like remembering the massive hunt they'd had a little more than ten years ago, seeking out a man who was kidnapping teenaged girls, raping them and leaving their mutilated bodies strewn across Edinburgh and its outskirts. Four girls had died in all; it had been a heartbreaking assignment. "We were able to get something from friends back then. I'd have never realized that there were two people involved if one of the witnesses hadn't mentioned that the last time she'd seen her friend alive, she'd been giving directions to a lady on the passenger's side of the car. Even then, I doubted myself at first."

He hadn't; he was lying. It had been frightening, how much of a connection he'd had with the killers. There was a point, on a day when they had stood on a hillside just outside of the city, when he had suddenly known that the killer couldn't be acting alone, known that there had to be a woman involved, as well. How else could the killer have managed to lure girls who knew to be on the lookout for any strange *man*. From then on, little clues fell into place. Tire tracks had indicated a return to the city. The area around one of the schools had provided one pub, and he had taken to spending his time there, watching. A handsome young couple who held hands across the table and whispered constantly like foolish, snickering lovers had garnered his attention. He was never sure if he heard their conversation, imagined it or re-created what it might have been in his own mind. But suddenly he'd been certain, so he'd followed them.

One afternoon he tried to imagine the route they'd take if they had, indeed, been stalking the girls together. Getting his car, cruising the area of the school, he put himself into the man's mind, made himself think and feel as the killer had done. There had been the thrill of the chase and, aye, some brutal treatment to his wife.

Eventually he was certain he knew just how and when the couple had moved. How the wife, claiming to be lost, would lure the girls, ask directions, come back once the girl was on her way home, alone, and coax her into the car. There she was drugged. Traces of morphine had been found in the body, so he didn't consider that any great divining work on his own. Then she was taken to their flat, a ground-floor apartment in a working man's area where the husband wouldn't be noted taking in a roll of bedding or carpet. Inside, the woman had held the girl at the man's command. And after he abused the terrified child, he'd have sex with his wife, as well, the girl still alive but unconscious. Then the poor wee lass would be taken into the bathroom and killed in the tub, so that the blood could be washed away.

He gave the scenario to his superiors, who thought that he was daft. And even if he wasn't, they couldn't arrest a couple because he'd seen them in a pub and followed them to their flat.

But after a storm, he'd gotten a friend to take a cast of the tire marks left by the couple's car near the pub. They matched those found at the site where the girl had been found. It was not enough for a conviction, or even a trial, but enough to get them what they really needed through the court system—a DNA sample. The case had taken months, eating into his soul—and into his last precious moments with Meg.

Her illness had been the reason he had given for resigning. His proximity to the mind of the killer had been the reason he had never gone back.

"Aye, who would have figured that such a man would have a wife just as eager to perform that kind of cruelty on another." Robert shook his head with disgust. "They had a case like that in Canada, not long ago. The wife got ridiculous leniency. Her defense attorneys claimed she was a victim herself. Looks like no one is accountable for his or her actions anymore. Even in the Highland Hills case, the husband was locked up for good but his wife may be out in as little as ten years! But the point is, *you* made the difference in that case."

Bruce felt a moment's severe discomfort. "Back then, the authorities were on it with a passion. Robert, you know as well as I do that if these were prominent lasses, the press would be having a stink and Jonathan wouldn't be halfheartedly sending a few men out to look around in the forest."

"That's sad, and always the case," Robert agreed, drumming his fingers on the table. "Aye, for a small country, we've had our share of loonies." He lifted his hand, indicating the town. "Edinburgh. It's where Burke and Hare practiced their ghastly trade, killing when they found out just how profitable it could be. Five years ago a fellow on the outskirts of town was killing one immigrant a month, in honor of social justice, so he claimed! He didn't like the fact that we weren't so 'pure' anymore. Tillingham, though…there's not been much violence there in centuries, as you are well aware. And what tragedies took place there always had to do with war, or feuding clans. This is definitely not clan retribution. Although… Jonathan does seem to have his share of troubles when it comes to that forest. At least a dozen teens, intent on some hanky-panky, have come out of it screaming their fool heads off, convinced there's someone, something, there. The superstitions grow. The local forces don't like going in there, so they only halfheartedly look for anything. Look, I'll see that the central office gets a crew out to search the forest. Will that give you any reassurance?"

"Aye, it will," Bruce told him.

"Now, as to the other…your American invasion?" Robert asked.

"They have rental forms and permits that look as legal as an international peace accord," Bruce told him, grinning. "I'm wondering if they're still not halfway convinced that I've been deprived of my land through some nonpayment of taxes and can't accept the fact that it's no longer mine."

"No!" Robert said, laughing.

"Yes, actually. Just such a scenario was suggested by one lass."

"They don't know what you do, or who you are?" Robert queried.

"No, not even the Scotsman among them. Frankly, I found that rather suspicious."

Robert shrugged. "In this day and age? Maybe. And maybe not. In Glasgow, folks tend to get into being… well, from Glasgow."

Bruce arched a brow at him.

"Now, Bruce, you know my own hometown by the Loch—'tis nothing there! Longing to be a police officer, there was nothing for me to do but come to the city. You know that's true. But don't worry on that front. If he's a Scotsman, I can trace his past for you by tomorrow. Actually, I can run traces on your entire group, though it might take a wee bit longer with the Americans. And once I've gotten copies of their documents, we can set the boys in the white-collar crime units on the trail of whoever is renting properties and taking euro-checks for them. Euro-checks, eh?"

He shrugged. "That's what she said."

"Not pounds sterling?"

"I didn't pursue that yet. My hearing is quite good, though, and she did say euro-check. This agency has probably purported itself to be something of a European finding facility, so I doubt that the use of a euro-check—even for a property in Scotland—would have seemed that strange."

"And you didn't send them packing immediately?" Robert said.

Bruce shook his head. "It was late Friday night when I found the folks putting on their show."

"Actually, it's a rather clever idea," Robert mused. "They're making a mint on graveyard tours and the like here, you know. People are ghoulish, that's a fact. They like a nice little chill, with the safety of knowing that the evil fellows practiced their wicked deeds centuries ago."

"I believe they were in Edinburgh when they got the idea," Bruce said.

"And how long ago was that?" Robert inquired.

"I don't really know."

"So these folks have been to Scotland before?"

"Aye, so they have. Why? Is that important?"

Robert shook his head. "Just a point of interest. I suppose there's no reason to think that they'd know much about the wee hamlets and villages, even if they'd been several times before. And from what you say, they've done well. Your castle was in need of serious repair."

"Aye, I've let it go. But every time before…well, it had been Meg's dream to go with all guns blazing and make it a showplace. When she was gone…"

"That's been more than a decade."

"I know, and I don't need any speeches. I've gone on with my life. I function well. I travel the globe. I do my best to steal from the rich and give to the poor. It was just the castle where I fell short."

"So your guests—for want of a better description—don't know what you do, who you are or that the castle isn't really what you call home?" Robert said.

"No."

"Are you keeping these things a secret for some reason?"

"Not really. No one has asked. I don't know. Maybe," Bruce said, correcting himself. "We might all be a bit wary of one another. They certainly appear to be exactly what they say. Still…let me tell you, it was strange to come home and hear what they were up to, then to have Toni Fraser tell me that she had made up her story, but even the name of Bruce MacNiall's wife was exact."

Robert waved a dismissive hand in the air. "That happens all the time. People hear things, forget them and then think that they're original thoughts."

"Well, that's what one would assume," Bruce agreed. "But I've talked to her, rather extensively. She's convinced that she made it up. And something more."

"What?"

"She's scared by it. She's having nightmares about my ancestor standing at the foot of her bed with a dripping sword."

Again Robert was unimpressed. "That's easy enough. She's in the old laird's castle."

"Easy enough—unless you've been there and seen the way she looks when she wakens from such a dream."

Robert arched a brow at him. "She's an actress, right?"

"Aye."

"Do you think that maybe, just maybe, a scam is being played on you?"

"Not unless it's the best one in history."

"Granted, you're not the kind to be taken," Robert mused. "A lot of this is outside my jurisdiction but, naturally, I'll get on it."

"Thanks."

Robert's phone went off, and he excused himself to answer the summons. Bruce watched his friend's face go from surprise to concern.

He clicked off, staring at Bruce.

"I'll head back with you right now," he said.

"What's happened?" Bruce asked, an uneasy feeling already seeping into his bloodstream.

"They've found a body."

Bruce's blood chilled. And yet, he wasn't surprised!

"Is it—Annie O'Hara?"

"I don't know. One of my sergeants saw the alert and called me right away. Jonathan and the medical examiner are heading out to the scene now. Even if the body is not at a severe stage of decomposition, I doubt they can be certain until they've brought it out and performed an autopsy."

"Oh, God. They've found her in the forest?"

"Aye. More than that." He was looking at Bruce strangely.

"What?"

Robert shook his head, rising. "I'll tell you on the way. I want to get out there before they botch anything up."

"Dammit, Robert, what is the 'more'?" Bruce demanded.

"She was found by your guest. Miss Fraser."

Chapter 9

A strange calm had descended over Toni. By the time she'd reached the village and a lazy deputy had accepted the fact that she wasn't hysterical and had contacted Jonathan Tavish, she was already ruing her actions in regard to Eban. There was no reason to suspect the fellow. Away from the green darkness of the forest—and the sight of the pathetic remains—she felt stronger.

When Jonathan arrived, she gave him a description of walking into the woods, seeing the branch and moving it. They sat in his office. He was just feet from her, looking almost like the boy next door in his casual Sunday attire.

"Toni, lass, what were you doing walkin' so deep into the woods on your own? I explained this morning why you shouldna be doing so."

"I saw Bruce," she said.

Jonathan shook his head. "I don't think so. After I

left you earlier, I saw him in the coffee shop. Said he was taking the drive to Edinburgh to have lunch with a friend."

His comment chilled her, but it didn't create the panic it might have just hours before.

"Well," she murmured, letting her lashes fall over her eyes. "I thought I saw him."

He sighed. "I hate to ask this of you, but you'll have to come back into the forest with me. I need you to guide us to the site."

"Certainly."

So she wound up not in the minivan, but in the constable's car with him and one of his deputies. Another car following behind them was filled with police tape and other paraphernalia needed to protect the integrity of the site.

At the scene, photos were taken before anyone touched the remains. The medical examiner—an almost absurdly kind and jovial-looking little fellow named Daniel Darrow—carried a small recorder and made comments into it as he made a preliminary inspection of the site and the skeletal corpse.

Toni stood some distance away, glad that the area was teeming with people. Even then, she felt as if she were being watched, and she kept herself from looking into the trees, somewhat afraid that she would see eyes observing her. Watching. Waiting. *For what?*

She heard Dr. Darrow speaking with Jonathan. "Well, it's not the missing Annie O'Hara. That's for certain."

"No?" Jonathan said.

"Definitely not."

"Aye?" Jonathan said. "How can you be certain?"

Darrow nodded. "This lass, if I'm not mistaken, has been here for centuries."

"Centuries!" Toni heard herself say.

"So I believe."

"And you know it's the body of a woman? If it's been here centuries, how do you know?"

Darrow smiled dryly. "Well, there are remnants of clothing left, even now. Don't think we had too many drag queens back then, eh? Then there are the medical reasons, as well, Jonathan, the pelvic bones of a woman being entirely different from those of a man, the delicate nature of the facial bones, stature, breadth of the ribs... Don't worry, we'll do all the proper procedures back at the morgue, but I think I'm safe in referring to our poor corpse as a lass! I'm going to try to excavate a bit here, rather than just remove the corpse. And we'll have to have a forensic anthropologist in. This is really most remarkable. She must have been buried deep in the muck to be as preserved as she is. Oddly enough, the lass's means of death is rather apparent."

Toni and Jonathan both stared at him blankly.

Darrow nodded, using a stick to point to the corpse.

"See there? It's a scarf, ascot, handkerchief...something of the like, used as a ligature. Poor wee thing was strangled."

Toni wasn't sure that she saw, but then, Darrow certainly knew this business better than she did.

Jonathan sighed. "At least it's not Annie O'Hara, though I don't know whether that's good or bad."

Darrow looked at him sharply. "I thought you'd searched the woods for Annie O'Hara? You might have discovered this old grave site."

"We did search for Annie O'Hara," Jonathan said flatly. "As you'll note, this is a dark area. And I'm certain that only the recent rains could have caused this— these remains—to suddenly rise to a point of discovery.

And Miss Fraser reported that she only discovered the bones when the branch was moved. Hell, Daniel, I'd need more men than I have here to move every branch in this forest!"

Toni was impressed with Daniel Darrow. Details had gone into his recording, and, despite the fact that it seemed she had found an ancient corpse, he made a point of keeping everyone else out of the immediate area.

She had no idea how long they had been at the site when Bruce MacNiall came striding to it with a grave fellow in a suit that identified him immediately as a professional lawman of some variety.

The men stopped at the yellow tape stretched around the immediate area. Bruce looked as imposing in the forest as ever, and yet somewhat haggard. His eyes pinned first on the cordoned area where the remains lay, then on Jonathan. Then he looked around until his gaze fell on where she stood by the trees.

"Toni!" His voice was harsh, yet there was an underlying emotion to it that she found gratifying. His long strides brought him to her in seconds. His hands fell on her shoulders; steel-gray eyes assessed her with pointed concern. "Are you all right?"

She nodded, glad of him there, wishing that his presence didn't make her feel a sense of tremulous weakness again. "Of course," she told him.

"I'll get you out of here," Bruce told Toni. "Can you give me another minute?"

"Bruce, I'm fine," she said. "I'm the one who came upon the remains, and I've seen quite a bit already, as you can imagine. And, Bruce, this isn't a recent victim of a serial killer. Dr. Darrow says that she's been here for centuries."

His brow furrowed and the muscles in his face tightened in confusion.

She nodded. "Centuries," she repeated.

He turned away from her, striding toward the others.

"Bruce," Jonathan said, his tone wary. "I'm here. Daniel is here. And now Robert is here, as well. You don't need to be."

"Aye, I do," Bruce said harshly. "The castle is the closest location to this forest. This corpse is ancient?" he asked, looking at Darrow, both incredulous and relieved.

"I believe. I'm not an expert, but I'd wager she was put here hundreds of years ago," Darrow told him. "I told Jonathan, what we really need is an excavation." He glanced at Toni, and she wondered if she had been staring at him with horror or dismay, because he quickly added, "We'll not be leaving her here. No, we'll see that she is brought out intact—as intact as possible—with the muck, as well, so that the experts will have all this to help them determine just what happened." He offered Toni a smile. "Miss Fraser, you've given a hand to history here today. This lass was strangled, that's a fact."

"Annalise!" Jonathan said suddenly, staring at Bruce. He seemed almost pleased. "Looks like the hero of many a Royalist battle might have strangled his wife after all!"

"Maybe, and maybe not," Bruce said evenly.

"Centuries old, so Dr. Darrow says," Jonathan persisted.

"Aye, but that doesn't mean the laird did her in, even if it's possible to prove that this is Annalise. The autopsy will take place in Edinburgh," Robert said.

"This is my jurisdiction," Jonathan replied testily.

"And it's a national situation," Robert reminded him.

"You're not the one to make that call," Jonathan said.

"Now, Jonathan, it's the right call, and we all know

it," Daniel Darrow said evenly. "This really is a piece of old history we've found here. Naturally, with what's been happening…well, we all thought that Miss Fraser had stumbled upon someone else. And even though this pathetic wee one isn't who we thought, it's pretty evident that we have something very serious on our hands." Darrow's voice made it clear that no one could fault Jonathan for being frustrated—or for a lack of investigative technique. Everyone involved had been tense, certain that the discovery would be a recent victim of violence. But Jonathan apparently felt under the gun, nevertheless.

"For now," Darrow continued, "I'll get the boys to help me dig her out and get her to the morgue. Perhaps, Jonathan, Robert, y'll both give me a hand. We need to see to it that an expert is brought here."

Toni didn't know much about the laws regarding jurisdiction over a corpse—especially a centuries-old corpse, or the remains of one—but Darrow's solution seemed to satisfy everyone. In fact his calm approach somewhat soothed all tempers—if only as far as professional and outward appearances went.

Bruce didn't go past the tape, but he hunkered down at a distance again, looking at the remains.

Toni's own gaze was drawn to it then, and her stomach catapulted.

Death was never kind. The angle of the skull made it appear as if the neck had been broken, as if she had been left in pieces, as if the violence done to her had continued—even after death.

She couldn't help but look, though empty eye sockets stared back at her.

"How is that she is in pieces, and yet there are bits of flesh and bone?" Bruce asked.

Darrow hunkered down next to him. "I'd say that she was buried deep. The muck preserved her."

"'Tis a pity it didn't do so for our more recent victims," Jonathan said.

Darrow looked around. "The air is what often causes decay. If the recent rains shifted an old grave, she's not been exposed long. Aye, poor lass! Certainly looks as if she met her end by strangulation. The marks and—" He produced a small flashlight. "There! Y'can see how this was tied about her." He flicked off the light. "Pity! I can tell more on this lass already than we've gleaned at autopsy on the girls killed within a year or so!"

Bruce stood. Whatever he had seen, it had been enough. "I'm getting Toni out of here," he said, looking around to adamantly defy anyone who might protest. No one did.

"Aye, good," Jonathan said simply. Toni wondered if he really thought it was such a good idea that she be taken from the area, or if taking her out meant that Bruce would be out of his way, as well.

Robert turned to Toni then, offering her a hand. "Robert Chamberlain. Detective Inspector Robert Chamberlain. Strange circumstances here, but it's a pleasure to meet you, Miss Fraser."

"Toni," she murmured, taking his hand. "Please. And yes, it's a pleasure, Detective Inspector."

He offered her a wry smile. "Robert, if you will."

"Robert," she murmured.

"I'll come to the castle before I leave," Robert told Bruce.

"Aye, and thanks," Bruce said, slipping an arm around her shoulder and leading her from the site.

They walked in silence along the brook, exiting to

the road area where there were now at least a half-dozen cars parked, along with the medical examiner's hearse.

It wasn't until they were out of the woods that Bruce said suddenly and angrily, "What in God's name were you doing in there—that deep, especially!—in the first place? I told you to stay out of the forest."

She stared at him, startled, feeling a tinge of anger herself, ready to tell him that she had followed him. But he'd call her a liar, or worse, say she was mad. And she was feeling somewhat insane herself. If he'd headed straight for Edinburgh that morning, he couldn't have been on his horse, in the woods, beckoning her to come.

But what if he had purported to be making the drive to Edinburgh, then doubled back, taken the horse out, lured her into the forest, left her there and driven on to Edinburgh? Was the timing possible? Maybe. Just maybe.

And far more probable than seeing a phantom on horseback!

"I thought I saw you," she said simply.

"Me?" he demanded.

She shrugged. "I must have been mistaken."

"Why would I lure you into the forest when I keep telling you to stay out of the damned place?" he demanded angrily.

"Hey! I thought I saw you. I was mistaken," she said, shaking off his touch.

Evidently he caught hold of his temper. "I'm sorry. You've been through a lot."

"I haven't really been through anything," she said softly. "It's not as if I found... Please, don't treat me like a frightened child. I'm all right." She felt a twinge of anger, as well. "And you might have explained to us

that the bodies had been found in Tillingham Forest—
and that you were the one to discover a victim."

"I had thought it would suffice to make your group
understand that there were murders taking place. I had
also assumed that, since it's my castle and I'm allowing
you to stay, my directive to keep out of the forest would
be respectfully observed," he said.

"Bruce, honestly, I thought you were there and that
you were calling me in."

"Don't follow anyone, even me, into that forest."

A strange surge of unease filled her, teased along
her spine, then disappeared. She couldn't believe that
he intended any ill to her.

"You're trembling," he said.

"I'm fine."

"Are you? Perhaps you didn't come upon Annie
O'Hara, but such remains are still…disturbing. And
I assure you, I wasn't so 'all right' the day I found the
first body in the woods," he said.

"That was different."

"This was pleasant?"

Her lashes fell over her eyes. "No! Of course not!
Okay, I'm shaken. But I'm all right."

"Let's get back to the castle," he murmured, indicating his car. "How on earth could you have thought that
you saw *me?*"

"I was mistaken!"

She felt stiff, even awkward as she walked the few
feet to his car and got in. *So…she was lying now. Well,
not really. She had followed someone she thought to be
him into the woods. Maybe she should have told the constable that. Maybe there was someone who looked like
Bruce MacNiall, who was playing games, luring people*

into the woods, for a psychotic reason all his own. Or maybe it had been Bruce!

But she couldn't really believe that. And just as she had felt earlier, a strange calm descended upon her.

"Please believe me, I'm okay. Yes, it was startling. Scary. But now, more than anything, I just think it's very sad," she told Bruce, looking at him as he drove. He nodded, but his features were still tense. Despite the niggling suspicion of *possibility* that teased at the back of her mind, she found herself admiring the hard, sculpted line of his profile, the determined set of his jaw and the gravity with which he considered the situation. He might have let his castle go to hell, but he had a deep concern for this, his home territory, and a decent and humane care for those found here who had suffered so cruelly.

He was also upset, she thought, because of Jonathan's certainty that they had found Annalise and that she had, indeed, been killed by her husband all those years ago.

In a matter of minutes, they pulled up to the castle.

Gina, Ryan, David and Kevin came bursting out the front doors. Gina rushed for her first, exclaiming, "Oh, Toni! You poor dear!"

David was behind her, hugging her. "Eban came and told us all about it."

Ryan brushed back a thick strand of his long brown hair, hovering awkwardly by her side. "We wanted to come to you, but Eban said the authorities were with you and that they wouldn't want anyone traipsing through the woods then. At least, I think that's what he said."

"Toni, how about a drink?" Kevin suggested. "I think a drink would be the best thing in the world right now."

Toni took a deep breath, offering a rueful smile and returning the hugs. "Guys! Honestly, I'm fine. Please, I'm not a hothouse flower."

"Neither am I," Gina said. "But still, I can't imagine... Bruce, we're so sorry, by the way. Such things are always so horrible."

"Sorry?" he said.

Gina looked awkward, uneasy. "Well...we hadn't realized that the murder victims were discovered right here, in Tillingham, one by you and one by Eban. And though he was relieved that the corpse didn't belong to that missing girl, Eban indicated that the discovery probably means that a sad part of your family legend is true. Either way, we're really sorry. I guess our murder scenes have been in bad taste. And, of course, we will stay out of the forest—as Toni should have done."

"Aye, everyone needs to stay out of the forest. Except for the police," Bruce said. "As for my family legend, finding a body doesn't prove how it got there."

David slipped an arm around Toni's shoulders. "Toni! Seriously, young lady! What were you doing so deep in the forest? Laird MacNiall told us to stay out of it!"

She inhaled very deeply. She'd be explaining this forever, she thought. "It was a mistake, that's all. A trick of the light. I thought I saw Bruce there, beckoning to me."

They all stopped, staring at her. "Bruce left very early this morning, Toni," Gina said, looking at both of them. "I told you that, remember, when we were planning the picnic. You did leave, right, Bruce?"

"Aye."

"Hey, it's a forest, a trick of the light!" Toni repeated, and headed inside to get away from their questioning stares.

The others followed, automatically heading into the kitchen, where it seemed they always gathered. Kevin immediately went about preparing drinks. "This is one of those occasions that calls for tea and whiskey," he said, as the rest of them took a seat around the table.

"Thayer hasn't come back yet?" Toni said, suddenly noticing that her cousin was absent.

"No, he's still off," Gina said.

"He's got his cell, so we could call him," David said. "But we thought we'd let him finish out his afternoon before telling him about...this."

She realized then that the group was once again nervous about Bruce, and the ramifications of what had happened that afternoon. He had been concerned about their show, and the fact that very real murders were occurring, but he had allowed them to stay so they could make some of the money they had poured into the place. Now it seemed that they had found Annalise.

Bruce, too, realized what was weighing on their minds. And he wasn't the type to keep anyone in suspense. "You can continue your tours," he said, eyeing them all one by one. "But no one strangles anyone, is that clear?" He stared at Toni. "There will have to be a new spin on your 'history.' Figure it out, and all will be well."

Gina cleared her throat. "Bruce, do you think that the bones Toni found could have belonged to MacNiall's wife?"

Bruce sighed. "The bones may prove to be Annalise, and they may not. My ancestor may have killed her in a fit of rage, and he may not have done so. I hate assumptions, that's all. And while the tests and research are going on, I'd just as soon not capitalize on the sensationalism, even if we are trying to make some of your money back."

A collective sigh could be heard around the table.

"Thank you," Ryan said simply.

Bruce nodded, then he finished his drink in a long swallow and rose. "Gina, when you have a chance, get all your documents together. I've a friend coming who is with the force in Edinburgh. I'd like him to see them. Naturally, his office and his resources are better equipped to deal with an international fraud situation than the department here."

"Yes, of course," Gina said. She, too, hopped up.

"We can hold dinner for your friend," Kevin said. He was of the firm belief that a good meal, served well, could help solve all problems.

Even Bruce quirked a smile at that. "We'll see if he can stay," he told them. "And now if you'll excuse me, I'll be in my room if you need me."

When he departed, they all talked at once.

"Thank God!" Gina breathed.

"He really is a great fellow," David said.

"You poor thing!" Kevin said, shaking his head sympathetically at Toni. "It's so terrible, what happened to her. It was chance that you found her, certainly."

"Toni, are you all right with all this, after...?" Ryan asked.

Toni rose, feeling the weight of having gone through the forest, the bits of mud that had stuck to her that she hadn't noticed before. The tea and whiskey had been good, but more than anything, she wanted a bath.

"Guys, I'm fine. Thank you all for being so caring. But I've really got to clean up! I'll be back down in a bit."

"And I've got to get back out and see to the roan!" Ryan said. He shook his head. "I don't know what on earth could have made old Wallace so ill!"

Toni paused. She had forgotten about Eban telling her that the horse was doing poorly. "The vet came out?"

Ryan nodded. "When we came back from our picnic, he was here. He's doused the fellow, but he seemed a little confused himself. Said it must be something the horse ate. But Wallace is in there with Bruce's stallion, and Shaunessy is doing just fine. I only bought the best—you know how I feel about horses."

The roan had been another investment, but of course, he was much more. And although she hadn't Ryan's expertise or knowledge, she had been the one to choose the horse with him. Ryan had looked for all the good points in a horse, for what they needed—a docile nature being among them—whereas she had simply liked the roan because he had liked her and he loved to have his nose stroked. Besides that, his name had been Wallace, which was wonderfully historical for their venture. He'd seemed like an omen of good fortune.

"I'll go out and see him later, too," she said, feeling troubled.

"The vet is excellent, at least," Ryan said. "I guess out here they have to be top-notch, since folks depend on their livestock."

"That's good to hear," Toni murmured. "I'll be back down soon." And she left them, hurrying up to her room.

The door to the bath was closed. She knocked gently on it, but there was no answer, so she opened the door. Glancing across, she saw that the door to Bruce's room was closed, as well. Not locked, but closed.

She made the conscious decision not to lock it as she poured herself a hot bath.

Stripping off the clothes she had been wearing, she knew that she was never going to wear them again. Leaving them beneath the sink, she added bubble bath to the tub and climbed in.

Grateful that no one else had taken a shower or bath lately—and used up the hot-water supply—she sank back and let the heat soak into her. She hadn't realized just how damp and cold she'd felt. The water was good. The steam rising around her seemed to permeate the icy feeling in her bones.

She closed her eyes, resting her head on the rear of the tub, and before long she was back in the woods.

She saw again the man beckoning to her, saw the bubbling water, the tiny whitecaps formed when it struck upon the rocks. Then she saw herself coming upon the branch again, lifting it. Tension gripped her, but she couldn't escape the image she was suddenly seeing. For it wasn't that of ancient bones, the remains of a centuries-old crime.

She pictured a different body. Complete, intact. The body of a young woman, naked, facedown in the mud and water, hair encrusted with the black muck, tendrils of it betraying that once it had been blond and long.

She pictured herself turning the body, seeing the face. Pictured the eyes looking up at her, glazed with horror. And she wanted desperately to escape the grasp of the vision, but she could not.

Suddenly Toni had an image of the girl that haunted her as she had been in life, standing on a street corner in Edinburgh. She vaguely recognized the locality, not on the Royal Mile, but a street that was off the main drag, very dark, shadowy, the lights flickering. From somewhere she could hear the sound of music, muted as it came from a pub. There was also the sound of laughter, voices, distant, as well, merrymakers drinking quite a bit. She could see the girl's face, the eyes, and almost enter her mind.

Money. She needed money. And standing on the street corner, she wondered if she should go back in the pub and seek out a man there...except that she had been in the pub already and had seen no familiar faces. And no prospects. She had chosen a working man's place that night, and the fellows had all been the kind down with the economy. So she had come to the street. She had to be careful, of course—she didn't want to advertise to any of the bobbies who might be cruising about—but she also had to stand in such a way that the right fellow would know...

She was dressed in a plaid miniskirt to show off her legs, which she knew were very good. And her blouse wasn't ridiculously low-cut, but low-cut enough.

She hesitated, wondering if she had chosen the right street corner. For a moment, a brief moment, she wondered what she was doing. How on earth had she chosen this way of life? Then she knew. She hadn't really chosen this life. She had just known that she had to get out of the life she would have lived, scrubbing floors, working in a factory or serving burgers in a fast-food dive. She had no real education, and she would have married some fellow who would also take a menial job. She would have had a dozen children and lived in poverty.

She still believed that with a little more money— and learning to stay out of the pubs!—she could make it down to London. And once there...well, something would work out.

She shouldn't be doing this, but she didn't have a whole lot of options. Besides, she had learned...even with an ugly, smelling, fat old fellow, all she had to do was close her eyes, get it over with. Then it was done. And she had learned how to forget.

Maybe tonight she could find one who wasn't quite so fat, so gross, a fellow who didn't smell of stale whiskey, or worse yet, sheep.

Maybe there would be no one...

She heard the car before she saw it. It drew up next to her. She bent down, looking into the window and her heart soared. He was really quite a handsome brute. Great smile.

She climbed into the car.

"Toni!"

Her eyes flew open. She jerked up. All images faded in a snap, as if they had never been. Only a whisper of unease remained with her, a slight trickle of fear.

Bruce MacNiall was just inside the doorway, a deep frown creasing his forehead. She stared at him, aware that the bubbles around her were dying and totally heedless of the fact.

She had consciously made the decision to leave the door open. At the moment, though, she barely remembered that as she tried to recall what she had seen in her mind's eye.

She had clearly seen the girl's face, her eyes, with far too much detail! And she had felt things for another, stepped into a different life.

"I'm sorry, I didn't mean to intrude," Bruce said, his voice deep. "I was afraid you were drowning in here."

She was suddenly so glad of his appearance that she could hardly bear it. She scrambled to her feet, almost tripping in her haste to leave the tub, startling him when she flew, soaking, into his arms.

"Hey!" he said, very softly and apparently heedless of the water that soaked from her naked body onto him. His arms wrapped around her for a moment, giving her all the warmth, security and life, vital reality that she so desperately needed. Then he drew back slightly, lifting her chin.

"I thought that you were all right?" he queried gently.

"I am," she said, and she was. At that moment, in his arms, she was fine. When he held her close, she was not afraid. She did not become blind to her visions, nor did she forget them. But she felt a sense of well-being. And more. Suddenly, despite what she had seen—or perhaps because of it—she wanted to feel all the heat and eroticism promised in the electricity that burned between them every time they spoke, every time they touched.

He arched a brow, then said, "If you're afraid, Toni, I'm pleased to protect you, to offer whatever company you may need. But don't come to me in such a way unless it's what you really want."

She nodded, and a wistful smile came to her lips. "I need you."

"Aye, and I'm here."

The curve to her lips deepened. "I know that you'd... keep me company with nothing more required. And this may sound very strange indeed, but I'm not afraid anymore. I want to be with you. So...you know that thing about me jumping you? Well...?"

He hesitated for a minute and a wave of uncertainty washed over her, almost a sense of panic. He would push her away, she thought; she was acting like a fool.

But then he lifted her chin and met her eyes with an intensity burning in his own. "I just don't want you jumping me because...because you need someone to sleep with."

She stared up at him, shaking her head. "Not *someone*. You."

"Ah," he murmured, still studying her.

"So...you *don't* want me jumping you?" she queried.

"Aye, lass, that I do," he said, and the ragged tremor in his voice alone sent shock waves of hunger and anticipation streaking through her. "I do, that I do. I want you jumping me because you just can't stand it anymore. Because you're thinking I'm the sexiest thing that's ever walked into your life. Because you want my hands all over you, everywhere. Because your every thought regarding me is totally sensual, simply carnal." His voice deepened still further, and the steel of his eyes was silver, the heat in his hold, in his body, almost staggering. "I want you jumping me because you're dying to get your hands on my bare flesh, because you're absolutely fascinated by what a Scotsman's got under his kilt."

"You're not wearing a kilt."

"Ah, lass, if this is really what you want, I don't intend to be wearing anything."

She reached up, stroking his cheek, marveling at the texture of his flesh, wondering, in that moment, how she had kept so long from doing this. She breathed him in, feeling the deep-seated power in his chest and everything that was so strikingly male about him—the sense, the feel, the color of his hair, the set of his features and all that she couldn't quite touch.

"I want to crawl into your skin," she whispered honestly, meeting his gaze.

He stepped back, and for a moment again, she felt the vulnerability of having laid her heart on the line. Or the absolute extent of her desire, at the very least. She felt her nakedness then, and her eyes betrayed a need too deep.

But he hadn't left her. He was simply getting out of his shirt so quickly that a button went flying.

"My skin is all yours," he said. "All of it."

She smiled, throwing herself against him once more, taking a moment to delight in the feel of his flesh against her own, her breasts pressed hard to him, the erotic pressure of muscle, the tease of dark hair upon his chest.

His hand, massive, the fingers so long, caught beneath her chin, lifting her face to his. His lips formed upon her own, his tongue bold. The first kiss was no gentle sway but a staggering force that eclipsed the world and created a staggering acuity in her senses. She was so keenly aware of where he touched her, and where he did not. And every inch of her naked length longed to be stroked by him, longed to come closer and closer. His tongue entered her mouth with a thrust and power that created a staccato pulse of all that was to come. She seemed to lose air and all thought of breathing. She felt like a bow, stretched tight and quivering, and she was afraid her knees would give at any moment.

Maybe he knew...

He lifted her against him. Again, every brush of sensation seemed to be acute. The feel of the fabric of his jeans, his belt buckle, his hands, his flesh, the force of his erection against the denim. It occurred to her vaguely that she'd known him two days' time; it seemed like forever. His naked chest against her flesh was hot with a fever that seduced and entered into her soul, exotic, overwhelming. He laid her upon the ancient tapestry of his bed, beneath the brocade canopy, and when he moved to doff his shoes and jeans, she was bereft, left cold and aching. In seconds he was back, upon her, straddling, creating a new wave of frenzied fire as she felt the bareness of his sex against her flesh. *Then* would have been fine. She had never wanted anything more. But he leaned low, eyes meeting hers again, fingers finding her arms, tracing their length, drawing them above her head as his lips found hers once again.

And from there...

The wet pressure of his lips, tongue, mouth, the feel against her breasts, nipples, was almost more than she could bear. His hands slid down to caress her torso; her fingers threaded into his hair. She writhed beneath him, gasping. "I am supposed to be jumping you!"

For a moment, his eyes touched hers, steel and silver, both hard and bright. "Ah, but jumping on me now could cause serious damage, and not further the cause at all." His face burrowed against her belly then, his tongue teasing her navel. Lower. Laving the hollows of her hips. And his hands...between her thighs. His fingers...a stroke never hesitant, a touch...followed by his kiss...

She cried out, stunned, catapulted to an urgency that was pure anguish. Reeling with the impact, the sensual sensation so staggering, she jackknifed beneath him, reaching a climax that rocked through her with astonishing speed, staying with her, gripping her...

And feeling him again, the slide of his body against her own, the insinuation of his sex and the length of it within her, so that before she had drifted down she was soaring up once again. She was moving with him in a state of blind, desperate bliss, so very aware of his scent, his heat, his vibrancy and every detail of the sheer physicality of their union. Heaven and earth seemed to fade away. There was nothing but entwining arms, limbs, the slick feel of naked flesh, the rise within her and the pounding, pulsing desire to reach the pinnacle once again.

She had thought herself stroked, sated, to the point of wild ecstasy before, had thought that nothing could ever shock or exhilarate her to such a fantastic sensual delight and combustion again. She had been wrong. His ragged pulse, stroke, thrust, touch, evoked and elicited a wildness in her she had never dreamed. Cries escaped her; she clung to him, writhed beneath him, arched and thundered, indeed, as if she could get into his skin…and the wild violence with which she exploded then into climax was shattering. As it ripped through her again and again, she trembled, awed, weakened, shaking, barely aware of the world around her. He held her still, damp, hot, the pulse that had thundered through the beat of her heart, slowing, bit by bit…

His arms, fast around her, his hair, a tangled thicket of ebony over his forehead, his eyes…silver, so sensual. His words…

She waited, barely breathing, longing to know what he would say.

And then…they both heard it—the rapping on the door.

"Bruce? You in there?"

The flicker in his eyes became one of resignation and amusement.

"Robert Chamberlain," he murmured with regret. "I told him to come by."

She certainly wasn't a child, had every right in the world to do what she was doing, to be where she was. Yet Toni found herself leaping to her feet, offering him a grimace. "Right," she said simply, and fled through the connecting bath.

Chapter 10

Darkness had descended and done so deeply by the time Thayer returned. As he headed up the driveway, he slowed, noting the cars at the foot of the hill by the forest, all with law-enforcement markings on them. There was the constable's car, and a few from farther afield—as far as Edinburgh and Stirling.

It didn't take a rocket scientist to figure out what had happened.

Still he slowed the car. An officer in uniform seemed to be standing vigil out by the cars. He walked to the driver's door of Thayer's vehicle as he slowed.

"Evening, sir!" the officer said.

"Evening."

"Heading for the castle? If you're here for one of the tours, I'm afraid there isn't one tonight."

"Actually, I'm with the folks giving the tours."

"Ah!" the fellow said. He peered more intently at Thayer.

"Heard it was Americans, giving tours on Scottish history. You from Glasgow?"

"Aye, that I am. Kin to one of the Americans. They're giving good tours," Thayer said. He didn't know why he was sounding defensive. He certainly didn't want to be challenging any law officials. Especially with what he had in the car.

"What's happening here?" he asked the officer.

"The news will be gettin' out soon enough, I wager," the officer said.

Thayer tensed.

"They've…found a body?" he asked.

"Aye!" the officer said gravely.

"In the forest again, eh?"

"Aye, again!"

"So…" Thayer said slowly, feeling a sheen of sweat break out on his upper lip. "They found the missing girl?"

The officer suddenly frowned, shaking his head. "Is that what you thought? Ach, well, and why not, since the other poor wee lasses were found here," the officer said. "Nae, what they've found is a very old corpse… well, bones and pieces, at the least. They're thinking she was the wife o' the laird of the castle, but there are fellows in there now from the university, as well as from the law! That's all I know. So, if you've legitimate business up at the castle, you go on up. Take care around here, eh? They haven't found the poor lass gone missing last in here as of yet, but with the discoveries made of late, well, they still may be doin' so. Aye, and if you can think of anything that you've seen around here out of the ordinary—other than a flock of Americans!—you be sure to tell the constable right away."

The officer thought that he was amusing. Thayer cracked a weak smile.

"Seriously, report anything suspicious right away," the officer said.

"Aye, right away," Thayer promised him.

The officer patted the car's hood. Thayer gave him a wave, put the car into gear and started up the path to the castle.

He parked in the driveway and hesitated. He hadn't realized that he was sweating, that his palms were clammy, that he had been shaking inside, right down into his boots.

Did he look as flushed as he felt? he wondered. And why not? He'd just been told that a body was found in the woods.

He sat a second longer, then exited the car. He started toward the castle, then turned back and stared at the vehicle, and made sure that the locks had clicked.

He slicked back his hair, and started on in.

Actually, he told himself, there was a bit of a thrill to it all.

"I didn't catch you sleeping at this time—and under these circumstances?" Robert said, looking up as Bruce made his way down the stairs.

"Sleeping?" Bruce repeated. "Ah, no." *Frankly, old chum, you just interrupted one of the finest moments in my life,* Bruce thought dryly. Then again, he'd asked Robert to come by. "Shared shower these days," he said briefly. That kind of explained, with a grain of truth. He wasn't so sure Toni would want their intimacy either known or broadcast at this moment, so he went on quickly. "Have you met the others?"

"I have," Robert told him. "Including Miss Fraser. She's the one with whom you share the shower?"

"Ah, yes." Bruce grimaced. "Where are they off to at the moment?"

"In the kitchen. The Glasgow fellow, Thayer, just returned. Everyone is talking at once in there, trying to tell him what's happened, and why the base of the hill is covered with police vehicles. When it winds down to a soft roar, Gina Browne is going to copy the documents and give me the original ones. She's trying to pull up the corporation on the Internet again, but naturally, there is no such place anymore, so we'll have to get the cyber experts on it. You were right, their papers look absolutely legal and authentic, but I suppose that's not a difficult thing to accomplish, if you're of a criminal bent."

"They're making copies here?"

"I guess you haven't wandered into Mrs. Browne's domain," Robert said. "She has a computer, printer, fax and mobile phone line. Quite an amazing display of 'have electronics, will travel,' actually."

Bruce nodded, not really surprised. "They trust you, then, I take it?" he queried.

Robert's eyes sparkled for a moment. "Well, there is the fact that I'm accepted by the dozen crime-scene experts down the hill, though I'm pretty sure that Mrs. Browne called Edinburgh and checked on my credentials."

Bruce smiled ruefully. "Well, good. I think they really believe that I own the place now, too."

Robert arched a brow in amusement.

"Was anyone able to glean anything more from the site?" Bruce asked him.

Robert shook his head. "Not at the moment. It appears that the remains must have washed up very recently. Darrow is actually excited, which is something I don't think he gets to feel often when he's found a body—or pieces of one. Due to our discoveries of the past, I made a very thorough search of the area myself. I guess I was actually hoping to find Annie O'Hara, but there was no sign of her—or anything else, for that matter. As for footprints, I could follow those of Miss Fraser, and the tracks of our officers, but nothing else. They were still scouring the area when I left—since all those men are there, it seemed a fine time for a very thorough search—but so far, nothing. Not a cigar butt, a broken branch, nothing. Darkness is on us, though. The woods do need a good scouring, but Jonathan is right about one thing—it's a damned big forest."

"That it is," Bruce agreed.

Robert angled his head, regarding Bruce carefully.

"Jonathan got your goat tonight, didn't he?"

Bruce offered his friend a slow, wry smile. "The rumor that our local hero murdered his wife in a fit of rage and jealousy has been around for years. Perhaps it's true. Maybe these bones will turn out to be those of one of my ancestors. It's only Jonathan's pleasure at turning my blood kin into a monster that riles me." He shrugged. "We're still friends, I believe. Have been, all these years."

"He's jealous of you, always has been."

"That's foolish. I may own a derelict castle and bear the old title, but it doesn't mean all that much these days."

"I don't think it's the title that bothers him," Robert said.

"Then what?"

"Your reputation," Robert said. "For solving a national mystery, all those years ago."

"I've been out of it for a decade."

"And he's still a small-town constable."

"Well, if he harbors ill will, it's his problem, and his foolishness," Bruce said, shaking his head.

"So you won't be greatly disturbed…if this proves to be the long-gone Annalise?"

"A mystery will have been solved," Bruce said simply. "Whatever it was, I can't change history."

"Nae, not a one of us can do that, ancient or recent," Robert said with a sigh, and Bruce knew he was thinking that if they could only catch the killer, they might well change the history of life for many a poor lass. "I've been invited to supper," Robert told him suddenly. "I was sent to retrieve you."

"Ah."

"But Miss Fraser is still upstairs?"

"I believe she'll be right down."

"Is she doing all right?" Robert asked.

"Yes, she seems to be just fine. Come on, we'll head on into the kitchen."

Robert was watching him somewhat strangely, but Bruce ignored the look and led the way. By the time they reached the door that led through the secondary hall, they could smell the succulent aroma of the meal. Pushing through the doorway to the kitchen, Bruce found the table handsomely set, Gina pouring wine, Ryan at her side, Kevin carving the roast and Thayer and David rushing about to find the proper bowls for the accompanying vegetables. With a tray of meat and tiny pearl onions in his hands, Kevin turned and saw Bruce.

"Laird MacNiall, thanks for coming down. I know

it's been a sad and traumatic day, but while we live and breathe, we have to eat, right?"

"Right. It looks like a fine supper, Kevin," Bruce said.

Kevin set the tray on the table.

"Where on earth is Toni?" David fretted, setting down a plate of broccoli, then running his fingers absently through his dark hair.

"On her way, I'm certain," Bruce assured him.

"I think we'll really have to start without her," Gina murmured. "It will all grow cold."

"I think I should go up," David said.

Kevin set a hand on his arm and nodded. "You should."

"They'll just take longer, chatting up there together," Thayer warned as David started out.

"David is very dear to her," Gina said, finishing with the last glass, surveying the table, seeming pleased. "If she's at all upset…well, David is close to her."

"We're all close to her!" Ryan protested, staring at his wife.

"Yes, dear. But David and she… Just let David handle it," Gina said. "Inspector Chamberlain, we're so pleased that you could stay!" she added, smiling at Robert as he walked in.

"Not to mention, grateful for your help," Ryan said. "Especially when the fact that we've been fleeced can hardly mean much in comparison to the plethora of bodies to be found about."

"A plethora! Ryan!" Gina said, horrified by his choice of words.

"I'm sorry. I mean, bodies…in the forest. Ancient, new… Sorry!" Ryan said again.

Robert waved a hand in the air. "Actually, I won't be

handling your problem myself—we have people who specialize in computer fraud and international crime. And you needn't be grateful to me in any capacity. Enforcing the law is my work, in no matter what capacity. We'll get your case into the right hands, which, admittedly, are not my own. The supper smells delicious."

"Thank you!" Kevin said, beaming.

"Actually, he's the meat wizard," Ryan protested. "Potatoes and broccoli are creations perfected by my lovely wife," Ryan informed him.

"To everyone involved in the effort, it looks—and smells—quite divine," Robert said. He flashed a glance at Bruce, indicating that he considered his household of Americans quite an amusement.

"Robert, we put you here, opposite the laird of the castle!" Gina said, trying for a light note.

The group assembled, minus David and Toni for the time being. Kevin cleared his throat. "Shall we say grace?" he asked, looking at Thayer for guidance.

Thayer offered an amused smile. "If you wish."

"Um…sure," Ryan murmured. He lowered his head, but his eyes were open as he looked around.

They were a fairly spiritual group, Bruce thought, decent folk, but not necessarily the ones in the front of the church every Sunday morning. Like Thayer, he was slightly amused, and yet he admired the group for trying to gauge the proper etiquette for a Scottish Sunday meal.

But no one spoke.

Kevin looked around, apparently a bit panicked, since it had been his idea.

"Um…is it proper for the laird of the castle to speak?" he inquired.

"I think it would be quite proper for the American cook," Bruce said.

"Ah," Kevin agreed. "Okay. Dear Lord, thank you for this meal, for the generosity and kindness of our host and for the help of our host's friends. We're aware that there is famine and real tragedy in the world—like the poor old soul found in the forest this time, and those other girls—but please, oh, Lord, help us in our endeavors, as well. We really meant all the best. We love Scotland! We mean to help—"

"Amen!" Gina cut in firmly, glaring at Kevin.

Robert simply laughed out loud. "A lovely grace, Kevin," he said. "But don't you have the same one in the States that we have here? Simply quicker. 'God is great, God is good, thank you God, for this food. Let's eat'?"

Kevin flushed as the rest of them laughed.

"Let me pass the meat!" Gina said quickly.

Toni had just set the hair dryer down when she heard the knock at her door and David's voice. "Toni?"

She opened the door. "Hey, I'm sorry. I've taken too long, huh?"

"Kid, you can take all night if you want. I came up to make sure that you were all right. The concern about a hot meal doesn't really compare to the discovery of bones in the forest," he assured her sympathetically.

"I keep saying this, though no one seems to believe me, but I'm all right," she said. "It's just…"

"Just what?" he asked gently.

She walked on into the room and sat on the side of the bed. He joined her, slipping an arm around her shoulders.

"Are you still envisioning a long-dead Scotsman with a bloody sword?" he asked.

She shook her head quickly, but then flashed him a glance.

"David," she murmured.

"Talk to me," he said. "That's why I'm here. Look, you're a good actress. You have everyone else convinced that you're relieved because it wasn't that missing girl, turned up dead. But I know you, and I know you're upset about those bones."

"She's dead," Toni murmured.

"What?"

She looked at his handsome, caring face and shook her head. "Nothing."

"Toni! Please, you know I never repeat a word you say to me."

"But do I know that you won't have me committed to an asylum?" she asked.

"Never," he assured her.

She inhaled deeply. "David, I could have sworn that I saw Bruce go into the forest."

David frowned. "Toni, he did leave the castle very early."

She nodded. "So I've been told. And I know travel here can take some time, but still…"

"Did you ask Bruce?"

"He was in Edinburgh. With his friend."

"And you trust in that, of course."

"There's something about him that…yes, I trust him."

"Then…?"

"David, I think I'm seeing things again." Her words suddenly started to pour from her. "This afternoon… if it wasn't Bruce, then it was the man that I invented, that Bruce from centuries ago. Or else, someone who dresses up like him and has access to a big black horse. Or else, I'm going crazy."

"Toni," he said slowly, "you're not going crazy. We'll rule that out right off the bat. When you came in tonight, you said something about it being a trick of the light. Isn't that possible?"

"I suppose," she murmured.

"But you don't believe it."

She shook her head. "There's more."

"Go on."

She shook her head. "When I was taking a bath… David, it was suddenly as if I was *her*."

"Toni, you're losing me. Her—who?" He shook his head. "The long-gone Annalise?"

"No. And that's what one would have thought. I mean, after everything else I made up that turned out to be true, I should have been imagining what it had been like for Annalise. But no, it was suddenly as if I were…the missing girl."

"Annie O'Hara?" he said with surprise.

She nodded gravely.

"What do you mean?"

"Well, it was as if I was where she had been, as if I could follow her thoughts the night she was taken. And killed. I could see outside a pub where she was drinking. She was even weighing in her mind what she was about to do. And then a car came up, and she was pleased and excited, because it wasn't some creepy old man about to pick her up."

"Did you see him?" David asked sharply.

"No." Toni shook her head. "No, I didn't. I—I was distracted. I don't know if I would have seen the fellow or not."

He sighed, rubbing her shoulders. "Toni, you do know that the mind can do bizarre things—especially under the stress of suggestion?"

"Yes, I know. Oh, God, David! Don't you think I'm

looking for every possible rational reason for what I'm thinking, feeling…doing?"

"Toni, please don't go getting all paranoid. Honestly, think about it. Everything happening here is very suggestive. And hey, maybe there is some idiot in the village who hates Bruce MacNiall and is trying to get the man into some serious trouble by dressing up like him."

"You think someone else might have a big black horse?" she queried.

He smiled. "I sure as hell think that's possible. They breed horses all around here. And big hairy coos!" he added, trying to get her to smile.

She did smile, but the effort faded quickly.

"Ah, Toni!"

"I'm still…scared. Well, not exactly scared, but worried. Unnerved, I guess."

"Toni! You found a body, the human remains of someone. That's pretty traumatic."

She shook her head. "No, you don't understand. Yes, it's horrible and disturbing, and I think I've had the reaction most people would—out-and-out pain and sympathy for the poor girl. And I also feel that distance most people would. Whoever she was, she died years and years ago. But it's this connection I feel to Annie O'Hara that's so unnerving! I don't know how to explain it."

"Still, it's natural that you would feel for another soul, and that your mind might play tricks," David said.

"David, I told you about the things that happened when I was a child. I had pushed it all back—so far back!—for years. It's terrifying to see these things."

He was silent for a minute. "Toni, don't say this to anyone else."

"They'll see that I'm locked up, right?"

He didn't smile or even reply right away. "No, that's

not what I mean. It's just…you shouldn't say things like this to anyone else. It could get out."

"I don't intend to! I didn't even intend to say anything to you. But if you're not worried about them all thinking that I'm crazy, what are you worried about?"

He hesitated. "Toni, you might have stumbled upon old bones, but there is a very real killer out there. He's probably a psychotic and far away, but people talk."

"So?"

He exhaled and looked straight at her. "Toni, people like wild stories. Newspapers will pick up anything. And whether they think you're a crazy, headline-hunting American or not, they could print something. Most people will think you're nutty. But there is a killer out there, and if you scare him, make him think that you can see things others can't, then you could be considered a real threat."

She stared at him, slowly understanding just what he was saying.

"A threat, Toni! Do you understand? You could put yourself in danger!"

She shook her head at first, in denial, then she felt the chills snaking down her spine.

"Don't worry," she whispered after a moment. "Trust me, I won't say a word to anyone, anyone at all. As I said, I didn't even mean to talk to you."

"But I love you, and I'm your best friend," he reminded her. "Well, Gina likes to claim that she is, but we both know it's me," he teased.

Toni laughed. "You're both the best friends in the world," she assured him.

"You can talk to me whenever you're feeling frantic, and I promise, I'll never make you think that you're crazy. I'll always be around when you need me," he said, giving her another hug.

"Thanks!" she whispered, and hugged him back fiercely. "Okay, I'll give it to you this time. You're the best friend in the world!"

"I'm the best friend, but Laird Bruce is still the hottest guy around, huh?" he teased.

She felt a flood of color soar to her cheeks.

"Hey! I have hit on something there, haven't I?"

"We'd best get downstairs," she said.

"I told you, he is a hottie," David said, watching her with keen interest now, a curious light in his eyes.

"Yes, yes, he's attractive," Toni murmured. "Shall we go down?"

He agreed, and rising, he took her hand and escorted her toward the door. When they reached it, he turned back, looking around the room. "Hmm. The bed is way too neat," he said. "And there I was, thinking that… But wait! There is another room, right? Through the bath?"

He started to walk back into the room, but Toni caught him by his shirt. "Out! You—we—are not going snooping into his room!" she said, trying to put some indignity into her tone.

"Snooping? I don't think you were snooping earlier!" David teased.

She groaned aloud. "Downstairs. Food, dinner, remember?"

"I want details!" he teased.

"You're not getting any."

"Aha! So there are details to be gotten?"

"Dinner!" she insisted.

"That's okay, I'll make up a better story than you could give me," he said.

She paused for a minute, aware that he was making her squirm—and laugh. He really was the world's best friend.

"There is no better story!" she said, putting up a hand. "And that's all you're getting! Let's go down."

Laughing, he followed her as she hurried toward the stairway.

"There's really a lot of activity in the forest," Thayer said, taking a piece of the meat and passing it on. He watched Bruce MacNiall, and the new man, Robert Chamberlain, with interest.

He'd heard of Chamberlain, of course. The man was ostensibly with the Edinburgh police, but had been called around the country often enough, and was held in high esteem by the government and his fellow law-enforcement officers. From what Thayer had read about the fellow, he'd thought the man a better diplomat and politician than detective. That evening, he felt as if he might have been wrong. There was something about the bloke.

"And judging by the number of cars, they've called in people from all over. It's funny, but I got the impression that the constable is a little proprietorial."

"Jonathan is all right," Robert said, glancing at Bruce.

"There is simply no way for a village such as this to have the kind of technology available in the larger cities, obviously," Bruce said.

"So," Thayer continued, "the folks out there now combing the forest are specialists? Forensics fellows, lasses, whichever?"

"Yes," Robert said.

Bruce nodded. "I think they were contacting the university, hoping to get out some anthropologists and specialists."

"Aye, then, that's good," Thayer said. "Maybe, while they're digging up old bones, they'll find out more about the fellow killing girls now, and be able to put a stop to the bloke."

"We will put a stop to him," Robert said.

"Pity that Toni didn't stumble upon Annie O'Hara," Thayer said.

They all stared at him.

"Sorry! I didn't mean that I'd wish such a thing on my own kin, or that we should give up hope that the girl is alive. But…if she'd been found, it may have helped the effort to catch the killer, right? It's bad business. No one even knows if Annie O'Hara is only the third victim."

"We don't know that she is a victim," Robert said.

"Has this guy been at it for such a long time?" Ryan asked with a frown. He flushed slightly as he looked over at Bruce MacNiall. "That sounds so callous. I'm sorry. I guess I just didn't really realize how long it's been going on. I don't know why it surprises me— we've had serial killers at large for years in the United States. Nowadays we're always hoping that they're… well, caught quicker. If you watch *CSI* back home, you get the feeling that a crime can be solved in a night."

"Sadly, it doesn't often work that way," Bruce murmured.

"The first woman disappeared over a year ago," Robert said, glancing at Bruce. "She was found in a sad state of decomposition. The second, just a bit more than six months ago. She was also found in a very serious state of decay. We've had little, if nothing, to go on."

"Dead men do tell tales," Kevin murmured.

"It's definitely true that the dead can speak, through medicine and science," Robert said. "But to make comparisons, you have to have a suspect."

Kevin set down his fork.

Bruce MacNiall stared at Thayer. "Surely, Thayer,

you might not have heard my name—or known anything about the castle or the forest here—but you must have heard about this killer? When the first girl went missing, there was barely a notice, until her body was found in the forest, by me. But there was national coverage when the second girl went missing, and then when she was found in the forest, this time by Eban."

Thayer was alarmed by the strange chill that snaked down his spine. What did MacNiall think this was, a bloody game of Clue? "Aye, *I've* heard about the killer. I do read the papers. But we've had other crimes, as well, about the country."

"But you didn't remember the name of the forest?" MacNiall persisted.

"This was advertised as Castle Keep," Thayer said, trying hard not to sound defensive. "Nothing in the documents we all read and signed mentioned anything about Tillingham Forest."

"I see," MacNiall murmured, not sounding convinced.

Toni walked into the kitchen then, followed by David, who was grinning broadly, until he sensed the tension in the room. "Is everything all right?" he asked.

"Yes, absolutely," Thayer said, thankful for the interruption. He lifted his glass. "We should be toasting Kevin's fine meal. And our host, Laird MacNiall, and his good friend, Detective Inspector Chamberlain."

"A toast!" David said. "Yes, indeed." Still standing, he lifted his wineglass. "To Kevin, great meal."

Gina cleared her throat.

"To Gina," David said, laughing. "Great veggies, as always! To Detective Inspector Chamberlain, with our deepest thanks, and to our host, more gratitude and admiration than he can ever imagine!"

"Here, here!" went around the table.

Then Thayer watched as Toni took her seat next to Laird Bruce MacNiall. He saw the flash in her eyes and the smile that curled her lips. And he saw the way that MacNiall looked back at her. Though it was subtle, it was still one of the most telling exchanges Thayer had ever seen.

Something had changed between the two. It wasn't a great mystery. His muscles clenched and tightened. His stomach hurt. So…they'd slept together.

Toni, with her huge, deep blue eyes, generous, sensual lips, damned plethora of blond hair, lithe height, supple curves, intoxicating laughter and scent…

Thayer could be nothing but her cousin, her friend. They were far too close, she said. Like hell. He remembered when they had met. He could have told her the truth—the real truth. Instead, he had tried to emphasize just how many times "removed" they were as relations. But it had done no good.

Face it, fellow, he told himself. *She just didn't find you attractive. You might as well have been a eunuch— or of another persuasion, like Kevin and David. You fool. You've dreamed, you've drooled. You thought you'd give it time. And there she is, sleeping with the bloke after only forty-eight hours?*

His fingers knotted around his wineglass.

He could see the two of them, Toni, with those eyes on him, his eyes somewhere else. Hell, the great MacNiall, the fellow with the castle, the title, the fookin' bulging biceps and cast-iron chest.

Suddenly the glass snapped in his hand.

"Thayer!"

Toni was the first to jump up with alarm, running to his side, her napkin in her hand.

"It's all right, it's all right!" he said quickly.

Her eyes were on his, deep with concern. "Must have picked up the handle wrong!" he muttered.

"You're bleeding. Let me make sure there's no glass in it," Toni said.

"I'll get the first-aid kit," Gina said.

"No!" he said, standing.

It had been a bark, he realized, for everyone in the room was staring at him. And was there suspicion in the eyes of the great Detective Inspector Chamberlain, and those of the even-greater Laird MacNiall?

He forced a wry grin. "Sorry, I'm feeling the worst fool, such an oaf," he muttered.

"Thayer, it's all right," Toni said, still concerned. "But you are bleeding."

"A scratch. If you will excuse me, I'll just see to it. Ach, I hope I didn't get glass in any of the food," he said, causing them all to look at the table.

"None of it even near any food, old chap!" David said cheerfully.

That damned David, always working to make everything fookin' copasetic! he thought.

"Thayer, are you sure you're not cut deeply?" Gina asked, concerned.

He shook his head. "Embarrassed is what I am," he said. "I'll be back in a moment."

Gina and Toni were picking up shards of glass.

"I really don't think we have to worry about any of the food," Gina murmured. "I think we're getting it all."

"Aye, don't worry none," Robert said. "If there's a shard there, your host will be seein' it."

"Good eyes, eh, Bruce?" David said.

Thayer found himself pausing just beyond the doorway, ignoring the blood that dripped from his hand.

"His eyes are the best," Robert informed them all. "Hell, when he was with the force, Bruce was run ragged. We dragged him in on everything."

There was a startled silence.

"You were a *cop?*" Ryan said to Bruce.

"Aye, for a time," Bruce said. There was a slight edge to his voice, as if he hadn't particularly wanted the information known.

Thayer remained in the hall, feeling as if he was very nearly baring his teeth. *Aye, the fellow was a copper! You never knew, you fools. Never suspected.*

But how would they have known? Only a Scotsman would have read all about it.

Chapter 11

Gina tidied up the business area in the bedroom she and Ryan had chosen. She'd liked it especially because of the large expanse of window it offered, looking out on the valley. Probably, at an earlier date, the room had been the domain of a chief guard, or something of the like. The window—evidently put in sometime after the turn of the nineteenth century—looked out over the hillside. From this vantage point, any invader seeking to come upon the castle would have been in clear view.

She stacked the copies of their documents and at last turned off all the machines.

Ryan was already in bed. She gazed at him with a deep and abiding love. She had known from the moment she met him that he was all she wanted in life. He could be fun, sweet—and aggravating at times. And though it appeared he deferred to her, it was only because she really did have an incredible business sense. But beneath it all… Ryan ruled the roost. He always had.

His hands were folded behind his head as he lay on his pillow staring up at the ceiling. The white sheets of their bed were drawn to his waist. His shoulders and chest were bronze, and she felt the thrill that she always did when looking at him. She truly loved everything about him.

It should have been their day for total relaxation, but it just hadn't gone that way. She was tired, anxious to crawl in beside him. He was pretty damned cool beneath the sheets, as well.

She walked to the doorway and turned off the main light. With the moonlight that filtered in, there was just enough light to…

She paused at the foot of the bed, feeling the need for intimacy, and ready to play with it. In that mood, she slowly shed her shirt, then her bra, and made a real act of shedding her jeans and panties. Ryan should be both amused and titillated.

Coming around the bed to crawl in, she realized that he hadn't even glanced at her—not once.

He turned to her then, frowning.

"Just what the hell are we going to do?" he demanded.

"Do? We're 'doing' it," she reminded him.

He shook his head.

"What the hell are we going to do about *Toni?*" he demanded.

She felt her blood grow cold.

"What do you mean…about Toni?" she said with a swallow. "She's—she's just Toni. There's nothing to *do* about her at all."

"There has to be!" he insisted angrily.

"Why?" she whispered, frightened by his tone, knowing it all too well.

"Because she's dangerous," he said flatly, harshly.

The chill in her bones deepened, and it seemed that her blood turned to ice.

Toni went up first that night, leaving Bruce still talking to Robert Chamberlain. She found herself industriously brushing her teeth, washing her face…and finding the white nightgown, aware that it kept her covered, but not all that covered.

She had made the first move, and it had been far from subtle—since catapulting yourself out of a bathtub, naked and dripping, into a man's arms could really never be considered less than big-time brash. Certainly he would come to her tonight. He had to!

He was slow in coming up. She lay on her own bed, torn. He couldn't feel quite the way that she did—desperate to feel again what she had just experienced—and linger so long. He was unique in her eyes. Maybe she wasn't so special in his. Hell, a naked woman throws herself at you, what else would a red-blooded male do?

She flushed, wondering if she hadn't made a fool out of herself, wondering if he wasn't downstairs pondering how to extricate himself from any further intimacy with her.

She closed her eyes and gritted her teeth, wincing. There was more to it. She didn't want to be alone. She didn't want to dream, imagine, envision or see things. And there was something about him that was rocklike and solid, something that defied fear and mist and things that could go bump in the night.

But that wasn't the only reason she had gone to him. Like David teased, he was…hot. Those eyes, a slate enigma, searching into her, sweeping over her, his hands touching her...the set and structure of his face...

She tossed and twisted around. How long had she been up here? An hour, more?

She rose, walked to her door and cracked it open, trying to ascertain if she could still hear voices from below. She couldn't. Looking up and down the hall, she saw that it was empty.

Cautiously at first, not wanting to run into anyone else and appear foolish, she made her way down the hall to the second-floor landing. She stood in the spot she took up when she told her tale about Cavalier MacNiall, the great hero, the battle laird who, it now appeared, had come home from victory to murder his wife.

Then she saw him.

He was standing at the great hearth, leaning against the mantel, looking pensively into the embers of the fire. For a moment, it didn't register that he had changed, that he was no longer in the jeans and tailored shirt he had worn at dinner. He was in a kilt. A swatch of his family plaid was stretched over his shoulder, held in place by a large crest brooch.

He must have sensed that she was there, for he looked up at her and smiled slowly.

Any words she might have said froze on her lips. She felt as if she were on the outskirts of the woods again. She didn't think that he really spoke, yet she heard him clearly.

Come, please. I need you.

Instinct warned her not to go, to remain where she was, but there was no denying the flutter in her heart, the compulsion to follow.

She started down the stairs. As she neared the bottom, he turned away from the great hearth and started toward the secondary hall.

"Bruce!" she managed to say.

He hesitated before disappearing, pausing to beckon with his hand.

"Damn you!" she breathed, following, even though she knew it was insane. She was more frightened for herself than ever, not because he might lead her somewhere terrible, but simply because she was seeing him. And because she had to follow.

"Stop, please!"

But he didn't. He disappeared, and she fled across the expanse of the great hall to the secondary one behind it.

He was there, waiting at the rear of the room where there was an ancient door with rusted hinges. It had been bolted tight, so that they hadn't bothered with it. It led underground, probably, Thayer had told them. A castle such as this one would have a crypt—or simple basement space.

Toni was now certain that it was a crypt, because the door was open, and she could see the winding stone stairs that led below.

She walked to the doorway and took the first step. It should have been dark, but there was a glow of light. And in that glow, she could see Bruce MacNiall, heading down the stairs.

She took a step…and then another step. She expected dust and cobwebs. Rats, even. But no spiders clung to tenuous webs in the rafters. There were no old, musty rushes on the floor, no dirt or dust. It seemed it had been kept clean—far cleaner than the main castle.

There were a number of corridors and alleyways, all with arched ceilings overhead, as if she had entered the ancient catacombs of an old church.

"Bruce?" she whispered. Then she saw him. He was down one of the corridors, watching her. Waiting.

She started to walk toward him, but he kept going, into the shadow at the end of the hallway. She hurried along, swearing again beneath her breath. She came to the end of the hallway, and only then realized where she was and what lined the walls.

Tombs.

There was nothing really eerie here. There were no bones turning to brittle dust on family shelves. Every member of the family had a marble flat across their final resting place. Their names were then engraved upon them, along with inscriptions in Gaelic. Wives were proclaimed with their own clan names, as well. *Mary Douglas MacNiall* was inscribed on one freestanding sarcophagus; she had died in the early eighteen hundreds, and she had been, according to her inscription, born to the great family of Moray.

Turning slowly, Toni realized that tombs surrounded her. She couldn't help the natural fear that came from being alone in the dark and the shadows with the dead.

When she turned again, she could see the end of the hall more clearly. There was a nook there, and in it a grand tomb with a marble effigy atop it of the laird, arms folded across his chest, his great sword at his side. A severe tremor shook her, turning her blood to ice. The effigy was so good. She could see the cheeks she had so recently stroked, carved in marble. It was Bruce, the Bruce she knew...

How could any man look so very much like an ancestor? A stone ancestor at that!

Another tomb was at its side, but there was no effigy. And though bold words proclaimed Bruce Brian Mac-Niall, Laird of Tillingham, victor against all tyranny, the great laird of the true Scots and the true king, there was nothing at all on the other tomb.

She stared at the grave for long moments. The cold in the crypt seemed to creep around her. The light was fading. The shadows, as if they were living beings, began to creep across light once again.

"Bruce?" she called out. Her voice was definitely tremulous.

She turned and ran back down the long hallway of the dead, racing for the stairway. In her wake, shadow covered all that had been light.

She ran up the stairs, terrified that she would reach the doorway and it would be bolted again, shut tight on its rusty hinges. She felt a sense of hysteria coming on then. *What if she was locked down here? What if the shadows kept coming, if they swallowed her, if they sucked her into a miasma of the death and terror and tragedy that had come over the centuries?*

She rammed against the door—and went flying into the open space of the secondary hall, spinning, stumbling and landing on the floor.

With a deep breath, she got hold of herself. Then she was angry.

She stood, looked ruefully at the tear in her gown, and swore that she wasn't playing this game anymore. It was Bruce who had lured her down. It had to have been. And Bruce had been in the forest earlier. Maybe he wanted to get even with them or teach them a sick lesson, so he was seducing her and tormenting her at the same time!

Furious, she started up the stairway to the second-floor landing. Her strides were long as she walked the hallway to his bedroom door.

She didn't knock, just burst in. And then she froze.

He was there, seated in the chair by the hearth, studying a book, in the jeans and shirt he had worn to dinner.

Eban Douglas stood outside the castle, down the driveway, looking up. He cocked his head, as if listening.

"They've found her!" he said, his voice a half whisper, half cackle. "They've found yer bride, Laird MacNiall. The wee lass. A horrid sight, so they say. Bits o' hair and flesh and…well y'd not want to be hearing that, wot, eh? They didna let me see her. Me, who might care for her so tenderly!"

A wind seemed to rise as he stood there. Clouds raced over the moon, throwing it into shadow.

He cast his head back and began to laugh. "Aye, the lasses, the lasses! They be in the forest, them, all of 'em strangled and gone, pretty, pretty maids…but with wicked ways. Ah, Laird MacNiall, I be beggin' yer pardon. Fer she was maligned, eh? Yer lady wife, she were. But not the others. Nae, not the others."

He shook his head sadly. "Poor wee sinners! Lost and alone."

Tears suddenly fell down his cheeks. "Nae, not the others!" he whispered.

Then he sighed. His shoulders fell. Dispirited, he turned away from the castle on the hill and started for his cottage, his own wee cottage where he lived, thanks to the kind graces of the great Laird MacNiall. He'd do anything for the great MacNiall. Aye, anything. Things, maybe, MacNiall didn't even know that he needed done himself.

He'd lie, steal or cheat. Indeed, he'd kill for MacNiall, he thought.

Ruefully, he smiled to himself. Aye, that was that.

Time to retreat to his little cottage, where he was a little man living a quiet and secretive life, barely even noted by others.

Toni felt as if she hadn't moved in hours, as if she had just stood there, frozen in time. And yet...could it have been so long?

He rose, his eyes on her. Tenderly? she wondered. Or mockingly?

"There you are," he said quietly, and smiled. "What were you doing? Raiding the refrigerator? Actually, I was about to come searching. You weren't here, and you weren't in your bed." His smiled deepened. "Or in the bathtub."

She couldn't move. Or speak. Her mind raced.

He was just a damned good shyster, tricking her downstairs, then running back up, changing clothing again. Was he trying to scare them out of his castle? And why would he? He seemed to have the legal right to it. All he had to do was tell them that they had to go!

It couldn't have been Bruce by the fireplace. But it had to have been—or else she was seeing ghosts.

His eyes narrowed sharply as he stared at her. He snapped the book closed and walked over to slide it into a drawer of his desk. Then he walked across the room to her and took her by the shoulders, staring into her eyes, his own a silver sheet of concern. "Toni? What's wrong?"

She shook her head, unable to speak for a moment. She was going crazy. No need to tell him so. It was unlikely that many men wanted to have an affair with an insane woman. Or was she just giving free vent to imagination? Was it all *suggestive,* as David tried to assure her.

She blinked, trembling, knowing that nothing mattered when he came to her, when he looked at her that way, when she felt the security of his hands upon her.

"Toni?"

She shook her head, gaining strength. She was an actress of some merit, wasn't she?

"I...was thirsty," she lied. "I went down for a drink."

He shook his head, frowning. "Toni, I have drinks up here. Not just brandy and such—there's a mini refrigerator, water, some sodas."

She moistened her lips. "I didn't know."

"You're white as a ghost," he said.

"Am I?"

He was still staring at her with the greatest concern. *As if...she weren't all there.*

Subtlety be damned.

"I want something," she whispered.

"Aye?"

"To be with you."

"I've been doing nothing but waiting," he said, the words so quiet, and yet so sincere, that they were like a caress against her.

She wasn't aware that she moved, or that he did, either, but she was suddenly melded against him. He was very much alive, a vital block of heat and fire, warming the ice that had seized hold of flesh and blood and bone. Her head fell back and she met his eyes just a split second before his mouth descended to hers.

This time, he stripped back the covers before he laid her down. And as he moved away, she rose back up herself, tearing the gown from over her shoulders, making her way on her knees to the place where he sat at the foot of the bed, shedding clothing. She edged against his back, lips, kisses, tongue falling against the breadth of his shoulders. And when he turned to her, naked at last, she could not be held away, but continued her wild, near frenzied search and exploration of his flesh.

He caught her by the midriff at last, pulling her against him, and she felt the full force and passion of his kiss, as driving as any power or rage of lust. They fell back together, entwined, hands and mouths seeking as if they were both mad. She tried to crawl against him, and he murmured to her, his voice deep and husky, "Ah, careful, lass. With that jumping, we're bound to have something bent or broken!"

She found herself laughing, still desperate, smiling as she was drawn beneath him, then breathless and silent as he thrust into her with a strength she sincerely doubted could ever be bent or broken.

She vaguely felt the sheets beneath her, the softness of the bed, vaguely heard the crackle of the dying fire. The room was bathed in a red and burnt-orange light, and it flickered upon his face and shoulders and chest. Then everything seemed to blur into a shadow blaze as the need within her spiraled and rose and, once more, seared into her with cataclysmic wonder.

She was wrapped in his arms, aware again of the feel of the sheets, damp now, the sound of the fire, a softer rustling still, and the glow of the embers. His weight eased from hers, but not his hold. No, never, please God! she thought. He pulled her against him, flush with his form. She was aware of his chest, chest hair, breath, the cradle of his hips, the now flaccid pressure of his sex against her. His fingers smoothed back her hair.

Time passed in a glory of soft sounds, gentle caresses, light...

"You are..." he murmured.

She waited, but nothing came. Then she smiled. "You are, too," she whispered.

His arms tightened. She felt the way their hearts beat then, almost together, just enough out of sync so that she knew there were two.

When she slept, it was without dreams. And when she woke in the night with a start, she felt his arms around her still. So she closed her eyes again, and her sleep was deep and restful.

"He's weird, and that's all there is to it," Gina said, shivering.

"Eban?" Toni asked, startled.

They were in town. Despite the fact that Robert Chamberlain had the original documents, they were taking a set of copies to Jonathan. Though they had more faith in Robert Chamberlain, they had a bit of sympathy for Jonathan, as well. The castle, and the forest, fell under his jurisdiction.

At the moment, they were seated at a wrought-iron table in the garden section of a pub known as Angus's Alley. It did a fair business, drawing a luncheon crowd from tourists and folks visiting from the larger cities. Bruce wasn't with them; he'd left early on business. They were their own little sixsome again, which was pleasant because, among one another, they didn't have to take care regarding what they said.

And Gina wasn't hedging her opinion at the moment.

"Eban, yes!" she hissed. She jerked her head to the right. He was not far from them, just off the road, feeding a dog. He was talking to the animal.

Ryan winced, his eyes light as he looked at his wife. "I talk to horses."

"Yes, and Toni talks to any animal she comes across. I've seen the two of you."

"So what's the difference?" Kevin asked her, biting into a piece of steak. "Yummy. There should really be more gourmet Scottish restaurants in the States."

"There is one in New York," David told him absently.

"What's the difference?" Thayer said, repeating Kevin's question, and staring at them as if they were a bit daft. "Don't you all ever let anyone answer a question before you go on into another train of thought entirely?"

Kevin shrugged.

"The difference?" Gina said. "Watch Eban! It's as if they're communicating back to him. Yes, Ryan, you and Toni speak to any mammal you come across, but you don't expect the animals to give you answers back!"

"'E's just a wee bit touched in the head," Thayer said. "I feel sorry for the poor old boy."

"I don't," Gina said, not even attempting to hide a shiver. "I feel...scared."

"I'm sure he's harmless," Toni said, yet she remembered how terrified he had made her, just the day before. But that had been because her imagination had gotten the best of her.

Had last night been her imagination, too? Or insanity. That morning, the door to the crypts had been bolted, just as it had always been. But she knew, if she insisted it be open, that she would find everything below just as she had seen it.

"Eban works very hard. We've seen him work!" she added.

"Thank God, I'm married," Gina murmured. "I think I'd be scared in my castle room if it weren't for Ryan."

"Great," Ryan said. "She keeps me around because she's scared."

Gina flashed him a warning stare, but Ryan just grinned.

"Eh! If the old man starts giving you too much trouble, lass, remind him I'm around!" Thayer said, winking.

"There you go," Gina told Ryan.

"Well…if worse came to worst, David and I would let Gina have the old Duncan Phyfe sofa that's in our room," Kevin said.

Gina shuddered. "I don't think I could take the activity in your room!"

"All right, all right, the lot of you! Break up the lust fest. A few of us—" Thayer paused, glancing at Toni. "Okay, maybe it's only me these days, but there's no one sleeping in my room, so I'd rather not hear about the writhin' and strainin' going on around me, eh?"

Gina burst out laughing. "Thayer, you could have your pick of girls! I've seen the way they look at you when we go in pubs and the like."

He shrugged.

"You're too picky," she told him.

He was thoughtful for a minute. "That I am. And I've decided I want an American lass."

"And why is that?" Toni asked him.

He shrugged. "I like the American way. Free from the shackles of tradition, and all that rot."

Gina laughed. "But you were willing to go in with us on the castle?"

"Well, in truth, that's all changed now, hasn't it? It seems like we're on a borrowed pound at a roulette wheel, eh? Just trying to make back our bet."

"We'll make it back," Gina said determinedly.

"Thanks to the largesse of our host," David murmured, and he stared across the table at Thayer suddenly. "Hey, did you know that he'd been a cop?" he demanded.

"How could he have known he'd been a cop?" Toni demanded. "He hadn't even known that he'd existed."

"Oh, yes, right," David said.

"You're starting to sound British!" Kevin told him. "Right-o, cheerio and all that!"

David looked at him and sighed.

"Well, when in Rome, you know," Ryan offered.

"But Laird MacNiall—a cop!"

"*Was* a cop," Gina said. "I wonder what he does now," she mused, looking around at all of them.

"Hey, don't ask me!" Kevin said. "I didn't know that lairds were…well, anything. I just thought they sat around being…lairds!"

"I don't think it works that way anymore, does it?" Toni asked Thayer, smiling.

"Well, these days, anyone who owns enough land collects rents," he said.

"Does he own a lot of land?" Gina asked.

Thayer shrugged, still looking at Toni. "The constable said that Laird MacNiall owned half the village, remember?"

"Hmm," Gina murmured. "So…he's simply rich."

"Strange, if he has money you'd think there would be servants swarming around the family home," David murmured.

"And instead, no one," Ryan mused.

"There's Eban Douglas!" Kevin reminded him.

"And he's weird!" Gina said again.

"So we're back where we started," Ryan said, standing. "Gina, we should get those documents over to Jonathan's office."

"We were supposed to see Laird MacNiall's deed today, remember?" Thayer murmured. "I guess now we just have to accept that it's legit, huh? After all, he wound up not being with us."

Gina sighed. "Ryan and I will go to the constable's. I'm sure we have to fill out a police report, as well, but I imagine that, for the time, one of us giving the information and signing the report will be all that's required."

"Two of us," Ryan reminded her.

"Two of us. The rest of you can wander. Toni, you said that you wanted to walk around the old kirk and graveyard, right?"

David groaned. "Don't you want me to take the documents to the constable's office?"

Toni stood up. "David, go shopping. And Kevin and Thayer...you can sop up some more ambience at the pub, if you like. I'm fine on my own."

"I would like to see if we can't find some...classier paper products for our tea and scones," David said.

"They're definitely not into paper plates the way we are in the States," Kevin agreed. "But they've lovely shops. Maybe we can find something."

"I don't mind going with you, Toni," Thayer said.

"You sure?" she asked him.

"Not at all," he assured her.

"Well, then..."

"Hey! Someone remember to pay the bill!" Gina said. "And don't take more than a couple of hours. We'll meet at the pub at the base of the hill at four, okay?"

They all started out in their different directions. Ryan and Gina headed west, in the direction of the village square. David and Kevin went no more than a few feet before being caught by a store window, and Thayer and

Toni headed east, slightly up a hill, toward the kirk and the surrounding graveyard.

Thayer seemed distracted. Toni set a hand on his shoulder. "You all right?" she asked him.

He flashed her a smile. "Aye, fine, why?"

She shook her head. "You've just seemed...not you, lately."

"Since our bubble was burst?" he asked.

"I guess."

He smiled, and pointed toward the kirk. "I can give you some local history. It was begun in the twelve hundreds, and the current structure and form dates back to the fifteen hundreds. Naturally, it was built as a Catholic church, and is now a part of the Church of Scotland. It has some remarkable stained-glass windows. It also has some beautifully carved tombs on the interior—Italian artists were brought in to honor various statesmen, poets, knights and ladies, and so on. In the truly dour days of Cromwell, the reverend was a plucky fellow who managed to hide most of the treasures, so little was destroyed."

She smiled at him, impressed. "Have you seen it, then? I thought you'd never been in this area before we arrived."

"Never been in it in m'life, cousin. I looked it up on the Internet. They've actually got quite a decent Web page."

Toni laughed. "Great."

A small stone fence surrounded the kirk and the graveyard, and there was a white picket gate, which Thayer swung open for Toni.

When they entered the kirk itself, she was awed and amazed. For such a small village, it was really phenomenal. The stained-glass windows surrounding the length of it were in blues that would have done Tiffany's proud. Picking up a flyer at the rear as they entered, Toni read that the pulpit had been carved from a single huge oak in the 1540s, and she walked to it, marveling at the intricate lion designs that graced it.

"Incredible workmanship, huh?" Thayer whispered to her.

She nodded. "Gorgeous."

"Come see some of the MacNialls buried here," he said.

"I thought…" For a moment she hesitated. "I thought that they were buried in a crypt at the castle," she said.

He shrugged. "I'm sure some are. But come here. Look." Pointing, he showed her a fairly modern tomb that occupied space against the western wall. "Our Mac-Niall's grandfather, or a great uncle, certainly. 'Colonel Patrick Brennan MacNiall, RAF, born April 15, 1921, died June 8, 1944, on distant shores, serving God and Country. May he fly with the angels now.'"

"He must have died just after the D-day invasion in World War II," Toni said. "How sad."

"Very. For thousands of men," Thayer commented. "Look, here's an older one. 'Laird Bruce Eamon Mac-Niall, a great protector of men and honor, born October 4, 1724, and gave his life for right and freedom, Flodden Field.'"

"They had a tendency to be on the wrong side of a battle, huh?" Toni murmured.

"History always decides the wrong side of a battle," Thayer murmured.

Toni nodded. "Quite true. And we have a tendency to romanticize many a lost cause."

"Shall we wander around outside? Or did you only want to look for MacNialls?" Thayer asked.

Toni was startled, but when she looked in his eyes they seemed guileless.

"I'd love to wander around outside."

"What's your fascination with cemeteries?" he asked her, and grinned. "I did this with you in Glasgow, too, remember?"

"The art, I think. And the poems and epitaphs."

"Like at the theme parks? 'Dear old Fred, a rock fell on his head, now he's dead, dead, dead,' or something like that?"

"Not that bad!" Toni protested. "The problem is, time erodes stone, lichen sets in and they're often difficult to read." They were outside now. The graveyard was the kind that always fascinated, with beautiful marble funerary art and huge stones rising at awkward angles created by the passage of time. "Here's one!" she told Thayer, rubbing the mold from the stone to read it better. "'Justin MacClaren. Once I ran, fast and hard, had a wife, ignored the lass. I gave all strife, ne'er went to mass, and now, lonely to this grave, I am cast.'"

"Hmm. That's almost as bad as dear old Fred with the rock on his head," Thayer said, making her laugh.

"But that's just it—they really give a little slice of life, as it was," Toni told him and smiled. Two young women had just entered the cemetery, wandering as they were, one a pretty redhead, her friend a brunette.

"Hello," Toni said pleasantly. "Good afternoon."

"Ta!" the redhead said cheerily. "You're American then, are you?"

"I am," Toni said. "Thayer is from Glasgow."

"I'm from Aberdeen myself, but I've taken a cottage here for a while," the redhead said. "I'm Lizzie Johnstone. And this is my friend, Trish Martin, up from Yorkshire to spend her holiday with me."

"Lovely," Toni murmured.

"Ah, the English are invading again," Thayer teased. He offered a hand to Trish first. She was very pretty, with large dark eyes, long pale hair and a beautiful peaches-and-cream complexion. He was, however, equally polite when he turned to Lizzie, who looked far more Irish with her wild red hair, spattering of freckles and bountiful smile.

"Thayer Fraser here. And the American invader," he added teasingly, "Toni Fraser."

"Ah, a couple are you then?" Lizzie said, obviously a bit disappointed.

"A pleasure to meet you," Toni told them. "And no, we're not a couple. We're cousins."

"Ah!" The young woman looked at Thayer with renewed interest.

Thayer smiled. It was a slightly awkward moment in which body language was too easily read. Lizzie liked Thayer. Thayer liked the blonde.

"So you like poking around old graveyards, too?" Toni said.

"You'd think I'd tire of them, but I never do," Trish said. "Much more interesting than the ancient sites that everyone is all atwitter about these days! They're nothing but rocks in the ground, while these old places…"

"They tell stories," Toni said.

Trish gasped suddenly. "I know who you are! The group doing tours at the castle!"

"Indeed!" Lizzie said.

Thayer nudged Toni. "We're famous!" he teased.

"Or infamous," she murmured beneath her breath.

"Oh, no! There was a bit in the Edinburgh paper today…y'can buy it down at the Ioin's place, that little newsstand-café down at the base of the hill, if you wish to see it," Trish said. "It's a good blurb, I believe you'd like it. Says you do a lovely little piece of drama while bringing back the past, and suggests that even locals would enjoy the fun of it. You'll have to get the paper. I'm afraid we've left ours at the café."

Toni looked at Thayer and shrugged, a smile creasing her lips. There was pleasure and wry regret in her expression. "Thank you for telling us," Toni said.

"Didn't know we had a reporter in either of the two groups we've taken through so far," Thayer said.

"Well, now," Lizzie said, "a reporter would want to slip in unknown and unnoticed, right? Get the same treatment as everyone else, eh?"

"Now, that sounds true enough," Thayer agreed. "I'd thought our folks were all Americans, though. We've been working with a tour company that does the promotion and packaging. They just book the tours, but they've been targeting Americans."

"What? Just because we've grown up with the history, it means we don't enjoy a good time?" Trish said, batting her lashes at Thayer.

"Well, now, we all enjoy a good time, don't we?" Thayer said, his voice soft and a little husky. Toni was glad for him. He seemed to be enjoying this flirtation with the attractive women, even if they happened to be in a cemetery.

Toni had noticed an older woman, slightly humped over with the beginnings of osteoporosis, making her way through the crooked stones and monuments. The others noticed her, as well, and fell silent.

Toni stepped back, realizing that although they stood among weathered markers that might have been about for hundreds of years, there were new plaques around, as well.

The woman was heading their way with a bundle of flowers.

"I believe we're intruding," she murmured. Thayer took her elbow, and they edged farther out of the way. They remained silent with respect, rather than make an obvious departure that might be loud and distracting.

The old woman was followed by a younger couple, a slightly balding man and an attractive, slender woman of about forty-five.

"Afternoon," the man said, nodding to them. The old woman ignored them, but the man's wife offered them a pleasant smile.

The old woman bent down with her flowers, and said her prayer by the grave. Then she rose slowly, using a headstone to help herself up, and turned, acknowledging that they were there.

Toni noticed that the woman's eyes, a faded blue set in the time-worn creases of her face, seemed to fasten right upon her.

"Yer from the castle," she said. It wasn't a question, it was a statement of fact.

Toni and Thayer nodded. Despite the interruption, they were still basking in the pleasure of having heard about such a good review of the tour. But as those faded blue eyes assessed her, Toni felt a sure stirring of unease.

The woman pointed a long bony finger at Toni.

"Y'know it, don't ye?"

"Pardon?" Toni murmured.

"There's greater trouble ahead, eh? They've found the lady, missing all those years. Disturbed the past! Dug up a ghost. And they wonder wot's goin' on in that forest! He killed once, and set her in the ground. Now she's dug up. He'll kill again, and again, and again. *We've* known that he roamed here all these years. Aye, that we have! Roamed his castle and the woods, betrayed and seeking his vengeance. Now he's risen, and he seeks it about the countryside. You!" Her finger shook in Toni's direction. "You know it! Know that he is up and about, wakened and furious! You know it! Bruce MacNiall is up and about, and killin'. And if ye tread upon the past any longer, y'll be the lass in the water. Aye, y'll be the lass in the water!"

Chapter 12

Bruce arrived at Darrow's office not long after noon, surprised by the urgency and excitement in the message the man had left on his cell phone.

It was quite a mystery, since Daniel hadn't left any details about why he was concerned that Bruce come in. And though Bruce should have accompanied the group into town, gone straight to the office of records as planned and shown them the deed, there really seemed little urgency to do so anymore. They had accepted the fact that he indeed owned the castle.

And Darrow's message had been just too intriguing.

Tillingham was one of those places where, most often, death came naturally, and to the aged. The surrounding countryside, at the base of the Highlands, was rich farmland. Those who hadn't made their way into larger cities or towns earned their living by producing some of the finest wool, dairy products and beef available. For the most part, they loved their corner of the earth, the land and a way of life that was almost ancient, yet far better than what it had been in centuries of servitude and strife.

Bruce owned large tracts of land and a number of the buildings in town where merchants sold their wares, but his holdings hadn't all been inherited. An education in the States at UCLA had taught him a great deal about the American stock market, and he had gambled—for that's what he considered it—well over the years. Even in hard times, he'd had luck with getting in and getting out. Still, his father had ingrained in him a certain tradition. Heredity—and the return of Charles II to the throne of England—had made them lairds. That meant a responsibility to the village of Tillingham.

There was another factor, of course. The area was home. He loved it. There were still thatched-roof houses that served as cafés and shops, apartments and single-dwelling residences. The farmland wasn't far from the center and the castle sat atop a hill as it had for centuries. Whatever the history associated with the place, good and bad, it was his.

Darrow's facility was on the square, near the constable's office and the beautiful old medieval building that housed the records and licensing bureaus, among other legal offices. When he had decided to hurry on down to see Daniel Darrow, he had refrained from mentioning that he'd be near the group, intrigued to see the medical examiner on his own.

Rowenna, Darrow's secretary, greeted him pleasantly, and with a little sparkle to her eyes. "He's agog with excitement!" Rowenna told Bruce, rising to lead him into the mortuary room, where Darrow tended to the dead of Tillingham and the surrounding areas. "He hasn't even told me what's got him so excited," she said.

He thanked Rowenna when she opened the door to admit him to Darrow's work area, and she gave him another wave and smile as she closed the door behind her.

The M.E. employed two assistants at all times, but most often they were temporary, eager to work their way to larger facilities or higher positions in other small villages. Neither of them seemed to be about that afternoon. Bruce realized that this must be something of a pleasant change for the man. Darrow had a very different case of a discovered "body" on his hands.

Darrow was wearing a headlight and huge glasses, studying the remains that were stretched out in proper form on the autopsy table before him. He looked up, seeing that Bruce had arrived, and his eyes seemed enormous behind the glasses. In his lab coat and paraphernalia, he gave the appearance of a mad scientist.

"Bruce!" he said with pleasure. "You're here?"

"How could I resist such an invitation?" Bruce said.

Darrow nodded and said, "Well, my good lad, if you've ever loved me before, yer about to adore me now."

"Oh?"

He beckoned Bruce closer.

It was a strange feeling to look down at the remains. On the one side, all that time had rendered had taken away something of the humanity that once belonged to the woman. The empty eye sockets were eerie, as were the remaining tufts of hair and mummified flesh. Some bones were not actually attached, yet they had been laid out in anatomical order. Blackened pieces of fabric gave an odd cast to what she must have worn during her last moments of life. The skull itself was devoid of flesh in places, while in others, that fragile bit of her one-time life remained.

Time could play good tricks with the mind, as well. He couldn't feel what he had experienced when he found the body of the murdered girl in Tillingham, because her life had been far more recent, far more real. And yet it occurred to him that this was one of his ancestors, and that if it hadn't been for her life, he would not have had his own.

"She's truly an exquisite find!" Darrow said, studying the upper region of the remains again.

Bruce cleared his throat slightly. Darrow looked at him and then seemed to realize the association. "Sorry, dear boy. I keep forgetting…well, centuries have gone by, you know."

"Aye, of course," Bruce said.

"It's the state of preservation," Darrow said. "Well, we've some naked bone, but I haven't actually cut into her, taken samples. We do have experts on the way."

"Daniel, what is it, then?" Bruce said, afraid that the doctor was getting so involved in his discovery again that he was going to forget to explain.

"There!" Darrow said. He focused the lights of his headgear on the ligature that remained around the neck.

There? Bruce stared, but he saw only the muddied and blackened ligature, nothing else.

"I'm sorry, Daniel. What are you showing me?"

Daniel let out an exclamation of surprise. "Now, I'm not giving it to you that easy, boy! You were a detective once."

Bruce looked up at him, arching a brow, and then back to the remains.

And then he saw it.

It was impossible to decipher the weave of the cloth

tied around the neck; the rich mud had seen to that. But it had once been emblazoned with a raised crest, embroidered into the fabric. And it wasn't the MacNiall crest.

Though it took a moment's study, the encrusting mud had actually made the crest and surrounding letters more visible beneath the light. He couldn't guarantee it, and wouldn't bet on it, but it seemed that elaborate letters, *GD,* sat above a peregrine falcon atop a sword. Bruce instantly felt a thrill of excitement himself.

Any schoolchild who had grown up anywhere near the village was aware that the *GD* with the peregrine on the sword had been the battle emblem chosen by the traitor, Davis, who had brought down the great MacNiall.

"So…!" Bruce said.

"Aye, quite so!" Daniel said cheerfully. "Looks as if Grayson Davis did in the Lady MacNiall, and not her laird husband. Well, certainly, there could be those arguing that Bruce did it with Grayson's colors, but what would Bruce have been doing with such a garment from his enemy? Nae, now, I'm no historian, but it seems as if our local hero has been vindicated!"

Bruce looked up, smiling. "Well, we'll see what your experts have to say, Daniel."

Daniel nodded.

"You're definitely right about one thing," Bruce told him.

"Eh?"

"Well, I've always loved you, Daniel, old boy. But I do adore you now."

"Ach, now, Ma!" the man said, stepping forward to take the old woman's arm. "Now I know y'see the old fellow about now and then," he said, tenderly bringing

her to him. "But y'll be scaring away these fine folks!"
He rolled his eyes at the group around him.

"They don't be seein' it, none be seein' it!" the old
woman said.

She was still staring at Toni, her watery, faded blue
eyes seeming to see things that no one else could.

"Y'must take care!" she whispered feverishly.

Toni nodded, her throat tight, dismayed by the chills
that iced her limbs and bloodstream. The old woman
was senile, she tried to tell herself. A victim of super-
stition, of a way of life.

Thayer's arm came around her shoulder. Even Lizzie
and Trish, whom she barely knew, seemed to be standing closer to give her assurance against the strange on-
slaught.

"Ma, come away, now, the flowers be at Da's feet,"
the younger woman said, flashing them an apologetic
smile. "I'll get y'some o' the fine scones down the street.
We'll have a wee spot o' tea, eh?" With a last look of
apology, she gently became the escort, taking the old
woman's arm. She started from the cemetery, looking
over her shoulder to smile at the group, that simple look
explaining all.

The old woman was daft but theirs, and they loved
her.

"Enjoy your tea!" Toni said, feeling the chill the old
woman's words had given her fade, and anxious to say
something just to let her daughter or daughter-in-law
know that it was lovely the way they guarded and cared
for the woman.

The man lingered a moment, shaking his head.
"Finan MacHenry," he told them. "And I do apologize,
miss. Ma can give one the willies, sure enough. But
take no note, please. I am so sorry. The townsfolk here,

well, we've done a bit o' watching—no one here could reckon with the fact that Bruce had rented the place!— but y're doin' us all a service here, and we're pleased." He grimaced ruefully. "I own a pub, and yer tour folks have spent a good deal there, just in the few nights' time. Please don't be listenin' to me ma. She's always thought she saw Bruce MacNiall—not our current laird, but the old Cavalier—in the forest. And she's a wee bit disappointed, being of the thought that he was innocent. Now, with the bones found and all…"

"Thank you, Mr. MacHenry," Toni said, extending her hand. "You and your wife and your mother seem very dear, and we're grateful that you've taken the time to tell us that you're glad we're here."

He inclined his head. "My pleasure. And again, I'm so sorry about Ma givin' ye that kind o' fright. She's—" he didn't say *off the wall, daft* or *crazy as a loon.* "Ma's just old, and she's really dear. I imagine she was just thinkin' y're a fine young woman and worryin'. Well, I'll let you folks get back to yer day. I'll be havin' me tea and scones then," he said. "Good day!"

"Good day," they called in unison as he departed.

"Well, that was interesting," Thayer murmured. "Toni, you all right? It was strange as bloody hell, the way that she looked at you!"

"She's just old," Toni murmured, repeating what Finan MacHenry had said.

"Aye, and a bit daft. But it was unnerving, to say the least!" Trish offered.

"Giving you the evil eye, or whatever!" Lizzie said, and shivered. "I'm glad she didn't look that way at me! Oh, I am sorry."

"It's all right, really," Toni said. "Actually, it was quite touching, to see the way that they take care of her."

"Well, that's the Scottish for you," Lizzie said. "A bit of the superstitious and whimsical, and then the good hard logic that we're famed for, as well. Let's be putting it behind us. Honestly, we'd certainly love to be part of a tour, though, even if we're not American, and can't quite make it on a bus from elsewhere!"

"Tomorrow night. Come a bit early if you like," Thayer said.

"I'm not the management end of things," Toni said, "but I'm sure we can arrange something special for you both."

"We've got to catch up with 'management' soon," Thayer said. "Why don't we head to the pub now. We'll buy you lovely ladies a drink, and we can talk about tomorrow?"

Lizzie looked at Trish, and Trish looked back. They must have come to a silent agreement because they both looked at Thayer. "Why, that would be lovely."

"I think I'll let the three of you go on," Toni said. "I was going to wander around here a bit more, if you'll allow me to beg out."

Thayer looked at her with a slight frown, as if he were afraid the ladies would beg out also if she didn't come with them.

"I'll be right along, of course, and our other friends will be arriving bit by bit," Toni added quickly.

Trish shivered. "You want to stay in an old cemetery alone, after that?"

"I like these places," Toni told her.

"All right, then," Thayer said, anxious to move on with the women. But he had come with her, so he hesitated one last time. "You're sure? You're sure you're all right?"

"Absolutely. We are just right off the street. If a hand

shoots out of a grave, or the like, I'll be out of here faster than a speeding bullet."

The three laughed.

"Shall we order you anything?" Lizzie asked.

"No, thanks. I'm sure service is quick enough," Toni said.

"Well, then…shall we go?" Thayer asked.

"Oh, aye, then," Lizzie said. "See you in a bit, dear!"

When they were gone, Toni felt a shudder seize hold of her again. So much for being right off a main road. She couldn't even see anyone on the streets, and the day was darkening early. This was insane. She should catch up with Thayer and the girls, and hurry down to the pub where the beer was warm, but company and hospitality warmer still. After all, here she was in a cemetery, filled with the long dead, and she already thought that a ghost was leading her around a castle.

Then she gave herself a shake. She was fine. She'd wanted to be alone, and she was *not* going to be afraid. This *was* the type of place she had always loved, the very old combining with the present, a piece of living history, since the kirk offered Sunday services now just as it had for centuries. So she turned back to look through the graveyard, absolutely determined to put the old woman's strange actions and words behind her.

One monument in particular had caught her eye earlier. Usually she was drawn to the very old, but this one was new, and more ornate—and functional—than most. At the base, it created an arched, marble seat that faced a garden well tended by someone. At the top was a magnificently carved, flying angel. When Toni came closer, she marveled at the detail in the sculpture. The angel's face looked down in sadness. Below it, etched in large letters, were the words *Margaret Marie MacMannon, beloved daughter of Rose and Magnus, departed this for a better world far too soon, yet the memory of her goodness remains.*

She had died at the tender age of twenty-three, just a bit more than ten years ago, Toni discovered, reading the smaller print. That she had been a teacher and a lover of history, music, dance and mankind was also immortalized.

As she sat and continued to read, Toni was surprised to find, in very small print, that the kirk thanked Laird Bruce MacNiall for the garden and memorial, to be kept in perpetuity.

"So you like old kirks and cemeteries, as well as castles!"

Spinning around, Toni was startled to see none other than Bruce MacNiall coming toward her.

He was wearing a leisure suit that day, and had doffed the jacket, which he carried casually under his arm. He was wearing sunglasses, as well, so his eyes were unfathomable, and his ebony hair was slicked back. He could have just walked off a page of *GQ,* rather than out of a crumbling stone castle steeped in history and lore.

"Bruce," she murmured, feeling as if she had been caught looking into someone's private diary. "Hi. Did… did you know I was here?"

He shook his head, joining her on the bench. "Actually, I didn't. But I'm glad to see you."

She smiled, still feeling a little shy. Then she decided simply to ask, "Who was Margaret?"

He didn't seem disturbed by the question. He simply looked up at the angel, as if he could see something that went far beyond it, then shrugged slightly. "The great love of my youth," he said softly. He looked at Toni, though she could still see nothing of his eyes beneath the dark shades. "She was a local girl with a great love for people, life…children. We were engaged, but never married."

"What happened to her?" Toni asked, afraid that she was prying too deeply now, and was about to hear a horrible story.

"Leukemia," he said. "I never knew anyone with a greater love for the simplest things in life. The sky, the hills, grass…trees. Children. She adored children. She wanted a dozen, and always said it would be fine because we were very wee in numbers here, and the world needed more Scots."

"I'm very sorry," Toni said. "It sounds as if she was really a lovely person."

He nodded and looked away. She thought that he had decided to say no more, but then he looked at her again. "That's why I rather let the castle go, I'm afraid. She loved it. She wanted to bring life back to it. She had a way of just making you glad that you were alive and breathing and…well, it seemed such an irony that her own life should prove to be so fragile."

"I am so sorry," Toni repeated.

"Thanks. She's been gone a very long time now. No excuse for me, really, to have let things go the way that I did." His lips curled into a dry smile. "Did you visit the rest of the family?" he asked her politely.

"I saw a few MacNialls in the old kirk, yes."

"And you're here alone?"

"We're all meeting at the pub at the base of the hill at four," she told him. "Ryan and Gina took copies of the documents to Jonathan. David and Kevin are shopping. And Thayer and I just met two lovely lasses in the cemetery, so the three of them headed on to the pub already."

"Good. I'm glad there's a bit of excitement for your

cousin," he said. And he smiled broadly at her. "I've had a bit of my own today."

"Oh?"

"I've been at the M.E.'s," he told her. "And we think we've made a discovery that will vindicate my ancestor."

"Really?" Toni said.

He nodded. "Looks like she was strangled with a scarf that belonged to his archenemy, a man named Grayson Davis. The fellow hailed from around here, but he wasn't the kind of man to fight for a losing side for long. It wasn't really such a terrible thing for men to be on opposite sides—throughout our history, Scots have fought Scots almost as much as they've fought the English. The thing with Grayson Davis was that he turned coat, and turned in many a man he had once called his friend. He was the one who brought down Bruce MacNiall, catching up with him in the forest and giving him a mock trial then and there. And, well, you know the rest."

Toni looked at him with surprise and murmured, "I wonder..."

"You wonder what?"

"Nothing!" she said quickly, shaking her head.

He took her hand, his thumb massaging the palm with an absent tenderness that stole around her heart. "You've done the family a great service, you know, finding Annalise. I've been telling you this all along, you know, but... I really do owe you."

"I'm delighted," she said, a little afraid of being so close to him and not sure why. "We really need to tell all this to an old woman who was through here a while ago. Apparently, everyone in town knows that Annalise was found. This lady was very upset, certain that your ancestor was running around, going off to the cities to abduct other women and strangle them in the forest, as well."

He frowned sharply. "What?"

She shook her head, startled to have gotten such an intense response from him.

"It was nothing to take seriously," she said quickly. "This old woman knew we were at the castle, and apparently, she's deeply distraught that Annalise was found in the forest. She wanted to believe that your ancestor was a hero, not a wife killer. Apparently she believes that Bruce MacNiall still roams the land."

He let out an impatient and irritated sound. "Elwyn MacHenry!" he said.

"Yes. She was with her son and daughter-in-law. They seemed like very nice people."

"They are, but Elwyn is more than 'touched,' as they call it here. She's been raving about Bruce MacNiall roaming the countryside for years." He looked at her with a trace of amusement. "However, he just used to ride in the moonlight. She never accused him before of going from town to town to strangle others, as he had supposedly strangled his wife."

"Elwyn will be happy, then, to learn the truth," Toni said.

He rose suddenly, drawing her up. "I love this place, but enough is enough. Let's go join the living, eh?"

The afternoon spanned into the evening. Bruce remained in an exceptionally good mood, and Thayer was riding high, as well, enjoying the company of Lizzie and Trish. Gina reported that Jonathan had been cordial, and he had told them it was good that they had given the original documents to Robert Chamberlain, since his resources were so great. In fact, they'd saved him the trouble of having to do it. And he was pleased to tell them that the locals were cheerful about the tours. The buses had stopped in the village both nights, and the tourists had bought all manner of T-shirts, stuffed draft horses, jams, jellies, jewelry, tartans, cashmere, ties, brooches, snow globes and miniatures of the castle.

Kevin and David had spent their hours in the shops looking for plates and plasticware, and they were delighted with all their little purchases.

Gina decided that they had to have haggis, since it was the national dish, but Bruce begged out of it being the meal for the entire table.

"Hate the stuff," he told her.

"But it's the national dish!" she protested.

"Aye, it's the national dish, and do you know why?" he asked her, eyes sparkling. "It's made from the cheapest pieces of meat—"

"Body parts," David put in.

"Aye, body parts, because we were too broke here most of the time to be using the best cuts ourselves. But, by all means, Gina, have the haggis. They actually do an excellent sirloin here, and the lamb chops are phenomenal, especially considering that we're in a local pub," Bruce finished.

Toni opted for the salmon, while Thayer, David, Ryan and Kevin went along with Bruce, ordering the sirloin. Lizzie and Trish decided to try the lamb chops.

"Sure you want haggis, Gina?" Ryan asked. "I'm not trading my meal with yours!" he told her.

She made a face at him, but when it came her turn to order, she asked their waitress, "What do you think of the haggis?"

The woman glanced at Bruce. "Should I be tellin' her the truth, Laird MacNiall?"

"Indeed, Catherine, aye," he said gravely.

"I think we keep it on the menu for the tourists," she said, causing everyone to laugh. Gina switched to the sirloin.

By the end of the evening, Thayer had planned to spend the next Monday driving Lizzie and Trish down to Glasgow to show them some of the sights there. Kevin and David were planning holiday decorations for the castle. Gina was ever so slightly crocked and affectionate in her husband's arms. And the light in Bruce's eyes offered amusement and a flicker of intimacy that Toni found both touching and seductive.

Whatever ridiculous doubts and fears she had regarding him—and the ghost of his ancestor—seemed to have dissipated completely. She couldn't wait to be back at the castle, and back in his arms.

But it wasn't to work out that way. When they arrived, Eban was there to meet them. The roan had taken another turn for the worse, and he'd been out with the animal, doing his best to keep him up and walking, but he was wearing himself out. Toni was ready to run out with Ryan, but Bruce stopped her.

"I'll tend to the roan with Ryan," he said.

"But it sounds as if Wallace is really sick," she said, upset. "And I didn't see him at first when I should have—"

"I'll be calling the vet, Toni. It will be all right."

"How are you going to get a vet at midnight?" she asked.

"The rewards of a small village, where everyone knows everyone," he told her. "It's all right. Toni, trust me, I know something about horses."

"Toni!" David set an arm around her. "It's best if you let them handle this, you know."

He was right. She would be emotional, and maybe in the way.

Bruce took her arm, leading her toward the castle. "Wait for me?" he queried. "Well, get some sleep, if you can...but in my bed?"

She looked into his eyes and nodded. The excitement she'd been feeling was definitely tempered now with worry for the horse, but there was something more that he gave her with his words and the gentle brush of his eyes—comfort and assurance.

"The doc will take care of old Wallace," he said.

So she went on upstairs and showered, then slipped into a gown and into his bed. Restless, she stood up and looked out the window. The lights remained bright in the stables.

She went back to bed, where she tossed and turned, her mind filled with the events that had occurred since their arrival. An hour passed, and she was still staring at the ceiling. Finally her eyes closed, and she slept. Then...she felt a touch. She opened her eyes, and he was there—at the foot of the bed.

His sword was not dripping blood this time. Instead, it was sheathed in the belt and holder that sat around his hip, on his plaid.

She sat up, staring at him, wishing that she could scream, make someone come running, making the apparition disappear. And though his face was Bruce's, she no longer thought that he was the Bruce she knew.

Staring into his eyes, she ran her hand over the sheets at her side, praying that maybe Bruce had come up while she was sleeping. But he wasn't there. And with the man at the foot of her bed looking so exactly like him...she began to question her sanity again. And to question the man with whom she was falling in love.

"Don't do this to me!" she whispered.

But he remained, turning and heading for the door.

"No!" she said.

He waited at the door until she rose and followed. Then he headed down the hall to the stairway.

Toni came along, barefoot, shivering in her gown. She didn't understand why she didn't scream then, or call out, waken someone else. If they didn't see him, then she was crazy.

But at least she would know for certain that he wasn't the man she knew, flesh and blood, playing tricks on her.

Yet, if they didn't see him, then she was following a ghost.

He paused at the landing, and a fierce tension suddenly gripped his features, as if he found it painful there. Then he looked back, as if to assure himself that she was following.

"You know," she said quietly, "you have a descendant here. You couldn't just appear before him, huh?"

There was no response. He started down the stairs.

Her heart was pounding. *Cry out!* she told herself. But still, she didn't.

He came to the great hall and waited again. When she neared the bottom of the stairs, he walked on to the secondary hall, and from there…to the door leading to the crypts.

"No, please!" she told him.

Nae, lass, the "please" be to you.

Did the ghost speak, or did the words just somehow echo in her head?

"I really don't like the crypts!" she whispered.

The door, bolted and rusted by day, was open. He went down the spiral stone stairs, and she followed. Once again, he led her to his grave. And then he was gone.

In the shadows, in the must and darkness of the dead, she spun around, frantically searching for him. "What do you want? Just what is it that you want? Annalise has been found. And they know…they know you didn't do it!"

But there was no answer, and she felt again as if the light began to disappear as soon as she lost him. She was incredibly frightened, and furious, as well. Why did he bring her here, then leave her alone in the shadows and cold, desperate to get back up the stairs?

She ran, nearly tripping in her scramble to regain the level of the hall. Once there, she burst out the door, across the smaller hall and then the great one, and up the stairs. She hesitated on the landing, thinking that David and Kevin would have to screw their sex life or intimacy that night because she was going to burst in on them and tell them that they were getting out of the castle then and there.

But as she stood on the upper landing, she heard someone humming. Looking down, she saw Ryan coming out of the kitchen with a cup of coffee in his hands. He looked up and saw her.

"Toni?" he said, and frowned.

She must have looked wild, she was certain. With him in the living flesh, walking across the hall, her panic subsided.

"I, uh, how is Wallace?" she asked.

"Fine for the night. The vet is convinced he's getting into something that's making him get this colic, though he can't figure out what. But he's good, Toni. Honestly, I wouldn't lie to you. You could have asked Bruce. He's up there now. In fact, he's been in for a while. You can go to sleep, and rest assured, old Wallace is doing well."

She smiled, glad to realize that he thought she was

standing barefoot and in a nightgown on the landing because she was so worried about the horse.

"Good night, Ryan. And thanks," she said.

She turned and fled back down the hallway, bursting into Bruce's bedroom. He had showered and was in a towel. He seemed distracted, and when he looked up and saw her, his face was filled with tension.

"I was about to gather a search party," he said. "I told you that I'd tend to the horse, Toni. And he's doing well."

She nodded. "Yes, thanks."

She was still standing in the doorway.

"Are you coming in?" he asked her.

She nodded, but didn't move.

"Toni, what on earth is the matter with you?"

She swallowed. "Bruce, you weren't standing at the foot of the bed in a kilt about fifteen minutes ago, were you?"

"What? I was out with the horses, with Ryan." He sighed. "You're dreaming again?"

She shook her head. "No...no, I don't think that I'm dreaming. I think that I'm seeing the ghost of your ancestor." She gritted her teeth, watching the astonishment and total incomprehension that spread over his features.

"Toni, ghosts don't exist," he said.

"I'm seeing the ghost of your ancestor," she said firmly. "And he keeps taking me down to the crypts."

"That door is bolted," he said harshly. "I keep the only key."

"Come with me," she told him.

"Toni, I'm wearing a towel. I'd have to get dressed. You're barely dressed yourself, you know. That thing is entirely see-through."

"Come now," she insisted.

"In a towel?"

"We're the only ones up," she said, and turning, she went back down along the hallway.

"Toni, dammit!" he said, but followed behind her.

She realized she was almost running. He caught up with her on the stairway, swearing as he gripped her arm—he'd almost lost the towel.

"Toni, this is insanity."

"I'll show you!"

She wrenched free, and tore through the main hall and the secondary hall. At the door to the crypts she stood dead still. It was closed.

She grabbed the handle and tugged, but it was firmly bolted. She felt him behind her, felt his doubt and skepticism. And then her own.

She turned into his arms. "I saw him!" she insisted. "He opened this door, I went down it!"

"Toni, please, let's go to bed?" he said.

She was shaking, cold as ice. He lifted her, hugging her close to him as they traveled back the way they had come. He tried to tease her. "Don't wiggle too much. I'll lose the towel."

She wasn't wiggling. She wasn't moving.

"Toni…!" he murmured, distressed by her fear. She shook her head, curling her arms around his neck.

He opened the door, still ajar, to the master's chambers with his foot, and closed it the same way. He laid her upon the bed and told her, "I'll get you some tea… brandy? Something?"

"No!" she said, rising to throw herself into his arms again. "No, no, don't leave me, even for a second."

"Toni, it's all right here—"

"No, just hold me. Make love to me, be with me, alive, vital, flesh and blood. Do what you do so well, make everything else in the world fade away!"

"Toni!" he whispered again, his slate eyes searching her own.

"Now, please!" she begged.

And with that, he complied. His lips found hers, and tonight they were gentle, slow, even hesitant. But she wouldn't have it. Not that. She was fevered, clinging to him, pressing the kiss until it became one of the most volatile passions. She ripped away his towel, frantic to be against him, to rid herself of every barrier between them. She was frenetic, electric against his flesh, needing every bit of heat and warmth, fevered, chaotic...

Until he caught hold of her, bore her down, gripped her wrists and began a far slower, far more sensual seduction, bathing her flesh with fire, with the brush of lips, teeth, tongue, hands, all eliciting a deep, slow hunger and anguish, and making her feel cherished, taken...

And as she had longed for, ached and needed, the world faded. Every thought was gone except for the perfect fit of his body to hers, the thunder of heartbeats, the drive of his sex, his hips, the frenzied arch and writhe of her own.

She soared, flew and exploded beneath him, then felt the burst of searing warmth within her that was his climax. And still, there was the feel of him within her, growing softer, a part of her...his arms, holding her.

"Toni..."

"No, not tonight. Please, don't talk tonight!" she begged. "Just...hold me."

And so he did.

Interlude

"Bruce, please. Before God, I do not know what this man has said to you, but you are my life, and I'd not betray you, ever. Dear God! I love you, Bruce!" she whispered.

And looking down into her eyes, those pools of blue, sapphire with sincerity and the sweetness of the bond that had been theirs forever, he knew that she spoke the truth. He drew her to her feet.

"Ah, so he lied, and has not come as yet. But he will come, Annalise. Perhaps the Lord Cromwell has not taken to ordering the demise of the families of men such as myself, but neither would he punish a man, here, in what he considers the wilds of Scotland, a land of savages, who took a captive…and misused her. Our son is safe enough, following the young king in France. You can stay here no longer."

"Where would you have me go?" she whispered.

"To the Highlands. To the clansmen there, honor-bound to protect you, my love."

"We could bring danger upon those men. And here, the castle—our son's inheritance—could fall to the enemy."

"A castle is mortar and stone, no more. And though no troops have come, in their eyes, the property is confiscated by the government, as it was. Nae, our hope is in the return of the king. And whether we are here or not, the day the king returns in triumph as Charles II of England will be the day we are justified, and all is restored."

She shivered suddenly. "What if that day never comes?"

"It will," he declared staunchly. He stroked her chin, reveled in the soft feel of her flesh and the beauty of her fine features. And more. Something that transcended anything mortal. The way that she looked at him. And all that they shared.

"I must get you away. Tonight."

"As you wish," she told him.

He held her against him, taking a brief moment to feel the heat between them, the beating of their hearts, a pulse that slowly melded, as well. He inhaled the scent of her, and thought that this, being together so, loving a person with such great passion and being loved in return, was heaven. And he was humbled.

He pulled away from her.

She smiled, her lips damp, wistful and sensual.

"There's not so much as a night we could spend together first?"

"Not in this house," he told her, ruing the words. "We must get into the forest."

She nodded. "I'll get my things…"

"Bring little. We must travel fast."

She was quick, and she knew that his words were wise. As she prepared, Bruce spoke with his steward and his men, explaining that he was taking his lady away, and that, until the world was right again, the people mustn't give their own lives in a battle. But if they came, to allow the troops of the Protectorate in, let them do what they would, take what they craved, even unto the very stone of the castle. When Annalise came down to ride with him, many wept, but she gave them her cheerful, beautiful smile, swearing that all would be well.

And they rode together, both of them upon his great black mount.

He brought them into the forest. Finding a cove deep in the security of ancient oaks, he laid out his mantle, and there, surrounded by the softness of the night's breeze, the verdant richness of the woods, upon a bed of pines, he made love to her. As the moon waned high above them, he held her against his heart. Entwined, they found a night's rest, beauty and peace.

As the sun rose, he heard the snap of a branch. Leaping to his feet, he grabbed his sword. Somehow, they had been betrayed.

The sound was distant still, so he fell to his knees, waking her, his finger to his lips. "Dress, quickly. I'll leave the stallion. Take him ever north and westward, climb to the Highlands and await me."

"Where are you going? What are you doing?" she demanded with alarm.

"Leading them astray."

"No!" She threw herself against him.

"Annalise! I wage battle constantly, I know what I'm about. You must be away. Please, if I know that you are safe, I can fight any man!"

She rose, finding her clothing, scattered about, as he kilted himself into his tartan in silence. He held her then, once more. One last kiss.

"Go!" he urged her.

He bent low and moved silently, at first, until he had put distance between them. Then he let his presence be known. And he heard the activity in the forest, heard the horses, moving now far more carelessly through the trees.

He knew that his enemy waited before him, and his path veered just in time for the men to jump out from their hiding places too late.

His sword felled them both with a mighty swing.

But there were more.

Suddenly he was surrounded.

He found a path through the trees behind him, drawing them on. He was caught, and he knew it, but he fought like berserkers who had long ago come to Scotland, joining their Norse and Danish blood with that of more ancient tribes. He fought, not for his life, but for time—time for Annalise to depart to champions in the north.

That day, he brought down man after man. Yet, to no avail. For his enemy had amassed quite an army, and the men were bitter and incensed at the losses they had sustained in previous battle. Alone, he bore their assault, sustained wound after wound, and battled on.

Finally he stood in a field of corpses, but his great sword had been broken, and he was on his knees, blood dripping down his forehead into his eyes. The men around him backed away as Grayson Davis strode into the copse.

"Not such a hero now, are ye, man?" he demanded.

MacNiall looked up. "A hero? Always. For a man

who believes in his ideals, and does not shift with the winds of fortune, will always be remembered as such."

Davis strode closer to him.

"Do you know how you are about to die?"

"Aye, that I do."

"You will scream with pain, beg for mercy, before I am done. I swear it."

He further inflamed his foe's wrath by smiling. "There is nothing you can do to me now that will cause me to cry out."

"Nae?" Grayson said. "Well, then, let me show you what you must see before you even begin to die!"

Chapter 13

By morning, Toni fully intended to talk to Bruce. Despite the fact that she was going to sound crazy, she meant to tell him that she was definitely seeing his ancestor, that a ghost had led her into the woods and was now leading her down to the crypts. But when she awoke, he was already gone.

David, sipping coffee and reading the paper in the kitchen, told her that he'd gone into town to see Jonathan.

"You all right?" he asked her.

"Yes…why?" She glanced at him, helping herself to the coffee.

"Why?" He shook his head and looked toward the doorway, assuring himself that they were alone. "Because you're seeing…entities. Ghosts. A disturbing presence, or something." He cleared his throat. "And Thayer told me that an old woman gave you some kind of look yesterday, and then said something absolutely horrible about *you* being found in the forest."

"She was just an old, superstitious woman," Toni said.

David set his paper down and patted the chair next to him. "Sit. Talk to me. So, she didn't scare you at all, huh?"

"She put the fear of hell and damnation right into me!" Toni said, laughing. "But only for a minute. She has cataracts, so her eyes were a little…eerie. After she was gone and we talked with her son…well, I was fine. Even stayed in the cemetery by myself."

David smiled. She decided not to tell him about her nocturnal trips to visit more grave sites deep in the bowels of the castle. He was too worried about her already.

"Laird Bruce is certainly in a fine mood, so it seems," David said.

"Well, I don't suppose the old legend had much bearing on his day-to-day life," Toni said. "But yes, I guess he's really pleased to find out that his famous ancestor most probably was innocent of the murder of his wife."

"And, apparently, we are good for the village." He was silent for a moment, studying his cup. "You know, I had been afraid that we'd be somewhat ostracized here."

"For being American?" Toni said.

David winced. "No, not exactly. And when I said 'we,' I meant Kevin and myself. For being of a different persuasion," he said lightly. "But people are wonderful. We had a great time in the village yesterday. Certainly, some of the older folks, gents, mainly, looked at us with a great deal of curiosity, but…everyone was curious and intrigued. We're actually going to get a lot of the locals up to the castle to see what we're up to, I think."

"That's good. I'm glad."

"But we don't really have a right to the place, so who knows how long Laird MacNiall will let it go on?"

Toni looked downward. *Yes, how long could it go on?*

"Well," she said, looking up. "In light of Laird Mac-Niall's pleasure over the vindication of his ancestor, I've thought of a way to change that particular bit of history in our tour."

"Oh, yeah?"

She nodded. "We have the great laird ride in just as before. He climbs the stairs to meet Annalise. It's glorious, a dramatic confrontation. Annalise pleads her innocence, then the two come running down the stairs—just as the bad guy rides in!"

David arched a brow to her. "Oh, Lord. Don't make me be the bad guy!"

She grinned. "No, it has to be Ryan. He's the only one with a prayer of controlling Wallace when Shaunessy is in the hall." She frowned suddenly, starting to jump up. "Wallace is…better, right?"

David nodded. "Sit. Finish your coffee. Wallace is right as rain this morning."

She sat. "Well, what do you think?"

"I like it. And MacNiall will like it. Ryan will love it. He'll have a chance to play the knight again."

She nodded. "I've got to run it by the others. And Bruce, of course."

Kevin came walking on in.

"What are you running by the others?"

With a sigh, she went through her idea again.

"Works for me!" Kevin said. "Want breakfast? What have we got? You know, David, we bought all those supplies yesterday and what we really need is to go grocery shopping for ourselves again."

"There's eggs," David said. "Plenty of them."

"Omelettes, then."

"Um, want help?" Toni asked.

"No!" both of them said in unison.

"I'm not that bad a cook!" she protested.

"As long as we're not getting too elaborate," David said, "Kevin and I work best alone. Go on out and see old Wallace, why don't you? Assure yourself that he's doing all right."

"Good idea!" she agreed, and started out.

The morning was crisp, clear and beautiful. As Toni walked from the castle to the stables, she found herself looking around, hoping that Eban wasn't about. She hated herself for still feeling so uneasy around the man, but she did. She was always ready to defend him in public. But inside, he made her uneasy.

She didn't see Eban as she walked on into the stables, but Shaunessy was gone. Bruce must have taken him. Wallace, however, was in his stall. Standing. He snorted as she walked toward him, and she thought that the horse was glad to see her.

She patted his nose, looking at his eyes, checking out his length thoroughly. "You're looking good this morning, fellow!" she told him. "Very good, as a matter of fact."

He stuck his head over the stall gate and pressed his nose against her chest, pushing her, as if he were looking for some kind of a handout.

"No, I didn't bring anything for you, boy," she told him, patting the downy nose. "We don't know what's making you sick! Maybe you're allergic to apples or carrots. Hmm. I wonder if that's possible. I haven't met this vet of yours yet, but when I do, I'll have to ask him about that."

The horse's huge brown eyes were on her, as if he really listened. He prodded her chest again with the tip of his soft nose, as if saying that such delights as apples and carrots couldn't possibly cause a problem.

"You are such a sweetie!" she told him.

She was startled when his ears suddenly went back flat. Turning around, she saw nothing. But she couldn't believe that the horse had suddenly become angry with her!

Then she heard a noise, a scraping sound from the rafters above her. A tingling of instinctive wariness vibrated throughout her limbs.

A ladder led up to the rafters. It was between her and the exit to the stables.

She inhaled deeply. *So? Someone was up there. So what?* It was probably just Eban, shelving hay, or…doing something.

The sound stopped, but she was still on edge.

"Well, Wallace, dear boy, I'm going to leave you to… enjoy your time off, stand around, do whatever horses do in their stalls," she said aloud. But she didn't walk out. Instead, she silently slipped the latch and entered the stall, standing by the horse's side. Still. Waiting.

At first, there was nothing at all. Then she heard movement above her again. She remained where she was, not breathing. Someone was coming down the ladder. She stayed hiding behind the horse, watching.

From around Wallace's flank, she saw a man coming down the ladder. He was in jeans and a casual denim shirt. She saw the back of his head first, his sandy-colored hair.

Thayer.

He jumped the last few feet to the ground, dusted his hands on his jeans and looked around. He seemed to sigh with relief. Then he walked to the stable doors and hesitated, looking out. After a moment, he made a quick exit.

Toni remained with the horse for a moment, puzzled. Why should Thayer be nervous about being in the stables? He had as much right to come out here as any of them.

"Good boy," she murmured, patting Wallace's neck. She slipped back out of the stall, walked out down the aisle of stalls and found herself looking up the ladder.

What the hell had he been doing up there?

She was just about to set a foot on the first rung of the ladder when she was startled by a voice.

"Eh, he be lookin' well and fine this mornin', miss, don't ye think?"

She swung around, almost in a panic herself. Eban was just inside the doorway, looking toward Wallace's stall.

She swallowed hard, forced a smile. Despite herself, she noted that he blocked the doorway.

"He looks very good, Eban. Thank you for watching him with such concern. He's really a wonderful horse."

"Aye, that he is," Eban agreed.

He didn't move from the doorway. If she was going to make an exit, she would have to walk by him.

"Well, thank you again," she murmured a bit awkwardly, striding toward the exit. She passed him, painfully aware of his presence. She was afraid that he was going to reach a hand out, stop her.

But he didn't. Instead, he caused her to pause with his words.

"'E's trying to talk to ye, miss, ye know."

She felt almost as if she had been physically gripped. And so she turned back to him.

"What?"

"The laird. Not everyone is able t'see him. But ye… y've got the way, y'know. The touch."

He came closer to her and whispered, "Aye, y'must take care, grave care. Don't be lettin' 'em all know it. There's those out there, always, who would do evil. But the laird…the laird would tell ye things."

She felt every hair on her body stand on end. Her smile was about to crack.

"I don't know what you're talking about," she said firmly, and turned.

Her footsteps were slow, but, by the time she neared the castle, she was nearly running.

As she entered the main hall, Ryan was coming down the stairs. "You went to see Wallace. Isn't it great, the old boy bounded back like a trooper!"

"Right. It's great."

She started up the stairs, anxious to hurry past him.

His hand fell on her arm. He stared at her quizzically. "Where are you going now? Kevin just shouted up to say that breakfast was ready."

"I—I just want to wash up," she said. "I'll be right back down. Don't wait for me, though. Everyone just eat, okay?"

Almost jerking free, she ran past him. She went straight to her room and found her purse. She dumped the contents on the bed, heedless of any mess. She dug into her wallet and found the card she had carried with her always, swearing that she would never use it.

She looked around, glad to realize that she'd remembered to plug her phone into the wall with the European adaptor on Saturday.

She punched in the country code for the United States, hesitated, looked at the card and then dialed.

* * *

"I've heard about the great discovery old Doc Darrow has made," Robert said, greeting Bruce as he came into the pub. "Congratulations!"

Bruce took his friend's hand and shook it as he slid into the booth. They were in Stirling, on Robert's suggestion that they meet there.

"Might be a bit absurd to feel so elated about something so long ago, but…" Bruce said with a shrug. "Sure, I'm happy. It's a fine thing to discover that your heroic ancestor wasn't a wife killer."

Robert grinned.

"Why Stirling?" Bruce asked.

"Didn't want to make you come to Edinburgh. I had some business here, and I don't really want our man Jonathan to know that I'm meeting with you so often. Don't want to step on his toes there, you know? We need too much cooperation."

Bruce nodded. "Well, then fine. So?"

"Want to order first?"

"Sure," Bruce said, glancing around with a slightly arched brow. The pub was rather dingy, considering that Stirling offered a lot of really fine establishments. Actually, Bruce considered the city a true gem of the country.

"They have the most delicious fish and chips in the world here. Full of fat and cholesterol," Robert said. He grimaced. "Service is slow today. The old fellow who owns the place has lost another waitress. They all quit on him. He's a bloody bugger, he is. Still, the fish and chips make it worth the wait."

"How long a wait?"

Robert grinned. "Not too long for me. He knows who I am." To prove his point, he lifted a hand. A fleshy man in an apron made his way over.

"Aye, then, what'll it be, Detective Inspector?"

"Fish and chips for me." He looked at Bruce.

"Fish and chips, and a stout," Bruce said.

"I'll be puttin' a rush on it," the man said, and he shook his head. "Lasses these days! Dependable as shite!"

"Lost another one, did you, George?"

"Came in Sunday mornin', took off Sunday afternoon, haven't see the lights o' her eyes since!" Muttering, he walked away.

"Someone should just tell him one day that he's a nasty bastard," Robert said.

George came back swiftly, nearly throwing a pint of stout down before Bruce.

"So?" Bruce said, when he was gone.

"Actually, I didn't dig up much. It's rather the coincidence of things that made me call you so quickly," Robert explained. "First, our Glasgow fellow, Thayer Fraser. The man has a record."

"Anything serious?"

"Some busts for drugs when he was young. Clean slate for the last several years. Played with a band, the Kinked Kilts, and his last gig was at a piano bar."

"As he said," Bruce murmured.

"He worked some shady places," Robert said. "Suspect, but not criminal."

"That's all on the man?"

"Aye, so far."

"And the others?"

"What I've gotten in from checking legally accessible records is rather strange. Apparently they're all exactly what they appear to be. I've found the college records from NYU, and some references to work. Not one of the Americans has a police record of any kind.

But, as a point of interest, two of them are natural computer whizzes."

"Lucky for them," Bruce said. "Which two? And why is that important?"

"Well, we're following two mysteries here, wouldn't you say? For them to have gotten the permits and licenses they have, there had to be some truth to their rental agreements. That means that someone did have a hell of a lot on you, such as information regarding your actual title, your numbers in our old British society… information that only you, as an individual, should have had. A crack computer hacker can get all kinds of information on someone, which is why identity theft is getting to be such an issue these days."

"So, in other words, you're telling me that one of them might have known about me, gotten into my records, faked being me and rented the castle to them?" Bruce asked.

"Well, it's a possibility."

Bruce shook his head. "But whoever did must have known that I'd eventually show up."

"Right. But if the person had done it just to get money out of the others and knew how to make the computer site disappear…well, what would he, or she, care at that point?"

"What about Thayer Fraser?"

"So far," Robert said, "I only know that he has one hell of a Web page—oh, and that he's big into computer gaming. Medieval game playing on line, you know, the kind that goes on forever and forever, with one guy at a computer in Glasgow playing with someone in London, New York, Moscow…or maybe just in Stirling."

Bruce nodded, taking in the information. "Still, none

of the Americans has a criminal record. That is a piece of good news."

Robert parted his folded hands, refolded them. "Aye, sure. But then there's this, as well. And…this probably doesn't mean a thing. I just found it interesting."

"What?" Bruce said.

"Well, there's a strange time line here. It has to be a coincidence, I imagine."

"What?" Bruce said, exasperated. Robert didn't often beat around the bush.

"Helen MacDougal disappeared from Glasgow on June third, a year ago."

"And I found her on August thirtieth, in the water," Bruce said, frowning.

"Mary Granger disappeared November eleventh, last year."

Bruce's brows furrowed to a deeper degree. "Aye, Eban found her in early January. In worse shape."

"January tenth, to be precise."

"Robert, what are you getting at?"

"Annie O'Hara disappeared, we think, just a week or more ago."

"Aye…so? Are we goin' somewhere here, Robert? If so, I don't see where," Bruce told him.

"You know hotels ask for passports when you check in," Robert said.

"Aye, of course."

"Well, your friends—Toni, the Brownes, Kevin and David, at least—were in a hotel in Glasgow, June of last year."

Bruce frowned. "They've said they've vacationed here, many times."

Robert nodded and drew out a folder by his side,

flipping a page. "November last, Mary Granger disappeared from Stirling."

"And you're going to tell me my friends were in Stirling?"

"No. Glasgow."

He accepted that, frowning. "And two weeks ago?"

"They were back in Edinburgh, making the arrangements for licenses and the like."

Bruce shook his head. "Robert, if you're trying to draw a connection here—"

"I'm not. I'm just letting you know what I found out. And the coincidence regarding the dates just happened before my eyes. I'd be remiss not to mention it to you."

"Aye, you're right, but—" Bruce shook his head. "Think about them, one by one. Toni? A murderess of prostitutes? Kevin and David—they don't fit the profile at all. Gina and Ryan? Frankly, I just don't see it."

"We don't actually have a profile—"

"But we know what it would be. White, heterosexual male, young, twenties to thirties, day job, probably menial, maybe even a wife or steady girlfriend."

Robert nodded. "Aye, you've a point there. But profiles have been off. You know that yourself. Remember, years ago? What profiler, no matter how good, would have come up with the real scenario, a husband and wife *killing team?*"

Bruce shrugged. "Robert, I think we're grasping at straws here. If we had to go through a roster of every foreigner who happened to be in the country at the times of the murders—or disappearances—I think we'd have some numbers to go through. And if we're looking at opportunity, I'm afraid we've a nation full of people to look through, as well."

"Bruce, you don't need to be defendin' the crew. All

I'm telling you is what I happened to see when I made inquiries—which I did at your behest."

George hurried over, nearly tossing down their plates. "Damn, but if I could just get meself a decent lass!" he swore.

Bruce frowned suddenly, catching the man's arm when he was hurrying to move on.

"George?"

"Aye? Sir, be quick, would ye?"

"Your girl just walked out on you? Or just didn't show up? She didn't quit, I mean, let you know she was leaving?"

George waved an impatient hand in the air. "She was another wanderer on the loose. Strange accent—looked more the Norse type, which she should. Lass came down from Orkney. And quit? Resign? Have the courtesy to let a fellow know she wasn't coming back? Are y'jestin'? Hell no! She didn't show up, and that's that. Got herself enough money and hurried on to the next town, no doubt. Now, sir, I've got food piling up in the kitchen!"

Bruce stared across the table at Robert. "You might want to make some inquiries here," he said softly.

Robert looked down at the table and shook his head. "Aye," he said, and pushed away the plate of fish and chips he had been so anticipating.

Toni called the number she swore she'd never dial, only to find that Adam Harrison was out of town. When the young man answering the phone asked if she'd like to leave her name and a message, she nearly hung up. But she had her own cell phone with her—it wasn't as if he'd call back and leave a message on a line that anyone might answer. After hesitating, she left her name and phone number.

"Oh, hi!" the voice on the other end said. "Toni Fraser... Adam said to pay sharp attention if you ever called. Someone will be right back with you."

Someone?

Toni didn't feel particularly comfortable with that information, but she thanked the young man anyway and rang off.

For a moment, she pondered her next move. She nearly jumped sky-high when her cell phone, still in her hand, began to ring. She fumbled with the little buttons, nearly hanging up on the caller.

"Hello?"

"Hi. Toni?"

The voice on the other end was feminine.

"Yes?" she said carefully.

"My name is Darcy. Darcy Stone. I work with Adam Harrison."

Toni was silent. It had been one thing to contemplate talking with Adam, a man who knew her. The gentle soul who had been there when a young child's world had fallen apart. The man who had come to see her one-woman show, but didn't press it when she said that she was just fine, not having any more nightmares, no more visions...

"Toni?"

The woman's voice was crystal clear; she might have been in the next town.

"Yes, I'm here."

"Listen, please don't worry, Adam isn't shuffling you off to anyone. You can speak with him in a few hours—he's on a plane right now. It's just that he has your name on a special list, and he's always said that if you called in, we were to get back to you immediately. Please, nothing you say to me will ever go any further than me. And again, no matter how insane it might sound, don't be afraid to say anything. Anything at all."

Toni stared at the phone slightly skeptically, as if by looking at it she could somehow fathom the truth of the words being said.

"Let's start at the beginning," Darcy Stone said, from across the miles. "Where are you?"

"Scotland. A small village known as Tillingham. At—at the castle there."

"A castle. In Tillingham?"

"Yes." Toni took a breath. "I think I'm seeing a ghost," she said.

"Then you probably are," came the matter-of-fact answer.

"I am?"

"Yes." Darcy chuckled. "I'm sorry, I'm afraid you'll hang up on me when I say this, but… I see many ghosts."

Toni *was* tempted to hang up.

"Please, don't hang up, and do talk to me," the woman said, as if entirely aware of Toni's every thought and action.

"I rented a castle with friends in Scotland, rented with a lease option to buy," Toni said. "Except it turned out that we didn't really rent it, at least, not from the owner. We were told the family had died out, but there's a very current laird. I made up a story about an ancestor of his, and it turned out to have happened, right down to the name of the laird's wife." She hesitated. "I dreamed, or woke up, a ghost. The man in my nightmares, or ghost in reality, is the exact image of the living laird. I thought at first that maybe I was being taken, as we had been taken in by the corporation supposedly leasing the property. But then, there are the murders."

"The murders?"

"Women have been disappearing. Three to date, I believe. And two have been found in the forest bordering the castle. I went into the forest one day, led by the… ghost. I found bones. Everyone assumed it was the third victim, but it looks as if it's the old laird's lady, dead now for centuries. He wasn't an old laird, he just lived in the sixteen hundreds. I'm not making any sense at all. I'm—" Again she hesitated, thinking that she really was losing her mind. This wasn't even Adam she was talking to, and she was spilling out way more than she had ever planned. "I've quickly fallen into a certain involvement with the young laird, the *contemporary* laird, who certainly has been decent enough about this whole thing. We rented, or thought we rented the place to do theatrical tours—"

"I saw your production of Queen Varina," the woman interjected. "It was wonderful."

Toni had never liked to think that she overreacted to either criticism or praise. But at that moment, she decided that she definitely liked the woman on the other end of the phone.

"Thanks," she said softly. "Um…he—the laird, that is—doesn't see ghosts. Or the ghost." She hesitated. "There's only one."

Darcy was silent for a moment. "Women have been found in the area, dead. But the ghost brought you to the remains of his long-dead wife?"

"Yes."

"Have you seen him since?"

"Yes. Now he keeps leading me to the crypts."

There was no way she could ever describe this conversation to anyone.

"There's a simple answer," Darcy Stone said from the other end.

"And that is?"

"He wants her by his side. Now that you've found her, he wants her buried where she should be—at his side."

Toni was startled to feel a rise of excitement. Lord, yes! That would make so much sense. Well, if the fact that she was seeing a ghost made sense, then his leading her to the crypts after she had found the bones would definitely align, at any rate.

"Yes," she murmured.

"Of course, it might *not* be that simple," Darcy warned.

"Now that you've said that to me, it has to be!" Toni said. "I saw him at the foot of my bed, and then going into the forest. And then...into the crypts. Oh!" She groaned.

"What?"

"They think she's an incredible historic find. His wife, the lady I found. I'm afraid they'll want to study her, put her in a museum."

"Well, that's easy enough to handle. And I don't think this is one you're going to have to worry about at all. Her descendant just says no! But still, there might be a lot more going on there."

"Not in this residence," Toni said. "There are terrible things going on—"

"The victims found in the forest weren't associated with the castle?"

"No, definitely not. They were part-time prostitutes at the very least, and kidnapped from three major cities, Edinburgh, Glasgow and Stirling."

"You're certain there can be no association?"

"That would be impossible. Really. We haven't been here that long. And aside from us, there's the laird and a fellow who works for him."

"I see."

Toni hesitated, aware that she should mention the fact that Eban scared the wits out of her. And that, at times, she'd almost convinced herself that the current laird was dressing up as a ghost. *She had never seen the both of them at the same time!*

"I can come right over."

"What? To Scotland? That's not…necessary," Toni said. She was ready to groan out loud. What had she done? If she brought anyone else in here—especially some kind of an occultist who claimed to speak to lots of ghosts!—they'd definitely be thrown out. She couldn't begin to imagine Bruce MacNiall standing for such a thing.

"Your situation sounds a bit complex." Darcy hesitated, then her words spilled out. "Toni, Adam has talked about you. He's says that you're…you're one of the most amazing mediums he's ever encountered."

"Medium!" Toni said, shocked.

"You see things," the voice on the other end said.

Toni gripped the phone so tightly it might have snapped. She swallowed hard, forcing herself to breathe. "I'm sorry," she said then. "This was…a mistake. I'm not a medium. I had a few unusual—very unusual— dreams as a child, but I am not a medium. I don't want to be a medium. And please, do not—I repeat—do not come over here. We're in a tenuous situation, at best. I appreciate your time. I'll see to it, somehow, that the woman is buried next to her laird. Thank you for all your help. It's truly appreciated. But do not come here! Thank you and goodbye."

She hung up the phone, threw it on the bed and stared at it as if it might turn into a serpent and bite her. She waited, half expecting the woman to try to call her back. But the phone lay on the bed, silent.

She turned and hurried out of the room. One of their group had to be somewhere about. She wanted company very desperately. Someone among…the living.

Chapter 14

It was time for the buses to come rolling up, and Bruce had not returned.

"You had it all figured out!" Gina said with dismay. "Now what are we going to do?"

"Someone else will play Bruce's part, that's all," Toni said.

They were standing in the great hall, dressed for the various roles they were going to play. Everyone stared at Toni.

"What?" she said.

Kevin cleared his throat. "Really, no one else can play Bruce's part."

"He's not even an actor!" Toni protested.

"That's just it," David said. "He *is* the great Mac-Niall."

Toni shook her head. "Come on, guys! We never

planned on having him to begin with. He's worked with us, but he's not on the payroll."

"We don't exactly have a payroll, right now, do we?" Thayer inquired.

"Thayer, you can be Bruce," she said.

"I can't ride that horse."

"And now," Ryan said, "I'm supposed to be the bad guy. I've been practicing my evil sneer all day."

Toni sighed. "He isn't here. So we have to do something else."

"I know!" Ryan said. "Okay, here's the deal. I'm not so sure I can ride his horse, either—"

"You can ride any horse," Toni protested.

Ryan shook his head. "That fellow *knows* his master. But Wallace is right as rain now. I'll ride him in, then I'll come up the stairs as the very personification of good and evil. You know, a dramatic Jekyll and Hyde number. I fight with Toni, and myself. It will be great."

Again, they were silent, staring at him.

"Thayer," Toni said, staring at her kinsman, "you'll have to be Bruce—without the horse. Burst into the castle on foot, run up the stairs. Ryan will come riding in as the bad guy."

"We could just do it the way we had originally," Gina said.

"That's a definite plan," David said. "It's actually the most logical."

"It is," Kevin agreed.

Toni shook her head stubbornly. "We can't go back, because now we know that we were maligning someone."

"Toni, we were never maligning anyone, because we didn't know he had really existed!" Gina protested.

"But now we do," Toni said. "And I don't want to play

it the way we had it originally. Guys, we know the fellow was innocent."

"Well, we don't know it," Kevin said.

"Yes, we do," Toni insisted stubbornly. "So, Thayer walks in, and Ryan rides in. Agreed?"

"Sure," Thayer said.

"I don't know," Ryan protested, shaking his head. "I think my Jekyll and Hyde thing could have been really, really good."

"Alas! We'll never get to know!" Gina said, and winked at Toni.

There was a knock at the door.

Kevin clapped his hands. "Places, everyone. David and I get to open the doors now!"

"No, no! Not yet," Thayer protested. "It's just Lizzie and Trish. They were coming early."

He went to answer the door. It was indeed the girls. They came in, excited and exuberant, oohing and aahing over the castle alone. "And you all are living here! How wonderful," Lizzie said.

"Actually, yes," David murmured, looking around. "We should be grateful, for whatever time we get, huh?"

Ryan sighed. "We thought we'd have it for all of our lives."

"Or as long as we wanted, anyway," Gina said.

"Well, it's lovely, truly lovely," Trish said, catching Thayer's arm and squeezing it. "You're lucky, for whatever."

"Yes, I guess we are," Gina said.

"Buses!" Kevin said. "I can hear them. Let's move, children. Trish, Lizzie, just follow the crowd around. We can all chat when the last bus leaves."

Toni disappeared up the stairs, awaiting her cue. Leaning against the wall, listening to activity below, she smiled, pleased to hear the audience reaction as they played out their parts and gave their histories. She didn't know if the fact that Lizzie and Trish were out there, determined to have fun, spurred their tour to greater enthusiasm, or if they were just all getting into it so deeply that they naturally brought their listeners along. But the night was going wonderfully.

When she came out on the landing, clad in her white gown, ready to become the Lady Annalise, she found that she was "on" that night herself, wound up by the stories the others had told. Her voice rang through the hall. Her passion for the heroism of Laird MacNiall was strong. And when she announced his return, she was stunned when Bruce came riding in on Shaunessy, perfectly on cue.

He strode up the stairs in anger as he had before. She found herself falling to her knees, and to her own ears, it sounded as if she really begged for her life.

Then his anger abated. If she hadn't caught the flash of humor in his eyes as he fell to his knees before her, accepting her words of loyalty, denying any fault thrown upon her by others, she would have thought the passion and ardor that he offered were real.

Ryan came riding into the hall with an expert display of horsemanship. Bruce rose, striding down the stairs to battle with Ryan.

Toni was amazed herself. Ryan, of course, had used swords in his previous work. It didn't seem a shock that Bruce might have learned something, as well. But they had never practiced. And usually, such a display was meticulously choreographed.

They were wonderful. They shouted back and forth, playing off one another's ad libs. And in the finale, a strike by Bruce's sword brought Ryan's flying across the floor—toward the hearth, away from their group. Bruce left Ryan for dead on the floor, coming back for Toni. As he reached her, Ryan slowly rose. With Bruce's back to him, he staggered up the stairs, catching Bruce by the shoulders, throwing him downward. Then he put his hands around Toni's neck. He winked as he strangled her.

After all that she had witnessed, she sprang into character, making her death scene as spectacular as the fight she had just witnessed. She lay dead on the stairs. Ryan fell at the feet of them.

Silence reigned in the hall.

Then, Lizzie, bless her, yelled out "Bravo!" And the room burst into applause that never seemed to end.

"Tea and scones! Into the kitchen, everyone!" Kevin commanded.

"This way!" David said, helping move them all along.

Toni sat up. Ryan and Bruce both were rising. "Oh, my God! We pulled it off!" Ryan said. "I thought you were crazy, suggesting that we could do this without a single practice. But that was incredible."

"I'll second that," Thayer said, coming forward. Gina, too, was running down from her place at the landing. She jumped up and down, kissing her husband, then planting one on Bruce's check before settling down in embarrassment. "Sorry, Laird MacNiall!"

"Nae, now, it was a lovely moment, Mrs. Browne," he told her, then turned to Toni. "Sorry I was late. I was—tied up."

She shook her head. "Why on earth would you want to be sorry? That was really phenomenal. The two of you…together. Purely amazing."

Bruce inclined his head to her. "Thank you, Lady Annalise."

She smiled but gritted her teeth, aware that no offense had been intended, but she was uneasy being called by the name. The strangeness of the day came rushing back to her—and the memory that, just that morning, she had so desperately wanted to talk to him.

Instead, she had called an agency that investigated ghosts.

She looked into his eyes. There had been laughter in them, and fun, but she was surprised to realize that he actually seemed a little distracted, as well. She had thought he was entirely into the act, but maybe he had just been going through the motions.

She turned away, disturbed. "I should really give Kevin and David a hand," she murmured, heading toward the kitchen. "We've an incredibly full house."

"I'll take the horses," Ryan said.

"Look after Wallace. I'll tend to Shaunessy," Bruce said.

Gina and Thayer followed Toni into the kitchen. Since there were so many people there, Toni was glad they'd come in, though Kevin was so well prepared that he probably could have handled a crowd of a hundred. The scones were in baskets, there were a number of stations with cream and sugar, and he'd had the tea prepared well before the crowd came filing in.

The crowd was always eager to talk, but tonight, more so than ever. News about the discovery of the ancient remains had traveled fast, and the group was excited to be the first ever to see their little drama played out with the great Laird MacNiall portrayed as innocent.

Finally the buses left, but Lizzie and Trish remained. And after everyone pitched in with the cleanup, Toni decided that Thayer was going to have to be his charming self and deal with their guests. She excused herself and went upstairs.

"Have you ever seen anything like it?" Ryan said.

Bruce, putting up the last of Shaunessy's tack, glanced over at him. Ryan was patting the roan's nose, studying his eyes and the great head of the horse.

"Quite frankly, I haven't," Bruce said, realizing himself for the first time that it was the absolute truth. He knew horses, and he'd never seen anything like this. The vet believed that the roan had gotten into something. Eban had seen to it that the stables were swept completely, lest it be some kind of infection caused by molding hay or bad grain. But only the roan had been infected. The vet had commented that it was akin to a child eating something disagreeable, having a bad night and clearing his system, waking up just as good as ever.

He walked over to study the roan himself. Wallace's eyes were clear and sharp, a sure sign that he was over what had plagued him.

"He's doing well now, it seems," Bruce said. He patted the horse. "Good lad," he murmured, then told Ryan, "I'm thinking, come the weekend, we'll move him. You did a damned good job here of cleaning the place out, and Eban came in and did more, but we might move both the boys and I'll get a real crew out here. These days… well, you get some kind of a germ or bacteria and you can't tell quite what's going on. The vet took some blood samples, too, so maybe we'll know more soon enough. Good thing is, he's looking fine right now."

Ryan grinned suddenly. "Hey, speaking of fine, we were something, eh? In the States, we couldn't have attempted such a thing! If one of us had nicked the other, there would have been law suits and all that. Where the hell did you learn to do all that?"

"Well, over here, we have mock tournaments and such, just like you have Revolutionary and Civil War reenactments."

Ryan grinned. "Well, I don't mean to brag, but damn, were we good!"

"Aye, that we were." Bruce gave him a wave and started back to the castle. He looked at the stone, climbing to the night sky, and realized that he had something very special. Time and reality had made him lose his appreciation. The Americans had brought it back.

Ryan followed him, and when they entered the castle, they could hear laughter coming from the kitchen—not surprising since the car belonging to the two women they'd met in the village remained in the driveway. Bruce had actually enjoyed the night, but he wasn't anxious for any more company.

"Sounds as if we still have company," Ryan said.

Bruce nodded. "Well, enjoy," he murmured, heading for the stairs. It was his castle; he could opt out.

He entered his room to find Toni sitting by the hearth, staring at burned-out embers. She was wearing a contemporary cotton T-shirt nightshirt, her blond hair caught by the light, her features grave. When she saw him, she brought a pensive smile to her lips.

"What's wrong?" he asked her.

Her smile remained uncertain, though she shook her head. He came to her, taking a seat on the side of the bed. He tried to calculate the time he had known her. A speck of dust in the span of his life. But it seemed natural that she was there, and beyond the obvious of a great sexual relationship, there was something better in the fact, as well. He'd known he'd come up the stairs and find her waiting. And he'd liked it.

Apparently she tried to shake off whatever was bothering her. "You and Ryan...wow. You played off each other unbelievably," she told him.

"It wasn't half bad, was it?" He picked up her fingers, idly stroking her hand.

"Of course, if you'd worked for me in the States, I would have fired your ass," she told him, eyes sparkling as they touched his. "You were very latc."

He arched a brow. "I got held up with Robert in Stirling."

"Oh?"

He offered her a grimace. "We were at a pub and found out that one of the barmaids had failed to show. The fellow who owns the place is a bit of a bastard, so he wasn't in the least concerned, but we felt we had to look into it. We found out where she'd been living. It seems she packed her bags, so..."

"I'm glad," Toni told him. "Luckily, you don't need much rehearsal."

"We both know what we're doing."

"Apparently," Toni agreed.

"So that, in a nutshell, was my day. Thinking something might be wrong, finding out we were both getting a little punch drunk due to events. So, I repeat, what's wrong?"

She didn't answer right away, but stared back at the dying embers. "Bruce, is this place supposed to be haunted?"

He laughed, then sobered when she stared at him. Still, he couldn't quite help the smile. "It's a castle. Centuries old. What do you think?"

She flushed. "Well, it is haunted, you know."

He sighed. "Toni, I let the place go to hell. Aye, that I did. But from the time I was a wee lad, I knew the place was mine. I have spent a great deal of time here. Not a single ghost has ever darkened my door."

"I see your ancestor a bit too frequently," she told him.

He groaned. "Toni, I know the dreams are plaguing you, lass." He shook his head. "Is the castle supposed to be haunted? Aye, definitely. Bruce MacNiall supposedly rides the forest and wanders these old halls. There are other tales, as well, and we do have one bloody history. But that's just it. Somewhere in the past, you heard the stories. I believe with my whole heart that you came here *thinking* you made up the past. But there are all kinds of books out about Scottish ghosts. They're as prevalent as Scottish sheep. And someone may not have gotten the names or the place right, but the story has probably been written up. You simply heard about it."

She bit her lower lip lightly. "Haven't you ever…felt something? Had a sense of déjà-vu, a premonition?"

A premonition? Aye, and it was you in the water, face-down so I couldn't see your face, just the trail of your hair, and my heart was in my throat. And worse. Once, when I was a cop with the Edinburgh Police Department, working a sad case indeed, I was able to crack it because I could put myself in a fellow's shoes.

"Toni…"

She pulled her fingers from his light touch and gripped both his hands.

"Bruce, I need you to take me to the crypts."

"What?"

"Please!"

"Toni, I think it might be better if I don't take you to the crypts."

She shook her head. Her eyes were a true sapphire, touching his. Earnest, sincere and alarmingly desperate.

"Look," she said. "We haven't known one another long, but I admire you, and I've come to respect you tremendously. I've come to care about you, too, and I believe that you feel something for me. So I'm begging you…please, please, just humor me on this. I know it sounds crazy. But you have shown me a great deal more than simple tolerance regarding my strange dreams. You've helped me, been with me, made me feel sane. Help me with this, now… I'm begging you!"

"Take you to the crypts…*now?*"

She nodded. "I've been there at night."

"Toni, I keep that door locked—"

"I've been there," she insisted. "Bruce, I can describe it to you! There's a winding stone stairway almost immediately after the door opens. Then there are arched hallways, like in the catacombs of a medieval church. And there's a tomb and monument to Bruce MacNiall, the king's loyal Cavalier, at the end of one of the hallways. I'm assuming it was designed sometime years after his death."

Bruce stared at her with certain astonishment. It wasn't impossible that the group might have gotten in to the vaults, but…

"I don't particularly want a circus made out of the family crypts," he said.

"Surely even Thayer has let those girls leave by now!" she said, smiling. "I'm afraid he's been the odd man out here," she added. "We both used to be a bit on the loose, but since you returned to the castle…well, Gina and Ryan are as close and old hat as Ma and Pa Kettle, David and Kevin have one another, and once you arrived…"

He noted that she didn't say *And I have you.* But

Toni wouldn't. She would never be so presumptuous. And yet...

He reached out and smoothed a tendril of sun-blond hair.

"All right."

She smiled, her appreciation evident, and he thought he actually heard a thump in her heartbeat.

"Thank you," she said.

"Think we've given them enough time to clear out?" he asked.

"We can see."

He nodded. "I'll need the key." The great skeleton key was kept in a drawer in the wardrobe. The thing was ancient, as old as the door and the metal bolt.

He joined her, grimacing, and took her hand as they left the room and started out. They moved silently along the hallway to the top landing, then paused.

"Hear anyone?" he asked softly.

She shook her head. "They could still be in the kitchen," she said.

"We'll check it out. However," he reminded her, "they are my crypts." She smiled at that.

They walked down the stairs and into the kitchen. It was spotless—and empty.

"Want a brandy first?" he asked her.

"I'm all right, really," she said.

"I'm not."

"Okay, then I'll have a brandy."

He poured them each a small snifter, watching her as she sipped the fiery liquid. "There's something more you want," he said.

"I'll tell you when we get down there," she said, sipping the brandy. Again her eyes touched his, searchingly. She cast her head slightly at an angle. "You don't dress up like an ancient laird and run around in the middle of the night, right?"

He arched a brow. "Nae, lass, I really don't."

She swallowed the last of her brandy, then waited patiently for him.

"You really want to go down to the crypts in the middle of the night?" he asked.

"I really don't. But… I don't suppose I could make you understand. I can't make myself understand."

"All right, then." He set the glasses in the sink. "Shall we?"

He offered her a hand again and they went back into the secondary hall, to the door that led downward to the crypts. She winced as the old metal scraped and groaned. He pushed the door inward. "It is a winding stairway, with very old stone. I'll lead. Be careful."

"You still don't believe me, but I've been here," she whispered. Though there was really no need for a voice so soft, the night, the circumstances, seemed to demand it.

Bruce started down, hitting the light switch on the side of the wall. They moved down carefully. But at the foot of the stairs, Toni paused.

"What is it?"

"Nothing…well, there weren't cobwebs before, and I had no idea there was a light switch."

"We've had lights down here since the nineteen-thirties," he told her with a trace of amusement. There weren't, however, terribly powerful bulbs lighting up the place, and the medieval arches led to a natural state for shadows.

Moving slowly, they walked by shelves and effigies, until they reached the end of the hallway where the man history had recalled as the "great" MacNiall had been laid.

"You know what actually happened to him," Bruce said. "He met what they called the 'traitor's end.' But his execution was carried out by a mock court right out in the forest. When Charles II returned to claim his throne, he ordered that Bruce MacNiall's body be recovered from the forest and that a tomb be made. The king even paid for the marble and the artist's work."

Toni stood pensively for a moment, staring at the tomb.

"It's you," she whispered.

"I beg to differ. It's not me. I'm right here," he told her.

She flushed, glancing at him. "But it is uncanny. There are hundreds of years between you, and yet…the resemblance is so great."

He shrugged. "Maybe we see more than there is."

"I don't think so," she said.

"Genetics can be very strange."

"True," she murmured. "And yet, does it ever make you feel…?"

"Uneasy?" he asked, slipping an arm around her shoulders. "Never, since I grew up here. And I used to love to bring friends down. We'd tell ghost stories ourselves and run up the stairs screaming, and my da would get mad. We were typical kids. But the great MacNiall isn't still with us, Toni. He lived out his life. He lived hard, passionately, and he arrived here, as all men will. I like the history. I like the fact that the family he served with such ardent loyalty returned that favor in the person of Charles II, restoring him to his home. It's legend, Toni, history and myth, nothing more."

She smiled, inching just a bit closer to him, still staring at the grave and the marble effigy of his ancestor.

"Bruce, there's a second sarcophagus behind the first."

"I suppose they believed that one day they would find the bones of his beloved."

"They've been found now."

"Aye. But who knows when the forces that be will release the remains, eh?"

She turned to him, solemn, deeply concerned.

"Bruce, she needs to be given a proper burial, here, with her laird."

"Well, lass, I'm sure that she will be. In time."

Toni shook her head vehemently. "They may try to keep her. The levels of preservation were rather bizarre. Someone may want her in a museum. Bruce, you can't let it happen!"

He looked down at her, smiling a little. "Ah, Toni, so you think my ancestor comes back, hauntin' your dreams at night, to have his lady buried at his side? They'll want a bit of my blood, you know. To verify that the lady was my great, great—whatever!—grandmother. And then she'll come home. When it's proved she is my ancestor, I'll bring her home."

"I'd really like it if we could rush them as much as possible," she said.

His smile deepened. "All right, but…"

"But?" she queried.

"I've a bit of problem with it all, you see. I haven't always been the most religious of men, but I do have a rather deep-set belief that there is a greater power— God. And perhaps, because like all men, I don't want to consider myself merely mortal, I do believe in an afterlife. But I also like to believe that beneath it all, we're something finer than the weakness of flesh and bone. And that being the case…well, Bruce MacNiall did not want his bones to lie here for him to be legend, to find his peace in death, or whatever. And though, certainly,

I'd not want the remains of an ancestor treated with anything less than respect, I cannot believe that an ancestor of mine would haunt you, tease or torment you, over earthly remains."

"Maybe he doesn't think he's tormenting me," Toni said. "He just wants to make sure that the remains of what was once the living, breathing woman he loved are treated with the due respect to which you refer."

He swept his arms around her tightly, caught, even here, in the realm of the dead, by the sapphire sincerity within her somewhat anguished gaze.

"We'll see to it, eh?" he said softly. "Now…if you don't mind, it has been a bitch of a day. Shall we?"

She nodded, smiling, and led the way out of the crypts. But at the base of the winding stairway, she paused.

"What now, Miss Fraser?"

She flashed him a smile, and shook her head. "I… Nothing."

"What?"

"No, nothing, really. Just a sense of…"

He sighed. "Toni!"

She exhaled. "Just a sense that someone was behind us!"

"Shall we walk back?" he asked.

She shook her head. "No."

They proceeded up the stairs. He followed her, watching the way the cotton clung to her curves. At the top, she stopped again, looking back at him.

"What?" she asked, perplexed.

"Keep going," he said.

Outside the door, he paused to close and lock the door. It creaked loudly.

"I did know what it looked like, exactly!" she whispered. "I told you, right? And I knew that the tomb would be there, knew that the old Bruce and you were spitting images of one another."

"Aye," he said.

"Well?"

"Well, what?"

"I don't know…exactly. Aren't you going to admit there's something a bit weird about it?" she queried.

He shook his head.

"No?" she said.

"Not tonight."

"Then why were you staring at me?"

He caught the innocent confusion in her eyes.

"I hate to admit to having feelings of a rather base inclination at the moment, but frankly, Miss Fraser, I was watching your hips, the machinations of the way you moved, and thinking I wanted nothing more to do with the dead, the old, the past. I find that my concern right now is extremely focused and has everything to do with the present. The immediate present. Dare I be crass? Madam, I was watching your ass."

The confusion left her eyes. She laughed softly, a breath of anticipation, of excitement in the sound that stimulated every sensual essence in his being.

He drew her against him then, allowing his fingers to ripple down her back and form around her buttocks as he drew her close. "This is my castle, and as laird here, I do have the right to every sexual fantasy known to man, as far as mind and place are concerned. Before the great hearth, in the kitchen, on the stair… But the place is filled with your associates and, God knows, they may well wander at night. And, truthfully, stone is quite hard on the back and the bones, so…"

"You do have a great bed," she mused.

"And you have a great—great assets," he assured her teasingly.

She escaped his hold, scampering ahead of him up the main stairway. In the hallway of the upper landing, she waited, looking back. Her smile was still in place, her eyes bright, her hair like a halo in the dim light. He was rather certain that she had chosen the cotton gown with the full intention of getting him to show her the crypts that night, that she had worn it in case they had, indeed, run into any of her friends.

She couldn't know how the soft fabric molded to her with sheer seduction, or that he would find her as appealing in burlap. Or that, even standing in the hallway so, she could arouse him to a staggering heat and hunger.

She turned, heading for the room, and he caught up with her just as she plunged into it, drawing a little cry of surprise from her. With her in his arms, held against him, he kicked the door closed, turned and found his way to the bed. They fell heavily upon it, and in moments, were tangled together.

That night he loved everything about her. It wasn't just that she was made beautifully, with the right assets, curves, flesh, breasts, skin, face, lips, or her innate ability to use all to the most erotic levels. No. Her seduction was in her laughter, the husky, silver whisper of it, and her eyes, conveying an excitement, a thrill, that elicited a masculine response of ego, that sheer, pulsing, hard, desperate, devil-may-care arousal.

Neither her gown nor his clothing actually left their bodies as they came together in a wild clash of fabric and flesh that needed no play, for that had come before, in the simple act of getting up the stairs and closing the door. In a smile, in a whisper, in the sapphire pools of her eyes. That time.

Then there was laughter as they untangled themselves from wool and cotton, kicked away sheets so that they could be drawn back up. There were the jokes about kilts, more words whispered, the sweetness of being close in the aftermath, eyes touching again, hands against one another, naked flesh against naked flesh.

It occurred to him then, almost in a corner of his mind, that he never wanted her to leave. Sex was easy to come by. She was not. Only once before had he felt...

Not at all ready for them, he pushed such thoughts aside. And when he made love to her again, it was slow, painstakingly slow, for himself, and yet...his fingers idled over her flesh, teasing long before she turned back to him, snaked herself against his body, moved down against him, caused him to erupt to fire again.

He thought that it was late, very late when they lay together and started to drift to sleep. But just when the darkness was about to overtake him, he opened his eyes. He didn't know what he had heard, but he had been attuned for years to listening. And he had heard...something.

He rose carefully, silently, taking up his swatch of tartan and quickly wrapping it about himself. Bare chested, he silently opened the door and started along the hallway. His feet made no sound against the stone.

He came to the top of the stairs and looked down to the hall.

Nothing.

He shrugged. One of his guests must have arisen and then gone back to bed. Until he'd had his "guests" here, he'd never even bothered to lock the great main doors. Tillingham had never really had such a thing as a crime ratio. None of the local teens would break in. If they were of that bent, they'd want to hit a store with a cash register. It was true, as well, that there were those who swore the place was haunted. Who wanted to chance the anger or vengeance of such a bloody legend as Bruce MacNiall?

He hesitated, then walked down the stairs. The doors were locked, as they had been when he and Ryan had come in after seeing to the stabling of the horses. So he walked back upstairs and slipped silently into the room, and next to Toni.

He pulled her against him. She sighed softly in her sleep. He let the silk and fragrance of her hair tease his nose, and he closed his eyes.

Toni didn't know why she awoke. She had been sound asleep, but suddenly she was wide-awake, staring. A chill gripped her. She wondered why, when she was in Bruce's arms, held tight against him.

She winced and stared toward the foot of the bed.

He was there.

That other Bruce. Come back, from a long ago time. He stood staring at her, his features hard and tense with what looked like sorrow...or concern. *Fear.* For her?

She exhaled. "Not tonight!" she whispered out loud. "Please, please, not tonight!"

She closed her eyes tightly, praying that the vision would go away. And when she opened her eyes, to her amazement, the vision was gone.

"Toni?"

The living Bruce, vital flesh and blood at her side, touched her, whispered her name. She snuggled more deeply against his chest. He absently stroked her hair.

They both slept.

Chapter 15

Bruce's phone rang first thing in the morning. He reached over from the bed to find it, thinking it was in the pocket of his jeans. But he'd come in with the swatch of wool around him he'd used for the tour, and his jeans were around somewhere. Not wanting the sound to wake Toni, he stumbled up quickly, and went searching around to find them. He fell upon them, and after some swearing and mishap, found the phone and answered it.

"Bruce." It was Jonathan.

"Aye, Jon, how are you?"

"Good, good. I've some information for you."

"Oh?"

"Can you come to the office?"

"Sure." Somewhat bleary-eyed, he tried to read his watch. It wasn't quite eight. "There's nothing you just want to say over the phone, eh?"

Jonathan sighed. "I'd rather you come in. What I've to say…well, I don't want to be coming there, and I think y'should come in."

"All right. I'm just out of bed. Give me time to shower." He rubbed his jaw. "And shave."

"I'll have coffee ready here," Jonathan said.

He hung up and glanced over to the bed. Toni seemed to be sleeping deeply, and he was glad. He frowned slightly, worried about her.

Strange that she had known the outlay of the crypts. He kept the door locked—and always had. It was one thing for locals and tourists to wander into the castle area, but another entirely for someone to come in, trip down the spiral stairway and lie injured in the cold, damp corridor of the ancient and the dead. But there were certainly plenty of people who knew what the crypts looked like. And every man jack from the village to the surrounding miles knew that the "great" Laird MacNiall lay at the end of a corridor, immortalized in marble by decree of the good old restored Stuart king, Charles II.

He showered, shaved and dressed quickly, quietly leaving Toni sleeping. As he closed the door behind him and hurried down the stairs, he could hear activity in the kitchen, but no one was in the great hall so he hurried on out and headed for his car. As he drove down the hill, he noticed the forest to his right, and felt again an anger and a conviction that they would eventually find the remains of Annie O'Hara there. And if they did not, she was there anyway, somewhere.

The remains of Annalise had gone undiscovered for centuries.

Parking, he looked up at the statue of his famous ancestor and shook his head. "You know, old fellow, if you are somehow haunting my American lass, I wish to bloody hell you'd stop!" he said, then became irritated with his own whimsy.

He strode on over to Jonathan's office. The constable was in his office, waiting for him.

"What, do you grow a beard all over your body?" Jonathan demanded.

"You woke me," Bruce told him with a shrug. "I'm here, what is it?"

Jonathan ran his fingers through his sandy hair. "Maybe nothing. Maybe a lot. I got this in from a computer fellow with the Lothian and Borders Police. Thought you might find it quite interesting, and that you'd be best out of the castle when you received it."

Bruce frowned, scanning the report.

The "corporation" the group had "rented" the castle from had a post office box in Edinburgh. But the computer site advertising his castle had been conceived and implemented from Glasgow.

He looked up at Jonathan. "Aye, so, it would appear the crooks are based in Glasgow."

Jonathan arched a brow. "Look into the next folder."

It was information Bruce actually had already. About Thayer Fraser's past. He tossed the folders back on the desk, grimacing. "Ah, Jonathan! The fellow has a shady background. And microchips are telling us that a person or persons committing fraud are based in Glasgow. We can't arrest a fellow for that."

"I know. But this, in itself, is damned suspicious. This fellow from Glasgow, a Scot, born and bred in the country, comes here with a group of Americans and claims he's never heard of you, that he has no idea there's a living MacNiall who owns the castle at Tillingham."

"It's a small castle."

"Ach! Bruce, you don't want anything to be wrong with the fellow, since he's the lass's kin, and that's a fact."

"True, maybe," Bruce admitted.

"Well, there's more. And I didn't actually get the 'more' legally. The fellow has a bank account with over a hundred thousand pounds."

"It's not a crime to have money, either, Jonathan," Bruce said. "And how did you come about this information?"

Jonathan shook his head. "No way that can be traced, should we go to court against him. I spent some time calling the banks, pretending to be a credit investigator."

"I see," Bruce said.

Jonathan shook his head, looking down at his desk, then back to Bruce. "You're my friend, Bruce. I took a few risks. Make some calls yourself, if you wish. Nae, there's no way I can arrest the fellow now, as is. But the fellows into microchips will be comin' up with more, I think. So, I wanted you to know. And not when you were in the damned castle with the fellow."

Bruce didn't let a flicker of emotion into his face. He nodded gravely. "Thank you, Jonathan."

"Keep an eye on the family silver," Jonathan said. "Or throw the lot o' them out. You've the right, y'know."

"Aye." Bruce rose. "But I think not, not yet. After all, if the computer fellows can get something real on him, we won't want him to have bolted on us, eh? As long as he thinks he's covered his tracks, he'll sit tight."

Jonathan agreed. "There's something about the fellow I never liked. Takin' up with Americans who think they can tell Scottish history!"

Bruce laughed. "Actually, they didn't do a bad job."

"What the fellow did was a serious crime, Bruce."

"What we think the fellow may have done is a serious crime."

"How else does a no-good bloke playin' a piano bar get that kind of money?"

"Well, we don't hang fellows in the square on suspicion anymore, Jonathan. I appreciate you calling me, and I thank you for the information. We'll sit tight and see."

He left the constabulary and decided to pay another visit to Daniel Darrow's office.

Rowenna greeted him in reception. "We've a team here, t'day, Bruce. Seeing to the lass from the past," she told him.

"The lass from the past would be my kin, Rowenna," he said lightly.

"Oh, aye! I meant no disrespect, Bruce, truly."

"I didn't think you did, Rowenna."

"They'll be glad to see you. Daniel said something about wanting a blood sample from you."

"I assumed they'd want one. My veins are ready and waiting."

"They've machines going in there. They're doing an MRI or the like on her, trying to see what they can before cutting up what tissue they've got. Mind waiting?" Rowenna asked.

"Not at all."

As he sat, he noticed the day's paper, and the headline. Still No Clues To Missing Girl. He picked up the paper and quickly read the article. It rehashed old news, then made mention of some of the old cases being reopened. Cold-case detectives were bringing up cases from as far back as 1977, trying to ascertain similarities to current crimes. But before he could read further, Rowenna came back into the room.

"Could you go in, Bruce? There's a Dr. Holmes from

Edinburgh in with Daniel. She's an anthropologist, but qualified to stick needles in your arms, as well!" Rowenna said cheerfully.

"Aye, I'm happy to bleed for you all, Rowenna," he said, and tossing the paper back down, he went in to do just that.

"Will you look at this!" David said, pouncing as soon as Toni walked into the kitchen. He had the Edinburgh paper in his hand.

She glanced at the headline, then at David and Kevin. The two had been alone in the kitchen.

"They haven't anything new," she said, staring at the two.

"Read," Kevin advised her.

She arched a brow, then read as Kevin brought her a cup of coffee. She thanked him while trying to decipher what they were so excited about.

The article was mainly about new technology being used by detectives so they could go back to old cases. In 2002, the South Wales police had at last identified the murderer of three girls who had been killed back in 1973, using a Familial/Sibling Swabbing science technology.

There were sad statistics on the number of heinous crimes never solved, and then a reference to the work by police that could be attributed to their dedication and professionalism—something that science could never go without.

The article went on to talk about Laird Bruce MacNiall and his time with the Lothian and Borders Police. It described the victims and the horrors of their deaths, and it commended Bruce. She read on, stunned to discover that the brutal slayings had been committed by a husband and wife, and that, in that instance, an officer's insistence on following his gut instinct had led to the solving of the crimes.

She looked up at David and Kevin. They were both staring at her, waiting for a reaction.

"We knew he'd been with the police," she said.

"Did you read the whole thing?" David demanded.

"Most of it."

Kevin sighed. "You didn't read the last paragraph? At the time, he'd told his superiors that he'd 'gotten into the head' of the man! Thought like him...moved like him!"

She looked at both of them a bit blankly. "Okay, isn't that what FBI profilers say they have to do when they're trying to solve crimes?"

"It's scary! That's what it is," David said.

"David! The guy was a good cop!"

"So why did he leave?"

"I don't know. Maybe he didn't like being in the head of a serial killer!" she said.

"Or maybe..." Kevin murmured.

"Maybe what?"

"Maybe it was too much like his own," David said.

"Oh, please!" Toni said, tossing the paper down.

"He found the first body," Kevin said.

"And the second body was found in the forest, as well," David said.

"You're sick, both of you!" she accused them.

"Maybe," David murmured. He hesitated, looking at Kevin. "But...he's a local hero-type here, Toni. I mean, if he was up to something, everyone in this village would protect him. Maybe he doesn't even know he's a lunatic."

She stared hard at both of them, then tapped the paper angrily with drumming fingers. "It seems to me that he saved a number of young lives. And with very hard and painful work. Good Lord! He caught a *couple.* Can you imagine that, a husband and wife working together, luring innocent young victims!"

Unfortunately Ryan and Gina chose that precise moment to come walking cheerfully into the kitchen.

"'Morning, all!" Ryan said, then stopped dead, his expression quizzical as he realized that the three were staring at them.

"What are you all doing?" Gina demanded.

"Reading the paper," Toni said.

"Seems our host captured some really serious killers at one time," Kevin said.

"A married couple."

Gina turned to the three of them, outraged. "So you're looking at us as if…as if being married makes us guilty of something?"

"No, don't be ridiculous," Toni said.

"That would be damned ridiculous!" Ryan said. "What? Gay people never kill other people?" he demanded.

"Sure, they do," Kevin said calmly, grimacing. "Statistically, they kill other gay people."

Toni groaned. "Don't worry, the Keystone Cops here aren't after the two of you. They're convinced now that I have to be careful around Bruce."

"I was just thinking that maybe you shouldn't be quite so close to him," David said with a sigh.

"As in sleeping with him on a nightly basis," Kevin added.

"I thought that he was the one who *caught* the killers?" Gina said.

"He was," Toni said flatly.

Gina arched a brow and looked at David and Kevin.

David threw his hands up. "Look, what do we really know about this guy?"

"Oh, let's see!" Toni said. "He's rich, owns half the village. People here are very loyal to him. He was with the police. And he's been damned decent to us, since he could have thrown us all out on our butts!"

David looked down his nose at her. "My dear, Toni! We know that you're solidly infatuated with the man. But let me ask you this. If he's so rich, why does he own a ramshackle castle?"

She sighed. "You two, it's just silly to be so worried about this guy. All right, let me fill you all in on something, having to do with the state of the castle. He was engaged once to a woman who was in love with the place. It was her dream to fix it up again, make it magnificent. She died, and he lost heart. And that's why he's ignored it. It's probably why he still spends so much time out of the area, even out of the country."

"It sounds...reasonable," Gina said.

"Oh, yeah, I just about hear violins," Ryan murmured.

"Hey! That borders on the entirely insensitive!" David protested.

"How do we really know anything around here, though, especially when it comes to our host?" Gina murmured.

Kevin glanced at David and then at Toni. "You've got to admit, we really don't know much of anything. And then...well, you do see the guy with a sword in your nightmares."

Toni instantly stared at David. "You—you traitor! You weren't supposed to say anything about things I told you in confidence."

"I didn't! Well, of course, I talk to Kevin. Especially

when I'm really worried about you!" David said, defending himself.

She groaned.

"Now I really don't know what any of you are talking about!" Gina exclaimed.

Toni groaned again, laying her head on the table.

"Somebody better tell us," Ryan said.

Toni lifted her head, not about to let David do her explaining. "I've had some nightmares, very real nightmares, about the legendary Bruce coming back and standing at the foot of my bed with a sword, okay?" She glared at David. She didn't want anything else about her past spread any further than it had already gone.

"And see, there's the thing. Thayer told us about the old woman in the cemetery the other day," Kevin said softly.

"Now Thayer has a mouth on him, too!" Toni muttered.

"Oh, yeah! That's right!" Ryan said. He looked at Gina. "Remember? He was talking about how he and Toni had just met Lizzie and Trish, and then this weird old bat comes in with her son and daughter-in-law, and rambles about the old Bruce being up from his grave, running around the countryside, finding women and strangling them as he had his wife."

"Dammit!" Toni said. "We know now that the old Bruce didn't strangle his wife, one of his enemies did it."

"We don't *know* that for a fact," David said softly.

"Right. Before he gets chopped to minced meat himself, he asks his executioners for a woolen scarf so that he can kill her first?" Toni said sarcastically.

"No, but maybe he stole his enemy's scarf."

Toni threw her hands up. "You're being ridiculous," she told them. "I can't listen to this anymore!"

"Toni!" David said. "I'm sorry, honestly! I'm just afraid for you, that's all. Maybe you don't have to…to sleep with him. Well, sleep with him, but don't *sleep* with him. Not until we find out a little more about him."

She shook her head with disgust and exited the kitchen.

Bruce wound up staying far later than he had intended at Darrow's office; it was impossible not to do so. With a full team in tiny Tillingham, fascinated with the discovery of Annalise and armed with modern technology, he found himself involved. He looked at half a dozen scans, and was there when they painstakingly removed the ligature from around the throat of the remains. The scientists were fascinated with the quality of the weave; he couldn't help but remain pleased with the evidence suggesting that his ancestor had *not* been the one to murder his wife.

When he returned to the castle, it was afternoon. He looked in the kitchen and found David and Kevin working on costumes. They looked at him like a pair of cats that had just filled up on canaries. But when he questioned them, they both said that they were fine—a little too quickly—and went back to work, telling him that Ryan was probably out on Wallace somewhere and Gina was upstairs working with the numbers to find out just what it would take to get them out of the hole. Neither of them had seen either Thayer or Toni for hours.

He couldn't find Toni upstairs, so he headed out to the stables. Shaunessy greeted him with a whinny.

He heard someone working above him and backed away, trying to see who was in the rafters. Eban was there, studiously working hay piles.

"Ah, Laird MacNiall!"

With a smile, the funny little man dropped his rake and came down the ladder. He was agile and quick, dropping the last few feet as easily as a monkey.

"Afternoon, Eban," Bruce said.

Eban gave him a gamine's grin. "The roan is doing fine. I bin keepin' an eye on him, now, I'ave."

"Thank you, Eban."

"I bin thinking, y'see, that someone is walkin' round," Eban said gravely.

"Walking around?"

"There's them that say it's yer ancestor. Y'know, *the* MacNiall."

Bruce exhaled with patience. "Ah, Eban! The dead don't walk around."

"And they don't go making a healthy roan sick, either, so they'd say!" Eban muttered, shaking his head. "There's someone walkin', and that's a fact."

He set a hand on the man's shoulders. "Myth, Eban. Legend. Good stories for a dark night. If *the* MacNiall were about, don't you think he'd be pleased to see his castle so well tended?"

"As y'should ha' tended it all these years."

"Aye, Eban. True."

"She sees him, too, y'know. 'Tisn't just me, Laird MacNiall."

"She?" he asked.

Eban nodded gravely. "The lass, the American lass. A fellow such as me, I see it, I do. I see it in her eyes. She be one of the 'touched.'"

"Eban, you know I don't believe all that."

Eban grinned. "Believe or nae, what is, is. Anyway, I just wanted y'to know, the roan will be well. I'm watchin' now, I am."

"Thank you, Eban. You do good work."

"Ach, Laird MacNiall! Like the days of old. Y'give me a home. A place. Others might not ha' been so kind. And I know it." With his strange little smile in place, he started back for the ladder. "'Tis like the days of old. Whether the eyes see or not, what is, is," he said, shaking his head as he went back up to the rafters.

A noise at the door alerted Bruce to the fact that someone was coming into the stables. He turned quickly. Thayer.

He felt his mouth tighten and his muscles tense. He might have refused to let Jonathan see any of his concerns regarding the man, but he felt them, just as he had from the beginning. He didn't think it was ego to wonder how the man could have lived in Glasgow and never heard his name—or known that he existed. And if he had been living with his head in a pint, he should still have known something once he heard the name of the property his group was renting.

"Bruce, you're back," Thayer said.

"Aye."

Thayer looked uncomfortable. He hadn't expected to come here and find his host.

"Well, I was just going to look in on the roan," Thayer said.

"He isn't here. Ryan must have taken him out. But actually, I'm glad you've come. I've gotten some news. I thought I should share it with you first." He meant to take grave care with just what words and what information he "shared."

"Oh, aye?" Thayer said carefully, hovering in the doorway, as if he could make a quick escape.

"They've traced the origins of the Web site that advertised this castle," Bruce said.

"Aye?"

The man looked as tense as a drawn bow.

"Glasgow."

"Glasgow?"

Bruce nodded, watching the man.

Thayer shrugged. "Well, then. That would explain a bit of it."

"What do you mean?"

"Well, there were advertisements about, as well. Flyers in a few local pubs, you know, like broadsides on walls, at bus stops, I think."

"Ah," Bruce said.

"I'm glad. I hope like bloody hell they catch the bloke," Thayer said, staring straight at Bruce.

Actors. It was a crowd of actors, Bruce told himself.

Thayer frowned suddenly. "Ryan isn't out with the horse," he said. "At least, I don't think, anyway. I saw him upstairs in his room, talking with his wife, not twenty minutes past."

"The horse is gone," Bruce said, frowning, as well. Then he realized that Toni had the horse out, and an unreasoning sense of panic set into him.

Thayer, too, seemed alarmed for reasons of his own. "Toni!" he said.

"I'll find her," Bruce told him, already turning to lead Shaunessy from his stall.

With landscape and terrain this beautiful, Toni wasn't sure why she hadn't been out riding before now.

One benefit to growing up in rural Maryland had been the little pinto her father had bought her. But as an adult working in the city, she'd had to leave Barto, now twenty-two, with her old neighbors. It was good for Barto, though. He was hardly ever saddled, was loved like an old dog, and given the best of everything.

She seldom saw him, and with the move to Scotland, she had given up the idea of ownership altogether, and given him to the Andersons' granddaughter. He was a gentle soul by then, just right for a child, as she had been.

Wallace was definitely a fine fellow, heavy enough for Ryan with his armor and weapons, and still sleek enough for a good ride. Whatever had ailed him, his recovery had been all but miraculous. He wasn't just glad to be out; he was feeling his oats.

Her mood had been angry and wild, so she hadn't bothered with a saddle. She'd just slipped the bit into his mouth, the bridle over his head, and chosen a path down the hill. There was plenty of countryside. Beautiful spaces. They passed slope after slope, scattering a few sheep as they raced along, but the longhaired cows they passed didn't seem to mind.

She wasn't sure how far she'd gone when she noticed that a white car marked Tillingham Constabulary was parked by a fence. Curious, she rode in that direction, and saw Jonathan out in the field. He appeared to be inspecting one of the sheep.

Nudging Wallace, she rode down the little slope that led to the valley where the car was parked. Jonathan heard the horse, looked up, released the sheep and dusted his hands on his uniform pants as he walked toward the fence, calling out a cheerful greeting. "Aye, now, lass, good t'see you. That is the way to really enjoy this countryside," he told her.

"Hello! And, yes, it's really beautiful. How are you?" she asked him.

"Well and fine enough, Miss Fraser. So…all is working well for you? Your friends were in, you know. And though I've not the resources of the big department, we are working hard for you, through the folks that know their business. I just told Bruce this morning, they've traced the site on the Web page to Glasgow."

"Really? I haven't seen Bruce today," she told him. "Glasgow," she repeated. "I'm delighted, naturally, and grateful that they've traced it so far already, but I suppose they'll need to learn much more to actually catch someone."

"Aye, Glasgow," he said. She thought that he was looking at her strangely, as if that should mean something.

"It's a very big city," she murmured.

"Aye, that it is." He was still staring at her strangely.

"I'm sorry, should that fact mean something to me?" she asked him.

"Your cousin is from Glasgow," he reminded her.

She instantly felt defensive bristles grow up around her. "It's a very big city," she reminded him.

What was it today? Was there something in the water? People attacking everyone who meant something to her?

"You're right," he acknowledged. "A very big city. I just thought that you wanted the truth. No matter what the truth may be."

"We do want the truth. Sorry, I didn't mean to bark. But I don't think the fact that something originated in Glasgow is any aspersion on Thayer at all. That would be like me being guilty of something because it happened near Washington, D.C."

"D.C. is much bigger than Glasgow," he said with a rueful grin.

"Still the point," she said.

"And well taken," he told her gravely.

"Well, I do thank you. Very much."

"You're quite welcome, but it is my job to uphold the law, even if it falls into unfamiliar realms. We've good police here in the old country, y'know. I feel somewhat guilty, I do. I should have known, before your group put the work into the place, that he'd have never rented out the place. But then, he hadna' been about himself for some time, so…it would be his right to do it, had he chosen."

"Please, there's nothing for you to feel guilty about. And actually, he's been quite wonderful."

Jonathan glanced down. "Oh, aye, the fellow is… magnanimous, isn't he?" he queried, looking back up at her.

She nodded, not wanting to go any further in that vein. "Are these your sheep?"

"Aye, that they are."

"You've beautiful land."

"Well, quite frankly, it's not my land. But I pasture here. Heard there's been some trouble with that roan there, but he looks fine to me. I thought I'd be wise to take a look at these fellows and lasses, assure myself nothing was getting into the herds."

"He's fine. The vet said he must have gotten into something, but he's come through just great. Like a little boy with a bellyache who'd eaten too much candy, I guess," Toni said.

"Well, you're right, must have been something… Anyway, the sheep look fine and healthy, too, lass. I guess I'd best be getting back into town."

"It was nice to see you!" Toni told him.

"Enjoy your ride!" He waved and started toward his car. Toni headed Wallace back up a slope. He seemed to want to run again.

She let him do so, mulling over her encounter with

the constable. On the one hand, it seemed that he did want to do what he could for them. But on the other hand…he seemed more concerned with how their business affected him. The foreigners have a sick horse, so he checks *his* sheep?

Then, of course, there was that ridiculous conversation she'd had with the others back at the castle, and… there was the ghost. A ghost that should be happy now! A ghost who kept appearing at the foot of her bed.

She leaned low against Wallace, and let the wind rip by her. She wanted *not* to think for a while.

She didn't know how long she traveled the hills and valleys before she realized that, even if Wallace was feeling frisky, she might well be pushing him too hard. After all, they'd had to send for a vet to see him twice in the past week. Patting his neck, she slowed him down, leaped off for a moment and came around to take a good look at his eyes.

He stared back at her and snorted, sending a sneeze and some mouth foam flying over her. "Wallace!" she chastised him. "Ugh! How could you do that to me? There are times when you *should* do it to Ryan, but I'm your friend. I think I am, anyway. You need a drink. Well, we should walk a bit and then get you a drink."

She looked around, trying to ascertain where she was, then wondering how on earth she could have turned herself around so badly. Although she could still see sheep, there was no sign of a house, a cottage or even a road.

Listening, though, she could hear the bubble of a brook. It was to the right, through a field of trees—and the path—a great canopy of trees arced over pine needles— looked inviting. "We'll wander in and find the water, eh, boy?" she asked, rubbing his nose.

As he tended to do—with true love and affection, she was certain—he nosed her in the chest, gently prodding her, as if he understood her words.

Plenty of light dappled through the trees. The shadows and patterns that fell around the trees and bushes were quite beautiful. The trails seemed broad and well used, yet when she followed the sound of the water and came to it at last, she felt like a fool.

"You know what? We're back in *the* forest."

It was all right. She definitely hadn't come that far, walking the horse. All she had to do was retrace her steps. She wasn't frightened, and she wasn't even worried. When Wallace had drunk his fill, she'd start back. But just when the horse lifted his head, the rain came.

"Son of a bitch!" she swore out loud, drawing a snort from Wallace.

It wasn't the rain. She didn't care much about getting wet. But the air was cold, and she hadn't set out with any kind of jacket, waterproof or otherwise.

"You know, it rains a lot here!" she told the horse, angry with herself for not being better prepared. But she'd left the house angry and disturbed, and decided on taking a ride on the spur of the moment.

In seconds, she was soaked. And what had been light and beautiful was now gray and...murky.

She determined to go back the way she had come. It should have been easy, but it wasn't. In a matter of minutes, she was entangled in the trees.

She looked at Wallace. Surely, it was close to feeding time. If she just gave the horse his head, he'd take her home.

"It's up to you, buddy," she said.

By the time she had leaped up on his back, making three attempts—because of the slickness, she told herself, not a lack of coordination—the rain had slackened. But the gray and the murk remained, and there was a low ground fog, as well. The whole atmosphere was…creepy.

"No!" she said aloud. Because now, she was feeling the eyes again, the eyes of the forest, watching her.

"Home, Wallace!" she said out loud, hoping the words would dispel the sense of eeriness that had crept around her. She *was* being ridiculous. These were *trees,* for God's sake! Trees, bushes, natural bark, leaves, the sound of rushing water…

Given free rein, Wallace simply stood dead still.

"Traitor!" she told him.

He whinnied and shifted weight from hoof to hoof.

"What kind of a horse are you? You're supposed to know the way back to the barn!"

The eyes…she could feel them.

"All right, forget it," she said, and gathered up the reins. She didn't know how far it would be, but since there was only one forest, she could hope there was only one stream. She'd follow it out.

The water was very shallow. She led the horse straight through it, then along the embankment when it deepened. She tried whistling, but she couldn't keep her lips wet enough. And as she rose, she fought a sense of sheer panic that could do her no good. But images kept floating before her mind. A picture of a man, a warrior, a Cavalier, in armor, kilted, dirty, worn, tired… A sword that dripped blood in his hand. The same man, standing before the hearth, watching the flames, then beckoning her down into the crypts.

Yesterday. The voice on the phone. The word *medium.*

She gritted her teeth. She was not some kind of a

vessel for horrid messages about things that she could not change or see through! Unlike the girl on the phone, she had no desire to see lots of ghosts!

She bit into her lower lip. The rain had stopped completely, but the mist continued to rise from the forest floor. She was soaked to the bone, completely chilled. And she continued to feel watched. *Stalked*.

Each time she hesitated and looked around, she saw nothing. The forest was big. Hadn't she heard many people say that? She glanced at her watch, again, seeking a sense of normalcy in the action. Yes, the forest must be very big. She'd been following the stream, she estimated, for nearly two hours, and suddenly realized that she wasn't just stiff, she was in agony.

She turned, setting a hand on the horse's rump, trying to see anything that she could behind her. Any movement. But all she saw was the fall of shadows.

"Hurry it up a bit, shall we?" she murmured.

They trotted forward, and when she looked back, the feeling that a darkness followed her, reaching out, started to recede.

Finally she could take it no more. She had to stretch, change her position. It might have been a nice day to choose to take a saddle, she reflected, but it was too late for that, far too late.

"Whoa, boy," she told Wallace, reining in lightly. She looked behind her uneasily, thinking that if she saw anything, anything at all, she could turn, slam her knees against Wallace and race away. But there was nothing, just the coming darkness.

She needed a quick moment's rest, then she needed to move again. So she slid from Wallace's back, wincing slightly. She walked a few steps, stretching. "I guess it is a big forest, if troops, outlawed by the powers that be, used to hide in here," she murmured. She led Wallace over to a large oak set up on a little hillock of grass, just above the stream, and sat down, leaning against the tree, ruing her stupidity.

"Wallace," she said, "you really aren't much help."

Still, she was very glad of the horse. He seemed to be her link to reality, to normalcy.

Tired, she closed her eyes for a minute. When she opened them, Wallace suddenly lifted his head, his ears pricking as he stared off toward her left. The horse was still, yet it appeared that his flanks were trembling. He snorted. She stared at him curiously, the animal's fear snaking into her, and realized, too late, that he was about to bolt.

With another snort, he did so, leaping forward like a show jumper. The reins, held too loosely in her one hand, snapped free from her hold in seconds.

She leaped to her feet. "Wallace!" she cried angrily. Then she fell silent, aware that the animal had run because something had frightened him. She stood very still, feeling the odd awareness, the *fear,* which the animal had passed onto her.

She listened. She could still hear the echo of the horse's hoofbeats. And then…the cry of a bird. And then…a rustling.

From somewhere far away, the faint wail of a bagpipe sounded, but not loud enough to dampen the sound of twigs snapping. Someone was near.

She moved against the oak. Then…she could see a figure, a man with a dark tam, his head down. He wore an old suede jacket.

She stayed still, not daring to breathe. But a sound of surprise came to her throat as the man stopped, dusted dirt from his hands onto his pants and looked around. She saw his face clearly. It was Eban.

Call out! He'll get you home, she told herself. But something warned her to remain still. *What had he been doing in the forest? Burying the remains of some poor girl? Was that why his hands were dirtied?*

No, stop! She told herself. She was being cruel, judging when she shouldn't judge.

But no sound would come to her lips. She remained quiet. Only when he was gone—gone, way past her—did she start walking again, following the stream. After a minute, she quickened her pace. If she'd seen Eban, she had to be close to the castle.

"Toni!" she heard her name called. There was thrashing ahead of her. Someone was in the forest, looking for her.

"To-ni!"

"Here!" she called out.

"Toni!"

That time, the sound of her name seemed to come from behind her. The voices, she realized, looking around, could have been coming from anywhere, she was so disorganized. She started to run, directly in the stream, which was shallow enough here. Water kicked up around her. It didn't matter in the least.

"Here!" she cried again, then paused suddenly, startled. The light was bad, very bad. The silver mist still lay close to the ground. But ahead of her, maybe thirty, forty feet, there seemed to be something in the water. She blinked, looking that way.

There was a thrashing sound ahead of her.

No, behind her...

She started to turn.

She saw the branch...

Saw it, tried to turn from it…
And went down, her skull filling with pain.
Her vision filling with the mist…
And then darkness.
And something else.

Interlude

Grayson Davis's man had Annalise by the hair, dragging her into the copse. She did not come easily.

Bruce's heart cried out as she was thrown down upon the ground, a cry wrung from her lips as she went to her knees where she was cast, sliding until she came to a stop before Davis. *Ah, and there she is, yer lady, Laird MacNiall. Filled with foolish pride, as ye would be. Ach! Y'd thought y'd bought her time, out of the forest, eh? Nae, foolish fellow. So now it is time fer heroes and legends to die, and fer rich men to die poor.*

Her eyes met his. He pleaded with her silently, begged his forgiveness. *Do whatever he asks. Live. The day will come when you will be set free...*

She smiled at him and shook her head slowly.

"Annalise!" Her name was a cry of anguish.

Grayson Davis swaggered before him, gripped Annalise by the elbows and pulled her up to face him. "Ah,

Annalise. We have come to a moment of truth. Will it be the laird there, half-dead as we speak, with none but torture ahead, or…they can take you from the forest before it begins. You can await me."

"Obey him!" Bruce pleaded. "Before God, obey him!"

She looked at Davis, as if weighing his words. She had never appeared more beautiful, proud or elegant, despite the mud caking her clothing, the scratches upon her cheeks, the wildness of her hair.

She seemed to deliberate long and carefully, then she looked back at Bruce and smiled again, a slow, sweet, wistful smile.

"Time, my love. Time will tell the tale," she said. Then she spit in Grayson Davis's face.

He struck her. Bruce roared with rage, but to no avail. The force of the blow sent Annalise down again, but her head remained high.

"Bitch!"

She smiled, eyes even, leveled upon him.

"Y're judged! He is judged. Condemned."

She shook her head. "Ah, Grayson, what a fool. There is a far greater judge. And my laird husband and I can truly be judged in His eyes alone."

"Not on this earth. Not on this earth! You had your chance!"

"And chose not to take it."

"Annalise!" Bruce cried again.

But her eyes, her steady gaze, had been the last straw against Davis's temper. He wrenched the colors from around his shoulders and drew them around Annalise's neck. Her fair neck. Slender, graceful, delicate…

"Nae!" The great MacNiall, humbled, hung back his head, bitterly fighting the arms that held him, nearly fighting off the men. He watched as she gasped, choked, shuddered, jerked…death brutal despite pride. He struggled free from the arms that held him. He raced forward, then staggered in the mud, almost reaching her.

An ax had landed in his back.

But he did not die. Not quickly enough. He saw as Grayson Davis picked up his wife, limp as a cloth doll, and cast her facedown into the stream. He cried out in anguish and in rage, saw the blood before his own eyes…

"Fool! Who put that ax into him? He mustn't die, not yet!" Davis commanded. He walked to where Bruce had fallen at last, arms outstretched in the mud. He rolled him, forcing the blade more deeply into him, relishing his enemy's anguish.

"First, castration. I want you to live for that! Then yer innards, great laird! Set to blaze before yer eyes. Eventually…yer head. And if y're living then, I'll see that the blade is dull and moves slow."

He stared at Davis, shaking his head. "It matters not what y'do to kill me. I am already dead. And yet, I will live, Davis, fer y're cursed now, and I will live to see you fall!"

"Cut him!" Davis roared.

Mercifully, the ax had done its damage.

The great MacNiall stared into the trees as the blood blurred his vision. But in his mind, his heart, he was with her already.

Chapter 16

Bruce was deep into the forest when he heard a heavy thrashing.

"Toni?" he called.

From a deep thicket, the noise continued, as if someone was hurrying toward him. He reined in on Shaunessy and waited, watching the area of lush growth. The green waved and jiggled. And the roan, Wallace, appeared. Riderless.

He quickly dismounted from Shaunessy, hurrying over to the roan. There was a scratch on his nose, but that had most probably come from a brush with a branch. The horse seemed all right, just spooked.

"Did you throw her, boy? Did you throw Toni?"

He shook his head, looking in the direction from which the horse had come. Toni could be out there, unconscious, bleeding. He gauged the direction; she'd been trying to follow the stream.

"Go on home, boy. Go on home," he said, giving the horse a sound smack on the rump.

Quickly remounting Shaunessy, he drove through the thicket at the spot where Wallace had just appeared. An overgrown, slender trail brought him back to the embankment.

"Toni!"

He felt his sense of panic rising. Nudging his horse's flanks, he quickened his pace, mindful of the rocks, stones and slippery embankment.

Ahead, he could see that the mist was still high over the bubbling water. He reined in, eyes narrowing. There seemed to have been a shadow moving through the mist. A shadow…in human form. Then he heard the sound of a grunt.

"Toni!"

Dismounting from Shaunessy, he hurried on foot through the mist and water.

"Toni!"

He heard a soft groan. Then…

"Toni? Bruce?"

Disappointment, dismay, washed over him. Thayer. Thayer was ahead of him. Still, he kept going. "Aye, I'm here. Toni!"

The mist still lay before him. And the water.

He suddenly saw her, saw her…as he had seen the body of the dead girl. Facedown in the water. Long trails of blond hair no longer lustrous, but caked in mud and grass and tangled with twigs.

No! That was only in his mind's eye, a remnant of a dream.

"Toni!" His voice ricocheted through the woods, vibrant, loud.

"Bruce?"

Her voice was barely discernible in the rush of water and whisper of breeze.

"Where are you?" he cried.

"Toni!" From somewhere, he could hear Thayer's voice, as well.

And then he saw her. She was seated on a fallen log, drawing back sodden tendrils of her hair.

She wasn't facedown in the water. She was seated, alive and well. A bit bedraggled, nothing more.

He let out his breath in a rush of relief. His knees were weak, and his voice came out like crackling thunder. "Toni!"

Then, just seconds after he had seen Toni, Thayer came crashing through the brush from the opposite direction. Seeing Toni, and then Bruce, he, too, went still.

"Toni!" he breathed.

She rose, distracted, offering Bruce a weak smile and then a quick defense. "Bruce!" She turned. "And Thayer. Thank God. And wait, please, no one yell! I probably should have spent some time riding with someone else before taking old Wallace out on my own. I didn't come into the forest on purpose. I wound up riding some fields on the other side and didn't know where I was. Then it started to rain, as you can see," she put in wryly. "Actually, I think I would have made it out eventually, except that Wallace decided to desert me, and I walked smack into a major branch over there, and..." She was looking from one of them to the other. "Hey! Bless you both, thanks for coming!" She gave Thayer a quick hug first, then turned to Bruce, a question in her eyes.

He reached for her. She came into his arms. He felt the air wrap around them, and felt the chill in her body.

"Let's just go back now, eh?" he said. Then he drew away, looking at her. She was somehow reserved, despite the look she had given him and the way she had melded to him.

"You're really fine?" Bruce said.

"Nothing happened?" Thayer asked.

She looked at them both and shook her head solemnly.

"The horse didn't throw you?" Bruce demanded.

"Wallace? No, Wallace is a love. I was off of him, stretching." She winced. "I haven't been riding in a while, I guess. Didn't bother with a saddle, so... Did you see him? Is he all right?"

"He's on his way back to the stables now, I'm pretty certain," Bruce said.

"Well, that's what I assumed he'd do in the first place!" Toni said. She pressed her fingers against her temple. "I think I need some aspirin."

"Let's get back," Bruce said anxiously. "Come here, I'll lift you up on Shaunessy."

"No, no, that's all right," she said, flashing a smile toward Thayer. "We'll all walk out together."

"Toni, I can get out on m'own," Thayer assured her. "But you're soaked!"

"As I have been for hours," she said lightly, then added firmly, "We'll walk out, all together."

For a moment, she thought that Bruce toyed with the idea of arguing with her, even taking a medieval stance and simply throwing her over Shaunessy's haunches.

It wasn't a matter of the total political incorrectness of such a gesture that stopped him; it was Thayer. He was hesitant about leaving the man behind, when, despite her words, there was something strange about Toni, about the way she had been sitting on the rock, and the way she had touched her forehead.

"Fine. We all walk out together," he said. "I'll just lead Shaunessy."

As they started back, he pulled off his jacket and set it around her shoulders. She flashed him a smile of gratitude.

"Darkness is coming quickly," she murmured.

"And the buses soon, too soon," Thayer murmured. He looked at her. "You should rest. Gina can take on being you tonight. You could wind up with your death of a cold."

"I feel fine," she assured him.

"He may be right," Bruce said.

"When I'm not fine, Gina can run around like a madwoman. Right now, I'm fine." She glanced at him, her smile sweetly suggestive, her tone specifically for him. "Absolutely nothing that a hot bubble bath can't take care of."

"Ach, do I have to hear this?" Thayer demanded.

Toni laughed. "And I thought I was being so subtle." She stumbled slightly; the terrain wasn't level as they followed the brook. The rain had left exposed roots, and flooded some of the embankment.

"Man, this is quite a place!" Thayer murmured. "The friggin' forest primeval!"

"Aye, that's why people should stay out of it," Bruce said. He glanced at Thayer. "I'm amazed that you stumbled upon Toni as I did…and as quickly," he added, watching the man's reaction.

"So am I. I thought I was lost myself," Thayer said. He pushed a tree branch out of the way for the others to precede him.

"Look how quickly it gets dark in here!" Toni marveled. "Seriously, thank you both so very much for looking for me. I think I would have made it eventually, but I'm awfully darned glad not to be here alone, now."

"Aw, shucks!" Thayer teased.

Minutes later, they'd broken through, reached the bottom of the hill and were on their way up. The others were waiting anxiously by the stables. Ryan had Wallace by the reins.

"Toni!" Gina came rushing down the hill, hugging Toni, then drawing away. "Ugh! You're soaked."

"Toni!" Ryan was right behind Gina, hugging Toni, as well, then demanding to know, "What did you do to Wallace?"

"What did I do to Wallace?" Toni demanded. "He deserted me!"

Ryan looked from her to the horse. "Wallace! Shame on you." He looked back, glancing anxiously at Bruce. "Really, what the hell were you doing?"

"Getting lost, nothing more. And I'm fine," Toni told them.

David and Kevin were both there now, looking at Toni worriedly.

"I'll make tea," Kevin said.

"With a shot of something," David said.

"We have about an hour before the buses show," Gina said, sounding very much like the business manager. "So we need to hop to it." She glanced at Bruce and swallowed a little uneasily. "Um... Bruce, are you still willing to play this with us?"

"Who else could better do the old great MacNiall?" he asked her, allowing his own accent a practiced strength.

"I'm going up," Toni said, and she flashed him another quick glance that was almost a question. Was he going to follow?

Oh, aye, beyond a doubt!

As if on cue, Eban came striding out from the barn. "Eh, Bruce, shall I be taking Shaunessy, setting him up for his grand entrance?"

"Aye, Eban, thank you."

"Well, Wallace, I'll be cleaning you up a bit!" Ryan said.

Bruce left them and walked toward the entrance, aware that they watched him in silence as he departed.

Toni sat in the tub, simply glad of the steaming water that soaked into her, pure bliss after the hours of cold. But her mind was racing. *I'm on overload!* she told herself.

So much had happened, yet no matter how hard she tried to recall those moments in the forest, she couldn't. Something had struck her. When she'd risen after falling, she'd thought she hit a tree branch.

But had she? Because it had happened right after she had seen…something. Something ahead of her in the water, gone when she had found her seat on the rock, gone when they had walked back following the stream.

Then there was the time—seconds, minutes, longer?— she had been out. Knocked out or just…out. Seeing a picture of the past, coming alive in the forest. She'd seen… Annalise, on her knees. Bruce, shouting, raging, straining, anguish written into his features.

And in the vision, she had been screaming herself, just as she had when she'd been a child. She'd been so desperate not to see more, praying, *Please, God, don't let me see the execution…*

There she was, half in the water, half out, her temple killing her and the rock before her. And as she found her footing and then sat, she heard Bruce and Thayer again, calling to her. The forest had been as it was, trees, pine carpet, bubbling, beautiful brook.

"I'm losing my mind!" she whispered aloud to herself. But she wasn't. And she remembered the woman's voice over the phone. *Medium. She was an incredible medium.*

No!

But she knew that denying something couldn't make it change. Maybe she had put it all past her for years and years, so far behind her that she'd never expected to know that kind of sensation again, that kind of fear. And yet, if she just accepted some of it, would the fear recede?

I talk to lots of ghosts, the woman had told her.

There was a tap; the bathroom door opened. Bruce came in, hair damp and raven-dark, features taut and concerned, chin hard-squared, eyes slate and sharp. For a moment, she saw the distant MacNiall, saw him as she had in the very strange interlude amidst a field of trees. The ferocity, the rage…and the undying devotion he'd given his Annalise.

She bit into her lower lip, watching him, and the warmth of the water was nothing compared to the searing tempest she felt when he was near. She started to rise from the water very slowly, stepping from the top, coming to him.

"Lass, you've been soaked. A bad day…"

"Then make it better," she whispered.

He cocked his head slightly. "There's not much time."

"Then we'd best use it well."

He wrapped his arms around her. For a moment, he held her tight, her frame taut to his. She felt the changes. And yet…it was as if he waited, waited to know what she really needed.

And then…he gave it to her. All that she wanted. A total abandonment of thought and worry, fears and visions. Reality, flesh, the senses…the feel of his hands and lips, body heat emanated, damp and slick, pure physicality, grinding, meshing. She had the longing again to crawl into his skin; they couldn't be close enough. And then those seconds of total constriction, the soaring, the touch of Elysian fields.

The man at her side was real, flesh and blood.

He stroked her hair for a moment, pulled her closer.

"The chill is gone?"

"I could never feel the slightest chill with you," she told him.

"It's not my show, you know," he reminded her gently, "but your buses are coming."

"I know," she said, but didn't stir. She waited a moment, thinking there was a tension about him, that he was about to say something. But he didn't.

So she did.

"I saw…what happened, in the past. Today, in the forest."

"What?" She felt his withdrawal, just slight and not physical.

She rose on an elbow, looking into his eyes. "I really didn't mean to be in the forest. I was furious with myself for being lost, but I was doing all right, except that that traitorous horse spooked at something and took off on me. Still, I was all right. I think I heard your voice first, maybe Thayer's, too. I turned to find you… and smacked into a branch. I saw stars, mist, darkness. Then—I know how this sounds—but it was as if I was back in time. Bruce, it was vividly real. There were these men, so many of them, and they had your ancestor. They dragged in Annalise, and the fellow strangled her there, in front of him. He broke free, but someone threw an ax, and he fell. They were about to do other things, but then I heard your voice."

He was staring at her as if she were stark raving mad. *Well, what the hell had she expected?*

"So you did bump your head!"

She sighed. "Bruce—"

"A conk on your head, and you...dreamed."

"No! That wasn't it."

"I knew you'd hurt yourself, the way you kept feeling your forehead," he murmured, thumb on her cheek then, shifting her head, looking for damage.

"Bruce—"

"My ancestor is not a ghost, a presence, ranging the forest, looking for victims!" he told her.

"I never said that—"

"Toni, you're dreaming, and that's all."

She turned away from him, rising, heading back to her own room.

He followed her. "Toni! Don't be angry with me. I'm trying to help you," he said, following quickly behind her.

She had the bathroom door halfway shut, but he stopped it from closing.

"Excuse me," she said coolly, "did you want the bathroom first?"

"I want you to listen to me!" he said. "Toni, suppose there was...a ghost. We all know that history was tragic. Okay, he led you to a tomb. He wants Annalise in it. So, we'll get her in it. I was at the autopsy today and I made it very clear that once my blood proves her my ancestress, I want her back. She'll lie in the tomb next to the great MacNiall. So why would this ghost still be haunting you?"

"He wasn't haunting me. He was showing me what happened."

"Why?"

"So that we know."

"Once they found the scarf, the truth was fairly evident."

"Maybe he just wanted the full story known. Bruce! It tore my heart out, really. When he was threatened, it didn't matter. He said that he was already dead, because his Annalise was gone. And he said something about vengeance, even though he was half-dead already."

"Dead men don't find vengeance, Toni."

"Damn you, I was glad that I saw it! I wasn't afraid in the forest then."

"You should be afraid in the damned forest. Someone—who isn't a ghost!—is killing women and discarding them there," he said. "Toni, your imagination is very vivid—"

"Do you know what?" she interrupted. "You're right. It's late. It's always your own business if you care to join us or not, but I owe a lot to this group. It is time I got ready."

"Toni—"

"If you're going to mock what I'm saying, or tell me that my imagination is too vivid, or that I'm losing a grip on sanity, you can just let it wait. Now, we do need to be ready. I repeat, did you want the bathroom first? It is your castle and your bathroom."

He didn't reply, but he closed the door sharply on her.

Toni winced at the anger she felt from him. Gritting her teeth, she turned the water on high and stepped into the shower, letting it cascade quickly over her. *Never! She was never sharing any of this with anyone, ever, ever again!*

* * *

Once again, his castle was full. Standing outside with Shaunessy, decked out for their grand entrance, Bruce looked at the tour buses with amazement. He'd have never believed that people would flock out like this—and pay the price charged—for a living history tour. But they did.

It still made him uneasy. But then, it had been a long time since he hadn't been uneasy, with regard to the castle—and the forest.

Shaunessy pawed the ground, as if he, too, was anxious to be at it, and over it.

"Hey!" Ryan came from the stables, leading Wallace. "I'm sure we've told you, but it really is damned decent of you to let us do this—and to pitch in." He cleared his throat. "We should probably do a legal contract with you, though. I mean, you didn't get the money, so we do owe you, but we can't pay you unless we're making it. Which we are. Gina has been meaning to talk to you. She just hasn't had the chance." He smiled awkwardly.

Bruce understood. Aye, he was helping them. But then, it was his property, wasn't it? And he could change his mind at any time.

"I'm sure we can work something out," he told Ryan.

Ryan let out a sigh. "I was so afraid I'd offend you," he murmured.

"I'm not offended."

"Good, thanks." Ryan inhaled deeply again. "I'm just thanking God old Wallace here has come through okay. If we'd lost our money on the castle, and then on the horse, too…well, it would almost seem as if someone was out there to get us!"

"Aye, it would, wouldn't it?" Bruce murmured.

A white flag was suddenly waved out the doorway.

"My cue," Bruce murmured.

"Go for it, man," Ryan said.

And he did.

There was always a fine line between acting and truth, he thought, as he played out the role, mounting the steps in a fury. Her words were right, her plea, brilliant. A pin could have been heard dropping from below. But her eyes… Aye, she was pleading all right. And she was still furious. He suddenly felt a great weight around his shoulders. He was sick to death of the myth and legend surrounding his ancestor, because it would start up all the rot about Bruce MacNiall roaming the forest. And since he and his ancestor were supposedly spitting images of one another, there would be those who stared at him, superstitious, thinking that the sins of the past were coming alive through him.

Except that she hadn't been unfaithful. And the great MacNiall hadn't killed her.

Staring down into Toni's eyes, re-creating history, he wondered if it had been like this. Had Annalise looked up at her husband all those years ago with eyes this blue…challenging and angry?

Ryan made his entrance then and they went into their mock battle. Soon, the tour group was moving on into the kitchen. Ryan, deeply pleased, clamped a hand with Bruce's. "Damned, but we're good. And we still haven't had a chance to choreograph anything. Toni," he said, looking up the stairs, "weren't we phenomenal?"

"Absolutely," she said, but she was hurrying toward the kitchen. "Big group. I'm going to give the boys a hand."

"She pissed at you or something?" Ryan asked Bruce. He shrugged. "You can tell?"

Ryan grinned. "I know Toni. Actually, I thought you

were going to be angry with her. For being in the forest again, I mean." He was studying Bruce's face intently.

"The remains of two murdered women have been found in those woods," Bruce said.

"Three, if you include your ancestress. She was murdered, too. Why, I'll bet you the place is full of bodies, considering the history here! Oh, man, sorry. I mean, I hope it doesn't have any more bodies."

"Thanks, Ryan. I hope it doesn't, either," he said. "I'm going to take old Shaunessy out and put him up for the night. Then I'm to bed. You can tell the others good-night for me, all right?"

"Yeah, sure. And thanks."

He departed, anxious to have his horse bedded down and himself upstairs before the tour group began filing out. He wasn't much in the mood to be pleasant to strangers.

In his room, he started a fire, stripped down and stretched out in his bed, lacing his fingers behind his head as he watched the logs catch.

Should he relent? Just say, I've had a few moments like that myself. It's all right. Hell, no! He'd never seen his ancestor prowling the place.

She was getting too carried away. It was dangerous. There were bad things happening, really bad things. Ryan's words came back to him—*It was almost as if someone wanted them all to go down*—and then his conversation with Jonathan Tavish that day.

Glasgow. It had all originated out of Glasgow. And Thayer was from Glasgow. Thayer had been in the forest. Helping him find Toni? Or trying to make sure that he didn't find someone—or something—else?

Toni had noted the couple in their tour group right away, simply because they were so attractive. She looked like she belonged on the cover of a magazine, and he was the tall, rugged-looking sort who could have walked through a Western and been instantly perceived as the real thing. And though they walked the tour with the others, there was something about them that struck Toni.

So she wasn't at all surprised when the woman followed behind and stopped her, catching up with Toni at the bottom of the stairs as she tried to make her escape.

"Toni!"

"I'm sorry, but if you'll excuse me, the others will help you. I had a—er—fall today, and I've got a terrific headache," Toni said, eager to keep going.

"I'm Darcy," the woman said.

"Darcy?" Even as she repeated the name, Toni knew who the woman was. Dismay filled her.

"Darcy Stone, we talked on the phone—"

"I know who you are!" Toni said, shaking her head. "But I told you not to come here!" Despite herself, she looked around. All she needed now was to have Bruce think that she was going to fill his castle with ghost hunters!

"I know. And please don't worry—we've not let anyone know who we are."

"We!" Toni gasped.

"Just me and my husband."

"Look, I'm certain you went through tremendous trouble and expense to get here, but I can't… You can't be here!"

"We've taken a little rental cottage in the village. Adam tried to reach you himself, but he wasn't able to get through. He's eager to talk to you. He's also afraid that things may be very serious if you've actually tried to reach him. So…here we are. It wasn't really such a bad trip. We made it in this morning."

She had a level tone, a sweet smile and a certain down-to-earth manner that belied her sophisticated looks.

"There is a presence here," she said.

Toni stiffened.

"Look, I'm leaving. But, please, I'm certain you need to talk to someone."

"I can't talk to you here, now," Toni said.

"I understand. Can we meet?"

Tourists would be pouring out from the kitchen at any minute. "Lunch, tomorrow," Toni said. "There's a pub at the bottom of the hill in the village. You can't miss it. Meet me there, say, one o'clock? And if anyone asks, I'll tell you frankly, I intend to lie. You're someone I met in the States."

"I did see you do Queen Varina," Darcy said with a smile. She glanced over her shoulder, aware they were going to be interrupted any moment. "Please, don't stand me up. Honest to God, I think I can help you."

"I'll be there," Toni told her. "But, please…"

"Good night," the woman said calmly.

Her husband was the first one to return to the hall. He glanced at his wife, and she gave a slight nod. The man then offered Toni a quick smile, slipped his arm around his wife and started for the main door.

Toni turned and fled up the stairs as quickly as she could. She went for Bruce's door and then hesitated. She was the angry one! She backed away and went into her own room. She tapped at the bathroom door, but there was no answer, and the door to his bedroom was closed, also.

Turning away, she brushed her teeth, washed her face and found her nightgown. She hesitated again. She could just go in, but what if he was angry now?

She turned, went back to her own room and crawled beneath the sheets. Fear suddenly set in. What if the old Bruce, with his bloody dripping sword, appeared again tonight?

The solution was simple. She was going to go to bed, close her eyes and not open them again until morning.

But sleep didn't come easy. She spent the first minutes wishing that Bruce would suddenly come into her room. And finally, she drifted off.

Then she awoke. *Don't open your eyes, don't do it!* she told herself. But she opened them, anyway.

She expelled her breath with a sigh. The room was empty. And yet…there was a *feeling* in it, a feeling of… sadness?

She sat up, remembering that, just after she'd *seen* what had happened, she hadn't been afraid.

Though she couldn't see her visitor from the past, she still somehow *felt* him. And she just wasn't ready to deal with it.

She rose, walked into the bathroom, hesitated, then opened the door to his room. She walked to the foot of the bed, biting into her lower lip, trying to see in the deep shadows. He was probably sound asleep. Should she dare take the next step and just climb in next to him?

"Are you coming in here?"

His voice, out of the darkness, caused her to jump.

"Well, are you coming in, or do you just intend to spend the night there at the foot of the bed, staring at me?"

"I'm coming in," she said. Her voice sounded ridiculously prim and sharp.

She crawled in, and his arms came around her.

"Toni—"

"No! Don't talk. Please don't talk!" she said.

"Toni—"

"Please!"

"Any way you want it," he whispered. And he, too, sounded ridiculous, sharp and cold, especially considering the way he held her.

Chapter 17

The couple were already seated in a booth at the pub when Toni arrived, and the lithe blonde introduced Toni to her husband, Matt. It might have been just a lovely meeting of Americans in a foreign country, where even casual acquaintances could suddenly become best friends.

"So you're Toni," the man said. And though the smile he offered her was warm and encouraging, she still didn't feel terribly assured.

"You saw Queen Varina, too?" she asked him.

He shrugged, looking at his wife with a half smile. "I am the Southerner," he said.

Toni shook her head. "You both came to the show with Adam?"

"Yes, actually, we did," Matt said.

"Adam has talked about you a lot," Darcy said.

"So I gathered," Toni murmured.

"And then, of course, when he discovered the castle was here, and that the owner was Laird Bruce MacNiall..." Darcy said with a shrug.

"Wait a minute. You're going to tell me that Adam knows Bruce MacNiall, too?" Toni demanded.

Matt Stone inclined his head and she realized that the barmaid had come to stand before them. "I'll take a pint of anything," Toni said, noting that the two were drinking beer.

"Lamb is great today," the barmaid suggested. "And there's a lovely chicken entrée."

The three opted for poultry, and the barmaid smiled and moved on.

"Adam knows Bruce?" Toni repeated.

Matt inclined his head again; her beer was coming. She decided that, with his smooth, cultured Virginian accent, he might have made an interesting twist on James Bond.

She thanked the barmaid for her beer.

"Please. Are you going to answer me?" she asked.

Darcy smiled. "He doesn't know Bruce MacNiall. He knows *of* him. He's been watching him. Bruce is actually on our register, as well."

Toni stared at the two of them with a certain outrage. "He's on the *register?* This is beginning to sound a lot like Big Brother!"

Darcy shook her head. "I never do begin well, do I?" she said to her husband, who smiled. She looked back at Toni. "It's nothing like that, honestly. Adam is the most humane, caring individual I've ever met. His son was incredibly gifted, so Adam started doing research. Most people who have...well, I guess around here they call it 'the touch,' others call it a gift and many call it a curse. Call it what you will, most people who have it are afraid of it. And they don't want to use it."

Toni inhaled, watching her silently.

"Like you," Darcy continued. "What child could endure such things happening, seeing such things in dreams? Adam said that you retreated, but that you were incredibly strong-willed and appeared to have put it all behind you. However, he always felt that you would call one day."

"As I did," Toni murmured.

"So," Matt said. "Want to give us the whole story?"

"In a minute," Toni said, still wary. "What were you talking about regarding Bruce? You said that he was on the register."

Matt leaned forward. "There was a case here, years ago—"

"Yes, I recently heard about it. He'd been a cop. His work led to the arrest of a serial killer. I think that means he must have been a good cop."

"An excellent cop. And according to him, he simply used the methods employed by profilers."

Toni nodded, looking at him expectantly. "So?"

"There were some articles written at the time that drew Adam's interest," Darcy explained. "Apparently, he actually managed to *think* as the man."

Toni frowned. "So," she said, still skeptical, "there must be a lot of good cops on that register."

"Oh, there are," Darcy assured her.

Matt smiled. "You're still looking at us as if we're crazy. But that's what you want to think, isn't it? Toni, if nothing else, we'll listen to you *without* staring at you as if you're mad, and we may really be able to help."

She drew her finger along the line of her beer mug,

as if it were frosty, which it definitely wasn't. She'd actually grown accustomed to warm beer.

"If Bruce has any of the touch, he certainly denies it," she said, hoping that her voice didn't sound angry or bitter. "He thinks that I have nightmares, that I hit my head…anything but that I might really have seen a ghost."

Matt lifted his hands and grimaced. "Guys don't like to admit that they see ghosts," he said simply.

"I don't think that he does see this one," Toni said.

"Different people have sight in different ways. I think that when he was on the force, Bruce wanted to catch the killer—or killers—so desperately that he was able to call on reserves he'd never want to acknowledge he has," Darcy explained.

"And probably never will again," Toni said.

"You never know," Darcy told her. "So…please, try to tell us more."

"Well, for one, they have a very contemporary problem here," she said. "There's a serial killer on the loose. He abducts prostitutes from the cities and dumps them in Tillingham."

"Yes, we know," Matt said.

"Tell us more about the ghost," Darcy said. "Especially if anything new has happened since we spoke on the phone."

Toni arched a brow, staring at the woman. "Actually, something very new happened yesterday afternoon, not long before the tour."

"The entrées are coming," Matt warned lightly.

So Toni waited. And once the food arrived, she started talking. And to her amazement, she talked and talked.

"A ghost is usually trying very hard to say something," Darcy told her when she was done.

"Let's say I buy into that," Toni told her. "That I can even understand it! History didn't pinpoint him as his wife's killer, but legend and speculation certainly abounded. So now Annalise has been found. They're doing DNA tests, and if it's proved that she is Annalise, she will come back to the castle and be entombed next to her laird. He'll be vindicated. She'll be at rest. So this ghost should be happy and quiet now, right?"

"He should be," Darcy said.

"Unless…" Matt murmured.

"What?" Toni demanded.

Darcy exhaled softly. "Apparently, there's something else bothering him. And if you really want him to be at peace, you'll have to figure out what it is."

"We've company," Matt murmured suddenly.

Toni turned to find Bruce coming into the pub with Jonathan Tavish. They both looked grim. Toni felt guilty instantly, although she wasn't sure why.

Bruce saw them and headed toward the table.

"Hi!" she murmured, trying to sound casual.

"Hello," he said, and looked to the couple across from her. "I saw you two last night, right?"

"Yes. Strange, isn't it?" Toni said cheerfully. "Matt and Darcy Stone, this is the real Laird MacNiall. Bruce, Matt and Darcy."

"Nice to meet you. Our constable, Jonathan Tavish," Bruce said, and Jonathan, too, exchanged pleasantries.

"Did you know one another in the States?" Jonathan asked. To Toni's ears, he sounded suspicious.

"Toni didn't remember until I talked to her last night," Darcy said easily. "Matt's family home is in northern Virginia, so we often go into D.C. for the theater. We were there for one of Toni's performances of Queen Varina. We're staying in this delightful village for a few weeks, so, naturally, I begged her to join us for lunch."

There wasn't a lie in her words. Toni admired her smooth narration.

"Ah, so you're joining us in the village for a wee bit?" Jonathan said, pleased.

"It's gorgeous," Matt said.

"We've rented the Cameron cottage," Darcy told him.

"Well, we'll let you get back to your meal," Bruce said.

"Join us," Matt suggested.

"We've a bit of business," Jonathan said, "so we'll be beggin' out, if you don't mind. Another time?"

"Certainly," Darcy said politely.

"Seems the castle is bringing in the lunchtime rush," Bruce murmured.

Toni twisted in her seat. She was surprised to see Thayer just a booth away, lunching with Lizzie and Trish. And three booths back, Kevin, David, Ryan and Gina were biting into what looked like servings of lamb.

"See? It's all good for business," Jonathan told Bruce.

"Apparently," Bruce said pleasantly. "Well, excuse us, then. We'll say a quick hello to the others and have lunch, as well."

With a wave, he turned. The barmaid apparently knew both him and Jonathan well, for she jovially told them that their "usual" booth was available.

"Hail, hail, yes, the gang is all here!" Toni murmured as he moved away.

"Great," Matt said. "I'm anxious to talk to them all. So is Darcy, right?"

"Oh, yes," Darcy said. "Definitely."

* * *

Bruce let it go for the evening, and all through that night's performance.

But after he'd stabled Shaunessy, he went upstairs, built a fire and sat before it—waiting.

In time, Toni came into the room.

"What's wrong?" she asked him.

He turned to her politely. "Friends from the States, eh?"

"Yes," she said carefully. "Well, acquaintances, you know."

"You called a *psychic?*"

"What?" He could see her mind racing as she tried to figure out how he could possibly know.

"Small place," he told her, deciding to spare her and cut to the chase. "Jonathan looked them up."

"Jonathan looked them up?"

"Passports," he reminded her. "You are all visitors in a foreign land," he reminded her. "And with computers these days…well, it can be quite easy to find out almost anything."

"I didn't call a psychic and ask her to come," Toni said.

"You didn't?"

"Well, I called her. Actually, I didn't call her, I called a friend. And—"

"Planning on adding tarot readings to the tour?" he demanded. She was floundering. She had done it.

"You're being sarcastic and—and horrible!" she told him. She was staring at him wide-eyed—caught, one might say. And yet those sapphire eyes accused him. She was still Annalise, dressed in the ancient white gown. A flicker of something passed through him then. *She must actually be a lot like Annalise was, slim, blond hair cascading down her back, those eyes...*

He brushed away the thought, angry again that she was so convinced there had to be a ghost. The damned place wasn't haunted. Although he was glad his ancestor had been vindicated—and he didn't mind a good historical place—he sure as hell didn't want the family home to be ridiculed, chronicled on *Ripley's Believe It Or Not* or a novelty in a ghost segment of the Travel Channel.

"This is still my property, my home," he said icily. "And I don't want a séance here, or a woman reading a crystal ball, or anyone making light of the history of my home. Do you understand what I'm saying?"

"Yes, I understand," she said. "Don't worry. And don't blame the others. I'll see to it that neither Darcy nor her husband ever darken your door again. Frankly, they're here to help. But then, you don't need any help, do you? After all, you were a great cop. You've got a friend who's a constable, and another who is a detective. So, what the hell, you would never need the help of anyone who might in the least tamper with the great dignity of the place! I understand. But if you had even begun to understand me, and taken the slightest chance of *believing* something that I said, we wouldn't be having this conversation now. But like I said, there's nothing to worry about. I'll never mention the word *ghost* to you again, or your ancestors, as matter of fact. Hell, do what you want with the remains of Annalise! Sell them to a museum, indulge posterity, whatever. You've no right to be angry with me because you really don't understand anything at all!"

"They were here, weren't they?" he asked.

"Yes. But I didn't ask anyone to come here. In fact, I specifically asked that she not. We all know that we've kept this going by your great bounty alone," she said, and there was definite sarcasm in her tone. "I don't know why I'm bothering. Obviously, you don't believe anything that I'm saying."

"Should I believe you?" he asked. "On what basis? I mean, do we really even know one another?"

She stiffened. "I thought I knew you," she said.

"And I thought I could trust you."

"Trust me? You know you can trust me! And if you were willing to take the least chance on me—and yourself!—you'd give me the benefit of the doubt. Apparently there have been times in *your* life when some kind of a sixth sense kicked in. That's why you were such a great cop."

"What?"

"Are you afraid to admit there just might be something in the world beyond what you can see?"

He was going to get angry. He was going to deny her words again. And yet…

Dammit. He didn't want to remember what it had been like when it had seemed that he had entered the mind of another man. A killer.

It was all bunk. Shite. In his rational mind, he had to believe that there was reason, and nothing else. He denied himself. No wonder he denied her, too.

"When you choose to," she said coolly, "you'll trust me. Because when you choose to look at the truth, you'll know, beyond all doubt, that you can."

She spun around, leaving him. He heard the bathroom door slam—his side first and then the other. He stared at the fire, still seething—and sorry.

But neither did he want to be a fool. These people had invaded his home…well enough, they'd been taken, he'd understood. But he hadn't thrown them out. Instead, he'd let them work—even when it was beginning to appear that one of their number might be guilty of the fraud from the start. Credit cards had been involved, and they were being tracked now. But in doing background checks, Jonathan had informed him, they had discovered that Thayer Fraser reported a bank card missing just before it had all begun.

"Aye, it could have been stolen," Jonathan had told him. "But don't you think it's rather a coincidence if it was the one used with the Internet providers?"

"Maybe too much of a coincidence," Bruce had told him.

"Meanin'?"

"Could he really be that stupid?" Bruce had asked.

Jonathan had shrugged. "He's a Scotsman, Bruce. And, aye, it might well have been a Scotsman to have way more information on you than anyone else. Bruce, it's lookin' as if someone's really pretended to be you."

"They took my identity, but the Internet site was a total setup!"

"Aye."

There were still discoveries to be made. But they would be made.

He sat in front of the fire awhile longer. Jonathan had told him who the people having lunch with Toni that afternoon were. He'd done the research on them himself, and he'd been astonished. Low-key, low profile. Harrison Investigations didn't advertise on television, didn't promise to fix anyone's love life or connect anyone with deceased relatives.

Still, they investigated strange and unusual occurrences, trouble spots. Ghosts. Hauntings. No matter what the hell they wanted to call it!

As if they hadn't enough real problems around here!

He could be glad that a family mystery was solved, but there was a fraud in his own house. A killer, leaving victims in the forest. And the last damned thing he wanted around was a psychic!

He could hardly kick the pair out of the village, but he damned well could make sure that they weren't invited into his home! Yet as he stared at the fire, nothing of logic, truth or the simple fact that he did own the property seemed to mean anything. Her last few words stung. *I thought I knew you.*

She had been the one angry before, but she had come back. If he just waited…maybe she would come back again. Because she was frightened? he wondered, mocking himself. Ego or not, he couldn't accept that she had come back into the bedroom the night before out of fear.

He *could* go to her. Actually, he could *apologize. Except that he wasn't in the wrong.*

The fire continued to crackle. Time passed and he was still there, staring at the flames. At last he rose, turned out the lights and went to bed. But he didn't sleep. He realized that he wasn't sleeping because he was waiting. And after a while, he realized that she wasn't coming.

Donning his robe, he went through to the bath. She hadn't locked the door on her side of it. He tapped lightly. There was no answer, so he opened the door and walked over to the foot of the bed.

She slept, her hand curled beneath her chin, hair splayed around her. He wouldn't wake her, he decided. But as he stood there, she suddenly bolted upright, staring at him with alarm.

"It's just me," he said. "Real. In the flesh," he added. She still stared. "Not a ghost," he told her.

She nodded after a minute, still staring at him.

"Do you want to be alone?"

"Is that an apology?"

"Did you apologize last night?"

"Was I wrong last night?"

"Am I really wrong now?"

She looked down for a moment, lashes sweeping her eyes, the fall of her hair concealing her features. "Does it really matter?" she said very softly.

Those words touched him in a way he couldn't quite fathom, and did more than any argument. "I'm sorry," he murmured.

"For what?" she asked him, looking up.

He crossed his arms over his chest. "I really don't want a psychic here. I hate it when you see those programs with cheap special effects as a handheld camera follows a purported medium around a house. I think we have enough problems here. I'm sorry I spoke the way I did. And I... I wish I could believe you. I believe that you believe your dreams are very real."

She rose, brushing by him, heading for the connecting door. There she paused. "You really do have the better bed," she told him. He followed her.

They were awake another hour. Then, they both slept.

Toni awoke thinking that it had to be very late, or nearly morning. But the room was in deep shadow. The fire had died in the grate and the lights were out, except for one that remained on in the bath.

She felt Bruce's arm around her. But still, she had the feeling that they were not alone.

She looked to the foot of the bed. And he was there. Once again, standing, looking at her, sword hanging from his hand, bloodied. He looked at her, and she knew he wanted her to follow.

At her side, Bruce stirred. "Toni?"

"Yes?"

"Is he here?"

She didn't know if the question was mocking or not. She was staring at the apparition. She told the truth. "Yes."

She heard a soft groan, but he pulled her closer. "Tell him to go away. Tell him that *I'm* here."

She looked at the apparition. "Go away!" she whispered. Words formed then, unspoken on her lips. *Please. I don't know what you want!*

He inclined his head, as if bowing to her desires. Then, as she stared at him, he faded until he was nothing more than a shadow in the night. She lay back down, glad, gnawing upon her lip.

There had to be something else that he wanted...but what? What the hell *was* it that he wanted?

Toni was determined to find out, whatever it took, wherever it led. She would swallow fear and find out why he kept coming back...

With that settled, she moved in tightly next to Bruce. His breath teased her nape. His hand rested on her midriff. Her back was solidly to his chest, and he gave her tremendous warmth. Like a cascade of warm water, the touch filled her with comfort and ease. She closed her eyes and fell back to sleep. She didn't waken to darkness again.

In the morning, Bruce was up and gone when she awoke.

"You're joking with me, right?"

Bruce sat across the table from Robert Chamberlain at the pub, having received a message to meet him there at eleven. He was surprised that Robert wanted to meet in the village; he usually chose Stirling.

But he was even more surprised by his friend's words.

Robert shook his head gravely. "I've asked them to meet us here."

Bruce groaned. "I don't believe this. Not from you."

"Bruce, law enforcement has resorted to such tactics many times. I wouldn't have called over to the States myself—"

"Why should you? It's not as if we don't have our share of quacks in Great Britain," Bruce said.

Robert grinned. "I wouldn't have known that they were here if you hadn't logged on to the police line to investigate them. But since I saw your inquiry, I looked them up."

"Harrison Investigations," Bruce said, shaking his head. "They go into places where unusual events have taken place."

"They're discreet, but not secretive," Robert said. "There's no sensationalism regarding the corporation. They've been called upon by law agencies in many places. They've worked for congressmen and senators, even a U.S. president—"

"Whoever said that men and women in the government were sane?" Bruce asked him.

Robert shrugged. "Bruce, you have told me a dozen times yourself that we should be tearing the forest apart, looking for the remains of Annie O'Hara."

"The last two victims were found there," Bruce said. "That's logic, not intuition."

"I still think it was more than logic when you nailed the killers ten years ago."

Bruce shifted uncomfortably. "It seems to me that there's a great deal more we could—sorry, the law could be doing without resorting to…mumbo jumbo."

"Be polite, please."

"Hey, times have changed. I'm not the ruler of my own little kingdom. I own the castle and a lot of property. I have the title, but you can buy a title on the Internet these days. I can hardly order these people to get out of my village by sundown," Bruce said.

"On a more realistic note," Bruce said, "I met with Jonathan yesterday. The boys in computer tech are apparently having some pretty good luck tracking down information on the phony corporation that rented the castle."

Robert nodded. "I've seen the reports. I've kept out of it. Jonathan is the local constable."

"He's got it out for Thayer Fraser, I'd say."

Robert shrugged. "We can't make any arrests on what we have right now. But the man's bank account pretty much matches the amount the Americans put up. And he reported a bank card stolen. If it proves that the bank card was used at the Internet Café in Glasgow where the site was formed…well, then we'll have to bring him in for questioning, at the very least."

"Doesn't make sense. He'd have to know he'd be caught."

"Aye, but there's a certain defense in that, too. They're trying to track his money now, as well. That will help. Naturally we need legal resources to do all that." Robert leaned back. "You won't see this one in the papers, because we've been keeping the inquiries quiet, but I've had my men go a lot deeper into the disappearance of the barmaid in Stirling."

Bruce frowned. "She'd cleaned out her room. She was packed up, bag and baggage."

"But no one knows where she went. She didn't take a bus or a train. She's just gone. Annie O'Hara could have gone back to Ireland, but I don't believe that. And our boy, Thayer, was seen with the barmaid that same day."

"Wait, you're accusing him of fraud—and of being a serial killer?"

"I'm not accusing him of anything," Robert said. "I'm telling you what we've got."

"It doesn't gel," Bruce said. "It sounds like grasping at straws."

"Straws are all we've got."

"With a good attorney, the man could skewer the force," Bruce warned.

"We can't make an arrest. But since the fellow is living in your castle…"

Bruce shook his head. "The fraud is one thing. But to assume the man might be a killer because he was in a pub…that's pushing it, don't you think?"

Robert didn't answer. "They're coming," he said. He and Bruce stood as the handsome American couple strode over to the booth.

"Hello," Bruce said, shaking hands along with Robert. "What did you think of the tour at the castle the other night?"

"It was quite remarkable," the woman said.

Bruce stared at the man. The fellow didn't look like a quack. "So, did you feel anything in the castle?" His words were polite, but he couldn't keep his tone as cordial.

"No, but then, I'm not the one who would," the man said.

"Matt is actually the sheriff in a town named for his family," Robert explained.

Bruce cast Robert a dry stare. *Might have mentioned that before, old chap!* But of course, Robert had refrained on purpose.

"I didn't ask them to meet about the castle," Robert said.

"No, of course not."

"It's a beautiful place," Darcy told him. She wasn't obsequious, just pleasant. Still, he knew he had a chip on his shoulder regarding them.

"Saturday, I've got men coming in from a number of the surrounding areas," Robert explained. "We're searching for the body of a woman almost certain to be a victim of a serial killer. I was hoping that you would be willing to search with my men."

"Of course," Darcy said, glancing at her husband.

"Naturally." Matt glanced at his wife.

Robert nodded. "Naturally," he agreed.

Darcy Stone looked across the table at Bruce. "You'll be there, won't you, Laird MacNiall?"

"I will."

"Of course," she said. "You feel a responsibility."

"The forest borders my castle."

She nodded. "It's interesting, Laird MacNiall. You really haven't spent much time at your castle in the last decade or so."

He arched a brow.

"Well, there's the place you have in New York and the horse farm up near Loch Ness. You even have an interest in a breeding facility in Kentucky."

Bruce stared at her levelly. "All that," he murmured, "and you didn't even ask to see my palm."

He started to make a move, but she placed her fingers on his hand.

"We, too, have access to the Internet, Laird MacNiall."

"Ah," Bruce murmured, wondering why the couple made him feel as if he should be wearing full body armor. There really was no call for him to be rude. Robert wanted to see if they could help. It was on the wrong side of good sense as far as he was concerned, but they certainly appeared respectable enough. The woman was hardly dressed in black with a veil, nor did she carry a crystal ball. There was no reason to be so instantly hostile.

He wasn't so sure he liked the scrutiny they had put on his life, though. And he didn't like the idea that Toni had called Harrison Investigations in the first place. Despite the fact that he believed her conviction that she'd never heard the story about the great MacNiall before, he was sure there was a logical explanation. There was surely even a logical explanation for her knowledge of the crypts. And it was pure luck and circumstance that she had come upon the remains of Annalise after the rainstorm.

After all, it was luck and circumstance that he had caught the husband-and-wife team of killers, all those years ago.

"The castle is your ancestral home," Darcy Stone mused, "but it does seem as if you've spent years running away from it."

That was it, his cue to leave. He rose.

"It's been a pleasure," he said, "but you will have to excuse me. I have some business in town. I'll see you both Saturday, then. Robert, keep me informed."

He shook Matt Stone's hand and strode out of the pub, suddenly wishing to hell that he was in New York right then, on the streets somewhere, watching a flood of living, breathing, pierced-tongued, green-haired teens and young adults walk by in a hurry to get their next tattoos.

Beyond the pub, he paused. It felt as if he had shed a heavy overcoat, just being in the air again. He glanced around, considering a drop-in at Jonathan's constabulary, then a visit to Daniel Darrow. He eschewed both ideas, staring up at the statue of his ancestor. Marble, some steel and God knows what else went into a statue.

"Get out of my life!" he told the statue.

"So, the old laird is in your life," a soft voice said.

He spun around, damning himself for not moving more quickly. Darcy Stone had followed him out.

"Mrs. Stone, if you'll forgive me—"

"Please, just give me a moment of your time."

He crossed his arms over his chest. "A moment, then."

"First, Toni Fraser didn't ask that we come."

"Why did you?"

She wasn't ready to answer that one. "There is a presence in your castle."

"There are a lot of presences. Americans," he said.

She smiled. "Laird MacNiall, you made one of the most brilliant cases and arrests in the crime annals. And then you left the force. Why?"

He lifted his hands. "Because the work absorbed my life. I put off my wedding. My fiancée became terribly ill and died soon after that case was solved. I decided that I had put a little bit too much time into man's inhumanity to man. Not that it's really any of your business, but then, you seem to know everything else about me."

"Might that be only part of the reason?" she asked.

"I don't know what you're talking about."

"I think you do. I think you had a few moments during that case when you saw too clearly what the killers were doing. Maybe you even got into their skin—into their hearts and minds—far more than you wanted."

"Murder is ugly, Mrs. Stone."

"That's why it should be stopped, whenever possible. Why killers should be taken away from the public, locked up," she said.

"Is that all, Mrs. Stone?"

"No. I just wanted to say that if you want to talk, if there's anything I can do…well, I would really love to help you."

He wanted to tell her that he didn't need her help but he refrained. "I'll keep that in mind."

"I really would love to come back to your castle."

"I'll consider it," he told her. "Is that it?"

She shook her head. "Just one more thing."

"Aye?"

"You…you have real capabilities, I believe. If you'd let yourself use them."

"I'll keep that in mind, as well, Mrs. Stone. Now… if you'll excuse me?"

And he made a point of getting into his car.

Chapter 18

Gina was in the kitchen with David and Kevin when Toni came down. The three of them were studiously poring over a document.

"Toni," Gina said. "Want to take a look at this? I've written up a new rental agreement. Well, it's not exactly a rental agreement, since MacNiall will apparently be staying on his own property. And, of course, there's no telling how long he'll be willing to play his ancestor with our presentation. Anyway, I'm asking him for a six-month run. If we keep doing as well as we've been doing, we'll be able to pay him for the facility—and even give him a cut for his participation—and come out with enough to look into going home and getting new work, or looking for another property."

Toni poured herself a cup of coffee, then leaned against the counter and said, "Gina, I'm sure you've written up a good agreement. But what we have to do now is get it to an attorney—and past Laird MacNiall."

Gina chewed on a thumbnail, reading over her own document. "I hope he'll go for this. Otherwise, we're just living day to day."

"Actually, we all just live day to day, no matter what," Kevin said.

"Sage, very sage," Toni told him. "Where is everyone else?"

"Bruce went somewhere in the car this morning, but he came back and went riding," David told her. "Thayer muttered something and went out. Ryan is upstairs— he wants to drive into town and buy some kind of polish for his swords. Eban is…well, he's being Eban, out doing whatever he does."

Gina glanced at her watch. "We should get going. We always spend more time in the village then we intend. Toni, want to come with us?"

"No, I think I'll hang around here."

David frowned at her. "You should come."

She smiled. "I'm fine. Really."

"Ah, the nights are not enough!" he teased. "She's awaiting the return of Laird MacNiall."

She forced another smile. "I have a book I want to read," she told him.

"Um," Kevin teased. "The book of man. And it's partially in Braille."

"You two are terrible," she said.

"I'd rather thought last night that there was some trouble in tranquil waters," Gina said, looking at her somewhat sharply.

That caused David and Kevin to study her, as well.

"Oh?" she said.

"I heard your voice when I came up. You sounded a little sharp," Gina said. "Are you two arguing?"

Toni shook her head.

"Because we really need him to sign this agreement," Gina reminded her.

She sighed. "He will sign it, or he won't sign it. I'm not arguing with him."

They heard singing and Ryan came bursting into the kitchen, doing a version of "Oklahoma." He seemed cheerful. They all stared at him; he wasn't known for his vocal ability.

He stopped and stared back. "What?" he demanded. "Okay, so this is Scotland. Brigadoon! I feel a new song coming on."

"Let's get out of here, please!" David begged. "Toni, come on. I'll go read more headstones with you, if you want."

She laughed. "I'm fine here alone. I'll walk you to the car."

They started to trail out, but when David opened the front door, they were startled to find Constable Jonathan Tavish standing there. He looked grim.

"Constable," Toni said. "Hello. Can we help you? Bruce isn't here."

Jonathan shook his head sadly. "I'm sorry. I've not come to see Bruce."

"Then...how can we help you?" Ryan asked.

"I've come for your cousin, Miss Fraser." He hesitated a moment. "I'm truly sorry. I've come to arrest Thayer Fraser."

David was the one to gasp. "Why? For what?"

Jonathan Tavish shifted uneasily on his feet. He truly looked miserable. "Fraud," he said.

"Wait! Please, explain this!" Toni said.

"Is he here?" Tavish insisted.

Toni shook her head. "He may be about…we don't know where he is. But—"

"I'm sorry to say this, folks, but he engineered the whole deal. Set you all up. He created a fictitious corporation on the Web and arranged for the box as an address. He probably presumed that you'd all be out after the MacNiall returned…you'd have to go home, broke, and he'd have managed to make himself long gone. It's quite a surprise that he hasn't flown already, but maybe he thought he'd covered his tracks."

"Thayer!" Toni exclaimed.

"Your cousin?" Ryan said.

"Now, now, we may be able to retrieve a bit o' the money," Jonathan said consolingly.

Toni shook her head. "I don't believe it."

"You don't want to believe it," David murmured.

"What kind of proof is there?" Toni demanded.

"Enough for an arrest," Jonathan told her quietly.

"I still don't believe it," Toni said stubbornly.

"Y'are not certain the chap isn't about?" Jonathan asked.

"He could be. We don't know," Ryan said. He stepped back. "Come in… I can check his room."

"I'll take a look around upstairs," Gina said, "while Ryan goes to his room."

Toni stood awkwardly for a moment, then thought that she might know where Thayer was. The stables. Up in the rafters. She didn't know what he did up there. *And maybe she didn't want to know.* But she did want to see him before the constable got to him, though.

"I'll…look around outside," she said.

She walked out the main doors, gazing toward the stables. Despite the fact that he'd actually warned her just yesterday that a trace had been made to Glasgow, she was stunned. *You don't want to believe it!* That much was true.

As she started across the grass, she saw Thayer. And she was certain he had been up in the rafters of the stables. He was walking toward her casually, though, smiling, taking long strides, his arms swinging, as if he hadn't a care in the world.

She stood still, feeling the cool breeze lift her hair from her forehead. "Top o' the mornin' to you, cous—ach! That's Irish, eh?" he said teasingly. Then he stopped, seeing her expression. "Toni? What's the matter?"

"The constable is here."

"Aye?"

"To arrest you."

"Arrest me?" He appeared honestly stunned.

"For fraud."

"What?"

"For fraud. For taking the lot of us."

He looked toward the door. Something else passed over his features. Turning, she saw that Jonathan had come out.

"Bloody hell!" he muttered, and took off running.

It must have been a moment of blind panic for him, for there was really nowhere to run. Or maybe there was. If he could have gotten down the hill and into the forest, he might have managed a real disappearance. But he didn't.

Jonathan Tavish could run. Seeing Thayer's intention, he came out with a startling flash of speed and athleticism. Thayer hadn't gone more than twenty yards before the constable tackled him. "This is bullshit! Bullshit!" Thayer roared as the two scrambled on the ground.

Tavish was the stronger man, broader, and in better shape apparently. The scuffle didn't last long. Thayer was quickly cuffed. Dusty and disheveled, he was dragged to his feet.

As Jonathan led him toward the patrol car, he looked at Toni. "I didn't do it! I don't know what kind of crazy proof there is against me, but I didn't do it. Toni, you've got to help me."

"Tell it to the judge!" Jonathan muttered, shaking his head wearily.

"I need help, Toni!" Thayer called to her. "Legal help. I swear, I'm not guilty!"

"We'll get you a lawyer!" she cried out. "A solicitor… whatever you need!"

The arrest was not like on a cop show. Jonathan didn't protect his suspect's head and put him into the back. Instead he opened the passenger door of his vehicle and shoved Thayer in.

Thayer's eyes remained on Toni's, silently begging for help.

David, Kevin, Gina and Ryan were there then, aligned on either side of her. "My God!" Gina breathed.

"Well, Constable Tavish said that we could get some of the money back," Ryan said.

Toni spun on them. "He says that he's innocent!"

David looked at her sadly. "Toni, most people don't go around yelling out that they're guilty, you know."

She shook her head. "I believe him. And we've got to get to the bottom of this! He needs legal aid—whatever it is over here."

"They have a fair and judicial legal system," Kevin told her sympathetically.

"We should have never trusted an outsider," Gina murmured.

"Right, he's my cousin, my fault," Toni said angrily. "What if he's innocent?"

"Toni!" Gina argued, but gently. "They couldn't have arrested him without some kind of proof."

"I want to know what proof!" she said. "And I want him to have legal help, right away."

"Well, that's just great," Kevin said.

"Why?" Toni demanded.

"Because we're all broke!" he reminded her.

"Look," David said calmly, "we need to find Bruce. This is his place, and he always knows more than we do. We can get hold of his friend, Robert. He can tell us, I'm certain, what they really have on Thayer. Let's hop in the car and drive around until we find him."

"Great," Kevin said with a sigh. "We're going to try to help the guy who screwed us all royally."

"Whatever happened to innocent until proven guilty?" Toni demanded.

"We really need to put all this before Laird Mac-Niall," Ryan said.

"Could he have *ridden* down to the village?" Gina wondered.

"I suppose you can ride anywhere around here," Ryan answered. "Hey, David and Kevin—you two take the minivan down to the village, ask if anyone has seen Bruce. Gina, Toni and I can hop in the car and try driving around these roads, cover the farm paths and all that."

Toni backed away. "Thank you," she murmured. "But I'll stay here, in case he's not in the village, and you miss him on the roads."

"You're going to stay here? By yourself?" Gina asked her.

She shrugged. "Eban is around somewhere."

"Oh, great. Eban! That gives me a real sense of security for you!" Gina said.

Toni shook her head. "It's all right. It's broad daylight. I'll be fine."

"I don't like it," David said.

"Oh, for the love of God, will you please go! If Bruce doesn't come back soon, or if you guys don't find him, I'll just hop on Wallace and come down to the village," she said. "Please, let's all move. I doubt if they'll be keeping Thayer in the village. They'll want to take him to a jail in one of the larger cities. We really need to move on this."

"All right," Gina said. "But, Toni, you've got to accept the fact that he might have done it."

She nodded, then backed away, toward the castle. But when both cars had started down the road, she walked resolutely toward the stables.

Entering, she noted Wallace in his stall, walking to the gate, expecting her to come and rub his nose.

"Sorry, boy!" she murmured, heading straight for the ladder. She climbed quickly to the rafters and looked around. A layer of hay covered the floor. She walked the planked surface, thinking this was foolish. She couldn't find something—whatever it was that brought Thayer up here—if she didn't know what she was looking for.

Then she heard whistling and stopped short. Eban. She listened as he strode into the stables, walking straight over to Wallace. "He y'be, lad, yer special treat!"

He was feeding the horse something. But what?

It occurred to her then that the strange little man may well have been feeding the horse something that made him sick. After all, Shaunessy had never been taken in. But why would Eban do such a thing? To sabotage their efforts? Or maybe he thought, as Bruce had originally, that they were mocking Scottish history.

She held very still, listening.

"Ah, there, lad, aye, eat it all up!"

She forced herself not to move, not to breathe. She waited. Eventually, she heard him leave the stables. Even then, until the sound of his whistle was long gone, she waited. Then, in a fury, she began to kick the hay around, desperately…searching.

"You'll not get me on this!" Thayer told Jonathan. "I didn't do it."

"You should be ashamed! A Scotsman, doing such a thing!" Jonathan said.

"Listen, I'm telling you—"

"Don't be tellin' me!" Jonathan warned him.

"Listen to me—" Thayer began.

"I'm warnin' ya!"

"Aye, and I'm beg—"

The constable had no more patience. He lifted his elbow as he drove, slamming it against Thayer's head.

The blow hurt. Like bloody hell! Stunned, Thayer reacted to the strike. He swung his elbow back, and caught the constable on the side of the head. Jonathan's skull crashed against the glass. He lost control of the car. It began to careen down the hill.

Jonathan swore just as the car hit a large boulder—and flipped.

Toni kicked up a lump of hay and saw it—a plastic bag. She crouched down and picked it up, looking at the contents. Grass?

Running her hands over the floor, she found a second

bag. It held matches and brown cigarette wrappers. She sniffed the first bag, no longer puzzled.

So Thayer had been coming to the stable rafters to smoke weed. It seemed evident, but it wasn't the answer she'd been looking for. She'd wanted something to either convict him or exonerate him on charges of fraud!

Sighing, she returned his stash, thinking she sure as hell didn't want to get caught with it herself. Rising, she walked gingerly to the ladder, not wanting to run into Eban again. She crawled down quickly, then made a detour to Wallace's stall. She eyed the horse carefully and critically. He whinnied. "I don't have anything for you. And if that man is giving you anything bad at all to cause a colic, I'll punch him out myself, okay?"

She glanced at her watch. Though it had seemed like she'd spent aeons in the rafters, only fifteen minutes had passed since the others left. She hesitated for a minute, afraid, and then she purposely walked back to the castle.

She resolutely made her way upstairs, into Bruce's room, and sat in the chair by the cold embers in the fireplace. Then she closed her eyes and spoke softly.

"If you're here, this would be a great time for you to appear," she whispered. "Please, we're alone now. And…I'm going to trust you. I'm not going to scream or panic."

And when she opened her eyes, he was there, watching her gravely, sadly.

Come.

"Yes, as you wish," she said.

He turned, tartan swaying, taking large steps with his long legs. He exited the master chamber, heading out to the hallway.

Toni moved along the hallway, following. He led her to the landing of the stairs and paused there. She waited as he looked back, assuring himself that she followed. Then he started down the stairs and she came behind.

Once again, he paused in the great hall, assuring himself that she was following still. She knew where they were going. "Down to the crypts?" she whispered. He stared at her with silent gravity, turned again, and traversed the secondary hall.

As she had feared, the door to the winding stairway down to the realm of the dead was open. Once again, he awaited her.

She stared at him, shaking her head slightly. "Why me?" she asked softly.

There was no reply; she hadn't expected one. Again he turned and started down the winding steps. Toni followed quickly. This time, however, she turned on the lights.

The lights didn't seem to help much, though, not when she was down there by herself—with a ghost. She was grateful that the MacNialls had not chosen to lay their dead out in simple shelving, that there were no decaying shrouds resting upon bodies left to go to dust with the passage of time. Still, ancient marble and words etched in Gaelic, monuments and carvings all reminded her of where she was. There was a certain cold down here that defied all logic. And as she wandered through the crypts, alone in the castle, with only the presence to guide her, she wondered at her own sanity.

As she ventured deeper into the recesses of the hallway, the light seemed to fade. On her left, the tomb of a laird from the 1500s was adorned with the life-size figure of a Renaissance man, seated upon his coffin, head resting upon a hand, marble eyes staring. She looked away quickly, feeling as if the blank eyes were watching her. She knew where she was going—the end of the hallway in the crypt.

She arrived, and though she had followed the vision of the great MacNiall down to this point, he was gone. The far end was cast in deep shadow. She stared at the marble figure, too much like the Bruce she knew, and wondered why she was here again, what it was that she hadn't seen.

Her blood seemed to turn to instant ice as she saw what was different tonight.

The stone sarcophagus just behind his—which had been set beside his own in the niche hundreds of years ago by someone determined that one day Annalise's earthly remains would one day join those of her beloved in death—was ajar.

She frowned and whispered aloud, hoping that the ghost would hear. "But she will come home, you know. Bruce will see to it. She will come home and lie beside you!" Her voice echoed back to her eerily in the arched stone corridor.

She moved forward, stepping around the edge of the effigy of the great MacNiall in death, trying to ascertain how and why the simple slab atop the second vault had been left open.

The shadows were thick and heavy. At first she could see nothing. She started to press at the stone, thinking she could see better if she could move it, but the weight seemed far too great for her at first. Then she heard a scraping, stone against stone. It was giving, moving back.

And she saw what lay within the coffin.

A scream tore from her throat. Loud, shrill, terrible. It ricocheted off the stone and echoed with resounding horror.

Toni backed away from the tomb, turned and ran down the corridor, desperate to leave.

She had her answer. She knew what the great Mac-Niall had been trying to tell her.

Chapter 19

There was nothing like riding, especially a horse as fine as Shaunessy. And God forgive him a certain pride, but there really was nothing as beautiful as the hills of his native land. Drawing to a halt at the top of a crest, Bruce surveyed the lands—dotted with sheep and cattle—that stretched in shades of green and purple as far as the eye could see.

It was amazing to look out over the peacefulness and tranquility of the scene below him. So much tragedy, bloodshed and pain had come before in this very area, where ancient tribes had battled for the best land, where the early nationalists had waged war against imperialism and where, in later years, men had shed their blood again and again for their loyalties, ideals and pride.

The last gave him pause, for he was disturbed, deeply disturbed. And uneasy, as well. He felt a growing sense of something…about to happen. Something about to break.

"Foolish, eh, old boy?" he said aloud, as Shaunessy pawed the earth.

He turned from the tranquil setting of the valley to stare into the dark green depths of the forest. Ten years had passed, yet the case he had solved still disturbed him. *Why?*

He knew why. He had entered the mind of a heinous monster, and it had scared him. It had made him wonder if, in doing so, he could become a monster himself.

I do not believe…! he told himself. And yet…just as he had never forgotten the case, he had not, in the last days, been able to rid himself of the vision of Toni, face-down in the stream.

Ghosts and ghost-busters! he thought angrily. Aye, tricks could be played with the mind, and all of this was playing tricks with his own.

Darcy Stone had gotten to him. As had Toni. There had been such a serenity about her. No driving passion, no wild speech. And he couldn't help but wonder, as he sat there atop Shaunessy, what the hell he was doing? Because one thing was true.

The vision returned again and again, haunting him. And the sense of fatalism was growing.

Toni slammed against the door, absolutely terrified that she would find it locked. But it burst open as it had before, easily allowing her an exit.

The phone. She had to get to the phone.

Eban! Eban was around somewhere. Not in the main castle. He never came in…or did he?

Striding for the main hall, she came to an abrupt halt before she could turn for the stairs.

Thayer was standing in the doorway, looking dazed, wild. Like a madman. Blood covered his forehead and caked his hair. His shirt was ripped; he was filthy. The handcuffs he'd been wearing dangled from his one wrist.

"Thayer?" she said.

"There was an accident," he said.

"An accident?" she said carefully. What she had seen below was still so vivid in her mind that she realized she didn't trust anyone. An hour ago she had been defending him so staunchly. But now, the way he looked…

"What happened?" she asked thickly.

"Hit…the constable…bastard…hit me. I hit him back."

"Where? Where is the constable?" she asked.

He shook his head. "I crawled out. I… Toni!" He started walking toward her. Panic seized her. She'd been too trusting. He'd been up in the rafters, smoking dope, when they'd all been in a precarious situation. Can't hang a man for that! she chided herself. But the way that he was staring at her…

He grinned suddenly, but it seemed lopsided and eerie. "Toni, you look as if you've seen a ghost. Been prowling around in the castle graveyard, eh?"

That did it. Screw the phone. She was getting the hell out. When he walked toward her, she pushed him. Hard. He staggered back, falling. "Toni!"

Ignoring him, she raced toward the stables, thinking to get Wallace. But she came to a dead halt. Eban was coming from the stables. He had an oilcloth in one hand and a sword in the other. He was just cleaning the sword! she told herself.

"Miss Fraser!" he said. "Coomin' to the stables, are ye? Aye, and good. Y'can see to old Wallace, good old lad!"

She shook her head, trying to appear nonchalant. *Wallace! Good old Wallace. Was the horse dead this time? Had Eban poisoned him?*

"I'm off for a bit of a walk, Eban!" she said, and waved jauntily, hoping Thayer wouldn't appear behind her right then. But...maybe it would be best if he did. Both men couldn't be guilty of heinous things...

Or could they?

She quickened her pace, grateful that she was going downhill. A walk at first, a trot, a lope...and then she was running.

"Toni!"

She looked back. Thayer, menacing in his stagger and tone, was coming after her.

It was a long, long way to the village.

She paused, looking back, taking a deep breath. He might not have moved quickly enough when Jonathan was coming after him, but he was cutting some speed now.

She happened to glance to the other side of the slope and saw the constable's car, overturned, down below.

There was no other choice.

She turned for the forest, tearing into its dark shadows as quickly as she could.

Bruce rode back to find the stables empty, the cars gone and his front door open. Striding into the great hall, he shouted, "Toni? Gina... David! Anyone?"

A sense of emptiness was his only reply. Still, he strode through the second hall, thinking someone might be in the kitchen. But he never made it there. The door to the tombs was standing open.

His heart thundered in his chest. Damn her! Had

she gone down, fallen…scared herself into a state of catatonia?

He took the spiral stairs at a dangerous speed. "Toni?" There was no answer, but he knew the route she would have traveled. He strode swiftly toward the great laird's tomb.

He frowned at first, seeing only that the slab was shifted over. Then he got a whiff of the sickening smell just as he looked in.

He didn't reel; didn't fall back.

He'd been wrong, dead wrong. They weren't going to find Annie O'Hara in the forest. She was here. How? his mind shrieked.

At the moment, how didn't matter. Toni was nowhere to be seen, and his sense of panic was growing.

He bolted back up the spiral stairs, feeling an urgency to find her unlike any premonition he'd ever experienced before.

Premonition. Aye! For that's what it was. That picture of Toni, blond hair trailing…facedown in the water.

The trees shielded her from the first second she moved into the cool green darkness. She tore across the brook, heedless of the fact that she soaked her shoes and jeans up to her knees. The cold didn't mean anything, not at this moment. Then, finding the thick trunk of an ancient oak, she leaned against it, getting her breath, trying to think rationally.

She was certain that, this time, she had found the remains of a recent victim, those of Annie O'Hara. It actually made sense; it was logical. The other bodies had been dumped here, in the forest. And now a body was actually discarded, right in the castle. Bruce's castle!

That should make Bruce appear guilty. Except that...
it couldn't be!

She heard thrashing, and she turned around.

"Miss Fraser!"

It was Eban's voice, Eban calling her.

*Why? Why had he chased her in here? And where
was Thayer? He had been far ahead of Eban when she
had looked back. In fact, she hadn't even realized that
Eban had followed her.*

"Lass! 'Tis dangerous in here!" Eban called with dismay. "The laird doesn't want ye in here, y'know!"

Flat against the tree, she remained perfectly still until
she heard his footsteps moving on. She started to move
out from around the tree. But as she did so, she was
stunned to see Thayer, frozen, dead still, standing directly in front of her.

"Toni!" he said softly. "Ah, Toni, here y'are! Luv,
I've been lookin' for you. Ah, Toni! I'm sorry, really,
truly sorry!"

They nearly crashed into one another. If Kevin hadn't
shouted, David never would have stopped the car in
time.

Ryan braked to a halt and leaped out his side of the
car just as Gina came out of hers. They both rushed at
the minivan.

"Something's wrong! Really wrong," Ryan said.

"Yeah! You can't drive!" David accused, but Ryan's
look silenced him.

"What? What?" Kevin demanded.

"We were at the castle maybe fifteen minutes ago.
Toni is gone, the door to the castle was standing wide-
open and the door to the crypt is open!"

Ryan paused for breath, and Gina continued. "And

the constable's car is upside down at the bottom of the slope!"

"We just came up the road—Toni isn't on it. Did you find Bruce?" David asked anxiously.

They both shook their heads.

"Neither did we," Kevin ventured.

They stared at one another for several seconds. Then they looked to the dark green canopy of the forest. Kevin groaned.

"She had to have run in there!" Gina whispered.

"All right, all right, let's go!" David said. He and Kevin exited the minivan. The four of them stood together, looking at the forest. Then they walked in.

When they came to the brook, David said, "Kevin and I will follow it this way...you two go that way."

And they parted.

He couldn't possibly have the strength to hurt her, Toni thought. But she dared not take that chance. She stared at him a moment, then turned to run again.

"Toni, wait! For the love of God, lass, wait!" he cried.

For the love of God!

She ran. She thought she was leaping brush and dodging trees in a race to go deeper into the forest, but she came back to the water instead. Standing dead still, trying to think of her next move, she heard a groan. Her eyes darted to the water...to her left. Farther to her left.

There was someone in the water. Someone. Not a body, since the person was groaning. Male, or female? She couldn't tell. She couldn't even see clearly, the branches were so low, the green darkness so vast...

The groan sounded again. The mass was moving.

"Oh, my God!" she breathed, and rushed forward.

* * *

He rode Shaunessy hard down the hill, reining in when he saw the cars. The two of them, almost touching. The constable's car, down the slope.

He dismounted, leading Shaunessy quickly toward the entry and the brook.

Eban came out of the forest, shaking his head. Bruce strode quickly to him, catching him by the shoulders. "Eban, where's Toni?"

"In there!" Eban said, waving a hand. "But the lass won't come to me!"

"Eban, you're certain? Who else is in there? All of them? You've got to answer me, Eban. Thayer? Thayer… he struck Jonathan. He's in the woods now, right? Eban, listen carefully. There's a body in the crypts. Do you know how it got there?"

Eban stared at him, then frowned. "Laird MacNiall, there be lots o' bodies in the crypts."

Bruce prayed for patience. "One of the murdered girls is in the crypts, Eban. Do you know how she got there?"

Eban stared back at Bruce, shaking his head. "Y'don't keep up the place, Laird Bruce, if y'll forgive me sayin' so!"

"Get to the castle and call Detective Inspector Robert Chamberlain. Please. Quickly, Eban. Get him out here."

"Aye, Laird Bruce. Aye!"

Eban hurried toward the castle. Bruce cursed himself for not carrying his cell phone, slapped Shaunessy's haunches so he'd head back, as well, and plunged into the forest himself.

"Constable!"

Toni rushed to Jonathan Tavish's side, trying to help him up.

He leaned on her heavily to gain his footing. "Toni… Miss Fraser… I'm sorry, but he's a bad seed, that one, he is! Slammed me in the head, wrecked the car! And he's loose."

Toni swallowed hard. "Come on. We'll get out of here. There's much worse, Constable Tavish. The body of that last missing girl… I'm almost positive I know where it is."

"Oh, aye?"

He found some strength, straightening to look her in the eyes.

"In the crypt. The castle crypt," she said. "I—I don't know what it means. I can't believe that Bruce MacNiall… No, others had access, too."

"Aye, and who would that be? Your cousin, Miss Fraser?"

"Anyone had access to the castle," she said. "It wasn't locked when we reached it, before we knew about Bruce. And there's Eban Douglas, as well. He's a local, and your friend, but he's a strange little man. Think about it! Anyone had access."

"Aye, anyone had access," he agreed.

The sound of a twig snapping suddenly alerted them to another presence. They both looked ahead.

Thayer had found her. He looked steadier, and he stared at Jonathan with loathing.

"Toni…you need to get away from him."

She sighed. "Thayer, we'll still help you. We'll see that you're represented. We'll—"

"Toni! You've got to get away from him. He clubbed me in the side of the head! Law-enforcement officers don't do that!"

"You bloody bastard!" Tavish roared. "You clubbed me!"

"You're not right, Tavish! You're not right!" Thayer shouted.

That caught Jonathan's attention, and gave him back his full power. He rushed Thayer, slamming him down against the ground. She heard a grunt, saw that the wind was knocked out of Thayer, and that Tavish was about to slug him hard in the jaw.

"Constable, no!" she cried, running through the water toward him.

The blow landed. Thayer's eyes closed. Toni's heart leaped to her throat. Despite all that she had seen, something in her heart was denying it.

"We've got to get him help. You might have killed him!" Toni said angrily.

Jonathan Tavish straightened again and stared at her, brushing his muddied blond hair from his forehead. "Ah, lass!" he said, coming toward her. "Poor, wee, beautiful lass! I'd envisioned so much more for you!"

She backed away instinctively. Too late, she realized that Thayer had been right. Indeed, he'd been barely walking, but he'd dragged himself after her because... he had known that Tavish would be in the forest.

He took another step toward her.

Toni screamed, as loudly as she could. She screamed again and then turned to run, praying that Tavish was in worse shape than he appeared.

Fingers tangled into her hair, jerking her back. She went crashing down into the water. She tried to rise, but he had her by the throat. She desperately grasped his hands, nails clawing. He was extremely powerful. She saw the world going a darker green all around her.

Green...black...

She heard gasping, choking...no air.

She slammed a knee against his groin with all her strength.

Bruce burst out on the little copse that sheltered the stream. And he saw her. Toni. Facedown in the water. Blond hair trailing behind her, floating...

"Toni!" He roared out her name in anguish, heedless of anything else around him as he raced over rocks, embankment, and into the water, falling to his knees, dragging her into his arms. She was still, so still, cold, silent...

He pressed his mouth to hers, parting her lips, breathing in. He staggered up with her in his grasp, anxious to get her to the slick embankment to perform CPR. Yet even as he held her, she gasped, choked, coughed up a wealth of water. Then she opened her eyes.

"Bruce!"

It was little more than a croak, but it registered as a warning. He set her down, spun and caught the blow of Jonathan's billy club right against his temple. He staggered back, falling on his haunches, his vision fading.

"What...the hell are you doing, Jonathan?"

"Taking care of a bloody murderer!" Jonathan told him.

The pain in his head was staggering, the darkness, welcoming. But he fought it, fought to get back to his feet. "I didn't murder anyone, and you know it!"

"Eh? Like as not how the law will see it, Laird Bruce! There's a fresh one in your old crypt."

"Aye," Bruce said, warily meeting his eyes. "You know I did not put it there."

"Actually, I do. Y'know, Bruce, I'm a handsome fellow. But the girls never came to me quite as they come to you. And there was that castle, rotting on the hill! You never had appreciation, Bruce. Y'don't deserve such a place. Now, if I don't kill you, and your last victim, y'may wind up ruling some prison and gettin' out again. So y'll die here with the lass. I believe y've said yourself upon occasion, ye can buy a title these days. And a castle, on a hill."

"You've murdered people—to spite me?" Bruce said incredulously.

Jonathan reflected on that for a minute. "Nae, the killing came first. Or maybe not. Maybe y'were the cause of it all, Bruce, because of Maggie."

"Maggie!" Bruce said incredulously. "Maggie has been gone a very long time, Jonathan."

"Aye, a long time."

"She was my fiancée, Jonathan," Bruce said.

"But I loved her first. And there was a time when I was certain she loved me, too. But you came into the picture, Bruce, and it was as always—the spoils of life to the great laird of the castle! And then there was pity in her eyes when she looked at me. I just hungered from afar, but then…well, she died, and that an act of God. Still, she taught me about women."

Jonathan started to pace, getting caught up in the frenzy of his words. "You know, Bruce, I've always been a smarter man than y've ever given me credit for! I'm the clever one, always have been. You, the great MacNiall, know how to look up your stock reports! But I can do anything with a computer." He paused a moment, then continued on. "It wasn't after the first girl that I thought of what I could do. It was after the second. There were a few times when I thought I might have erred, so there had to be a scapegoat. Actually, it was quite easy. I set these people up to come. Ah, Bruce, the Internet!

What an invention. I knew everything about you there was to know, and you can sell anything at all over the Web, that you can. I thought y'd really show yer temper. Who knew? You might ha' thrown 'em out right on their arses. Then again, they might ha' been around when the last body was found. The lovely Miss Fraser might ha' been spared, but now…well, there will be a bit of a mess to clean up here!"

Bruce locked his jaw, thinking of the dizziness, the darkness that still gripped him. His so-called friend meant to kill them, there, in the forest.

Jonathan drew a knife from his pocket, smiling. "A law officer, attacked. I did what I had to do!"

Jonathan hadn't just resented him, Bruce realized, he had hated him with a pathological conviction for years. The man hadn't acted in any mad, sudden rage. He had plotted and planned, dreamed of this.

Bruce flew at him in a desperate tackle, bringing him down hard in the water. But Jonathan had some strength in him. He forced a roll, bringing Bruce beneath him.

With a cry, Toni threw herself at the man. But he was powerful, and he heard her. Turning, he sent a fist jackknifing out. Toni went flying, falling hard back into the water.

Bruce saw the knife raised high above him, ready to plunge, and forced his shoulder to twist, throwing the man off. But Jonathan instantly started crawling through the water again, intent on getting the knife into Bruce's chest. Bruce managed to lash out with a foot, catching him in the ribs.

He fell back, but was soon up again. Then…absurdly, he stood in the middle of the stream and stared at Bruce, then away, then at Bruce.

"Hold still, y'bloody bastard!" he roared.

Incredulous, Bruce stared back.

Toni was on her rump, edging her way out of the water. "Which one, Jonathan? Which one do you need to kill?" she demanded.

Bruce glanced quickly and sharply at her. They were both seeing...*someone.*

"This one, Jonathan! This one! He's leaping at you!" Toni cried.

And to Bruce's amazement, Jonathan went charging forward, determined to wrestle thin air. He found no hold, barely balanced, and turned again, ready to reach for Toni then, the knife silvery in the green darkness, his intent fierce and brutal.

It was Bruce's chance, perhaps his only chance. He gut-tackled the man again, bringing him down hard into the stream. He heard a terrible cracking sound and winced inwardly. They'd struck a rock.

Beneath him, Jonathan Tavish didn't move. He knew it had been self-defense, but he had killed the man. There was a terrible emptiness inside.

He rolled, letting the water of the brook, icy cool and fresh, wash over him. A second later, Toni was by his side, taking his hand. Her eyes, sapphire and glittering with tears of relief, touched his. The death of any man was a tragedy. They both knew it. Yet, they had survived. For her life, he knew, he would have given his own. And for their future, he couldn't rue the fact that they had both lived.

Not without help.

"He was here, right?" he whispered to her hoarsely. "The great MacNiall. He appeared in the forest. Jonathan saw him, too, and didn't know which of us to kill?"

She nodded.

Bruce closed his eyes. "Thank him for me."

Chapter 20

"It's still beyond my comprehension," Bruce said, sitting across from Robert Chamberlain at the coffee shop. "Why? Why would anyone spend a lifetime wanting nothing more than…well, revenge, I guess, for not being born the laird to a castle?"

"In a way, I can almost feel pity for Jonathan. Whatever his hatreds, real or imagined, they festered in his heart. Along with the sickness that tore into him. Who is to say just what caused what?" Robert asked. "It might have begun with Maggie, and it might have started before she fell in love with you."

"She never rejected Jonathan for me. There was never anything between them," Bruce said, shaking his head.

Robert sighed. "But he believed she would have loved him if it hadn't been for you. I'm no psychologist, but when he finally started killing, he might have been looking for women who somewhat resembled Maggie—in the dark, at least. Getting even with her. He chose prostitutes because they can disappear far more easily than your average office worker, wife, mother or schoolgirl. In the main cities, they would just see him for a fairly decent-looking bloke, nothing scraggly or ugly about the man. They wouldn't hesitate to go with him. Disposing of the bodies in the forest was a way to get to you. Imagine how delighted he must have been, ready to wait and watch, when he snared in that group of Americans— and Thayer. It was nothing for him to slip the money for the payment on their lease into Thayer's account, and make it look as if Thayer had been the one committing the fraud. He was good with computers. Brilliant. It's a pity he couldn't have put it to good use. The fellow is all right, by the way?"

"Ah, yes, fine. Absolutely fine. Toni was nearly hysterical to reach him, once Jonathan was dead. Then the others arrived, and he was helped out of the woods. And, well, you know the rest." He grimaced. "Here I am, forty-eight hours later, still barred from my own castle while the forensic teams finish with all their work."

"Bruce—"

"Hey, I was a cop, remember? Take all the time you need to see that everything is processed." He exhaled with a grimace. "There I was, thinking that Jonathan was incompetent when he was really a master criminal. And I was certain there was something really evil lurking in Thayer Fraser. I'm sure Toni and her friends were just about in terror of poor Eban. I even began to wonder at times if we weren't looking at another husband-and-wife team of killers. And all along I had inspired this terrible hatred myself."

"Whatever you do, don't blame yourself," Robert cautioned him. "You didn't do anything to Jonathan. No one knows what really causes that kind of short circuit in the mind and soul. Maybe he was born with a capacity for evil. Or maybe he let it grow inside. Anyway, here comes your crew. And I have work to do."

Toni and the others had arrived, having taken a bit longer to get ready. They were staying at the Thistle and Crown, just down the street, and though it reeked with charm and hospitality, it lacked a great deal in water pressure.

They all greeted Robert affectionately, but he demurred and told them that he had business when they implored him to stay.

As he was leaving, Matt and Darcy Stone arrived, and he went through a series of goodbyes once again.

About to actually depart, Robert stopped suddenly. "Oh!" he said, offering them all a grin.

"Oh?" Bruce said.

"Now I can't believe I forgot to mention this! The barmaid, the young barmaid from Stirling we thought to be missing—do you remember?"

"Oh, aye," Bruce said.

"Indeed," Thayer muttered. "Katie."

"Well, she's not going to be found in the forest," Robert said. "Seems she turned up in London. She had a date with a young man who convinced her that she was worth more than being a lackey to a mean man. She's working in a clothing shop and going to school. She was horrified when the London bobbies stopped her. She'd had no idea she'd been reported as a missing person."

"Thank God!" Thayer said.

"Well, now, there's a truism, all right. Good news, for once. Ta, now, folks, for real."

They were all gathered at the table and the waitress came to take their orders. For several minutes, there was a certain amount of chaos, what with decisions on what to eat and drink being made. Then there was a silence.

So far, all they had done was apologize to one another for their suspicions, worry about one another and talk about what had happened. But as of that night, the forest and the castle had been the domain of the police. Evidence was being gathered, and both forest and abode were crime scenes, off-limits. Even Shaunessy and Wallace had been moved to the stables in town. And Eban, loath to leave his little cottage, was now in wonder at the friendly service he received at the little hotel.

So now there was the future. It would be tinged by the past, but as always, the future would be what they made of it.

They were all staring at him.

"Here's how I see it should be done," Bruce said. "The tours will be stopped—for a few weeks. The police still have possession of the castle. And there will be articles in all the papers, so a little time should definitely pass out of respect. But then, knowing how people really do seem to love the gruesome, you'll probably be so busy, you'll be turning people away."

Gina made a funny sound in her throat. "You're… going to let us continue?"

He shrugged. "For about half a year."

"And then?" she whispered.

He didn't get a chance to answer, because Thayer suddenly burst out with, "Who'd ha' figured! Him, Jonathan…a *constable.* A man y'd know all yer life, Bruce!"

The past…yes, it would remain with them awhile. Even when they thought they had talked it out, it came back. Like a ghost from a not so distant time.

Toni looked at Darcy Stone. "Darcy, could Jonathan have been... Grayson Davis, living out another life?"

Darcy smiled and shrugged. "I don't know. Maybe, maybe not."

Matt added, "There aren't always answers, you know, from the living, or the dead."

Bruce spoke up. "Maybe he was just a man who resented me all his life—and had a penchant for power and murder, as well. There's nothing that will excuse his actions, but I can almost understand his hatred for me. I had everything he wanted—the castle, the title. Despite the fact that I was seldom here after Maggie died, I was the laird, and that meant something to the people in the village. Then there was Maggie...my fiancée. I'd never known that Jonathan had been in love with her. She always thought they were friends. Apparently, he thought that he'd been rejected. Maybe there's a whole slew of psychological explanations. And then again, maybe he was Grayson Davis, living a new life, without really having learned from the old."

Gina shivered suddenly and stared at David and Kevin. "And you! You little rats! As soon as you read about that case Bruce had solved in Edinburgh, you were staring at Ryan and I as if we were capable of such horrors."

"Oh, now, that's not true!" David protested.

"As if Gina would allow another woman next to me, much less find one for me," Ryan said.

Gina stared at him in reproach.

"You are jealous," he told her.

"My foot!" she said.

Bruce laughed. "Hey, come on now, Ryan. I've seen you hug Toni."

"Toni..." He waved a hand in the air. "Toni's my friend."

"Chopped liver!" Toni said, amazed that she could smile and laugh.

"I hug Toni, just like I hug David and Kevin."

"Ooh! Sexy!" Kevin teased.

Ryan groaned. "Ignore him, please," Ryan said to Bruce. "So…you'll let us stay and work for six months. And then what? Are you going to keep working with us, as well?"

"Aye, after the first month."

"After? Why after? What's happening before then?" David asked.

Bruce turned to Toni, a smile halfway curling his lip. "I thought I'd get away for a bit. And though I know Toni has a true love of Scotland, she might need to get away, too. Somewhere brand-new, very commercial, with a beach and lots of sun. Cancun, the Florida Keys, Aruba… Disney, maybe, though we'd definitely avoid the Haunted Mansion." He arched a brow to her.

"Toni can't go!" Ryan said. "Then all we'd have is Gina, and she can't do all the female roles. Ow!" he complained at the end as his wife elbowed him.

"There's Lizzie and Trish," Thayer said. "They'd love to be part of this, though I'm thinking of opting out myself."

"What?" The question came from around the table.

Thayer grimaced. "You know what all this has taught me? I want to be on the right side of the law. I want to clean up my act, get in some training, learn to be a cop… and apply to be constable here." He looked at Bruce. "All right, you're thinking I've been something of a scumbag, not worth a hoot—"

"Actually, I was thinking you might be perfect for the job," Bruce told him.

Thayer sat up straighter, stunned and very pleased.

"Aye, I'd be good, I swear it." He was quiet for a minute, staring at Bruce. "And you…you should go back to police work, you know. Robert told me that you were an asset he sorely misses."

"Truly, Bruce, it is something you should consider," Darcy said.

"There are many different ways in which you could put all your learned and…natural talents to good use," Matt told him.

"Sometime in the future, maybe," Bruce said. "Just not immediately."

"Okay, great. You're going off, Thayer wants to be constable and we get to keep doing the tours, minus half the staff!" Ryan said.

"You've got yourself, David and Kevin, Gina… Lizzie and Trish. And we will be back," Bruce promised. He looked at Toni again. "That is, if you're coming with me?"

"Try to leave without me," she told him.

"Still, what happens after the six months?" Gina demanded, diverting his attention.

"I think I know," Darcy said lightly, grinning. "And it doesn't take a psychic to see the future here!"

Bruce's eyes never left Toni. "Well, the way I'm hoping it will go, there will be this magnificent wedding here. The bride will be incredible in white, the groom, traditional in his colors. And the bridal party…well, you all figure it out." He glared at David and Kevin. "No yellow!" He turned back to Toni, taking her hands. "I was born a privileged man. I ignored that, and my heredity, a long, long time. This castle should be a home. I want to make it so, with a wife, with children. Think about it, lass!" he said softly, his words earnest. "That poor fellow, the great MacNiall, spent all those years walking this place, watching out for his descendants. I owe him that, don't you think? A bride as fierce, as passionate, as loyal as his own…and great-great-grandchildren?"

It was somehow incredibly special to Toni that he had dared to say this, before them all.

"You said you didn't really know me the other night," she reminded him.

"I was wrong. I know now—as I knew then—everything about you that I will ever need to know." He paused, now a little unsure of himself. "I'm sorry, I'm rushing you."

She shook her head. "No, you're not. I think it's the most wonderful story I've ever heard—and I didn't even make it up myself."

"Oh, my God!" David exclaimed. "Does that mean you two are engaged?"

"Aye, precisely," Bruce said.

"Ach, then! It's time for champagne," Thayer said.

And so there was a toast. And they spent most of the day together, a group that would forever be linked by the strange events they had shared.

Then night came again, and Bruce and Toni were alone at last. Cozy in their little room, he gathered her into his arms, taking her chin, raising it, meeting her eyes. "This is what I haven't said yet. I love you. It's not that I was a monk after Maggie died, nor was I a roving lecher of any kind. I was just existing. And then there was you."

"My dear, dear, Laird MacNiall!" she returned. "You do have a way with words."

"You still know very little about me," he warned her.

She shook her head, delighted just to look into his eyes. "We'll have a month in Aruba for you to tell me everything."

"And?" he said softly.

"And… I think I fell in love with you the moment you came riding into the hall, the great MacNiall! As you said earlier, I know everything I really need to know about you. And I love you, for everything I know, for you being you."

He smiled and kissed her. And when the kiss would have become extremely ardent, with clothing being shed, he paused suddenly, staring into her eyes again.

"The great MacNiall?" he queried.

"I don't believe he checked into the hotel," she teased innocently.

"Toni…is he still around?"

"He's gone," she said simply.

"You're certain? For good?"

She nodded. "He did what he needed to do. He's at peace."

"Ah. Well, peace isn't exactly what I intend to give you, you know. I have a feeling there will be plenty of tempest ahead."

"I wouldn't have it any other way," she assured him.

Then he kissed her again. And the tempest began.

* * * * *

Also available from B.J. Daniels

HQN Books

The Montana Cahills

Wrangler's Rescue
Rancher's Dream
Hero's Return
Cowboy's Redemption
Cowboy's Reckoning
Cowboy's Legacy
Outlaw's Honor
Renegade's Pride

The Montana Hamiltons

Honor Bound
Hard Rain
Lucky Shot
Lone Rider
Wild Horses

Harlequin Intrigue

Whitehorse, Montana: The Clementine Sisters

Hard Rustler
Rogue Gunslinger
Rugged Defender

Whitehorse, Montana: The McGraw Kidnapping

Dark Horse
Dead Ringer
Rough Rider

Look for *Stroke of Luck*, the first book in
B.J. Daniels's new series, Sterling's Montana,
available March 2019 from HQN Books.

Visit the Author Profile page
at Harlequin.com for more titles.

WHEN TWILIGHT COMES

B.J. Daniels

When I decided to become a writer
I just wanted to tell stories. I'd never met a writer,
knew nothing about the business or the blessings
that come with it. One of the greatest gifts I have
realized is the friendship of other writers.
This book is dedicated to two of the best:
Amanda Stevens and Joanna Wayne.

Chapter 1

Seattle, Washington

Jenna Dante ran her fingers down the cold steel barrel of the gun in her jacket pocket as she parked in the darkest part of the estate.

Through the trees, she stared at the second floor bedroom window, willing the light to go out.

It took everything in her to wait another twenty minutes after it finally did so. Then she picked up the crowbar from the seat next to her and, making sure the dome light was turned off, slipped from the car.

Because she would be carrying a heavy load when she left, she'd taken the service road, parking at the back entry closest to the house.

The hired help had gone home hours ago. Lorenzo didn't like anyone staying on the estate at night. That was because he didn't want any witnesses.

The gun weighed down her pocket as she moved stealthily through the trees and darkness toward the servants' entry. She'd worn all black, and had picked this entrance because it was the farthest from the main part of the house.

At the door she pulled out the ring of keys, thinking she would have to use the crowbar. But the key she chose fit in the back door lock and turned. She stared down at it, surprised that she could still be shocked by Lorenzo's arrogance. He'd been so sure she would never use her keys that he hadn't even bothered to have the locks changed?

Or was he expecting her?

She froze, her pulse drumming in her ears.

With the crowbar in one hand, she turned the knob and pushed open the door. He hadn't reset the security system when he'd come home, either.

She felt a chill race up her spine as she stood in the rear entryway, fighting to calm her nerves. Desperation had brought her here. Desperation and anger. She drew on the anger now, reminding herself of everything Lorenzo Dante had done to her. He had taken her dignity, her innocence, her confidence. He'd hurt her every way possible. But this time he'd gone too far. This time he'd taken the one thing she couldn't let him get away with, no matter what happened here tonight.

She stood listening for a moment, then slowly closed the door and put down the crowbar. The arrogance that had kept him from changing the locks and turning on the security system would be his downfall, she told herself. Better to believe that than consider he didn't even see her as a threat.

The thought brought a fresh surge of anger. She needed it desperately if she hoped to succeed. Fear was a weakness, one she couldn't afford. Not tonight. But anyone who didn't fear Lorenzo Dante was a fool, and Jenna was no longer a fool.

Cautiously she crept up the stairs to the second floor. The carpet was soft and deep, her footsteps silent. She stopped near the top. She could hear music playing in the living room. Classical music. Lorenzo must be in one of his moods. He tried to forget his humble beginnings by pretending he was a man of breeding.

But during their marriage, Jenna had noticed that he played classical music when he was trying to convince himself he was somebody, that he wasn't just some thug who'd made a lot of money illegally, that he didn't have enemies who were more powerful than he was.

Tonight he must be feeling vulnerable.

The thought surprised and scared her. He was more dangerous when he was like this. She wondered why he was in this mood. He should have been on top of the world. After all, he'd struck another blow against her, one that he knew would destroy her.

Something was going on, she realized. Something to do with the business? Or her?

At the top of the stairs she looked down the long hallway. The door to the room she was most interested in was closed. Her fingers itched to open it and slip inside.

But first she had to know where Lorenzo was.

She pulled the gun from her pocket and crept down the hall, noticing that the door to the master bedroom was open.

Another piece of music came on. Over it, she heard the rattle of ice cubes in fine crystal. She felt another jolt of concern. Lorenzo was making himself a drink? Something was definitely going on.

Moving silently along the thick carpet, she crept to

the landing at the top of the stairs that overlooked the living room. She gripped the gun tighter in her hand as she held her breath and peeked over the railing.

Lorenzo stood in front of the fireplace with his back to her. He held a drink in his hand, his gaze apparently on the fire, an anxious set to his shoulders.

He was a large man. Just the thought of his big hands on her made her stomach roil. Her finger skittered over the trigger of the gun as she raised it and sighted down the barrel, pointing it right where his heart should have been.

You can't kill him. Not in cold blood.

She wasn't so sure about that. Not after five years with Lorenzo. Not after everything he'd done to her.

She thought about him turning and seeing her, seeing the gun. She could imagine the smirk on his face, could imagine him taunting her. He wouldn't believe she could kill him.

Even with a gun in her hand, he wouldn't see her as a threat. He thought he knew her so well, figured she would be too afraid to come after what he'd taken from her.

But she also knew him. Maybe better than he knew her. She knew his one weakness: arrogance. He'd been so brazen to come back here—to not even try to hide from her. Because he had the courts and the police where he wanted them. Jenna had learned the hard way that she couldn't beat him through the system.

And because of that, he thought he had Jenna where he wanted her, as well. That was her edge. That's why she had to move fast.

She lowered the gun, sliding it back into her jacket pocket, and turning, stole down the hallway again. As she started past the master bedroom, she noticed once more that the door was open. Lorenzo's suit jacket was lying across the bed. She slipped into the room and moved to the nightstand on Lorenzo's side.

Reaching into the space behind the table, her fingers brushed across duct tape and cold steel. She ripped Lorenzo's gun off the back of the stand and peeled the sticky tape from the grip.

She didn't need to check if it was fully loaded; she knew it was. Lorenzo was meticulous about that sort of thing. But she looked, anyway. Tonight she wasn't taking any chances.

The gun *was* loaded. She slid the safety off with a soft click. Pointed it at the open doorway, slipping her finger through the guard, caressing the trigger, getting the feel of the larger, heavier piece.

Then she lowered the gun, snapped the safety back on and stuck the weapon into the waistband of her black jeans, so it was covered by the tail of her jacket.

As she started to leave the room, she saw something that stopped her cold. When Lorenzo had thrown his suit jacket on the bed, something had fallen from the pocket. At first all she saw were the passports.

With trembling fingers she picked up the top one and saw Lorenzo's photograph, but with an entirely different name.

She began to shake harder as she picked up the second passport and opened it. Tears of fury sprang to her eyes at the sight of the photograph.

Bastard. He was planning to skip the country. That's what was up. That's why he was feeling vulnerable tonight. His "associates" must not know his plans, because Lorenzo belonged to an organization that knew only one type of retirement program: death.

Unless he had made some kind of deal to buy his way out.

But the passports weren't the only things that had been in his jacket pocket, she saw. She pulled out two airline tickets and had to steady herself when she saw the date Lorenzo had booked for a one-way flight to South America. *Tomorrow.*

Shaking furiously, she ripped up the tickets and threw them into the wastebasket beside the bed. Then she pocketed both passports and hurried down the hallway to the smaller bedroom. As she opened the door, she could see the slight rounded shape under the covers in the glow of the night-light. Her heart lodged in her throat at the sight of her sleeping child.

Jenna eased the door closed behind her and tried to stop shaking, angrily fighting back tears.

She moved quickly to her daughter's side. She couldn't let Lexi see her anger. Or her fear.

The silky dark hair was spread out on the pillow, the little face that of a cherub. Lexi had one arm around her beloved rag doll, Clarice. The other was looped around the neck of her cat, Fred.

Fred looked up as Jenna stepped deeper into the room, and let out a loud meow.

Jenna hurried to the baby monitor and shut it off.

Fred blinked at her with huge golden eyes.

"Lexi," she whispered as she knelt over the bed. "Wake up, sweetie."

Lexi's lashes fluttered, then suddenly flew open. Her dark eyes widened in surprise. "Mommy? Daddy wouldn't let me see you." Her lower lip pushed out into a pout. "He said you had gone away."

Jenna hushed her. "It's you and me who are going

away, sweetie. But it's a secret. We have to be very quiet, okay?"

Lexi nodded and threw back the covers as she sat up. She was wearing the little yellow ducks pj's Jenna had bought her. The same ones she'd been wearing last night, when Lorenzo had broken into her apartment and taken Lexi.

"I need you to be very quiet," Jenna told her daughter. "We don't want to wake up Daddy."

Lexi nodded and put a chubby finger to her lips. "Shh."

Jenna picked up her daughter, hugging her tightly as she breathed in the sweet smell. Lexi felt solid in her arms. Safe. At least for the moment.

"Come on," Jenna whispered. "Remember, we have to be really quiet, okay?"

Lexi nodded, clutching her rag doll. "Is Daddy coming with us?" she asked in a small voice.

Jenna looked at her daughter's face. "No." She saw the instant relief and her heart broke. "Did Daddy hurt you?"

The child shook her head, her lower lip pushed out again. "He yelled and made me cry."

Jenna hugged her. "Well, he won't make you cry again." She stepped to the door of her daughter's bedroom and started to open it.

"Fred!" Lexi cried. "I can't leave Fred."

Jenna groaned inwardly. She'd never been a big fan of cats. Lorenzo had bought the kitten for Lexi, knowing Jenna wasn't allowed to have a cat in the apartment where she'd been living with Lexi since the divorce.

"Alexandria will have to come over to the house to see her cat," Lorenzo had said.

Which meant Jenna would have to come as well,

since Lorenzo only had supervised visitation. He'd gotten the cat to force Jenna back to the estate—a place she had grown to abhor.

Now she stepped back into the room and, with her free hand, picked up Fred from the bed. He complained loudly as she hooked him into the crook of her arm.

She waited until he settled down before she opened the bedroom door and glanced down the hall. Empty. She could still hear the classical music.

She crept along the back hall, then down the stairs. She was almost to the back door when she heard an approaching car coming up the service road. Was it possible Lorenzo had called for a delivery this late at night?

Moving to the window, Jenna peered out as headlights flashed. The whine of an engine rose, then died as the car pulled in directly behind hers.

No! Whoever it was had blocked her car in.

The police? Or some private patrol?

But as she peered through the blinds, she saw that it was one of Lorenzo's "associates" who climbed out.

Franco Benito. He looked toward the house, making her step back and let the blind knock against the window frame.

She moved quickly down the hallway, stepping into the laundry room and partially closing the door. Motioning to Lexi to be quiet, she held both her daughter and the cat as the back door opened. Franco closed the door a little more forcefully than usual. She pressed herself and Lexi against the wall as the man stormed past. She caught only a glimpse of him, but he looked angry. Probably because Lorenzo had made him come to the service entry. Why had he done that?

She breathed a sigh of relief as Franco's heavy footfalls fell silent.

How was she going to get away now, though? He'd blocked her in. And what if he mentioned her car to Lorenzo? Lorenzo would know she was in the house—and he would know exactly what she'd come for.

Lorenzo Dante finished his drink and poured himself another as he tried to calm down. He glanced at the clock on the mantel, checking it against his watch.

Nine fifty-seven. Franco was twenty-seven minutes late. He hated people who weren't punctual. People who made him wait.

He gripped the glass, anger seething inside him as he looked around the country estate, reminded of all he had accomplished—and how little respect he'd garnered. He deserved to be treated better than this. Because Franco was taking his place in the organization, did he think he didn't have to treat him with respect? The glass shattered as he crushed it in his hand. Blood ran down his wrist and dripped to the floor.

Lorenzo stared at it in surprise, having forgotten he was even holding a glass. Opening his hand, he let the pieces tinkle to the Spanish tiles.

Two shards were stuck in his palm. With a kind of distracted fascination, he plucked them out, dropping them to the floor as he watched fresh blood run from the cuts down his wrist.

He turned at the sound of footfalls behind him. "You're late."

Franco Benito stopped in the middle of the floor, clearly startled by the sight of the blood and the broken wineglass.

Lorenzo smiled as he stepped to the bar and leisurely wrapped a wet cloth around his hand, all the time keeping his gaze on Franco, considering the best way to teach the two-bit thug respect for his betters—and the value of being on time.

"I'd take a drink if you haven't broken all the glasses," Franco said, clearly irritated himself.

Lorenzo smiled at the idiot's attempt at humor. Franco hadn't liked being ordered to come through the service entry. Too bad.

Without being offered a drink, Franco stepped to the bar beside Lorenzo. Franco was a good-looking guy, not really big, but strong. His one great flaw was that, because he was taking Lorenzo's place in the organization, he thought Lorenzo was powerless against him.

Franco was so clueless. He reached behind the bar and wrapped his thick fingers around the neck of an expensive bottle of bourbon. Taking a glass—the wrong kind for bourbon—he sloshed some of the amber liquid into the expensive crystal with arrogant abandon, spilling enough fine liquor on the bar to make Lorenzo wince.

Franco turned to face him, raising his glass in a mock salute. After drinking it down, he sighed and smacked his lips, smiling at Lorenzo, almost daring him to comment as he reached for the bottle to pour himself another. After tonight, Lorenzo wouldn't have any power in the organization. And Franco would.

But the night wasn't over.

Lorenzo grabbed the back of Franco's neck and slammed his face down on the bar, into the spilled booze. He heard the thug's nose break like a twig even over the howl of pain.

"Shut up. You'll wake my daughter," Lorenzo snapped as blood poured from Franco's nose, a stream of bright red.

Franco staggered as he let go of the bourbon bottle and fumbled for his weapon.

Lorenzo could feel himself losing control, and tried to pull back as he snatched the bourbon bottle off the bar and brought it down sharply, dropping the thug to his knees. It would have been so easy to finish him right there and then.

Franco had his gun in his hand, trying to find the trigger through the blood pouring down his face. With a swiftness born of survival in the dog-eat-dog, violent world Lorenzo lived in, he reached behind the bar and came up with the sawed-off shotgun.

Jamming the end of the barrel against Franco's temple, he brushed his finger lightly over the double triggers as he met the man's gaze. It was all Lorenzo could do to restrain himself. If he didn't, he would definitely waken Alexandria.

Franco glared at him, clearly caught between an irrational desire for retribution and the need to stay alive.

Lorenzo watched the ignorant thug weigh his options, and smiled to himself when Franco slowly dropped his gun to the floor.

"What the hell is wrong with you?" he demanded as Lorenzo lowered the shotgun. The thug plopped into a sitting position and leaned back against the bar to cup his hand over his broken nose. "Are you crazy?"

Lorenzo put the shotgun back behind the bar and poured himself another drink, glad he hadn't pulled the trigger. It wouldn't have just awakened his daughter, who was sleeping upstairs, it would have added to his problems with their boss, Valencia.

After tonight, though, Lorenzo would be free of Valencia. All he had to do was keep his cool, get the money he owed Valencia and give it to Franco. Just a few more minutes and it would all be over. He would have bought his way out of the organization and would soon be on a plane to another country. A new life. What did he care if Franco was acting too cocky? Or if Valencia was determined to stay legit now and thought he could run things without him? Let Franco try to take his place.

Lorenzo downed his drink. He unwrapped his hand and tossed the bloody bar cloth on the floor next to Franco. "Clean yourself up while I check to make sure you didn't wake my daughter."

"Just get the money." Franco glared up at him, then angled a look at his gun, lying on the floor within reach.

Lorenzo cut him a smile. "You'll get the money. If you live that long."

Franco gingerly picked up the bar rag and held it to his nose, leaning his head back, closing his eyes— disappointing Lorenzo by not going for the gun. "Valencia isn't going to like this."

Lorenzo considered kicking the thug, but feared he wouldn't be able to stop once he started. He walked past him, his expensive Italian shoe brushing Franco's calf, making the man draw his legs up and open his eyes. Lorenzo was rewarded by the fear he saw shining there. Maybe Franco wasn't as stupid as he'd thought.

But Franco was right about one thing: Valencia wouldn't be happy about this. Lorenzo didn't know what had gotten into him. He'd never liked Franco, never trusted him, and he sure as hell didn't like the idea that Valencia had picked Franco to take his place in the organization. Lorenzo didn't like what it said about him that Valencia thought someone like Franco could replace him.

As Lorenzo climbed the stairs to Alexandria's room, he felt his blood pressure start to come down, along with his temper. By tomorrow he would be on his way to a new life. No more Francos. No more Valencias.

And to make his new life even sweeter, he would have his daughter with him. He smiled at the thought of his ex-wife and how much pain that would cause her. Jenna deserved much worse. It would be all he could do to leave the country without killing her first. But he took pleasure in knowing Jenna would die a slow death just knowing he had Lexi, and that she would never see her daughter again.

At the top of the stairs, he glanced down the hallway, immediately on alert. The door to Alexandria's bedroom was partially open. He was positive he'd closed it earlier. Had she gotten up for some reason? She'd been upset earlier, wanting to see her mother. He'd had to spank her to get her to quit asking for Jenna. Was it possible she'd run away, thinking she could find her way to that awful apartment Jenna had rented after the divorce?

Or had someone taken Alexandria?

His step quickened as he told himself he had to be wrong. But even before he grabbed the doorknob and turned it, he knew.

As soon as Jenna was fairly sure that Franco wasn't coming right back out to his car, she pushed open the laundry room door, sneaked down the hall and slipped out the rear door of the estate. She knew she wouldn't get far on foot carrying Lexi and the cat.

"Mommy?" Lexi whispered. "I'm cold."

"I know, baby. Hang on." The child was growing heavy. The cat started to squirm. Jenna knew she couldn't put Fred down. He might run off. She had to do something and fast.

She glanced toward the four-car garage. What choice

did she have? She'd have to take one of Lorenzo's vehicles.

But when she opened the side door she saw that the garage was nearly empty. Lorenzo had sold all but one car: his large black SUV.

Of course he would have sold the cars. Because he was planning to leave the country. She should have known. He'd been too calm during the divorce, too agreeable. True, she hadn't asked him for anything but Lexi. Still, it hadn't been like Lorenzo to give up anything that he felt was his. He'd never planned to let her get away with Lexi.

Jenna stared at the large black SUV. Lorenzo always left his keys in it, as if daring anyone to steal it. Her heart leaped at the sight of Lexi's car seat in the back. Did she dare?

The ridiculousness of the question made her laugh. Lorenzo was going to kill her for stealing Lexi back. It wouldn't matter what else Jenna took.

She opened the rear door, set Lexi in her seat and Fred on the floor. The cat jumped up on the back seat beside Lexi as Jenna snapped the child in, before rushing around to the driver's side and slipping behind the wheel.

Once she opened the garage door, she would have to move fast. She reached for the key.

Lorenzo Dante let out a howl of anger and pain at the sight of the empty bed, the covers thrown back, Alexandria gone.

He couldn't believe what he was seeing. He glanced around, checked the bathroom, ran down the hall to his bedroom. No little girl.

Letting out a string of curses, he charged into his

daughter's room and ripped the covers from the bed, whirling them into the air in a rage as he crushed the fabric in his fists the way he would crush his ex-wife's throat when he found her.

It had to have been Jenna who took the child. Part of him still couldn't believe it, though. Jenna knew what he would do to her. She was smart enough to fear him. He'd made sure of that as soon as they were married. He'd gotten her young so he could train her to be the wife he wanted. She'd bent to his wishes from the start, because she'd had no other choice.

Until Alexandria had been born a year later.

That's when Jenna had started to change, he realized now. The pregnancy hadn't been her idea. In fact, he was almost certain she was entertaining thoughts of leaving him when he'd decided to change her mind by getting her pregnant. Foolish young woman that she'd been. As if he had ever planned to let her leave him.

She'd thought he didn't know about the birth control pills she had started secretly taking. He'd simply replaced the contraceptives with sugar pills, and was pleased when she'd quickly gotten pregnant.

He'd thought he had her exactly where he wanted her. Now she would obey him. Now that she was tied down with a baby. And it had worked for a while. He'd tried to act the loving husband and father.

But he'd learned the hard way that she, too, had been acting. He'd come home one day to find her gone. She'd filed for divorce, gotten a restraining order against him. She couldn't have thought he would ever allow her to leave him, let alone take his daughter.

Unfortunately, he'd gotten into some trouble inside the organization and needed to keep a low profile. At Valencia's urging, Lorenzo hadn't fought the divorce.

He'd let Jenna think she'd gotten away with it—and sole custody of Alexandria. He'd even let Valencia think he wasn't going to cause Jenna any trouble.

But no one walked away from Lorenzo Dante. No one took anything of his, either—and lived to tell about it.

Jenna had stolen his daughter. First in court, then again tonight. Just because he'd let her think she'd gotten away with it the first time, now she thought she could do it again? He blamed Valencia for tying his hands and keeping him from taking care of Jenna right away. If he had killed her the moment she'd taken Lexi and filed for divorce, he would have saved himself a lot of aggravation.

He flung the blankets back onto the empty bed, wanting to trash the room to relieve the anger that had started building downstairs with just the thought of seeing Franco tonight. Then Franco had been late...

Lorenzo reminded himself that the thug was still downstairs. Waiting.

It would be impolite to make him wait, Lorenzo thought with grim humor.

Wanting to finish his business with Franco so he could deal with his ex-wife, Lorenzo started out of the room, then heard a car engine.

He ran to the window and looked out in time to see his black SUV come tearing out of the garage. In the glow of the garage light, he saw Jenna behind the wheel. She'd taken his car, too?

Fury tore through his veins like a grass fire in a stiff wind. What did she think she was doing?

He started to charge out of the bedroom after her, already thinking he could take one of the other cars, chase her down, run her off the road and—

He stopped as he remembered. He'd sold the other cars because he was skipping the country. Just as he'd sold the house and everything in it. Because he planned to fly out as soon as he settled up here tonight. He didn't want any hired killers coming after him. That's why he was buying his way out of the organization.

The realization that he wouldn't be able to catch her hit him like a blow. He'd made Franco come to the service entry to show contempt for him and his new job. Even if he took Franco's car, he wouldn't be able to catch Jenna. She was on an entirely different road, was getting away, and there was nothing he could do about it.

He slammed his fist into the wall three times in quick succession. Franco called up an inquiry, which Lorenzo ignored as he tried to calm down.

That's when he remembered. All the air rushed out of him. The money. The money to pay off Valencia. He'd left it in a duffel bag in the back of the SUV.

No! He felt his knees go weak. He had to sit down on the edge of the bed to keep from falling. The room blurred in a haze of red as his rage sent his blood pressure soaring. His money.

No, not *his* money. *Valencia's* money. As if taking his money wasn't bad enough, she'd taken the money he owed a man who could crush him—and would.

He'd kill her. If Valencia didn't kill him first. Lorenzo swore and dropped his head into his hands. He'd never dreamed Jenna would come to the house and try to take Alexandria. She knew what would happen if she did. What the hell was wrong with her? The woman he'd married had been so shy and quiet, so submissive, so malleable.

Even during the divorce, Jenna hadn't asked for a

penny of his money in court, refusing even child support when the judge had tried to insist on it.

So what had happened to that woman? A woman who would never have taken his daughter, let alone his damn car, and worse, his money.

He pushed himself to his feet. He couldn't call in his stolen car to the cops. Not with the money in the back. Nor could he send the cops after Jenna for taking their daughter. She had sole custody. Not that he'd ever put much store in handling things legally, anyway.

His hands began to shake.

He would get the money back. That wasn't the problem. The problem was Valencia. Unfortunately, Valencia expected the money *tonight*. It was the reason Franco was waiting downstairs. Franco and his broken nose.

Lorenzo's mind raced. Valencia wouldn't believe that the money had just gone missing. Even if Lorenzo told him the truth—that Jenna had taken it along with Alexandria—Valencia wouldn't cut him any slack.

No, the boss would be furious that Lorenzo had taken Alexandria. Valencia had ordered him not to fight the divorce, not to seek retribution. That bastard had never even shown any sympathy for what Lorenzo had been going through with Jenna. It was one of the reasons Lorenzo had decided to secretly take his daughter, settle up with the organization and leave the country. And there had been a couple of previous disagreements over money with Valencia that had already caused some bad blood between them.

Lorenzo didn't need this.

Valencia had been willing to let him walk away from the business, from the past. But now Lorenzo might be considered a liability, someone who knew too much and couldn't be trusted, and therefore was expendable. Valencia might feel forced to kill him.

For an instant Lorenzo thought about just taking off, skipping the country tonight, running for his life. He had a passport in a new name and enough money hidden around the country to live on for some time.

He pushed himself off the bed and hurried down the hall to his bedroom. He reached behind the nightstand on his side of the bed, instantly realizing the weapon he kept hidden there was gone.

His gaze fell on his suit jacket. He grabbed it up, knowing before he searched the pockets that the tickets and passports were gone, as well.

He wrung the garment in his hands, wanting desperately to rip it to shreds. But even before he'd found the passports missing, Lorenzo knew he wasn't leaving the country.

Valencia would hunt him down like a rabid dog. Plus, Lorenzo knew that just the thought of Jenna getting away with not only his daughter, but also all that money, would drive him insane.

He swallowed back the bile that rose in his throat. No, he would have to stall for time until he could get the money back. But he would get it back. The money *and* his daughter. He could always get new plane tickets, new passports.

But he couldn't leave without making his ex-wife regret ever being born.

"Hey?" Franco called from downstairs. "Hey! Valencia's waiting for his money. He's going to be pissed enough when he sees my face."

Lorenzo nodded to himself in the empty bedroom. Franco had a good point. Valencia wouldn't be happy on either count.

As he left the room, Lorenzo stopped at one of the heating grates, pried it open and took out another of the weapons he kept hidden in the house—one that even his dear wife hadn't known about. He shoved the gun into the small of his back and descended the stairs.

Franco never knew what hit him.

Chapter 2

Jenna Dante had been driving for hours through the pouring rain and darkness when she came around a corner in the narrow road.

She couldn't believe what she was seeing. Water. It tumbled down the hillside from a rain-swollen creek, flooding the road ahead. The raging water ran over the highway and on down the mountainside like a river.

She slammed on the brakes, her fingers gripping the wheel. The SUV began to skid on the wet pavement, directly toward the deep water flowing onto the highway.

She wasn't going to stop in time, and once she hit the moving water...

She cranked the wheel, felt the SUV begin to spin out of control. *Lexi!* It was her only thought as the car crashed into the side of the mountain. There was a terrible sound of metal ripping, then silence.

For a moment, Jenna couldn't move. Her gaze shot

to the car seat in the back. Lexi was awake and looking at her. "Are you all right?" Jenna cried.

"What happened, Mommy?"

"We just went off the road. It's all right." She peeled her fingers from the steering wheel, shaking so hard she had to grip her hands together in her lap. "But we're fine." They were fine. Her air bag hadn't even deployed. But she could hear the water rushing by not feet from them. They wouldn't be fine for long.

The car engine was still running. She shifted into Reverse, praying that the car wasn't damaged badly, that she could drive out of here.

But the moment she pressed on the gas pedal, she realized they weren't going anywhere. Not in this car.

She shut off the engine and unhooked her seat belt. The rain seemed to have lessened as she climbed into the back and hurriedly got her daughter out of her car seat. Grabbing her purse, Jenna opened the door and climbed out, reaching back to lift Lexi and her rag doll in her arms.

"Fred!" Lexi cried, and grabbed for the cat.

"I'll come back for him," Jenna promised. But Lexi already had a death grip on the animal, so it looked as if they were all going.

Jenna wasn't even sure where they were. Somewhere in the Cascade Mountains. All she knew was that she hadn't seen a house or another car for miles.

"Mommy? Clarice is scared," Lexi whispered, one arm around the rag doll and Fred, the other squeezing tighter around Jenna's neck.

Jenna tried not to let her own fear immobilize her. The car was wrecked. They were out in the middle of nowhere. And Lorenzo would be coming after them. Could already be after them.

Fred let out a loud meow in her ear, as if agreeing with the rag doll. It was definitely scary.

"Clarice shouldn't be afraid," Jenna said. "She has you to make sure nothing happens to her. And you have me."

Right. She felt her stomach clench with fear at just the thought of how helpless she was against Lorenzo. But she had Lexi. And Lorenzo would take her again over Jenna's dead body.

She almost laughed at the truth in that. She never wanted to see him again and didn't think she probably would. He never did any of his own dirty work. Of course, this time he might make an exception. He would want to kill her with his own bare hands.

She shivered at the pleasure he would derive from it.

Jenna walked back up the road, away from the raging creek, trying to decide what to do. She had few options. The road was blocked, might even be washed out by morning.

Not that Jenna was going anywhere in the SUV. From what she could tell, the car was high centered on a rock. Or worse.

The rain had almost stopped. Fog rose from the pavement, and beyond that was nothing but darkness.

She tried her cell phone. No service.

Out here she felt so vulnerable. But they couldn't have stayed in the car—not with the water so close and possibly still rising.

She half expected to see car lights coming up the road. Half expected Lorenzo to be behind the wheel. Could just imagine the expression on his face. *Gotcha!*

In the weeks since the divorce, she'd often wondered why he'd let her go so easily. But in her heart she'd always known. He wanted her to think she'd gotten away.

Gotten away with her daughter. When in truth, it was just a cat-and-mouse game with Lorenzo. He'd known that he could end it in an instant when he was ready.

Had he taken Lexi knowing Jenna would come after her? Had he just been looking for a reason to come after her and kill her? Not that he needed one.

She shuddered, telling herself that nothing could change the course of events. And if she'd never married him, she wouldn't have Lexi.

Jenna's heart broke at the thought that she might not be able to protect Lexi from her father. It had been a last resort, taking her back from Lorenzo the way she had. Now she couldn't let her daughter down. No matter what she had to do, she thought. Shifting the cat she reached for the gun still in her jacket pocket.

"Lookee!" Lexi angled a tiny finger out into the darkness beside the road.

Jenna had to crane her neck to see where she was pointing. Lights glowed from out of the fog. High up on the side of the mountain she could make out the top spires of a building poking up out of the trees and mist.

And there on the hillside was a sign, barely visible in the gloom. The neon outline of a woman in an old-fashioned bathing suit, in a diving pose. Underneath her, the words Fernhaven Grand Opening. The date on the sign was in three weeks.

There was definitely something up the road—a huge building, the lights glowing faintly through the swirling mist.

"I want to go there!" Lexi cried. "Please, Mommy? Clarice wants to, too. She said she wouldn't be scared at all if we went there."

"I don't think it's open yet," Jenna said. Whatever it was. "But we'll go see."

As she moved forward, the glow of lights high on the mountainside became clearer. No wonder she hadn't noticed them earlier from the highway.

If she could get her daughter somewhere warm and dry, she could call for a wrecker. They just needed someplace to wait. It had to be close to midnight by now.

The freshly paved road wound up the mountain. They hadn't gone far when she had to put Lexi down and catch her breath. After that, the child insisted on walking. Thankfully Jenna had grabbed a sweater for her daughter. She put it over the footed duck pj's. Jenna carried Fred, but Lexi wouldn't give up her rag doll, Clarice. The going was slow, the darkness around them intense. Along the road the trees were dense and dark.

Jenna was beginning to think this was a mistake when they crested a hill and the road abruptly widened. There, shrouded in fog, was a huge castlelike building looming out of the night.

She couldn't contain the chill that moved over her.

Fred dug his claws into her arm, seconding Jenna's thoughts. This place gave her the creeps, too.

"It's a castle," Lexi cried.

If this was a castle, then an evil count lived here, Jenna thought. But then, she'd been living with evil for some time. She still wondered how she could have been so deceived by Lorenzo. Why hadn't she seen what kind of man he was before she'd married him? She knew the answer. Lorenzo was very adept at hiding his true nature. But living with him, she'd quickly seen through his facade right down to his black soul.

As tired as she was, she wouldn't have been surprised if the hotel turned out to be a mirage. But all the lights were on in the huge lobby, and she could see someone inside.

"Come on, Mommy," Lexi said, and ran toward the wide front steps.

The air was damp and cold. Jenna could hear a roar as if there was a waterfall nearby. She caught up to Lexi, taking her hand. As they ascended the wide steps, Jenna looked up.

The face of a man appeared at one of the third-floor windows. She had the distinct impression he'd been watching them as if waiting for them. Maybe the hotel was open to guests, after all.

She had little more than an impression of him before he was gone.

Harry Ballantine wasn't sure what had made him go to the window and look out. Just a feeling.

Even more odd was what he saw from the window: a slight-framed woman with a young child, and something in her arms. A cat.

So what had drawn him to the window after all these years?

Apparently the woman.

She was dressed all in black, her dark hair pulled back in a ponytail. She wore no jewelry of any great value, something he could tell even from this distance. Her face, pale in the foggy light emanating from the lobby, had the appearance of both strain and exhaustion, but also fear.

She was in trouble. Why else would she be banging on the door of a not-yet-opened hotel after midnight on a rainy night?

He saw no reason why he might be interested in her. In fact, there was every reason not to get involved in whatever trouble she was in, even if he could help her.

That's what made it so strange. He *was* interested.

Something had drawn him to the window. Just as it now drew him to the woman. What worried him was that he had no idea why.

Raymond Valencia called Lorenzo just before midnight. "What the hell?" he said by way of greeting.

Lorenzo had gone to bed, turning out all the lights, just as he would have if nothing unusual had happened tonight.

"Raymond?" he asked, pretending he'd been awakened from a sound sleep. He sat up, fumbling with the lamp beside the bed. "What time is it?"

"Where the hell is Franco?"

"Franco?" He yawned. "How should I know where Franco is?"

"You might recall he was at your place to pick up something of mine a few hours ago," Valencia snapped. "Or don't you know anything about that, either?"

"Actually, he was late. Didn't get here until almost ten, seemed...nervous. Smelled like he'd been drinking."

There was silence on the other end of the line.

It was all Lorenzo could do to keep from filling the space, but talking too much would only make Valencia suspicious.

"What time did he leave with the money?"

"Right away," Lorenzo said. "I offered him a drink, but he said he was in a hurry."

More silence. He could almost hear the wheels in Valencia's head turning. Franco was a man Valencia trusted so much he was going to let him take Lorenzo's place. And Franco knew firsthand what happened to anyone who crossed the boss. It was no wonder Valencia was having a hard time believing that Franco would betray him.

"He probably stopped off to see his girlfriend and lost track of time," Lorenzo said, yawning again. "Hell, he probably had a fight with her and that's why he was late and had been drinking. Women. They can twist a man up good."

"What girlfriend?" Valencia demanded. "I know nothing about a girlfriend."

"Oh yeah?" He shrugged, counted slowly to five. "I don't know her name. I just overheard him on his cell with her one day. She was giving him a hard time, from the sound of it. He was kissing her butt, trying to calm her down. Pretty funny, really."

Valencia swore. Even a man as cold and hard as Raymond Valencia knew the effect a woman could have on a man.

Lorenzo smiled to himself when Valencia slammed down the phone without another word.

He'd offered the bait and the boss had taken it. Lorenzo put the receiver back in its cradle and turned out the light, lying in the darkness, thinking about the way Jenna had messed him up.

His first impulse was to go after her. But he couldn't indulge that impulse. If he left town now, Valencia would become suspicious. More suspicious than he no doubt already was.

No, Lorenzo had been forced to put one of his former employees on Jenna's trail.

He'd called a man who was so dumb Lorenzo trusted him. Alfredo made Franco look like a genius. The man was all brawn and no brain, and because of that he was like a robot when it came to just doing his job without any questions. Alfredo didn't even complain about being awakened in the middle of the night. He said he would find Lorenzo's ex, not let anyone know where he'd gone, and "detain" her until Lorenzo could join them at a later time.

"Good. I want to handle this myself when the time is right," Lorenzo had said.

"No problem."

He'd hung up. He hated waiting, and here he was going to have to wait some more. But he had confidence that Alfredo would find her and the money, and that was all that mattered. As long as it was soon.

The problem was what to do once he had Jenna and his daughter and the duffel full of money. Maybe he would just tell Valencia the truth. Valencia would be furious at him for killing Franco, but Lorenzo figured it was something he could get over. Especially since Valencia would have his money back.

Or… Lorenzo could go with plan B. He could keep the money, take his kid and get out of Dodge. By then Valencia would be fairly convinced that Franco had ripped him off. Lorenzo could maybe plant some evidence, a trail for Valencia to follow that would make it even clearer that Franco had taken the money. Franco and his girlfriend.

What if Franco really did have a girlfriend? Lorenzo had had to lie about overhearing Franco on the cell phone with someone. But what if the stupid thug really *did* have a girlfriend? That could mess things up good.

Lorenzo swore, almost wishing he hadn't killed Franco. If Franco had a girlfriend, then Lorenzo would have to find her before Valencia did.

Chapter 3

Jenna followed Lexi up the steps and across the hotel's wide veranda, then knocked on the door. Earlier she'd seen someone moving around inside the expansive lobby, where several huge ornate chandeliers glowed brightly.

Lexi peered in, seeming enchanted by the place. It was definitely elegant, from what Jenna could see. Expensive, too. And apparently not open yet. Had she just imagined someone inside earlier? What about the man she'd seen at the third-floor window?

She pounded harder.

An elderly man appeared from out of the back. He seemed surprised to see her.

"We're not open for business yet," he called through the glass.

"My car went off the road down by the creek," she

called back. "The road is flooded. We just need somewhere to stay until I can phone for a wrecker."

He held up a finger to signal he would be right back. Good to his word, he returned with a key and opened the door. "Sorry. Come on in. The road's out?"

She nodded, and she and Lexi stepped in. The moment she entered she felt a brush of cold air move past her cheek. She shivered as she looked around. "What is this place?"

"Fernhaven Hotel. The exact replica of the one built in 1936."

That explained why the place had the feeling of another time. The lobby was huge, with massive planters of ferns and palms, rich fabric-covered sofas and chairs, Oriental rugs spread over hardwood and marble floors that gleamed. The crystal chandeliers sparkled. Through high arches she could see thick burgundy carpet running to the elaborate entrance of a huge ballroom.

"Nothing was quite like Fernhaven at the time," the elderly man said. "I remember my parents talking about the place. It opened during the Depression, but there were still some that had money and wanted to be with other folks with money in someplace isolated. Couldn't get more isolated than this," he said with a laugh.

"Do you have a phone I could use? I tried my cell phone but it doesn't seem to work up here."

"Sorry, didn't mean to talk so much. Gets lonely up here." He was tall and whip thin, with a shock of gray hair and thick brows like caterpillars over pale eyes. "You're welcome to use the phone in the office, but I doubt you'll be able to get anyone out tonight. The closest town is to the east, and if the road is flooded… Give me a minute. I should call the highway patrol first, so they can put up a roadblock at the creek."

He left her and Lexi, and went into the back. Jenna could hear him on the phone. When he returned he said, "The creek isn't the only stream flooding tonight. Sounds like there's more problems on the road you came in on. I'm afraid you're not going anywhere for a while." He glanced from her to Lexi.

Jenna realized what they must look like. Though the rain had stopped, there was enough moisture in the air to make them both damp and chilled.

"I can put you in a room for the rest of the night," he offered. "We're not officially open, but we have some suites on the third floor that are finished." He waved off her concern. "The rooms are just sitting up there."

She had no choice, she thought, gazing at her daughter. Lexi hugged her rag doll, looking both cold and tired. "That's very kind of you. I just don't want to get you into any trouble." She thought of the man she'd seen looking from the window on the third floor. "Did you say there is no one else staying here?"

"Just the three of us," he said, smiling down at Lexi. "I'm the security guard. Name's Elmer. Elmer Thompson. I'll be here until six, when the manager arrives with the rest of the crew finishing up the place. I'll let him know you're here."

Jenna had forgotten about Fred until he meowed and tried to jump down. "I'm sorry about the cat. He's my daughter's and she couldn't bear to leave him in the car."

Elmer smiled. "I think we can accommodate the cat, as well. The dining room isn't open yet, but I can scare up some canned tuna and a box with some sand from the construction site. How would that be?"

"Wonderful." Jenna found herself starting to relax. "I'll pay you, of course."

"You can discuss that with the manager in the morning," he said.

She noticed the old black-and-white photographs behind the registration desk. "When were those taken?"

"Opening night, June 12, 1936. The new owners rebuilt the place to make it exactly like the original, right down to the most minute detail."

"Rebuilt it?" She felt a chill as she squinted at the photo taken of a ballroom filled with people, the men in tuxedos, the women in fancy gowns and elaborate, expensive jewelry. "What happened to it?"

"Burned down opening night."

She jerked back from the photograph. "How horrible. Was anyone hurt?"

"Fifty-seven souls lost."

She felt her chest tighten. "These photographs...if they were taken during opening night..."

He nodded in understanding. "You're wondering how the photos survived. A newspaper photographer took the photos, then left to meet his deadline not realizing that the hotel was burning to the ground as he drove into town."

She glanced around unable to hide her shock. "Why would anyone want to build on this site, let alone make the hotel exactly as it was?"

Elmer shook his head. "I've never met the owners, but I heard they feel Fernhaven is too beautiful to lie in ashes. They don't build hotels like this anymore, true enough, but quite frankly, I think they did it because of the ghosts."

"Ghosts?"

He laughed. "Haunted hotels are the thing, they tell

me. It's a marketing ploy. Some of the crew have said they've felt them." He scoffed at the idea. "Cold spots in the hallways, curtains moving when there is no breeze, that sort of thing. The gimmick must work. We're booked solid for the grand opening in three weeks."

"It sounds ghoulish to me," Jenna said, and couldn't contain her shiver.

"I'm sorry. You're both chilled. Let me get you into a room." He turned to the wall of wooden cubbyholes behind the counter. Each held a pair of old-fashioned room keys. "I suppose I should have you sign in, if you don't mind. Make it official."

Elmer flipped open a thick book that looked not only old but charred in one corner, as if it had been burned. "From the original hotel," he said, seeing her shock. He swung the book around and handed her a pen.

She took the pen, but drew back when she saw the date on the opposite page: June 12, 1936. Seventy years ago. And the list of guests who'd signed in that night. She couldn't help but wonder how many of those people had died here.

"Is there a working phone in the room, so I can call for a wrecker in the morning?" she asked.

"Yes."

She noticed that his attention was suddenly fixed on the key to room 318, lying next to the registration book. He seemed surprised to see it there. She tried to remember if she'd seen him take it from the cubbyhole, and couldn't.

Frowning, he checked the book, then with a shake of his head and a small laugh, he handed her the key with 318 embossed on it.

"Thank you." Jenna looked again at the old photographs of people dancing in a large ballroom, others sitting in the lobby or standing at a long bar.

One of the faces jumped out at her. Her heart began to pound for seemingly no reason as she stared at a man from the 1936 photograph.

He was lounging against the bar, decked out in a tux, holding a champagne glass in his hand as he smiled at the camera, arrogance in every line of his body.

His hair was dark, with an errant lock hanging down over his forehead. His features were as chiseled as the broad shoulders under the tux jacket, his face handsome even with the thin dark mustache.

She felt a chill ripple across her skin. Something about the man reminded her of the image she'd seen in the third-floor window earlier, as she and Lexi had approached the hotel.

The man seemed to be looking right at her—and smiling as if he knew something she didn't.

"If you'll just sign the book…"

She dragged her gaze away from the photograph, surprised she'd been so drawn to it she'd completely forgotten to sign in.

She started to write her full name, then stopped. For a few moments, with everything that had happened, she'd forgotten what she really had to fear. Not ghosts, but Lorenzo. She signed her name as Jenna Johnson and made up an address in Oregon. Best not to even use her maiden name, McDonald. Lorenzo would be after her. Might already be hot on her trail.

"I'll bring up the tuna and cat box. If you like I can scare up something for the two of you to eat," Elmer offered.

"That is very kind of you, but not necessary." She

had some cereal and dried fruit in her purse for Lexi. "We'll be fine tonight." At least, she hoped so.

"Are your suitcases in your car?" he asked. "If you give me your keys, I'll run down and get anything out that you might need for tonight," he offered.

"Oh, that's not necessary. I feel like we have imposed on you enough."

"Please. I get bored to tears here. It's nice knowing there is someone else in this big old place. And you and your daughter are going to need dry clothing."

He was right, Jenna thought. "Thank you," she said, as she handed him the keys.

"The elevator to your wing is right down there," Elmer told her. "I'll be up in a few minutes with your things."

"Come on, Mommy." Lexi pulled on her hand.

"Thank you," Jenna said again to the security guard. She felt shaken and weak, stumbling around in a haze of exhaustion. A little rest and she'd be fine. Thank goodness the hotel had been here. She didn't know what she would have done otherwise.

Her daughter broke free again to skip toward the elevator, her eyes bright with excitement.

The lobby seemed too large and empty as Jenna followed. The elevator doors opened as if expecting them.

Jenna took Lexi's hand and stepped into the empty elevator car. But as the doors closed and the mirrored, wood-paneled cage began to hum upward, she had the strangest feeling that they weren't alone.

Harry Ballantine stood in the corner of the elevator wondering what he was doing. What had he expected? That there was some reason he felt drawn to this woman? That maybe she'd been sent here?

She was totally oblivious of him. Just like the little girl and the cat.

He noticed the diamond ring on the woman's left hand. She was turning it nervously with her thumb. True to his former profession as a con man and jewel thief, he assessed the diamond in the half second it took to do so. Not bad quality. An average cut. A carat and a quarter. Not worth stealing.

The thought surprised him. He hadn't thought about stealing anything in years.

His gaze went to the woman again. Who was she? But more to the point, what was it about her that had him thinking about the past again?

He'd almost forgotten what it had been like, the night of Fernhaven's first grand opening. Standing at the bar watching the men in tuxedos, the women in expensive gowns, all whirling around the spacious ballroom to the music of the Johnny Franklin Orchestra.

Those had been the days. Harry had been thirty-two and had never seen that much wealth in one room before. Not surprisingly, he'd been down on his luck—until he'd conned his way into an invitation to the grand opening.

June 12, 1936.

It had been nothing short of heaven for a jewel thief.

Until the fire.

The elevator slowed. The woman glanced in his direction, and for just an instant he thought she might have sensed him there.

Jenna leaned against the elevator wall, the past few days finally catching up with her as she stared at the empty space across from her, telling herself no one was staring back at her and Lexi.

Her reflection in the elevator mirrors made her wince. Not only did she look terrified, but there were dark circles under her eyes and her face was pale and drawn. Her hair hung limply from her ponytail.

The elevator ride seemed interminable but she was sure it only took a few seconds before the car stopped.

As the doors hummed open Lexi looked up, breaking into a smile as if there was someone waiting just outside the elevator. Jenna felt a cold draft curl around her neck. There was no one standing there. Nor did she see anyone in the long, lush red carpeted hallway.

"Did you see her hat?" Lexi asked. "It was purple."

Jenna had no idea what her daughter was talking about. She gripped Lexi's hand as the elevator seemed to fill with the icy invading air, and practically lunged out, dragging Lexi with her.

Before the doors closed behind them, Jenna turned to look back, expecting to see frost on the mirrors. The elevator was empty, her reflection mocking her fear.

"Come on," Jenna said in a whisper as she led Lexi down the hall.

Lexi took off, skipping along the plush carpet of the wood-paneled hallway.

"Wait!" Jenna called quietly, even though according to the security guard there were no other guests to disturb. The wing was deathly still.

She was so tired that just lifting each foot took Herculean effort. When she saw the room, she gasped in astonishment. Elmer had said it was a suite, but she hadn't expected this.

She looked at the magnificent rooms, half-afraid to enter. Lexi had already disappeared inside, making Jenna nervous. She stepped into the suite and closed and locked the door.

For just a moment she felt something—a cool brush against her cheek. She drew back, touching her skin.

She couldn't rid herself of the feeling that she and Lexi weren't alone, hadn't been since they'd entered Fernhaven. Jenna was afraid that somehow Lorenzo had followed her. She told herself that was crazy. Unless he had some sort of tracking device on the SUV...

Ridiculous. He had no reason to track himself. Unless one of his so-called "associates" had put the device on his car.

Jenna knew she was being paranoid. No way could Lorenzo have found them, let alone sneaked into the suite to wait for them.

Lexi came running out of a far bedroom, chattering to her rag doll as she climbed up to look out the bay windows. "Lookee, Mommy!" she cried in delight.

Jenna joined her to gaze down at a beautiful courtyard. Lights glowed golden on an exquisite fountain and a string of hot pools set among huge rocks with steam rising from them. Past the pools there appeared to be a path that disappeared into the foggy darkness and thick foliage of the mountainside.

It was all beautiful and eerie. Jenna hugged herself, trying to enjoy this extraordinary place as much as her daughter obviously was.

She told herself to be glad that she had Lexi back. That they were safe now. But the words were hollow. She knew Lorenzo. He wouldn't stop until he found her, until he destroyed her.

Lexi raced across the large suite to peer out another window. Jenna followed again and saw that this side looked down on the front of the hotel.

Beyond the small parking lot was the thick darkness of the forest. Jenna stared into the blackness, imagining someone staring back at her, then hurriedly pulled the drapes and turned toward the larger of the two bedrooms.

A knock at the door startled her. "Who is it?"

"Elmer Thompson."

She recognized the aging voice of the security guard from downstairs and felt foolish. Hadn't he told her that there was no one other than the three of them in the entire hotel tonight?

She opened the door and he rolled a cart in. She caught a glimpse of Lexi's and her suitcases.

Fred started meowing as Elmer handed her a can of tuna and an opener. She opened the can and fed the cat as Elmer took Lexi's small princess suitcase into the second bedroom, along with the box of sand.

"I took a look at your car," he said as he rolled the cart out of the master bedroom after unloading it. "I'm afraid the front axle is broken. It's definitely not drivable."

She would have to call for a rental car first thing in the morning and have the SUV towed to the nearest town.

"Sorry. You've had your share of bad luck tonight," he added. "But at least you're someplace warm and dry and safe." He smiled. "I'll be downstairs until six. Just call if you need anything else."

"You've been too kind," Jenna said, and tried to tip him.

"Thank you, but no. I'm just happy to help."

He left, and she got Lexi into some clean dry pj's and into bed.

By the time she entered the other bedroom, all she wanted to do was fall into bed still wearing her damp clothing.

But as she stepped into the room, she saw her suitcase on an ornate stand at the end of the bed. Beside it was a large navy blue duffel bag she'd never seen before.

She frowned, wondering where it had come from. It must have been in Lorenzo's car, but it didn't look familiar.

She stepped toward it, feeling a sense of panic as she slowly unzipped the bag and peeled back the top.

The duffel was filled with stacks of used hundred-dollar bills! There had to be thousands of dollars in the bag.

She stumbled back from it. *No. Oh no.* Her body began to quake with the realization of what she'd done.

She hadn't just taken Lorenzo's daughter or his SUV. She'd taken his *money*.

Chapter 4

"Mommy, you didn't tuck me in, the way you always do," Lexi said behind her.

Jenna jumped, clamping a hand over her mouth to keep from crying out. She fought back the tears of fear and frustration that burned her eyes as she turned to face her daughter, and tried to smile.

"What's wrong, Mommy?" Lexi asked, her lower lip protruding as she studied her face.

"Nothing. You just startled me, that's all."

Lexi looked as if she might cry.

"Everything's fine, sweetie," Jenna said, leading her back to the other room.

It was so late all she wanted to do was go to bed, but she was determined to try to keep to their usual routine for Lexi's sake.

But she knew she had to get the money back to

Lorenzo somehow, and quickly. Maybe if she gave it back…

She shook her head at even the thought that it would appease her ex-husband. Nothing would placate him but revenge. Still, she had to try. For Lexi's sake.

The question was how to get it to him. She couldn't just box it up and send it by UPS.

Lexi scrambled up onto the bed and began to jump up and down. "Three little monkeys jumping on the bed—" She broke off in a fit of giggles. The words were from their favorite book.

"No jumping on the bed! I don't want you falling off and busting your head," Jenna said, playing along.

Lexi plopped down, still giggling. "I like it here. I want to live here."

No chance of that, even if Jenna had shared her daughter's enthusiasm for the place. They had to keep moving. As much as Jenna hated it, they would have to leave the country. Even with the safeguards she'd taken, she feared Lorenzo would find them, though, because in her heart she believed she would never be free of him.

Unless she was dead.

Or he was.

"I want to live here with you and Clarice and Fred and—" Lexi's lower lip came out and tears filled her eyes "—a new daddy who's nice."

Jenna felt her heart break for her daughter. She'd stayed with Lorenzo as long as she had only because she'd wanted Lexi to have a father. She realized now that she'd been hoping that maybe Lexi's love could change her father. Jenna had been such a fool.

"You have sweet dreams, okay?"

Lexi nodded.

Jenna tucked her daughter into bed and kissed her

warm forehead, brushing back a lock of her hair. Lexi had her coloring, the light skin, the dark brown eyes and hair, although Lexi's hair was darker than Jenna's, more like her father's, thick and straight.

Lexi had taken after Jenna in personality as well, and fortunately didn't have any of Lorenzo's traits, including his need for perfection or his bad disposition. Jenna was thankful for that.

"Good night. Sleep tight. Don't let the bedbugs bite," Jenna murmured, after Lexi had said her prayers.

The little girl laughed. "There aren't any bedbugs."

"No," Jenna agreed. Not in this hotel. She was feeling better about staying here. Even Fred had come out from under the bed.

The suite, she had to admit, *was* beautiful, from the rich woods to the soft carpet and elegant furnishings.

Lexi snuggled down in bed, with Clarice tucked on one side and Fred on the other.

Jenna padded to the door and looked back at her daughter. She could hear Lexi carrying on a one-sided, whispered conversation with the rag doll. Her daughter had such an active imagination. She could entertain herself for hours. Lorenzo used to say it wasn't normal. That they should have another child for Lexi to play with. He'd tricked Jenna the first time. But she'd been too smart for him after that.

Studying her daughter from the doorway, she was just thankful that Lexi hadn't seemed to suffer, not through the divorce or her abduction by either parent. Since she'd never known "normal," Lexi didn't seem to realize that her parents *had* divorced. Or that she and her mother were running for their lives.

To the comforting sound of Lexi's sweet voice, Jenna checked the entire suite to make sure there was no one hiding there. Relieved, and finally starting to relax, she went into her bedroom and opened her suitcase.

She hadn't packed much, just a few clothes for herself, and most of Lexi's. She'd had to move quickly once she'd gotten the call from the private investigator, telling her that he believed her ex-husband had taken Lexi back to the home Jenna had shared with him.

"Let the police handle getting your daughter back," the private investigator had advised.

"I've already tried that route." The man obviously didn't know Lorenzo Dante. "This is something I have to do myself."

Stripping off the black clothing now, she tossed it aside and put on the complimentary thick white, terry-cloth guest robe hanging in the closet. She pulled it around her, snuggling into the warmth, trying to chase away the chill that ran bone deep, as she looked at the duffel bag full of money.

Hurriedly, she zipped it closed and stuffed it into the back of the closet. Tomorrow she would figure out a way to get it to Lorenzo.

In the meantime, she and Lexi were safe, she thought, repeating it like a mantra. At least for tonight.

She couldn't wait to soak in the huge old-fashioned tub. Maybe tonight, for the first time in a long time, she would be able to sleep.

Or maybe not, she mused, as she sensed that same strange charge in the air that she had earlier. It breezed past her, a brush of icy breath against her bare skin, leaving her with that sense of a presence in the room with her.

She checked the whole suite once again, unable to stop herself. There was no one there, just as there hadn't been earlier.

Back in her bathroom, she began to fill the enormous tub with hot steamy water and almond-scented bubble bath, compliments of Fernhaven.

She shied away from thinking about Lorenzo. Or the money in the duffel bag in the back of her closet. To her surprise, her thoughts veered to the man in the old black-and-white photograph from the hotel's opening night. Funny how she thought she could smell the smoke from his cheroot…

With a shudder she realized that the man in the old photograph resembled the one she'd thought she'd seen at the window of the third-floor hotel room tonight.

But that wasn't possible. There was no one else in the hotel, Elmer had said.

Jenna frowned. Lexi was the one with the overactive imagination, not her.

Exhaustion, she decided. What else could it be?

A low hissing sound directly behind her made her whirl around. Fred was crouched in the doorway of the bathroom, his wide-eyed gaze boring into the corner of the window seat across from her.

Jenna stared at the spot where Fred's eyes were transfixed. There was no one there, of course.

She snatched up the cat.

"Fred, I really wish you wouldn't do that," she said as she carried him back to Lexi's room. He protested as she started to close the door so he couldn't get out. "I'm not going to have you waking me up all night with that foolishness," she whispered.

He just stared at her with those big eyes, then looked past her, jumping as if someone frightening had just come up behind her.

She swung around, knowing even as she did that no one would be there. Then she glared down at Fred, who had stopped hissing, but seemed to be watching the doorway, as if whoever had been there had left.

"Honestly, Fred, you're really starting to annoy me," she whispered, scratching his ears. He began to purr, pushing against her fingers, golden eyes closed in contentment. "Oh, how quickly you change your tune, you old faker."

She moved to the bed to reassure herself that Lexi was sleeping soundly. The child's face was angelic in sleep. She had Clarice tucked in the crook of her arm. Jenna leaned down, needing to touch her daughter, to assure herself that she was real, that she was here, that she was safe.

Jenna pressed a soft kiss on her baby girl's cheek, then remembered the water running in the tub in her bathroom. Closing the bedroom door, she rushed back and hurriedly turned off the faucet before the tub overflowed. Then, unable not to, she looked at the spot Fred had freaked over. Nothing but an empty, sparkling tile bench.

That's what she hated about cats. They jumped at nothing and generally spooked her. Darn that cat. She couldn't help herself, but now she was scared again. She rubbed the back of her neck, unable to throw off the memory of that cold draft, and Fred's odd behavior.

But it wasn't just the cold. Or the cat. It was the feeling of being watched.

She stared down at the tubful of steamy water and glistening bubbles, smelled the almond-scented bubble bath and yearned to sink into it.

"You aren't going to keep me from this bath," she said to the empty room, then directed a challenging glare at the tile bench.

Still, she disrobed hurriedly, stepping in and sliding down into the hot water until all but her head was under the bubbles. Her gaze went to the corner of the window seat again as she tried to assure herself that she was alone in the bathroom, that no one was sitting in the corner, watching her.

Harry Ballantine sat on the tile bench, idly watching the woman through the steam.

The cat had sensed him. He wasn't sure what to make of that, any more than he was sure why he was here, in this room, with this woman.

The cat had spooked her. But she was no more aware of him than before, he thought with a disappointment he should have gotten over years ago.

She didn't know he was here. No one did.

Except maybe the cat. But who could tell with cats? They reacted to all kinds of things that weren't there.

Harry studied the woman.

He'd always been good at sizing up people. Had to be in his former line of work. He had been able to tell a lot by the way they dressed, their body language, their actions, the way they talked.

But his skills were rusty from lack of use.

She glanced toward him again, her big brown eyes dark and a little afraid.

What is your story?

Earlier, he'd watched her search the suite three times. Who did she think she was going to find here? Harry couldn't help but wonder what monsters she feared were hiding in the closet, waiting for her to turn out the light.

She was running from something. Someone. He'd bet everything he had on that. If he had anything to bet.

She was humming softly to herself now. Probably her

version of whistling in the dark, since it was a child's song she was humming.

He'd seen the way she was with her daughter, love shining in her eyes whenever she looked at the child. He'd felt something like loss as he'd watched her. He couldn't remember his mother ever looking at him like that.

Not that she'd been mean to him. She hadn't. She'd just been too busy cooking, cleaning and taking care of nine kids, along with working in the fields with his father.

Jenna moved on to Broadway show tunes. He smiled, watching her hum away, her breath making the soap bubbles glide across the water's surface like tiny white sailboats.

He could see she was beginning to relax. Steam rose off the water, making her dark hair curl around her face. She brushed it back from her cheek.

She was pretty with her hair wet, her face bathed in steam. Her eyes were a different brown. He tried to think of the color as she blew out a breath and sent more bubbles scooting across the water.

He wondered what kind of trouble she'd gotten herself into. And why he felt so strongly drawn to her.

Harry slid off the seat and moved to the side of the tub. Steam rose from the hot water. She looked soft and lush in all that warmth, her head tilted back against the white porcelain, eyes closed, her dark hair wet and slick, falling like a waterfall down the side of the tub.

He couldn't help himself. She looked so young, so appealing, so vulnerable. Her skin was fair, dotted with a faint sprinkling of golden freckles across her cheekbones. He brushed his fingers over her warm, wet cheek, trailing them like falling stars. He'd forgotten what warm skin felt like.

Her whole body went rigid, her brown eyes widening.

He touched a finger to her full lips to see if they were as soft as they looked.

She jerked up into a sitting position, her breasts bobbing above the bubbles, full and round, the peaks dark and dripping wet.

She had felt his touch!

He quickly stepped back as she looked in his direction, even though he knew she couldn't see him.

Her pulse throbbed in her slim throat. Her eyes were wide and dark, reminding him of a thunderstorm. She pressed a hand to her collarbone. He could see her listening like an animal, alert, prepared to fight. Or run.

She bit down on her lower lip. Her eyes filled with tears, and after a moment, her fingers came out of the bubbles to cover the spot where he had touched her lips. Tears threatened to spill over just before she ducked under the water and bubbles.

She had felt him! How was that possible?

He watched her dark hair float on the surface as he waited for her to come up for air.

Her head burst up out of the water and she gasped for breath, flipping her mane of wet hair back in a wave of warm scented water that splashed onto the floor.

Her eyes were closed, the lashes dark on her pale skin, as she wiped soap bubbles from her face.

In all these years, he'd never wanted to have substance and warmth—all the things that had once made him human—more than he did at that moment.

He stepped back, surprised not only by the strength

of that long-suppressed emotion, but by something else that had been foreign in him: desire.

He watched her grope for the towel hanging on the rod within inches of her fingers. Without thinking, he pulled it down so it fell into her hands.

Her whole body went rigid again. Holding the towel out of the water, she sat up, wiped the soap from her face and opened her eyes to look anxiously around the room once more.

Keeping the towel in front of her, she stood up in the tub. He backed out of the room. He hadn't realized how much he'd missed the feel of a woman's skin. Jenna Dante's cheek had been soft and warm, just like her lips. God, how he'd missed warmth.

In her bedroom, the covers were turned down. A long black nightgown lay across the pillow. Silk. He heard her pull the plug in the tub. The water began to drain noisily. Even the bedroom smelled of almond from her bath. He inhaled the last of the scent as if it was water and he was a man dying of thirst.

He felt a strange intimacy with this woman. Why, after seventy years of a kind of hell?

Her purse was on the nightstand. He could hear her in the bathroom, brushing her teeth. He knew without looking that she had dried her body quickly and wrapped herself again in the guest robe.

In her purse he found the usual female stuff, along with two grand in traveler's checks. Her driver's license said her name was Jenna McDonald. Not Johnson, the name she'd registered under.

In a manila envelope in her purse he found copies of vaccinations and medical histories for herself and her daughter. Also in the purse were her birth certificate and one for her daughter, Alexandria, two plane tickets in the names Nancy and Alicia Clark, and two passports with the kid's and her photographs, in the new names. The woman had to have a connection to get these—a criminal element.

He glanced toward the bathroom as she finished brushing her teeth and shut off the water. She was running away all right. Far away, from the looks of it, and not planning to come back. From the husband?

A quick search of her suitcase turned up nothing of interest. He glanced in the closet and spotted a large, heavy-looking, navy blue duffel bag on the floor. Interest piqued, he took a look.

The duffel was filled with hundred-dollar bills, used ones, banded together in what he would guess were ten or twenty thousand dollar stacks.

He'd never seen that much money in one bag before, but he'd always wanted to. He felt that old pull like a bad ache. Once a thief, always a thief.

Her black clothing had been thrown over the chair near the bed. He picked up the jacket, wondering what was so heavy that it pulled down one pocketed corner.

A gun. The woman had a gun! He didn't need to pick it up to see that it was fully loaded.

For all he knew she was running from the cops. Or even the feds, given that wad of money in the closet.

What kind of trouble was this woman in?

She came out of the bathroom wrapped up tight in the bathrobe, just as he'd known she would be. Nor was he surprised when she checked the suite again. He watched her open her daughter's bedroom door.

He could see the relief in Jenna's body as she knelt over her child, tucking the little girl in with a tenderness that touched him.

All these years he had felt nothing. Why now? And

for a woman who was in more trouble than Harry wanted to know about?

He hovered beside her bed, watching her fall asleep. Watching the rise and fall of her chest, the slight flutter of her eyelashes on her pale skin.

Her cheeks were still flushed from her bath. She smelled heavenly. At least what he thought heavenly would smell like.

He'd never really noticed her mouth before. It was bow-shaped. There was a light sprinkling of freckles across her nose and a tiny brown spot, like a fleck of chocolate, just below her left ear.

He wanted to touch her. He felt drawn to her in ways he didn't understand. But something told him he'd been waiting a lifetime for her.

He joined her on the bed, lying next to her, listening to the steady rhythm of her breathing, content for the first time in seventy years.

Chapter 5

Lorenzo was disappointed when he woke to realize that Jenna was still alive, still had his daughter and his money. Killing her had only been a dream.

Unfortunately, his current situation *wasn't* a dream, but a nightmare. Franco was dead. Valencia's money was gone. And the clock was ticking. Lorenzo needed that money found one way or another. And soon.

He also needed to make sure that if Franco really *did* have a girlfriend she wouldn't be talking to Valencia.

Getting up, he pulled a red silk robe over his naked body and went to the top of the stairs, stopping to survey the living room. He'd cleaned up last night. There was no sign of anything out of place—just the way Lorenzo liked it. He couldn't have gone to bed without sweeping up the glass and scrubbing the blood off the tile.

While he'd taught Jenna to keep his house immaculate, the way he insisted, Alexandria had driven him crazy with her toys and dropping food on the floor at the table. He'd blamed Jenna for not making their daughter behave better.

He had to admit his life was easier without Jenna and Alexandria. But once he had his daughter to himself he would teach her not to make messes. Jenna had always been too easy on the child. Lorenzo saw now that he should have been stricter with both of them.

He went to the drawer where he'd put Franco's wallet and cell phone—and the plastic gloves he'd worn to remove them from Franco's body.

Donning the gloves again, he went through the wallet, finding only cash and one gas credit card, in Valencia's name. No photographs. Nothing personal.

Lorenzo pocketed the seventy-five dollars in cash, thinking what a two-bit thug Franco had been. Didn't even carry enough cash to buy a decent meal.

Booting up the cell phone, he checked Franco's phone directory. Only one number in it. Not surprisingly, it was Valencia's. He checked the list of calls Franco had received. All from Valencia. Sheesh, Franco had no life.

Or at least no life he wanted anyone to know about.

Lorenzo then checked numbers dialed. For a moment it looked as if all of those would be to Valencia, as well. All except one.

He dialed the number, not holding out much hope. A woman answered and tore right in. "Franco. I was worried about you. I waited up half the night for your call." She stopped. "Franco?"

Lorenzo hit End and put the wallet and cell phone into a plastic grocery bag. He pulled off the gloves and disposed of them in his garbage.

Getting the woman's address proved easy. The number Franco had called was to a land line. He found her

through his computer's cross directory. Her name was
Rose Garcia. She lived on Beacon Hill. While still on
the Internet, he called up a map directory and printed
out a route to the woman's house—and ordered a rental
car.

Jenna had taken his only form of transportation. The
memory did little to improve his mood. Worse, she'd
left her car behind—but he no longer had a key for it.

The rental agency promised to bring him a car at
once, something big and black.

He then called a towing service. The sooner he got
rid of Jenna's car the better.

Under normal circumstances, he would have had a
leisurely breakfast and taken a soak in his whirlpool
bath before going out. But thanks to Jenna, nothing
was as it should be. Since he couldn't put off getting to
Rose Garcia before Valencia did, he'd be lucky to get
something to eat before noon.

Jenna, now that she had the duffel bag of money,
was probably eating a nice big room service breakfast
in some fancy hotel.

The thought ruined his day.

Jenna woke to rain. It plinked against the window,
driven by a harsh wind.

She rose at once and went to check on Lexi. Her
daughter was sleeping like an angel, and Jenna felt such
relief it brought tears to her eyes.

She climbed into bed next to her and snuggled close,
breathing in the sweet scent.

Lexi stirred, rolling over, her big brown eyes widening in surprise to find her mother in her bed.

"What are *you* doing here?" the little girl asked,
smiling.

"I got cold and got in bed with you," Jenna said. It was one of the excuses that Lexi used when she didn't want to sleep alone.

Lexi smiled, recognizing it, and gave her an I-know-better look. "I had a dream about the ocean," she said, and proceeded to tell about swimming in the salty surf. "I had a big dog that ran in the water and splashed me. The dog was black and white and had floppy ears and a big tongue." Lexi giggled at the memory.

Jenna smiled at her daughter, thankful that the dream had been a pleasant one. Her own dreams had been disturbing. "That sounds like a wonderful dog. But what did Fred think about that?"

As if on cue, Fred crawled over them to let out a loud meow, making it clear he wanted his breakfast.

Jenna hated that they had to get up and get going. She would have loved to stay in the bed, talking and giggling with Lexi.

Or go back to sleep. Back to the dream. It felt unfinished. She flushed with heat at the memory of the man in it. The dream had left her frustrated and aching for fulfillment. For release. Worse, she'd dreamed about the man from the old photograph.

How odd was that? But she knew she'd probably conjured him up because he was safe. The photo had been taken seventy years ago. The man had been about her age then. He was long dead, long forgotten. Safe.

Jenna swung her legs over the side of the bed and stretched. Her body felt too alive, her skin tingling as the dream refused to fade.

"I put some clothes out for you to wear," she said over her shoulder to her daughter as she headed for her own bathroom. "And no bouncing on the bed!"

The bedsprings instantly quieted, making her smile.

As she walked through the living area, she noticed that the hotel suite seemed less ominous in daylight.

She went to the window and looked out at the rain-drenched mountainside. The courtyard itself was still shrouded in fog. She dreaded just the thought of driving off this mountain in such poor visibility. Or was it leaving the dream that she dreaded?

She called for a rental car—and wrecker—and was told both would be sent as soon as possible.

"I don't want to leave," Lexi moaned from the bed. "Clarice and Fred don't, either."

Jenna looked back at Lexi's pouty face.

It was so cute, she had to smile. "We'll play a game on the way into town. We can have breakfast at the first café we see." She thought of Lexi's dream of running on the beach with a dog. She didn't see why they couldn't have a dog someday. Or why they couldn't live on the beach. "How would you like to go to the ocean?"

Lexi's eyes lit up as she scrambled to her feet and began to bounce on the bed again. Fred dug his claws in to hang on, making them both laugh as Lexi bounded off the bed, then jumped back on to retrieve her doll.

"We're going to the ocean," Lexi told Clarice. "That's where we're going to live. We'll have a new daddy, a nice daddy, and a dog." She turned to Jenna. "What is the name of our dog?"

Jenna could only shake her head, her heart breaking all over again at Lexi's wish for a new daddy. "You'll have to pick a name for your dog. Now hurry and dress so we can get going."

Lexi did so, mumbling under her breath to her doll things Jenna was sure she didn't want to hear.

As she padded to her bedroom, the dream hung around her like a cocoon, images flitting in and out, vague and muddled. But that desperate feeling of wanting, of needing, made Jenna ache.

The harder she tried to remember the dream, the more it evaded her. But she could still almost feel him. His presence, his touch, his essence.

"Sexual frustration," she said with a grin. Her laugh sounded hollow even to her own ears.

The dream had felt so *real*. The warmth of him. Lying in his arms, his touch arousing her in ways—

She stopped, staring down at the bed, as her body turned to ice. Her heart began to pound erratically.

There were two impressions in the down-covered mattress. One on her side, where she always slept. The other where someone else had lain next to her.

Chapter 6

There was only one thing Raymond Valencia hated more than being treated like a fool, and that was allowing someone to *think* he was one.

Lorenzo Dante's story didn't hold water. Franco wouldn't cross him. At least not on his own.

Raymond could think of only two ways in which Franco could be coerced into doing something so stupid as stealing from the man who'd picked him up out of the gutter.

One would be if he had no other choice. Like a knife to his privates. But even that was hard to believe, given that Franco knew Raymond would do far worse to him when he caught him.

Two would be by a woman. If Lorenzo was right, some female had Franco confused. Raymond knew that a woman could turn any man's head around. But Franco? Franco had women, of course. But he made no secret that they were only the kind he paid for, the kind a man could depend on not to let him down.

Was it possible Franco had an honest-to-goodness girlfriend he hadn't let on about?

"You know anything about Franco having a girlfriend?" he asked one of the two men he'd called the moment Franco hadn't shown up.

Both men, now weary from lack of sleep, shook their heads. "I never saw him with anyone," Rico said. Rico was small, wiry and deadly. Raymond never turned his back on the man.

"You never heard him talking on his cell to any broad?" he asked the other man, a massive Neanderthal everyone called Jolly, short for Jolly Green Giant. Jolly was anything but.

"I never heard nothin'," Jolly said.

Raymond studied the expressions of the two men: bored and half-asleep, but seemingly not hiding anything. "Okay, Jolly, I want you to find the girlfriend."

"There *is* a girlfriend?" he asked in surprise.

"That's what you're going to find out," Raymond snapped. "Rico, I want you to take over the tail I have on Lorenzo Dante. If he blinks I want to know about it. Got it?"

Rico showed only slight surprise. There had never been any love lost between Rico and Lorenzo. Probably because they were so much alike. Another reason Raymond didn't trust Rico. Both were capable of killing their mothers without the least bit of remorse if there was something in it for them.

Raymond couldn't understand that. He'd bought his mother a huge house, sent her on expensive cruises, made sure she had everything she'd ever dreamed of. A man had to have someone in his life who loved him no matter what he did. That, Raymond had realized a long time ago, was only one person: his mother.

Lorenzo hadn't understood that. He hated his mother and instead had attempted to find love through marriage. Raymond had tried to warn him, but the man hadn't listened. Not that Raymond hadn't liked Jenna. In truth, he thought of his associate's wife with a deep-seated envy. Jenna had been too good for Lorenzo. The man hadn't known how to treat a woman like her and Lorenzo had lost her—and his child.

Lorenzo was a fool. He had proved he wasn't reliable. Raymond had been relieved when Lorenzo had offered to buy his way out of the business and leave the country.

But Jenna...well, she was another story. Raymond still didn't regret that he'd helped her during the divorce. Otherwise Lorenzo would have ended up with his daughter. A man like that had no business with a child like Alexandria. Raymond knew he'd done the right thing helping Jenna get her divorce. And with fake passports, he had trusted that she would never tell Lorenzo who had helped her.

But Raymond wondered now if Lorenzo had somehow found out the truth. The thought brought a cold dread. It would make Lorenzo a liability that had to be taken care of immediately.

The problem was that Lorenzo had friends. It wouldn't be good for business to hit Lorenzo. Especially now that Raymond was legit. It would be better if Lorenzo just left the country as he'd planned.

But if Franco hadn't taken his money and run off, then who did that leave? Lorenzo. And if Lorenzo had taken it, then he obviously was waging war.

Raymond checked to make sure the security system was on and the guard dogs were patrolling the area inside the fence around his house, just in case. So he'd have to find out who had taken his money—and why. First he would try to find Franco and this alleged girlfriend. If that lead proved false, then he would have to deal with Lorenzo. If Dante had his money, Raymond would be justified in killing him. And killing him in the most painful way possible.

He started to pick up the phone to call Jenna. He felt a small thrill at just the thought of hearing her voice. But he was also worried. Lorenzo was a hothead. If he had found out that Raymond had helped Jenna, then the woman was in danger.

What would it hurt to call her and make sure everything was all right?

Jenna quickly packed up what little she'd unpacked last night, pulling the duffel out of the closet and putting it beside her suitcase. She couldn't stop shaking.

As she turned to put the last item in the suitcase she felt something brush by her. She caught her breath, freezing in place as the cool air caressed her cheek and trailed down her throat to the crest of her breasts above the silk gown. She leaned back, closing her eyes, caught again in the dream. She surrendered to it, washed with a yearning that made her tremble. And then it was gone.

She opened her eyes and looked around the empty room. My God, she was losing her mind. These feelings, this fantasy… Upset with herself, she finished packing and angrily snapped shut the suitcase. What was wrong with her?

It was the hotel. The old photograph of the man at the bar. What had she seen in him that made her call him up in her dreams? She hated to think. He wasn't anything like Lorenzo, she realized. He was dark like

Lorenzo and there was no doubt he had a confident air about him that verged on arrogance, but he was nothing like her ex.

How did she know that?

She felt a shiver. She couldn't know anything about the man in the photograph. But there had been a man who resembled him. The man she'd seen from the third-floor window when they'd arrived. Except according to the security guard, she and Lexi were the only guests here.

She'd imagined him. Because she needed someone to love?

Jenna scoffed at the idea. She wasn't sure she would ever trust another man. And the dream had nothing to do with love, but a whole lot to do with lust. She could well understand why she would imagine a gentle lover in her dreams. Even why she would draw him from out of the past to come to her. She'd never known a man's loving touch. Lorenzo had been a fierce, brutal lover who took rather than gave.

Better to have a dream lover.

Except, Jenna thought with a frown, last night he'd only frustrated her. Made her want him, ache for him. She shivered, caught between desire and revolt. She didn't want to need any man—even a dream lover, but part of her feared he would return in her dreams tonight. Another part feared he wouldn't. She had the oddest feeling that he only existed for her here, in this eerie hotel with its ghosts.

How pitiful that if she wanted a man to love her with any tenderness, she'd had to find him in a dream.

She looked down at her left hand, to her engagement and wedding rings. She'd put them both back on, thinking it would make it easier to pretend to be married when she and Lexi were living in another country.

But just the thought of Lorenzo... She painfully wrenched both rings from her finger and threw them into her purse.

Jenna glanced back at the bed that she'd hurriedly made, leaving no sign of the impressions she'd thought she'd seen earlier. Imagined? Just as she'd imagined the man from the photograph coming to her in her dream?

Suddenly she just wanted out of this place. It made her feel things, sense things, yearn for things she couldn't have.

This hotel scared her. It was as if it knew her needs and desires. She and Lexi would be safer on the road than here, Jenna told herself. She was sure of it.

Rose Garcia got up every morning and ran five miles no matter the weather. This morning it was drizzling. That's what she got for living in Seattle.

At the time she'd moved here, rain had seemed enjoyable compared to the winters where she'd grown up, in North Dakota. Her family had been Spanish royalty at some point, but her great-grandfather had gotten into trouble in Spain, been forced to catch a boat and light out for a new life. On the boat, he'd befriended some Norwegians and ended up a general store owner in North Dakota.

Rose stretched on the porch, listening to the drizzle turn to full-fledged rain as she prepared for her run. She loved living in Beacon Hill and had bought the house cheap because of the depressed area. But with the cost of houses around Seattle now, Beacon Hill was making a comeback. People like her were buying up the older houses and renovating them.

She'd done the work herself, watching those home improvement shows for tips. The guys she worked with made fun of her, but she could swing a hammer better than most and she was hell on wheels with a power saw.

She stretched her other leg, then quit stalling and bounded down the porch steps. As her luck would have it, the rain began to fall even harder. She ducked her head, burrowing down in her jacket, determined to do five miles even if it killed her.

It almost did.

A car came around the corner, moving too fast, as she was crossing the street. She lunged out of the way, feeling the bumper just miss her. The car's tire dropped into one of the potholes in the road. A wave of muddy water splashed over her, making her feel like a drowned rat.

She swore at the retreating car, noticing that it was black and expensive. The downside of an improving neighborhood, jerks like that one, she thought, and resumed her run, not worrying anymore about getting soaked by the rain.

Lorenzo Dante glanced back in his rearview mirror at the runner he'd almost hit and cursed her. Stupid health nuts. Why didn't they join a gym like normal people? Or better yet, buy equipment and stay home?

Not that he wasn't already in a bad mood. And then to have some stupid pedestrian almost dent his rental car... He swore and slammed his fist on the steering wheel. Damn Jenna to hell and back. This was all her fault.

He was so angry he missed Rose Garcia's house address the first time and had to turn around and come back, circling the block, driving down the alley.

It was a small house. There were potted plants on the porch, checked curtains at the kitchen window, a red-and-white Mini Cooper out back. A house that said a woman lives here—*alone*.

But still he drove around the block a couple more times before he parked down the street. This didn't feel right. Franco and the woman who lived in that neat little house? Didn't add up.

Finally, taking his umbrella, he walked through the pouring rain up the steps to her porch and knocked softly, thinking she might still be in bed, since the car was out back.

No answer. He knocked a little harder, then surreptitiously peeked into her mailbox by the door. No mail. Glancing in a window, he saw that the place was neat, freshly painted, nice hardwood floors, modest carpets but well tended.

This was definitely not the kind of woman who would have dated Franco. Lorenzo wondered if he was dead wrong about her. But how could he be, after what she'd said when he'd called her number? She'd been expecting Franco to call her. She'd been worried about him. Had stayed up half the night. Sounded like a girlfriend. One who had Franco on a short chain.

Lorenzo double-checked the address, but remembered that she'd also sounded about the right age. Late twenties, early thirties.

He tried the number on Franco's cell phone for her. The phone rang and rang inside the house. No answer. She wasn't home. Someone must have picked her up.

He walked around back, and almost started to break into the rear door, but something stopped him. What if she had an alarm system? He decided a window was safer and, using his elbow, knocked out a pane.

No audible alarm went off as he reached through and unlatched the window. He shoved it up and, cleaning off the jagged glass, stepped through, annoyed his life had come to this.

Dusting off his favorite slacks, he ventured deeper into the house just to make sure she wasn't home. Apparently she didn't have an alarm system. Stupid, trusting woman.

There weren't any photographs of Franco. No sign Franco had ever been in the house. Lorenzo was going through a desk drawer when the phone rang, making him jump.

He checked caller ID and recognized the number. One of Valencia's other thugs, Jolly. So Valencia had put him on the task of finding Franco's girlfriend. Lorenzo wondered how Valencia had latched on to Rose Garcia's number so fast without Franco's cell phone. Valencia must have supplied Franco with the phone.

Lorenzo couldn't help feeling relieved he'd gotten here when he had. Now if the chick would just get her butt home…

He'd barely had the thought when he heard footfalls on the porch. He flattened himself against the hall wall and waited as he heard the sound of a key in the lock. A gust of cool damp air brushed past him as he heard her open, close and lock the door.

If he'd guessed right, she would come walking by him at any moment. He waited. And waited. Then, straining, he heard what seemed to be her taking off her shoes at the door and cursing softly. He didn't have all day.

He peeked around the corner to see her stripping out of her wet clothing, and was shocked to realize that she was the runner he'd almost clipped with his car.

If only he'd known, he could have saved himself a lot of time and trouble. But then again, it would be better if she just disappeared. That would make it more believable that she'd talked Franco into taking off with the duffel bag of money.

She'd stripped down to a gray jogging bra and a pair of hot-pink bikini panties by the next time he stole another peek around the corner.

She wasn't what he'd expected, but he could definitely see why Franco had been interested in her. She was hot, late twenties–early thirties, in great shape.

She looked up as if sensing his presence. He jerked back, but realized he couldn't wait for her to come to him. Not now. Pulling his gun from behind him, he stepped around the corner of the wall.

"Hello," he said, pointing the barrel at her heart. "I'm a friend of Franco's. Scream and I'll kill you. Keep quiet and you get to live. Put your clothes back on. You and I are going for a little drive."

To his surprise, she didn't scream. She didn't move. She glanced at the gun, then at his face. "I'm not putting those wet clothes back on."

Why couldn't he for once find a woman who just did what she was told? No, he always had to find one that put up an argument.

It was his last cognizant thought before she took a tentative step, seemed to wobble as if tired from her run, and flew at him. He never saw her foot coming until it slammed into the side of his head. He dimly felt her painfully twist the gun from his hand an instant before her other foot caught him in the groin.

But by then he couldn't isolate the pain, and he was already headed for the floor and unconsciousness, anyway.

Rose balanced on the balls of her feet, hopping back, poised to kick him again if necessary. She had the barrel of the gun trained on a kill spot just in case he was still conscious and lunged for her.

She waited a few seconds, then nudged him hard with her bare foot. Out cold.

She released the breath she'd been holding.

Lorenzo Dante. She'd recognized him right off. Until recently, he had been Raymond Valencia's top lieutenant. She'd heard he was planning to skip the country, and thought he'd already gone. She wondered what he was still doing here. More to the point, what he was doing flat on his back in her living room.

Her mind worked up several scenarios before going with the one that seemed most likely. Only one person could have led him to her: Franco. And if that was the case, then Franco was dead.

She felt sick to her stomach as she stared down at the man on the floor. She'd known what she was getting into, but that didn't make it any easier now.

Whatever she did, she had to move fast. Had Valencia sent Lorenzo to take care of her, as well?

The phone rang, startling her. She edged around Lorenzo, just in case he decided to come to. She checked the caller ID and didn't recognize the number. A bad sign. The caller didn't leave a message. Another bad sign.

In the kitchen, she pulled a roll of duct tape from a drawer, noticing the window Lorenzo Dante had broken to gain entrance. Bastard.

It seemed a pretty good bet that if he didn't report in, someone would come looking for him. If they hadn't already. Best to make sure that Lorenzo didn't come to before she could decide what to do with him.

Back in the living room, she taped his wrists, ankles and mouth, then dragged him back into the kitchen, out of sight of the front door. She was chilled and trembling, her undergarments still soaked.

The hell with it, she thought as she ran upstairs, turned on the shower and stripped off the rest of her wet clothing before stepping in.

She would have loved to have stood under the hot spray long enough to really warm up, but that was too risky.

She shut off the shower and dried herself, listening for any sound that someone else had broken in. At least the next intruder would have easy entrance, thanks to Lorenzo Dante.

She dressed in jeans, a flannel shirt and boots, then took the packed small suitcase she kept for just such an occurrence. Back downstairs, she was relieved to see that no one else had shown up yet.

Lorenzo had come to, though. He was giving her the evil eye. She chuckled to herself, remembering her Spanish grandmother's evil eye. Lorenzo Dante, killer that he was, had nothing on Rose's grandmother, Rosamaria.

If he had found her, then she had to assume that Valencia knew, as well. She glanced around the house, bummed that she would have to leave her home. Even temporarily. As she headed for the back door, she heard Lorenzo trying to say something through the tape on his mouth.

Rose stopped. She knew she didn't have much time, but she couldn't help herself. She turned and went back, taking a perverse satisfaction when Lorenzo Dante, local tough guy, cried out in pain as she ripped the tape from his mouth.

"You bitch!" he screamed.

"I thought you had something important to say." She

put down her bag and started to rip another strip of duct tape to reseal his mouth.

"No. Listen, I don't know who you are but maybe I can help you," he said quickly. "Franco's boss, Valencia, knows about you and Franco. He'll kill you if he finds you here."

She raised a brow. "Like you weren't going to."

He took a breath, obviously in some pain from at least one of the spots where she'd kicked him. That's what he got for breaking into her house and holding a gun on her.

"I will give you money so you can get away from him."

"Why would you do that?" she asked suspiciously. She heard a car go by slowly, for the second time in the past few minutes.

"Look, do you want the money or not?"

"Not." She started to slap tape back on his mouth.

"Wait! I don't think you realize who I am."

"Lorenzo Dante, two-bit criminal."

He winced at the two-bit part, just as she knew he would. "All you women are bitches. You're both going to burn in hell."

She had started to tape his mouth again but stopped. "What are you talking about?"

He closed his mouth and gave her a look that said over his dead body would he tell. Fine with her. She gave him a hard jab with the blade of her hand along his temple, then another just in case he didn't get the message.

"You and my ex-wife," he cried out, grimacing in pain. "I'll see you both in hell."

That she could believe. She slapped the tape over his mouth as she heard a car door slam out front.

She half expected one of Valencia's men to be covering the rear. The doorbell rang as she slipped out the back door to her car. Getting into her Mini, she turned the car key. The engine purred. She tromped on the gas, speeding out into the alley.

She spotted one of Valencia's men, Rico Santos, running along the side of the house with a gun in his hand. She reached the end of the alley, hung a quick right and didn't look back as she tried not to think of Franco and what the bastards had done to him.

She kept her foot pressed to the gas pedal, roaring down street after street, zigzagging her way toward Seattle, the skyline a dull gray in the pouring rain. When she was sure no one was following her, she slowed, pulled out her cell phone and called work.

"When was the last time anyone's seen Jenna Dante?" she demanded the moment she got her partner at the Seattle Police Department. She was afraid she already knew the answer.

"The chief called off the officer we had watching her after reading your report," Detective Luke Henry said.

Rose swore. "Does he realize that he probably signed Jenna Dante's death warrant?"

"She did that when she married Lorenzo and then decided to divorce him," Luke said solemnly.

True or not, Rose felt responsible. She was the one who'd gotten close to Jenna Dante, close enough that she'd been able to report that Jenna didn't know enough about her husband's business to turn state's evidence against him.

"My cover's blown," she said, feeling sick. "I think they made Franco."

Luke let out a pained sound. "How do you know that?"

"He called me on his way to Lorenzo's. He said Lorenzo had sounded strange, almost angry. I think Franco was worried Lorenzo had somehow figured out who he was."

"Not possible. Not after spending two years undercover," Luke said. "Franco was in. Raymond Valencia trusted him like a son."

"Well, something went wrong," she said. "I got a call from Franco's cell and the caller hung up. Not long after that Lorenzo was holding a gun on me."

Rose swung the Mini toward the apartment complex where Jenna Dante had been living with her daughter.

"I just left Lorenzo trussed up like a Christmas turkey in my living room," she said. "One of Raymond Valencia's men had just arrived when I left. Rico Santos. You might want to send a squad car by so they don't tear up my house any more than they already have."

"Where can I reach you?" Luke asked.

"I'm going to try to find Jenna Dante." She hung up before he could remind her that she was on medical leave.

"Trapped?" Jenna echoed in disbelief. "For how long?"

Elmer shrugged. "Until they can get the road open again none of us are going anywhere. The rental company you contacted this morning just called back. They can't get a car to you. The crew working on the hotel couldn't even get through. A bridge washed out to the west of us and the road is still flooded to the east."

"Surely there must be some other way out of here."

He shook his head. "Not until they get a road open, but don't worry. There is food stocked in the kitchen and so far the power hasn't gone out." He smiled. "It could be worse."

Yes, she thought, it definitely could be. If she couldn't get out of here, then Lorenzo couldn't get to her.

Still, she couldn't shake the feeling that she wasn't supposed to leave here, that her ending up here wasn't an accident.

That was crazy.

No crazier than the dream she'd had last night. She could still feel the effects of it. Crazy or not, a part of her didn't want to leave. She wanted *him* to come to her again.

Elmer was saying, "You might as well take advantage of what the hotel has to offer. At one time Fernhaven was famous for its healing waters. Have you seen the pools out back? They're sheltered from the weather and the water is nice and warm. As for breakfast, just help yourself in the kitchen."

Lexi started jumping up and down, wanting to go swimming.

"I guess we're going swimming," Jenna said, hoping to make the best of it for her sake. "We can raid the kitchen later."

"I'm going to be checking the rest of the hotel to make sure there aren't any problems," Elmer said. "Make yourselves at home." He seemed glad he wasn't trapped here alone.

She stood at the door to the suite and watched him disappear down the hall. The hotel had seemed isolated before, but nothing like now. It was just the three of them and a cat and a rag doll. Part of Jenna wanted to curl up in the room and wait out the storm—and the opening of the road.

But one look at her daughter's face told her that wasn't possible. "Let's get your swimming suit on."

Jenna got them both ready to go to the pools. It felt strange as they rode down the empty elevator.

Lexi rushed off, excited. She didn't seem to notice the brush of cold air as they exited the elevator.

"Wait a minute," Jenna told her. "There's something I need to do first." She didn't see Elmer at the registration desk. He must still be doing his check of the hotel.

She stepped behind the desk to take a closer look at the old black-and-white photograph of the men at the bar—one man in particular.

A chill rattled through her. That *was* the man who'd come to her in her sleep last night. She hadn't noticed before, but there were names written under some of the photographs. Under his, in small print, was the name Bobby John Chamberlain. The name had a line through it and under that name was another in a different handwriting: Harry Ballantine.

"Mommy," Lexi whined. "Come on."

Jenna swallowed hard as she stared into the man's eyes, then turned as Lexi began to run in circles crying, "Swimming, swimming, swimming."

Hurriedly Jenna spun the large, partially charred registration book around and did a quick scan for the name Harry Ballantine among the guests registered in 1936.

No luck. She quickly made a search for Bobby John Chamberlain. There it was. Room 318. The same room she and Lexi were staying in.

Why had the name been scratched out and Harry Ballantine written in? She shuddered, trying to tell herself it was a coincidence that she'd ended up in the same room. Vaguely, she remembered Elmer seeming flustered last night, as if he didn't recall choosing to put her in 318.

"Swimming!" Lexi cried.

"We're going swimming," Jenna said, her voice breaking as she took her daughter's hand and headed toward the pools.

Her hands were shaking, and as hard as she tried, she couldn't convince herself that it was just a coincidence she'd thought she'd seen the same man watching them from a third-floor room last night. That she'd dreamed about him. That she and Lexi were trapped here.

It was as if forces far beyond her control had not only brought her here, but were trying to keep her here.

Chapter 7

Lorenzo jerked around on the floor, but as hard as he tried, he couldn't free himself. He'd never been so outraged in his entire life. And that was saying a lot. What made it unbearable was that Rico Santos, of all people, had to be the one to find him. He hated that son of a bitch.

"What you doin'?" Rico asked, standing over him, laughing.

Lorenzo mumbled a string of swearwords behind the thick tape on his mouth.

Rico laughed harder. "Sorry, I didn't catch that."

Lorenzo glared at him. If only looks really could kill.

And just when he thought things couldn't get any worse, Jolly showed up. Jolly and Rico had a good laugh, did some crude speculating on how Lorenzo had ended up on the floor, gagged and bound, in some woman's house.

Lorenzo fought to free himself. If he could get loose he would kill them both and deal with the ramifications later.

"Oh, hold still, man," Rico said as he reached down and ripped the tape from his mouth.

It hurt like hell, but Lorenzo would have died before he showed it. He licked his lips. "Cut me loose."

"Take it easy," Rico warned, beady dark eyes narrowing as a switchblade appeared in his hand, the long slim shaft catching the light. "You see—" Rico leaned in so close that Lorenzo could smell what he'd had for breakfast "—Mr. Valencia wants us to bring you to him. He'd be upset if we had any trouble with you."

Lorenzo took a breath and let it out slowly. He would kill Rico. If not today, tomorrow. "Just cut the damn tape," he said quietly. "My legs are starting to cramp up."

Rico spun the switchblade in his fingers for a moment, then with a sudden thrust, sliced between Lorenzo's ankles.

Finally able to straighten his legs, Lorenzo rolled over onto his side and thrust out his wrists.

Rico met his gaze, holding it, while he freed his hands.

Lorenzo rubbed his wrists, staying prone on the floor until Rico finally rose and put the switchblade away.

Jolly offered Lorenzo a hand up. Jolly he would kill quickly. Rico was another story.

"Mr. Valencia is waiting." Rico's look said he knew Lorenzo would be coming for him, and he would be eagerly waiting.

Lorenzo couldn't believe how his luck had gone south. A woman had just kicked his butt. Worse, she'd gotten away. But maybe he could make that work to his advantage. If he couldn't find Rose Garcia, then neither could Valencia.

And who said she hadn't gone to meet up with Franco? Nobody.

His cell phone rang. He checked it. Alfredo. "Tell Valencia I'm on my way," he said to Rico and Jolly. "I need to take this."

Neither moved.

"He wants us to bring you to him," Jolly said. "Now."

Lorenzo swore silently. He didn't want to take the call in front of these two bozos, but he also could use a little good news right now. And if Alfredo had found Jenna, then that would be good news indeed.

"Yeah?" he said, after flipping open his cell phone.

"Just checking in like you said." Alfredo spoke in a low monotone no matter what was going on. "Found a gas station northeast of Seattle where she filled up. Clerk remembers her. She didn't ask for directions or nothing like that, so you want me to keep looking? A lot of wild country out here."

Lorenzo tried to hide his disappointment. "No, don't bother. Just come on back and I'll call you later." He snapped the cell phone shut and looked at the two men standing in front of him, telling himself he could take them both before either of them knew what hit 'em.

But killing two more of Valencia's men didn't seem the best idea right now.

"So what are we waiting for? Let's go see your boss. I'll follow you in my car."

"I think not," Rico said. "Jolly will bring you back for your car after you see the boss."

Just the thought of seeing Valencia on an empty stomach made him weak. "Mind if we stop and get breakfast along the way first? I'm starved."

Rico chuckled. "Yeah, right."

"We could swing through a drive-up," Jolly suggested. "I could use a little something."

"Fast food? Forget it," Lorenzo said, wondering again what his ex-wife was having for breakfast and where. "I'd rather starve."

Rose Garcia flashed her badge at Jenna Dante's apartment house and got the manager to open up 4B.

The apartment complex was a dump on the wrong side of town. After being married to a man with as much money as Lorenzo, Jenna had definitely taken a financial nosedive.

The manager was a short, squat, middle-aged bald man who smelled of fried onions. His name, according to the piece of paper taped to the door, was Buzz Gerard.

"I got things to do," Buzz said, scratching himself after he opened the door to Jenna Dante's apartment.

"So go do them." Rose stooped down to pick up the newspaper lying in the hall. She checked the date. This morning's. "I'll lock up when I leave," she assured him as she stepped into the apartment and closed the door behind her.

The place was neat and clean, nothing like the apartment complex itself. No sign of a struggle, she thought with relief. Or a break-in.

But it also had an empty, I'm-not-coming-back feeling, just as Rose had feared. The kitchen was clean, holding only a few odds and ends, dishes and silverware, thrift shop stuff.

Rose opened the closet. Empty hangers, some looking as if clothes had been jerked off in a hurry. She

checked the daughter's room. Bed made. Room too neat.
The bureau empty just like the closet.

Jenna had cleared out. With the girl? It appeared so.
But where had she gone? And why?

Something must have spooked her.

Lorenzo, Rose thought. He'd sure as hell scared *her*.

Rose picked up the phone and checked caller ID.
Jenna hadn't received many calls. The most recent one
was from Flannigan Investigations. *Interesting*. Rose
jotted down the other numbers, then checked the numbers Jenna had called. One stopped her cold.

Raymond Valencia? Why would Jenna call Lorenzo's
boss?

Rose searched the rest of the apartment but didn't
find anything to indicate where Jenna had gone. Clearly,
however, she wasn't coming back.

Every instinct told Rose that Jenna Dante was in over
her head. Maybe in more trouble than Jenna knew, if
she was involved with Raymond Valencia.

Raymond Valencia was in his greenhouse when he
heard Jolly and Rico return. Rico had called to say they
were bringing Lorenzo Dante with them.

Picking several of the finer tomatoes for lunch, Raymond left the greenhouse, the one place he found any
kind of peace.

In the kitchen he gave the tomatoes to the cook, then
found Jolly and Rico waiting in the den. Lorenzo had
made himself at home in one of the leather chairs by
the fireplace. He was slumped down a little, an ankle
resting on his knee, his hand fiddling with the tassel
on his Italian loafers as if he was bored. Or nervous.

He stopped fiddling the moment Raymond walked
into the room. Nervous, Raymond decided. Very ner-

vous. What had Lorenzo done? Raymond hated to think. He motioned for Jolly and Rico to leave them alone.

As the door closed behind them, Raymond took a chair facing Lorenzo. Crossing his legs, leaning back, hands in his lap, he imitated the other man's comfortable composure. Only Raymond really was relaxed.

"Don't you think it's time you told me what's really going on, Lorenzo?" he asked quietly.

Lorenzo pretended not to understand.

"What were you doing at Rose Garcia's house?"

"Just trying to help find Franco for you."

Raymond nodded. "When I talked to you last night you said you didn't know Franco's girlfriend's name."

"This morning I realized that Franco had left his cell phone on my bar."

Raymond lifted a brow. "I thought Franco refused a drink last night."

"He did." Lorenzo had begun to sweat. "But I was behind the bar, so he came over to lean against it."

"Did he use the phone while he was there?"

Lorenzo seemed to consider that. "Not that I know of. But I had to leave the room to get the money. He could have called someone." He shrugged.

"Do you still have the phone?"

Lorenzo reached into his pocket, pulled it out and got up to hand the cell phone to him.

"You checked numbers dialed, right? That's how you found Rose Garcia?"

Lorenzo nodded. "I called the number this morning to make sure she was home."

"Why didn't you call me and tell me about this?"

"I thought I would find her, maybe get your money back and save you the effort."

Raymond smiled. "That was thoughtful of you." It

was the weakest defense he'd ever heard. As if Lorenzo Dante cared about anyone but himself. So how would finding Franco's girlfriend benefit Lorenzo?

"I understand this woman, Rose Garcia, got away?" Raymond asked.

Lorenzo nodded, looking sheepish. This, at least, appeared to be genuine. "She knew karate or some defense thing."

"Where is your ex-wife?"

Lorenzo's head jerked in obvious surprise. Raymond glimpsed panic in his eyes. "Why…what…why would you ask about Jenna?"

"Is there any reason she would leave town?"

Lorenzo blinked. "What makes you think she left town?"

Raymond said nothing.

Lorenzo's eyes widened. He shifted in his chair. "You think she ran off with Franco?" He looked dazed by the idea. "Jenna and Franco? You think they're together?"

The thought had never crossed Raymond's mind. "I thought you found Franco's girlfriend, this Rose Garcia woman."

"I guess I was wrong," Lorenzo said. "Jenna and Franco. Who would have known?"

Raymond tried to picture Jenna with Franco. Impossible. And yet Franco was gone with a bagful of money, and Jenna wasn't answering her cell phone.

And yet what bothered him wasn't how quickly Lorenzo had latched on to the idea but how he was taking it. Too calmly.

"That son of a bitch," Lorenzo spat, as if it had just sunk in. Or he'd just realized his reaction wasn't the right one. "I'm going to kill that bastard when I catch him."

"Not until I get my money," Raymond said, watching Lorenzo. This was all messed up. He couldn't have been that wrong about Jenna. Franco wasn't her type. But there *had* been a lot of money in that duffel. If Jenna had run off with Franco and the money, then it was out of desperation to get away from her ex-husband. Somehow this always seemed to come back to Lorenzo.

"I'll take care of it," Raymond told him. "I don't want you involved."

"But it's my ex—"

"Yes, it's your ex, exactly," Raymond said, cutting him off. "That's why I don't want you involved." He settled his gaze on Lorenzo. "You'd better hope this doesn't have anything to do with you."

"What?"

"If you're behind what is going on—"

"What? I'm responsible for Franco as well as a woman who divorced me?" Lorenzo looked angry as well as offended. "I let her divorce me just like you told me to. I even let her take my kid. How could I have been nicer to her?"

Chapter 8

Flannigan Investigations was in Ballard, just north of downtown Seattle.

Rose couldn't help but wonder why Mike Flannigan's call had been the last one Jenna Dante received.

Recalling that private investigator Mike Flannigan had once told her he usually ate at his desk, she'd waited until she saw his receptionist and partner both leave for lunch before she let herself into his office.

True to his word, he was sitting behind his desk eating what looked like a wrap.

"On that low-carb diet?" she asked, lounging against the doorjamb as she watched him almost choke on the bite he'd just taken.

"Rose?" he managed to croak after chewing and swallowing and quite possibly stalling for time to cover his initial startled reaction.

She didn't date a lot. She never went home with a

man on the first date. Mike had been the exception, and at the time she'd had her reasons.

That was three months ago. Destiny or not, she'd been trying to put it behind her ever since. Which would have been easy if that night hadn't been wonderful. More than wonderful. And if Mike Flannigan hadn't kept calling, trying to get her to go out with him.

Their one night together, she'd left right after he'd fallen asleep. Had called a cab from outside and gone home to her own bed. He'd phoned the next day. She'd thanked him, but made it clear it had been a one-night thing. He'd called again a few times, asked her to dinner, suggested maybe they could date, suggested the one night together had meant more than she wanted to admit. She'd been tempted. Oh God, had she been tempted.

"It's been awhile," he said now, tossing the wrap into its plastic container and leaning back in his chair.

She had the feeling she'd just ruined his lunch. "I need to know why Jenna Dante hired you." It was a shot in the dark, but she saw she'd hit her target.

One brow shot up. Part of Mike Flannigan's appeal was his sense of humor. That and his blond good looks.

"You really think I'm going to tell you?" he asked with a disbelieving grin as she stepped into the room and closed the door behind her.

"Jenna's in trouble. Her ex paid me a visit this morning. It seems his plan was to take me for a ride. Judging by the gun he was holding, I don't think he planned to bring me back. He mentioned that he'd see both me and his ex in hell. She might already be dead for all I know. I'm hoping not. If she is still alive, I have to find her. Warn her."

"*Warn* her?" Mike studied Rose for a moment, his

expression serious. He let out a curse. "You tried to get her to turn state's evidence and you think Lorenzo found out." It wasn't a question.

"She didn't know enough about Lorenzo's business, so I cut her loose." Rose glanced away, unable to meet his eyes. If Lorenzo had found out, then he'd gotten the information from someone in the department. It was no secret that Lorenzo had some pull down there.

Mike swore again. "As if Jenna Dante wasn't in enough trouble." He sounded angry with Rose. No more than she was with herself. But it had been her job to get close to Jenna Dante, find out if she could help put Lorenzo away. Rose should have known the department would pull off the officer keeping tabs on Jenna.

Rose met Mike's gaze, her chin going up as she straightened into her tough-gal cop persona. "We could do this the hard way. I could subpoena her file, have you thrown in jail if you don't give it up…" She stepped closer and placed both hands on his desk, leaning toward him. She could smell the wrap. Turkey and Swiss with cream cheese, avocado, sprouts. She would never have taken Mike for a sprouts man. "If she's still alive, I'm going to find her and help her. You going to make this easy for me?"

"I thought you were on medical leave," he said. "Something about a stab wound?"

He'd been keeping track of her? "It healed. My official leave unofficially ended this morning with Lorenzo's visit."

Mike shook his head and leaned back, studying her. "Lorenzo took the kid. There'd been other times when he'd 'forgotten' to return her after visitations. The police department gave him a warning. The court ordered that all visitations be supervised. So he swiped the kid from her bed in the middle of the night. He didn't even bother to hide. Just took the girl back to that estate where he and Jenna had lived together. He knew Jenna's hands were tied. The cops had backed off. The courts really couldn't protect her or her daughter. Not from a man like Lorenzo Dante. I offered to help her, but she wanted to do it on her own—"

It was Rose's turn to shake her head. "On her own against a man like Lorenzo?" What the hell had Jenna been thinking? Did she really believe she was any kind of match for a man like him? "Have you heard from her?"

Mike frowned. "She told me she'd send me a check. That was yesterday, the last time I talked to her."

"You should have gotten the money up front. I doubt the check is in the mail." Sarcasm went with the job. "I went by her apartment. Looks as if she took off. Or didn't return. Have any idea where she was going to go if she got her daughter back?"

He shook his head. "Run, I would imagine. If she got away. Otherwise…"

Otherwise she was dead. Rose studied Mike, wishing she could forget the night they'd spent together. She wondered if he remembered it the way she did. "If she calls, would you let me know?"

He rocked forward, his blue-eyed gaze locking with hers as he picked up a pen and notepad. "And you'll let me know what you learn?"

She nodded and gave him her cell phone number. He wrote it down, tore off the sheet of paper and folded it into a neat little square before sliding out his wallet and placing it inside.

When he finished, he settled his gaze on her as if waiting, letting her know he expected her to say something. Not about Jenna Dante. With their careers, they both dealt with the dark side of human nature on a daily basis.

Except Mike seemed to handle it better, seemed to find a way to distance himself from that part of his life—compartmentalize it so he could have more. That more, he'd told her, was a meaningful relationship based on love and friendship and hope.

Mike Flannigan thought he could have taught her how to make the two work, but she'd never given him the chance.

"I wish I'd gone out with you again, okay?" she said. "That night was—" she waved her hand through the air, meeting his gaze "—amazing."

He smiled as if that's all he'd been waiting to hear and, picking up his turkey-cheese wrap, leaned back in his chair.

She grinned at him, seeing that he knew how hard that had been for her to admit. "Thanks for the help."

"Good luck, Rose."

She would need more than luck and they both knew it. "You have my number."

He nodded. "Yeah, I do, don't I."

Jenna lounged in the wonderfully hot water as her daughter splashed in the shallows next to her. The outdoor pools were just as Elmer had said: enchanting. Carved out among the rocks and trees, they wound like a creek along the edge of the mountainside, providing a natural landscape and at the same time intimacy.

Jenna tried to relax in the hot water, pushing away thoughts of her dream. She had more to worry about than some man in an old photograph or the thought that she was losing her mind. The duffel bag full of money in her room felt like a noose around her neck. She had to get it back to Lorenzo. She wasn't naive enough to think she could use it to buy her freedom. But she knew that Lorenzo was moving heaven and earth right now to find her, more so because of that stupid bag of money.

She had thought about calling him and telling him where he could pick it up. That was before she got trapped here.

No, she decided, it would be better for Lorenzo to pick up the money at her apartment. She didn't want him knowing which direction she'd headed. With luck she wouldn't leave a trail he could follow—once she got him back the money.

"Look, Mommy!" Lexi called as she dipped her head under the water.

Jenna watched her through the steam, smiling and offering words of encouragement. All the time her mind was racing. Who could she trust to take the money to the apartment?

Only two people came to mind. She hated to ask either of them, afraid to involve them in her life—or worse, Lorenzo's. But if she did this right, Lorenzo would never know who'd put the cash in her apartment for him.

Once the money was on the way to her apartment, she could call him and tell him where to pick it up. He must be going crazy. He'd been too close to crazy as it was. Little things often set him off. This, she feared, was monumental.

Whatever she did, she had to make sure that Lexi was protected.

Lexi waved at someone at one of the other pools behind Jenna. Jenna feared it would be the imaginary woman in the purple plumed hat.

Bracing herself, she turned to look through the steam. She didn't see anyone. Nothing new there. That awful feeling began to settle in the pit of her stomach. "Who were you waving to?" she asked, fighting to keep the growing fear out of her voice.

"That man."

"Elmer. The nice man who gave us the room?"

Lexi shook her head. "The one with the funny hair on his lip."

Jenna's heart began to pound. "A man with a mustache?"

Lexi nodded and Jenna turned to look in the direction of the other pool, where Lexi had been gazing. "I don't see anyone." Her voice broke. "Is he still there?" she asked in a hoarse, scared whisper.

Lexi shook her head. "He's gone. I guess he didn't want you to see him."

Jenna couldn't breathe. "What do you mean?"

Lexi shrugged and bobbed up and down in the water, clearly losing interest in the conversation.

Fear compressed Jenna's chest, making it hard to catch her breath, let alone talk. "What did the man look like?"

Her daughter sighed, scrunching her face up in thought. She'd always been dramatic, using her hands and a variety of facial expressions when she talked. Now she let out a big sigh.

"Mommy," she said, throwing her arms wide, "he just looked like a *man*." She frowned as if she'd thought of something. "He was wearing funny clothes and his hair was wet."

"Wet?" Jenna thought of the photograph of the man in the tuxedo. His hair was oiled and combed straight back.

Lexi ducked under the water again, and despite the

warmth of the hot springs, Jenna shivered. It wasn't possible that Lexi had seen the man.

They had to get out of this place. Get the money to Lorenzo. Then she would take Lexi as far from here as possible.

"Did you see me go all the way to the bottom?" Lexi asked, bobbing up again.

"I saw," Jenna managed to say.

"Wanna see me swim?" Lexi didn't wait for an answer. She took off, paddling wildly, sending spray in all directions, then stopped to grin back at her mother. "Did you see?"

Jenna nodded and smiled, her heart a hammer. She tried to convince herself that she shouldn't be scared, that this was only a very imaginative, bright little girl. But she remembered how Lexi used to scare Lorenzo by seeming old for her age—and wise beyond her years.

Her preschool teachers said she was gifted.

Or maybe she just has the gift.

"Lexi, it's time to go." Upset and shaking, Jenna started to get out of the pool.

"No, not yet, Mommy!"

Weak from the hot water and her fears, Jenna let herself slip back into the water. "A few more minutes, but then no arguments, agreed?"

Lexi grudgingly nodded.

Jenna sank neck deep in the water, feeling cold now. Why had she thought these pools, this place, at all enchanting?

Harry Ballantine watched Jenna and her daughter through the steam rising off the pool, shaken.

The little girl had *seen* him. How was that possible? No one had seen him in seventy years. He'd been in a vaporous limbo, drifting in the wind. Nothing. Absolutely nothing.

Until the woman and child had arrived last night from out of the rain and darkness and he'd gone to the window. Was it possible the woman had seen him, too? She'd looked up as if knowing he was there.

My God, it was the first time anyone had seen him—let alone felt his touch. Did he dare hope?

He moved toward the pools, half-afraid.

The woman was in a deeper end of a pool, not far from her daughter. Her eyes were closed, but he could tell she was listening to the little girl chattering away to herself nearby.

He watched the woman brush a strand of dark hair back from her face. She really was lovely. High cheekbones, porcelain smooth skin, dark fringed lashes. There was an innocence about her that pulled at something deep within him.

You are beautiful, Jenna.

She stirred, her eyes coming open as if she'd heard him.

Can you hear me?

Her dark eyes widened and she looked around.

My God, she *could* hear him.

Don't be afraid. I won't hurt you.

He was so close now that he could see she was trembling.

Remember last night?

The pulse at her throat began to pound. She reached for the side of the pool as she tried to find bottom.

"Lexi, we have to go now." Her words came out choked with fear.

No, please don't leave.

"Mommy, it's not time. You said we could stay for a

little while longer," Lexi cried. "Please, just a few more minutes. Please."

He touched Jenna's shoulder and she froze, eyes wide with terror—and something else he recognized. Need.

She was losing her mind.
I'm here. It's all right.

She let out the breath she'd been holding. It came with a sob, and she dropped back into the water, suddenly too weak to pull herself out.

His voice was velvet. And familiar. She'd heard it last night in her dreams and had known it was the voice of the man in the old photograph.

She stared into the steam rising from the surface of the pool, knowing no one was out there and yet at the same time bracing herself for his touch, yearning for it, feeling terrified that, like the voice, it would be familiar.

"I can't..." She tried to climb out of the pool, but something pulled her back down.
You don't have to go yet.

She felt hysterical laughter bubbling up. "This isn't happening."
Yes, it is.

She sucked in a breath as she felt him pull her back down to him. She closed her eyes, telling herself this wasn't real. But it felt more real than anything she'd ever experienced.

"Tell me I'm not losing my mind," she whispered.
You're not. I'm here.

Her body revved up like an engine taking off. "If you knew what I was thinking..."

She heard a soft chuckle. *Don't I?*

She could feel him under the water, his touch cool. Familiar.

Sometimes things are exactly as they seem.

She shook her head, unable to accept that this was happening. How could she have feelings toward…what? A man from a seventy-year-old photograph? Or something else?

"Who are you?" she whispered, feeling tears well in her eyes as she pulled free of him. "*What* are you?"

You know me.

"No." She didn't know him. But she sensed things about him. Both good—and bad.

"Mommy, look!" Lexi called, breaking the spell.

Jenna jerked free and reached for the side of the pool. In an instant she had pulled herself out. "Lexi, come on. We have to go. *Now*."

From the shallow end of the pool the little girl started to protest, but Jenna hurried toward her, drawing her out. Holding her hand, she moved quickly to their towels.

It wasn't until she'd covered herself and Lexi that she turned to look back.

But of course there was no one there.

Chapter 9

Jenna scooped Lexi up into her arms and ran toward the lobby, praying that Elmer had returned.

"How did you like the swimming pool, little lady?" he said, smiling at her daughter. His gaze shifted to Jenna and his expression changed. "You saw them."

Her heart dropped. *"Them?"*

"I'm sorry but I didn't want to say anything to scare you, but I've felt them. Even saw one. Some old gal in a purple hat with feathers."

"She's nice," Lexi said. "She waved and smiled at me."

Jenna drew her daughter closer as she stared at Elmer. "You're telling me…"

He nodded. "From what I could learn, she was the hotel owner's wife. She was—" he glanced at Lexi "—lost opening night in 1936."

In the fire. Jenna took a ragged breath, her gaze

going to the photograph of the man from her dream. "What do you know about Bobby John Chamberlain?" she asked, motioning toward the picture.

Elmer stepped closer and frowned. "Bobby John Chamberlain." He reached under the counter, then stopped, his frown deepening.

"What's wrong?" she asked.

"There was a box of Fernhaven pamphlets under here. They seem to be gone." He looked confused and a little scared.

"Maybe you moved them and didn't remember," she said, wondering why it mattered. She'd obviously rattled the poor man.

"It's just…odd. But you're right, I probably moved them. Or someone else did yesterday and I didn't notice." He didn't sound convinced, but he seemed to shake it off as he reached under the registration desk and brought out a stack of photographs. He went through them, mumbling to himself, obviously still agitated over the missing box of pamphlets.

"The owners of the hotel got photographs from the newspaper archive," Elmer said. "A lot of the photos ran after the fire. It was big news as you can imagine."

Jenna held her breath as he drew out a photo and handed it to her. Like the other photo, the name Bobby John Chamberlain had a line through it, with "Harry Ballantine" neatly printed underneath in different handwriting.

"Who is Harry Ballantine?" she asked, afraid she didn't want to know.

Elmer nodded as if to himself. "I looked up some of those old newspaper articles from June 1936. It's funny you should ask about Harry Ballantine. There were a lot of famous people at Fernhaven that night. But Harry was without a doubt the most infamous. He was a renowned jewel thief in his day."

"A *thief*," Jenna said, wondering why she would be surprised. She'd married Lorenzo, hadn't she? Why not conjure up a jewel thief for a phantom lover? "Why was the other name under his photo?"

"The story came out after the tragedy that Harry had conned a rich Texan oilman named Bobby John Chamberlain out of his invitation to the 1936 Fernhaven grand opening."

"What happened to Harry?" she asked, her voice barely recognizable even to her own ears.

"Died in the fire. Ironic, isn't it? If he hadn't stolen the Chamberlain fellow's identity, he wouldn't have died. But then again, he was a thief, no doubt here to steal some of that jewelry in those photographs." Elmer sighed. "In a way, I guess he got his just rewards. Strange, though, how Chamberlain died right after that. An accident at one of his oil rigs. I guess he just couldn't beat death."

Jenna was speechless. Her pulse pounded in her ears, a deafening drumming. Her limbs felt weak as water. She stared down at the photograph of Harry Ballantine, a man she felt she knew. Dead for seventy years…

"He the one you're seeing?" Elmer asked.

She shook her head. "I didn't see anything."

Elmer nodded knowingly. "With the rain stopped, the highway patrol said they should have the road open sometime later today. I left a breakfast tray outside the door to your room."

"Thank you."

"They can't hurt you or your daughter," Elmer said. "You're safe here."

Jenna wasn't so sure about that.

* * *

Once inside the room, Jenna locked the door behind them and stood for a moment trying to get her heart rate back down. She was shaking, and not from the cold.

Fred came out Lexi's bedroom meowing loudly.

Jenna started toward her own bedroom and stopped. Someone had been in the room. She sniffed the air. That scent. She'd smelled it last night in the dream.

Unnerved, she tried to convince herself she'd only imagined it. Just as she'd imagined the voice, the feel of the man in the pool. Her body still tingled from the feel of him against her in the hot water. Harry Ballantine? Thief?

She thought of the duffel bag of money and raced into the bedroom. It was where she'd left it, and none of the money appeared to be missing.

She rezipped the bag, shoved it into the back of the closet and sat down heavily on the bed.

In the other room Lexi was talking to Clarice and eating the breakfast Elmer had sent up. From the doorway Fred was meowing loudly, as if trying to tell Jenna what had taken place while she'd been gone.

She tried to pull herself together. After a few moments she realized that Fred had gone into Lexi's room and was acting almost normal. Almost too normal for a cat. When she glanced into her daughter's room, she found Lexi was rubbing her eyes.

"Come here, sweetheart."

Lexi stumbled to her and let Jenna hold her.

"Why don't we lie down for a little while?"

Lexi nodded sleepily against her.

Jenna helped her daughter out of her swimsuit and into warm, dry clothing. When she tucked her into the bed, Lexi was asleep in an instant. Playing in the hot water, plus the interrupted sleep from last night, had tired them both out.

Unable to put it off any longer, Jenna left Lexi's bedroom door open and went to her own room to retrieve her cell phone. She hesitated. The road would be open soon. And the instant it was, she was getting out. She had to trust someone. Someone who would help her.

She was in short supply of friends. Lorenzo had seen to that. She couldn't call Raymond Valencia and ask for more help.

He'd helped her all through the divorce, even telling her who to contact to get fake passports. But she couldn't involve him again. She'd seen the way he looked at her.

Asking for his help again would only open her up to something she wasn't interested in pursuing—and possibly put her in more danger. Fortunately she'd met two women since she'd moved out and gotten the divorce. Charlene Palmer lived in the same apartment house as Jenna. She'd met the other woman, Rose Garcia, in the grocery store. They'd since run into each other at the park.

Jenna thought of the two women, both so different. Neither knew Lorenzo, or vice versa.

Jenna flushed at the memory of how she'd confided in both women, complete strangers. She'd been raised to keep her personal business to herself, and yet she'd opened up to Rose especially. Rose had been so easy to talk to. While Jenna had never mentioned Lorenzo's name, she'd told her new friend everything that had happened.

Even now she wondered why she'd done that, knowing how dangerous it was to talk to anyone.

But Rose had been so supportive and such a good listener. And Jenna had thought she'd never see her again.

As it was, she'd run into her on a half-dozen occasions. Rose had encouraged her to go to the police with what she knew, to try to put Lorenzo behind bars. Jenna had assured her she knew nothing about Lorenzo's business affairs, and shuddered at the thought of what her ex-husband would have done if she'd gone to the authorities.

"He has some of the police on his payroll," Jenna had told her.

Rose had been shocked and wanted to know who.

"I don't know. I just know that when I went to the police when he ignored the court's orders, nothing happened."

"He thinks he's above the law, but he's not," Rose had argued.

Jenna had laughed. "He *is* above the law. His power extends far beyond the police, believe me. He's a ruthless man who destroys anyone who gets in his way."

"Let me help you," Rose had insisted, pressing a piece of paper with her cell phone number on it into Jenna's hand.

Jenna had hidden the number in her purse, but she'd never called. No one understood just how dangerous Lorenzo Dante was. And she didn't want to drag anyone else into this.

Her other new friend was her neighbor, Charlene Palmer. She'd met Charlene one day after Lorenzo had broken the restraining order and come by, making loud threats and breaking things. Fortunately, Lexi had been in an afternoon preschool program up the street.

Charlene had come over right after Lorenzo left, and had asked if she could help. The walls were thin; she'd obviously heard everything.

Charlene was a large, soft woman with a kind face. She'd given Jenna a hug, gone into the kitchen and poured them both diet colas, then sat down and said, "Talk to me, honey. That bastard who was just here— your ex, right?" She hadn't waited for an answer. She'd just started telling Jenna about her own ex, who she said was doing time in prison.

Jenna had worried at first about befriending Charlene. Not that Charlene would have any reason to know who Lorenzo was. It wasn't as if he'd ever been arrested for his crimes and gotten his picture in the paper. And Jenna had rented the apartment in her maiden name, McDonald.

It seemed safe to talk to a woman who seemed to actually understand because she'd been in her shoes.

And Jenna liked Charlene. The woman had survived misfortune, was easygoing, had an attitude Jenna admired.

It had been Charlene's idea to keep Jenna's spare apartment key. "Honey, I had a husband like your ex. He beat me up so bad one night…" Tears had welled in Charlene's eyes. She'd brushed at them angrily. "Thank God I'd given my apartment key to a friend who lived next door. She waited until my old man left, then came over and took me to the hospital. I would have bled to death on the floor if she hadn't had a key. In our neighborhood you didn't call the cops. And you couldn't afford an ambulance."

The story had chilled Jenna. Lorenzo was capable of hurting her. Hurting her badly.

Jenna knew that either woman would help her. She pulled out her purse.

She dialed a number. It rang once, twice, three times. Jenna started to hang up, suddenly afraid she'd picked the wrong person to trust.

* * *

Charlene Palmer had her feet up on the coffee table, a bag of potato chips on one side of her and a box of cookies on the other. She'd just poured herself a large glass of diet cola and had settled in to watch her favorite soap. Life was good.

Her cell phone rang in her purse on the other side of the room. She eyed it suspiciously. It rang again. She swore softly. Her show was just starting, and when the phone rang it was never good news.

It rang a third time. And she had the oddest feeling that she should answer it. She shoved herself up from the couch and launched herself across the room, snatching up her purse, digging deep and coming up with the phone as it rang a fourth time.

"Yeah?" She was out of breath, heart pounding from the exertion of just crossing the room.

Plus it always spooked her a little when she got one of those "feelings." Her Grandmother Tyler believed she could see the future. Of course, everyone in the family thought her just a crazy old bat.

But one time Grandmother Tyler had stared into Charlene's eyes and said, "You got the gift, too, don't you, girl?"

Charlene had denied it. Hell, she didn't need that kind of gift. No way.

And yet even before she heard Jenna Dante's voice, Charlene knew that her "gift" hadn't let her down—at least not this time. Answering this call was the smartest thing she'd done in a long time.

"Charlene?"

Jenna Dante. She tried to catch her breath. "Hey, girl." She felt a sharp stab of regret as she hit the TV's mute button. She hated missing her show. "You all right?" Jenna hadn't come home last night and she'd been worried about her.

"You said if I ever needed help…"

Charlene looked toward the heavens and smiled at her luck. "I meant it. What can I do?" She glanced at her soap ruefully and just hoped nothing big happened on it today.

"I'm kind of in a bind," Jenna said on the other end of the line.

"It's that ex of yours, isn't it," Charlene stated.

"I'm afraid so. I have something of his I didn't mean to take. Now I need to get it back to him," Jenna explained.

Something of her ex's? Charlene held her breath.

"The thing is, this package that I need to get to my ex, I can't mail it."

Charlene let out the breath she'd been holding. "We're not talking drugs here, right?"

"No, no, nothing like that," Jenna said quickly. "It's just some papers I didn't mean to take." She sighed. "It's a long story. But I thought if I could get them to my apartment, I could call him and tell him where to pick them up." She paused. "You know, maybe this wasn't such a good idea."

Papers. Right. "Look, are you sure you shouldn't go to the cops? What am I saying? You already went to them. They can't protect you from him. Hey, I can get him the papers. Just tell me where to pick them up."

Silence. For a moment Charlene was afraid Jenna had hung up.

"Charlene, I'm not in Seattle. It's too far and you can't—"

"Hey, what are friends for? And it's not like I'm doing anything." She glanced wistfully at her soap opera. "I've even got wheels. A friend sold me her used car when she traded up." A small lie. At least for the moment. "And I'm up for a road trip. What else do I have to do? Just tell me how to get to you."

"Are you sure?"

"Absolutely." Charlene found a pen and turned over one of the bill envelopes on her coffee table. "Just give me directions."

"Well, there is one small problem," Jenna said, and explained about the bridge and the flooding.

"I'm sure I'll be able to get through by the time I reach there," Charlene said.

"It will be good to see you."

Jenna and Franco. Lorenzo couldn't believe how well this was all working out. Not that he could see Jenna with Franco. Not in a million years. But if Valencia found Jenna first, then he would find her with the duffel bag full of money. What else would he think? No matter what she said, Valencia wouldn't believe her.

And if Lorenzo managed to find Jenna first?

Little chance of that happening. Alfredo hadn't been able to locate her. Jenna could be miles from here by now. But didn't that mean Valencia wouldn't be able to trace her, either?

Lorenzo breathed a sigh of relief. He couldn't have planned this better.

His cell phone rang. He flipped it open, stared at the caller ID and smiled. Lady luck was shining on him today. "Yeah?"

"Mr. Dante?" said the female voice. There was a mocking lilt to the way she said the mister that he didn't like.

"Charlene," he said, and waited. The last time she'd

called it was to tell him that Jenna had taken off. By that time, he'd already figured it out. He had wondered why Charlene hadn't phoned sooner with the information. Wasn't that what he was paying her for?

"I just heard from Jenna," she said into the silence.

Well, maybe setting Charlene Palmer up in the same apartment complex to spy on his ex-wife hadn't been such a bad idea, after all. Charlene had befriended Jenna, as she'd been hired to do. But up until this minute, she hadn't given him anything that had been worth her rent, let alone paying all her expenses so she could sit around on her butt.

"She wants me to meet her," Charlene said. "I told her I have a car."

Lorenzo's smile faded. "A car?"

"How else could I meet her?"

She was holding out for a *car?* He thought about driving over to the apartment complex and showing her how he felt about extortion.

Charlene hadn't been wild about doing his bidding to begin with. But what choice did she have, with her brother in prison? Stan Palmer had worked for Lorenzo until he got caught hijacking a semi load of electronics. Lorenzo had the ability to make Stan's life in prison even less enjoyable if Charlene didn't do what Lorenzo wanted.

"A car," he said again. "What kind of car?"

"A newer model used one," Charlene said.

"Not a *brand-new* one?" He couldn't keep the sarcasm out of his voice.

She chuckled. "Now what would a woman like me be doing with a fancy new car?"

"Where is my ex-wife?" he snapped, tired of this.

"She says she has something that she took by mistake and wants to return to you. Some…papers? I'm to pick up the package as soon as I get a car and drive to where she is."

His *money*. Jenna wanted to return his money? He shook his head in amazement. She *did* have a brain. Not that returning his money was going to save her. If she thought that, then she was out of her mind.

And no way was he letting Charlene Palmer within a mile of that duffel bag. He'd never see her or the money or his newer model used car again. "I'll meet her. Just give me the address."

"It isn't going down that way. If anyone else comes, she'll skip and you can forget whatever it is she took from you," Charlene said. "You want it back? Then we do this her way."

Lorenzo gripped the cell phone so hard he heard it crack. "Do you have any idea who you're dealing with?" he demanded.

"Oh, yeah," Charlene said with another chuckle. "And so does your ex. I have to wonder why she would give you anything back. Must be pretty important."

Lorenzo swore under his breath. "If I have to come over there—"

"You really think I'd still be here?" There was a sound as if she was starting to hang up.

"Wait!" He gritted his teeth until his jaw ached. "We'll do it your way. I'll get you a car. You make the pickup. I'll have the title signed over in your name as soon as you give me the package and her location." Silence. "And I give you five thousand dollars to end our business arrangement."

"Make it twenty thousand, you put the title of the car in my name right away and I give you the location after I make the pickup."

He would kill her when this was over. "How do I know I can trust you?"

"You don't. Make it a red car. I like red. Something nice. Don't be cheap. You'll probably want to have it delivered as soon as possible so I can get going. Jenna isn't anywhere near Seattle. I'll call you on my cell phone when I have the package, and we can set up an exchange. I'd like that twenty grand in new bills."

He cursed the turn his life had taken. Women were now calling the shots? He'd been beaten up and hog-tied by a woman, his ex-wife had stolen his daughter and his money, and now this woman was telling him how things were going to be?

"You do realize the fine line you are walking here?" he asked Charlene in his most calm voice.

She chuckled. "I have nothing to lose. How about you?" She let out a long sigh. "The sooner I get the car, the sooner I get your *papers* back." She hung up.

He threw the cell phone across the room and immediately regretted it as the phone shattered in a spray of plastic. He'd have to buy not only a car but also a new cell phone.

Picking up the land line, he first called Alfredo, then a car dealer and ordered a car delivered to Charlene's address, the title in her name, plus a cash payment to be made from his bank account. The only red car the dealer had was going to set him back over ten grand. Lorenzo swore and told the dealer that the car had to be delivered immediately.

The doorbell rang.

"Screw the paperwork. Put the insurance under my name then. Just get the car to that address *now*," he barked into the phone, having to raise his voice because of the sudden pounding at the front door. "What the hell?" Lorenzo swore. He hung up and went to the door to look out.

Cops?

Raymond Valencia had sent Jolly and Rico over to Jenna Dante's apartment after numerous attempts to reach her had failed. They came back with the bad news.

"Looks like she skipped," Rico said, playing with the toothpick in his mouth. "Super said she left last night and didn't come back."

"How the hell does the apartment super know that?" Raymond snapped.

"Insomniac. Saw her leave with two suitcases, a large one and a small one. Seemed to be in a hurry. Her parking space was empty all night. No sign of her this morning."

Raymond pulled on his left earlobe, a habit when he was thinking. "No one has any idea where she went?"

Rico shook his head.

"And what about this Rose Garcia woman? Any word on her?"

Jolly shrugged. "Lorenzo scared her off."

It always came back to Lorenzo.

Rico pulled the toothpick from his mouth. "After a little persuasion, we found out that someone else had been snooping around the apartment." He paused as if waiting for a drum roll. "Some broad," he said finally, nodding and smiling. "A cop. Name was Rose Garcia."

Raymond stared at Rico, his mind reeling at the implications. He tried not to show his surprise. Or his distress at the news. A cop looking for Jenna. A cop whose number was on Franco's cell phone. Nothing about this situation boded well.

Was Franco working with the cops?

Or worse, was Franco a cop? If so, he'd certainly fooled him. Raymond had always prided himself on his instincts. If he was wrong about Franco, could he also be wrong about Jenna? If so, how did she fit into the picture?

"Tell me something," Raymond said after a moment. "You knew Franco. Can you see him with Jenna Dante?"

Rico laughed. "That broad was too classy for *Dante,* let alone a dunce like Franco. No way."

Raymond wanted to argue that Franco was no dunce. There had been intelligence behind all that attitude. In fact, Franco could have been smarter than Raymond had realized. He'd certainly fooled him. Raymond looked to Jolly. "What do you think?"

"I don't know, Boss. I've *never* understood women."

Rico laughed and even Raymond had to smile.

"I know what you mean, Jolly," Raymond said. "I've never understood women, either." But he'd thought he'd understood Jenna. He'd thought he knew her. More important, he'd thought he could trust her. Just as he had Franco.

Now he wasn't so sure. "You left a man watching Jenna Dante's apartment and another one watching Lorenzo?" Both nodded. "Rico, I want you on Lorenzo. You know the drill." Rico nodded. "Jolly, you take the apartment. I want to know if anyone comes or goes. *Anyone.*"

Rico's cell rang. He checked the caller ID, looked at his boss, then quickly answered. "Yeah. No kiddin'. Yeah." He snapped it off. "The guy I left at Dante's. He just called to say that cops are there. Had a warrant and everything. Got one of them forensics teams in there. And two detectives just took Dante downtown in handcuffs."

Raymond Valencia swore. Hadn't he known he would live to regret not killing Lorenzo?

Detective Rose Garcia cupped the cell phone to her ear as her fingers whipped over the computer keyboard at a Ballard Internet café.

"We got a warrant to search Dante's house, and picked up blood spatters in the tile grout on the living room floor," Detective Luke Henry said on the other end of the line.

"Franco's?" she asked scared.

"Maybe. Could be his ex's. Got the forensics guy on it and Dante in custody. He says the blood is from a cut on his hand. Has a fresh cut. Unless we find more evidence of foul play, we aren't going to be able to hold him, and he knows it."

Rose stopped typing and closed her eyes.

"You still there?"

She took a breath, opened her eyes. "Let's say he did the ex. Where's the daughter?"

"We found a bedroom upstairs. Had some little girl's clothes in it. Dante says he has visitation rights. Doesn't get the daughter again until the weekend. Claims he hasn't seen or heard from his ex since the last time he had supervised visitation."

"He's lying."

Luke laughed. "You think? But unless we have a body…"

"Yeah. I'm running her credit card right now to see if she's used it in the last twenty-four hours. Maybe we'll get lucky." Maybe by some miracle Jenna Dante had escaped her ex-husband. "Still no word from Franco?"

"No. Shouldn't you be home taking it easy?"

"I'm fine. It was just a little knife wound. The perp barely cut me. It wasn't like he shot me." She snapped her cell phone shut and stared at the computer screen.

Jenna hadn't used her credit card late last night. Rose felt a wave of disappointment. Now what?

Unable not to think about the blood Luke had found at Dante's house, Rose checked the police wire. If Lorenzo had dumped the bodies, maybe they'd been found by now.

One report caught her eye. A woman and child and elderly security guard had been stranded at an empty hotel in the Cascades. Highway patrol were unable to reach the three, but had talked to the security guard on the phone.

But what had caught Rose's eye was the model and color of the SUV the woman had been driving, information provided by the security guard. It matched one owned by Lorenzo Dante. But now that Rose thought about it, she realized Dante hadn't been driving it this morning when he'd almost hit her.

She called Luke. "Is Lorenzo Dante's black SUV out there?"

"No, hold on." Luke left the line and came back. "He says it was stolen. He hasn't had time to report it yet. He's driving a rental, and guess whose car is parked out back?"

"Jenna's," Rose said. "Bingo. I think she took his SUV, for whatever reason. If I'm right, I might be able to find her."

"Rose? Listen, I don't want you doing anything without backup, and there is no way I can back you up with you being on medical leave, do you hear me?"

"I won't do anything without backup. I promise."

She hung up. Her instincts told her she was on the right track. If Lorenzo Dante's SUV really had been stolen, he would have called the cops right away in a fury. But if Jenna had taken it...

Rose jotted down the name of the place. Fernhaven Hotel.

Opening her purse, she pulled out a map of Washington State. Based on the police report, she found the approximate location of the hotel. About two hours from Seattle.

She crossed her fingers as she dialed directory assistance and got the number for the hotel. But when she called the phone rang and rang, each ring causing her more concern. Rose couldn't shake the feeling that the woman and child stranded at the hotel were Jenna Dante, now McDonald, and her daughter, Alexandria—and that they were in more trouble than they realized.

As the phone rang, Rose studied the map. No close towns around, and according to the latest update, no way in. The highway was flooded to the east and impassable, and a bridge was out to the west.

Still no answer. She let it ring until it was picked up by voice mail. The message informed her that the hotel wasn't open for business but would be taking reservations next week, and that a grand opening was scheduled three weeks out.

She would keep trying the number. In the meantime, there had to be a way to get to Fernhaven. That country was crisscrossed with old logging roads. Not the kind of route she could drive in a Mini Cooper, but she knew someone who had a Jeep—and she did need backup.

She dialed Mike Flannigan's number.

Chapter 10

Jenna was still trembling after her phone call to Charlene. She had tried to convince herself she'd done the right thing. But now she feared she had only managed to put Charlene's life in danger.

And all to get the money back to Lorenzo.

Maybe she shouldn't have even tried. Would it really make that much difference? Something told her it did. No way would Lorenzo have that kind of money just lying around in a duffel bag in the back of the SUV. Especially since he was planning to fly out the next day. He would never have gotten that bag of money through customs.

So what had he planned to do with it?

Since she'd returned to the room, she hadn't heard any voices in her head. Maybe she'd never heard voices. Or felt someone in the pool with her.

Stress did strange things to a person. And with Lorenzo out there somewhere looking for her…well, no wonder odd things were happening to her.

She shivered at the memory and realized she was still wearing her swimsuit and wrap. Going into the bathroom, she turned on the water and stripped out of her wet clothing. To keep her mind busy she went over the phone conversation with Charlene again in her head.

Charlene had been so understanding. "Honey, the best thing you can do is get out of the country as soon as possible, right? You wouldn't have run unless you thought you had to, and I got to tell you, some bad-looking guys have been coming around hunting for you. Whatever it is that you accidentally took, give it back. Hell, you don't want any more trouble from that man."

Jenna knew Charlene was right. "You'll make sure you aren't followed," she'd said.

"Don't worry. Your ex doesn't know me from Adam. I'll be on my way within the hour," Charlene had assured her. "It will be great to see you, too. And don't worry, I'm sure the road will be open by then."

Had she made the right choice, calling Charlene for help? Jenna prayed so as she soaped her body. She found herself listening for him. Just the thought brought on an ache that was both physical and emotional.

She shook it off as she climbed out of the tub and pulled on the warm guest robe. Then she froze.

He was *here*. She could feel him in the room. Her heart lodged in her throat. "Who are you?" she whispered hoarsely as she stepped back, grabbing the wall for support.

She stared in horror at the steamed-up mirror over the sink as letters began to slowly appear.

HARRY
BALLANTINE

Raymond Valencia had been waiting by the phone. Jolly had called to say that the cops were still searching Lorenzo Dante's house. Jolly thought they may have found something.

"Let me know when Lorenzo returns," Raymond said, ruing the day he'd ever met Lorenzo. What had the fool done? Something bad enough that Lorenzo might try to make a deal to save his sorry self?

Raymond had hoped it wouldn't come to this, but clearly Lorenzo would have to be dealt with. Unfortunately, now that the police were involved, it would have to be done with some finesse. That left out Jolly and Rico.

"There is something I thought you'd want to know," Jolly said. "Her car is here."

"Whose car?" Raymond asked impatiently.

"Mrs. Dante's."

"*Jenna's?* Is she there?"

"I dunno. Doesn't seem to be. Cops are crawling all over the place and the only other person I've seen is Lorenzo. But her car is parked out back. The police just got through searching it. A towing company came to take it away, but the cops stopped them."

Raymond swore under his breath. "Let me know the minute Lorenzo returns." He hung up.

The phone rang. More bad news?

"You said to call if anything unusual was going on," Rico said without preamble. "Well, it's probably nothing, but the local car dealer just dropped off a nice red Mustang for one of the tenants."

"That's nice, Rico, but not exactly—"

"I wouldn't mention it, but guess who took ownership?"

Raymond wasn't in the mood for guessing games.

"Stan Palmer's sister. Stan, the guy who got sent up for jacking that semi a couple of years ago? The guy who used to work for Dante?"

"Stan Palmer's sister lives in the same apartment house as Jenna Dante?" Raymond asked in astonishment. What were the chances of that in a city the size of Seattle?

"I recognize Charlene from one time when I picked Stan up for a job back when we were both freelancing," Rico said. "You think she knows Dante's ex-broad?"

What were the chances Charlene Palmer *didn't* know Jenna Dante, he wanted to demand of Rico.

"The dealer just handed her the keys," Rico said. "She's all excited about the car, like it's a present, you know?"

Raymond knew.

"Last I heard, Charlene couldn't afford bus fare and was living at the women's shelter. Her lack of looks aside, she's too nasty toward men to have found herself a sugar daddy."

Hadn't Rico been around long enough to realize that not all men wanted sex from a woman?

"She went back inside after signing the papers for the car," Rico said.

"Go in and ask the super who's been paying her rent. Persuade him to tell you," Raymond said. "Then call me right back. Make sure she doesn't leave before you come out again."

"You got it." Rico hung up.

Raymond waited by the phone. He knew he wouldn't have to wait long. Rico had excellent persuasion skills.

"You sitting down?" Rico said without preamble.

"Just tell me," Raymond said through gritted teeth.

"Paid through a corporation called L.D. Inc.," Rico said. "The super gets a kickback for keeping his mouth shut."

Raymond let out a curse. L.D. Inc. "Lorenzo Dante."

"You got it. Hey, Charlene just came back down. She's carrying a bag, like an overnight bag. Should I stop her?"

"No. Follow her," Raymond said. "Don't lose her. Call me as soon as she gets where she's going." He hung up, wondering what the hell was going on.

Jenna fled the bathroom and would have fled the hotel if she could have.

Lexi was sleeping soundly, with Fred curled next to her, purring, and Clarice snugged under one arm.

Jenna closed her daughter's bedroom door. There was no place to run. Charlene was on her way to pick up the money for Lorenzo. Jenna couldn't leave here even if the roads were open.

She glanced toward her own bedroom, afraid to go back in there. Afraid the letters would still be on the bathroom mirror.

Outside, the day had darkened with the promise of more rain. *No.* She couldn't stay trapped here much longer or she feared she would completely lose her mind. If she hadn't already.

She turned on all the lights in the living room to chase away the shadows and the threat of a storm outside. Then she curled up on the couch, wrapping the robe tightly around her, determined to fight the voice in her head.

But it was silent.

Her eyelids grew heavy from lack of sleep last night, from the hot water of the pool and the shower. She felt herself drifting, and tried to fight it, afraid he would be waiting for her, her defenses down.

And yet a part of her knew he would come the moment she fell asleep. She drifted off, waiting for him, yearning for him the way she'd never yearned for anyone before.

Harry wasn't even aware that he'd touched her. Not until Jenna let out the smallest of sighs. He wished he could show himself to her. But even now he didn't understand how he'd been able to connect even this much with her. It was as if after seventy years something had come alive in him.

He focused his energies on his hands, not wanting his touch to be cold. He didn't want to repel her. He brushed a caress over her temple again, then across her cheek to her jaw. She stretched, arching her neck a little as he skimmed his now warm fingers down the slim column of her throat. She let out a low moan as his fingers stopped at the opening of her robe.

She rolled over on her back on the couch, stirred a little, then dropped back to sleep. He waited before he touched her again, waited until she was in a deep slumber. When he knew she would welcome him. She needed him as much as he did her.

His fingers went to the hollow just below her throat. He could feel her quickened pulse as he traced a path down between her full breasts. Her skin felt like fine silk, rich and lush and creamy smooth.

She smelled of the expensive soap from the shower. He breathed her in, moving closer as he concentrated on making his body warm. He slipped his hand under the opening at the top of the robe.

She shivered as he cupped one breast, being careful to do it slowly, tenderly. She moaned and turned her head away from him as she pressed her breast into his warm hand. The nipple hardened against his palm. How he ached to suck it into his mouth, to lave it with his tongue, to taste her skin, to kiss her warm flesh.

Carefully he untied her robe and let each side fall away from her body. Her nipples were rock hard, dark pink against her fair skin. He thumbed one, then the other as she arched against his touch and groaned in her sleep. Her skin was hot to the touch and her breathing short and fast.

What surprised him was his own reaction. He was aroused and he wanted this woman. He'd never wanted anything as much as he did her.

But as he looked down into her face, he knew there was something else going on here. Something Harry Ballantine could no more figure out than he could free himself from the hold she had on him, a hold she'd had from the moment he saw her come up the mountain to Fernhaven.

His fingers trailed down the flat of her stomach. She froze, and for a moment he thought she would awaken and be afraid again. He waited before he slipped his fingers over the slightly rounded mound to gently caress her. She didn't wake up. But she did respond, arching against his fingers, groaning once more as he skillfully took her higher and higher, her breath coming hard and fast, her body convulsing with pleasure until he took her to a climactic peak. She shuddered and sighed. All tension washed from her face. A slight smile curved her lips.

He drew the robe back over her as she turned onto her side again. Then he lay down beside her as if he, too, had been sated, he, too, had been released.

As Harry listened to her breathe, his heart ached. Only one of them would be leaving this place.

"Any idea where we are?" Mike Flannigan asked as he shifted the Jeep into four-wheel drive. Ahead Rose could see nothing but trees, with a narrow slash cut through them that looked nothing like a road.

Mike had already had to stop numerous times to get out and move a small downed tree. Or find another way around larger fallen trees.

She looked down at the map in her lap and the compass Mike had given her. "We're going in the right direction, kinda."

He laughed and looked over at her.

She felt her heart jump in her chest and wished she hadn't gotten him involved in this. "This might have been a mistake."

"You think?" He shook his head as he reached over to lay his warm palm on her shoulder. "We'll find the road that takes us to this place. Don't worry."

The last time she'd been able to get through to the highway patrol, the road wasn't open yet. That meant Lorenzo couldn't have gotten to Jenna—even if he had somehow found out where she was.

But still Rose couldn't relax. She knew how dangerous Lorenzo Dante was. With his connections, who knew what he was capable of?

She feared Franco had found out—just before he'd died. All attempts to contact him through the safe numbers she'd been given had proved fruitless. Her instincts told her he was dead, but she still held out hope that she was wrong.

The Jeep roared up the mountain through the trees, Mike deftly steering it around boulders and tree stumps from when the area had been logged.

She looked at the map. If she was right, they weren't that far from Fernhaven.

Lorenzo couldn't sit still. He paced the interrogation room, cussing cops. "How long can they hold me?" he demanded of his lawyer.

Anthony Cruise sat in the corner, a small man in a dark suit, with a pockmarked face and sharp features. "Depends on if they book you."

"They aren't going to book me," Lorenzo said confidently. "They're just trying to scare me. They haven't got anything on me."

His lawyer glanced at the mirrored wall as if to remind him that cops were probably behind it, watching the two of them.

Thank goodness he'd had the presence of mind to put Alfredo on Charlene before he'd opened the door to the cops, Lorenzo thought. All Alfredo had to do was follow her to Jenna and take care of things. Jenna had said she wanted to return his money, but he didn't trust her.

He thought of the duffel full of money as *his* now. If he could get to it before Valencia, he could take at least half and hide it. Let Valencia think Franco and Jenna had split the money. Made a lot more sense than the two of them being romantically involved.

Lorenzo thought he could sell a story that Franco and Jenna had hatched a plan to rip off the money and split it. Then Franco would meet up with his girlfriend, Rose Garcia.

Valencia might actually buy that. And Lorenzo would come out the winner on every count. Franco's body would never be found—or his half of the money, which was two hundred and fifty large.

But first Lorenzo had to get out of the police station.

When the door finally opened and the big cop, Detective Luke Henry, came in, Lorenzo snapped, "Charge me or let me go. I know my rights, dammit."

Jenna couldn't believe she'd had the dream again. She woke flushed, the robe sticking to her damp skin. She sat up, shocked to see that it was late. How long had she slept?

She swung her legs over the side of the couch and stumbled to her feet, disoriented and confused, the dream trying to drag her back.

Hurrying through the suite, she jerked open Lexi's bedroom door, afraid her daughter would be gone. The four-year-old was still snug in the bed, asleep in the dim light.

Jenna rubbed her arms against the instant chill. Once they got away from this hotel she would forget the man from the old photograph. Forget Harry Ballantine. He didn't exist except in her mind. In her dreams. She conjured him up in her need to be loved. And yet no man had ever felt so real.

Disoriented, she stood for a moment, just letting her heart rate come back down. What scared her was what the dream had left her with. It hadn't just been sex. Someone had made *love* to her.

And the dream had left her feeling safe…a dangerous thought. But nothing like the ones that came after it. The dream had left her feeling…loved. Cherished. Protected. Alive. Whole. Blessed.

She laughed at her own foolishness. What she was was crazy. Lorenzo had tried to push her over the edge, to drive her nuts, and now he'd succeeded.

She shook her head, clearing away those thoughts.

Charlene would be here soon.

Jenna had to get the money ready.

Then she would wake Lexi and they would leave with Charlene.

For now, Jenna closed the door to her daughter's room and padded barefoot to the living room. She picked up the phone and dialed the front desk.

"Elmer, I need a box and some tape for a package," she said.

"What size? I can scare up one and bring it to you," he said cheerfully.

She gave him the dimensions.

"I saw one in the kitchen that should work. By the way, the highway patrol called. Good news—they think they will have the road open soon."

"That is good news." Jenna hung up, telling herself that Lorenzo would be so happy to have his money back that he would leave her alone.

That once she and Lexi left here, they could put all this behind them.

She hurried into her bedroom to pack, but was drawn to the bathroom. The mirror had cleared, but the words were still there.

HARRY
BALLANTINE

She closed her eyes, willing away not only the letters, but the way he'd made her feel. Her body still tingled from his touch. She thought she could smell him in the small room, almost feel his breath on her neck.

Her eyes shot open. The scream caught in her throat.

Chapter 11

"Where are you?" Raymond Valencia demanded when Rico finally called in. "Do you still have Charlene Palmer in sight?"

"Stuck in traffic. And yeah, she's just a couple of cars ahead of me, stuck in the same roadblock. But the road is supposed to open soon. There's, like, a jungle on both sides of the road. Creepy, if you ask me."

"Where are you on the map?" Raymond snapped impatiently. He could hear Rico rustling the paper as he tried to get the map open.

Raymond tried to control his impatience. He feared he'd sent Rico on a wild-goose chase. And after hearing about the police taking Lorenzo down to the station, he feared Jenna might already be dead. Franco, too.

Rico finally gave him the road number and the last town he'd been through. "I'm headed east, but according to the map there isn't anything up here but some place called—" more map rustling "—Fernhaven."

Fernhaven? It took Raymond a moment to remember where he'd heard that name before. A few months ago he'd received an invitation to the grand opening of the Fernhaven Hotel. It was a recently rebuilt hotel in the middle of nowhere, with some tragic history that dated back to the 1930s.

Could that be where Charlene Palmer was headed?

"No towns close?" he asked Rico.

"Nope."

First Charlene got a car she couldn't afford and now not only was she headed for a hotel she couldn't afford, but the place wasn't even open for business yet. Or was it? He felt better about sending Rico after her. Raymond would soon be finding out what Charlene was up to. Obviously she was doing something for Lorenzo. Maybe the car, the hotel, were her payoff, along with the apartment rent. Raymond could well imagine what her duties might have been, given that Jenna lived in the same apartment house.

He would take the chance that Charlene knew where Jenna was. Or at least what had happened to her.

Either way, Charlene Palmer wouldn't be returning to Seattle.

"You're sure of your location?"

Rico made a disgruntled sound, accompanied by what seemed to be an attempt to refold the map. "It looks like we're finally going to get under way. They're removing the barricades."

"Listen to me. I think I know where Charlene's headed. When you get to where she's going, park somewhere so you won't be noticed and call for me. I'll take the chopper. I don't want Charlene to see you, no matter what. Have you got that?"

"Got it," Rico said, in a tone that said he wasn't stupid.

Raymond wished he could believe that. "I'll be there within the hour." He hung up and called the pilot to get the helicopter ready.

Once free of the cops, Lorenzo pulled out his new cell phone and called Alfredo. He answered on the first ring.

"What's going on?" Lorenzo demanded. "Don't you dare tell me you lost her."

"Nope, I can see her car up ahead. We're stopped because of some road problem. I tried to call you—"

"I had no cell phone for a while."

"She's got another tail, though. Picked it up right after we left the apartment. I've been following both her and the tail."

Lorenzo tried to calm himself. "Who else is following her?"

"Dunno. I'll take a look."

Lorenzo heard Alfredo's car door open, then close. He waited.

After a few minutes he heard the sound of the car door opening, the springs on the seat groaning, then, "Hey, can you believe it? It's Rico Santos."

Rico. Lorenzo swore. So Valencia was one step ahead of him. How? *Charlene.* Had she sold the information to Valencia? Lorenzo wouldn't put it past her. He swore again. "Tell me where you are." He took down the directions. "Did Rico see you?"

"Naw, I didn't think you'd want me letting him know I was following her, too."

"Good work, Alfredo. Now make sure Rico doesn't follow her any farther. When she reaches wherever she's headed, call me and wait for further instructions. I'm on my way."

He remembered that Jenna's car was still parked at the service entrance. The damn cops had turned the tow truck driver away so they could search her car. Lorenzo had told the cops that it had some kind of mechanical problem and that's why Jenna had left it there and called someone to give her a ride home. He didn't know who. He didn't care.

Now he would have to call the towing company again. They would charge him double. But he never wanted to see Jenna's car again. He should have dumped it in the lake the way he had Franco's.

He quickly packed his belongings. Charlene had promised to call as soon as she had the package. As if he would trust her to do that. A woman like Charlene would open the duffel—if Jenna was stupid enough to still have all that money in nothing more than a duffel bag.

From where Alfredo said he was stopped in traffic, it was a good two-hour drive. But Lorenzo had no choice but to head up there. Alfredo would buy him time by taking out Rico. And if need be, he'd have Alfredo take care of Charlene and get the money.

Jenna, though, was another story. As dangerous as it was, Lorenzo wanted to take care of her himself.

My God, she could *see* him.
Jenna stumbled back, a look of horror on her face.
It's all right. Don't be afraid.
Harry didn't dare move toward her. He still couldn't

believe that she could see him. He wanted to rejoice, to sing and dance and shout. *She could see him.*

"Please go away," she moaned as she backed up against the wall of the bathroom, then slid down to the floor, as if her legs would no longer hold her up. Tears welled in her eyes. She bit her lower lip and squeezed her eyes shut.

Is that really what you want? He stepped toward her, desperately wanting to touch her, to reassure her, to look into her eyes and have her gaze into his. He'd never dreamed this would ever happen. Not after seventy years of being nothing. Of not being heard. Or seen.

But now...

She tried to draw back as he cupped her cheek with his hand. "Please, don't." But even as she said the words, she turned her head to press her lips into his palm. Her tears splashed down over his fingers. He could feel them, just as he could feel her.

Somehow she had breached the barrier that had enclosed him all these years and kept him prisoner.

I don't know. I think you were sent here. For me, he thought. This woman he felt such intense emotions for had opened a door and released him. And now the ache to live again was so strong in him that he knew he would do *anything* to reclaim a place in her world.

Open your eyes. Look at me.

Mike Flannigan slammed on his brakes and swore.

Rose caught her breath as she stared at the cliff just feet in front of the Jeep. The logging road had ended without warning in a fifty-foot drop into a creek bed.

"I guess I should have taken the other road back there," Mike said as he carefully put the Jeep in Reverse and backed up.

Rose didn't let out the breath until they were far enough from the dropoff that she dared inhale again. Her hand went to her side.

"Are you feeling all right?" Mike asked.

She dropped her hand. She could feel the scar through the fabric of her shirt and realized that it had become a habit, touching it, almost as if it had become a reminder.

"The knife wound is healed. I'm fine."

"Right." Mike turned the Jeep around in a wide spot and started back up the road. "You really think you're up to taking on some really bad bad guys?"

"I'm just going to warn Jenna, that's all."

Mike chuckled. "Right. Lorenzo isn't already out on bail and tracking her, too. Probably hasn't sent any of his thugs after her, either." He shook his head and shot Rose a glance. "It isn't your fault she married him."

"People make mistakes," Rose said, remembering the young, gentle woman she'd met in the park. "Jenna made a big one. But she shouldn't have to pay with her life. Not to mention the price that little girl might have to pay."

Rose swallowed, willing back the tears that burned her eyes. She remembered Lexi from the park.

Mike seemed to let the silence lie between them for a moment. "You have a plan if Lorenzo and his gunmen show up?"

She had no plan. That wasn't like her. She preferred having a plan of action, if it was working on her house or working on a case. She was winging it and that alone should have scared her. "I'm going to get Jenna out of there before they can find her."

"There's something you should know," Mike said. "The word on the street is that a big payoff is missing.

Raymond Valencia is looking for Franco. Lorenzo is somehow involved. But there is a fear that there will be retribution. If there hasn't already been."

Was this about a missing payoff? Or about Jenna?

Rose closed her eyes. "I just can't shake this feeling that Jenna is in worse trouble than even having her ex after her."

Chapter 12

Charlene Palmer had taken every precaution to make sure she wasn't followed. In the busy traffic around Seattle she hadn't spotted any car twice.

But once on the two-lane road heading east she kept seeing a large black car behind her. She figured Lorenzo would have her followed. She'd hoped she'd lost the tail before now. Maybe she hadn't.

She wasn't that worried. Even if it was one of Lorenzo's men, he wouldn't stop her until she had the package, and since she had a backup plan...

She'd locked the doors on her car while waiting for the road to open and patrolmen to remove the barricades. There hadn't been but a handful of vehicles in line behind her, the black sedan one of them.

Now that they were moving again, she didn't see the vehicle. Maybe it had turned off. Maybe it hadn't been following her at all.

She tried to relax. She had a nice car. Soon she would have twenty thousand dollars to go with it. Actually, more than that if her plan worked. And unless she missed her guess, she would no longer be needed to spy on Jenna Dante. She'd never liked doing it, anyway.

Wisps of fog began to drift across the highway. She'd been climbing for miles. Up here, the trees were thick on each side of the road, walls of green that hemmed in the highway. Around the next bend, the fog grew more dense. She caught a glimpse of black clouds shrouding the tops of the mountains. A storm was coming in. She liked storms.

She turned on her headlights and slowed as she checked her rearview mirror. There was one set of headlights a good distance behind her, but she quickly lost them in the fog and trees as the road snaked up the mountainside.

Glancing at the mileage gauge, she saw that she should be almost to Fernhaven.

And there her life would finally begin.

Fear kept Jenna's eyes squeezed tight. *Hurry, Charlene. I have to get out of here.*

Jenna tried to remain calm. Charlene would be here soon. By this time tomorrow Lorenzo would have his money back. She and Lexi would be on a flight to some country far from here. Everything would be all right. She would forget this place and what had happened...

Jenna.

She shook her head and put her hands over her ears. She heard him chuckle.

You know that won't do any good. Look at me.

She felt a sob escape her lips as she opened her eyes. He was crouched next to her on the floor, looking exactly as he had in the old photographs downstairs. He wore a tuxedo, his dark hair oiled and combed back. His eyes were the most beautiful blue she'd ever seen. She felt a jolt as she looked into them.

He met her gaze.

Jenna's heart beat faster. It *had* been him in her dreams. She could see it in his eyes. He'd been here last night and again this afternoon. He'd made love to her. He'd made her believe that anything was possible. His touch had ignited a passion that had been missing in her life, and she didn't want to let it go. She wanted this phantom lover to come to her, to make love to her, to never ever go away.

As if he knew that, he reached out and pulled her into his arms, drawing her to her feet.

She closed her eyes, feeling tears well behind her lids as she leaned into him. He felt solid. Real. "What is going on?" she whispered.

"I'm not sure. This is as much of a surprise to me as it is to you."

She pulled away from him and stepped deeper into the room. "Who is Bobby John Chamberlain?" she asked, slipping her hand into her jacket pocket.

"Jenna—"

As she turned, she withdrew the gun from her pocket and pointed it at him. He seemed to shimmer in the light. Not a figment of her imagination. But not *real,* either.

Harry groaned and looked disappointed. "Put down the gun, Jenna."

"Who are you? *What* are you?" She gripped the weapon tighter.

He met her gaze. "You already know."

She shook her head. "No, I don't. Tell me I dreamed it."

"It isn't a dream," he said quietly.

She shook her head. "But this isn't possible."

"I don't know how or why, but you were sent here. Sent to me." He stepped toward her.

She raised the gun to point it at the spot where his heart should have been. "I have to know who you are."

"My name *is* Harry Ballantine, and part of me has been waiting my whole life for you. Isn't that all you have to know?"

She shook her head once more.

"Jenna, let me help you. Put down the gun. It won't do you any good. You can't kill me. I'm already dead."

"No." She recoiled, her hands trembling so hard she almost dropped the weapon. She stumbled back, losing her balance.

He caught her, gently took it from her and eased her down onto the couch. Flipping on the safety, he put the gun on top of the television cabinet, out of Lexi's reach.

Jenna felt as if all was lost. She'd lost her mind. Worse, she'd lost something else—a part of herself—to Harry Ballantine. No matter who or what he was, a part of her would always remain here with him, whatever happened now.

"I'm sorry." It was all Harry could think to say. Because he was sorry in more ways than she could ever know.

She was shaking, her eyes glittering with tears. He didn't know how much time he had. She could still see him, but he didn't know for how long.

"You came here so I could help you," he said.

She shook her head yet again, her eyes wide as she stared at him. Her face had blanched white and he could see the fear. The disbelief. He'd been there and understood how hard it was to accept some of life's—and death's—little surprises.

"I think I knew the moment I saw you," he murmured. "You have to let me help you. It's the only way."

"Why should I believe anything you tell me?" she demanded, her voice breaking.

"Because a part of you knows how I feel about you," he stated. He could see her fighting it.

"I don't understand any of this," she said with a sob.

"Listen to me, Jenna." He gripped her hands. "I know you're in trouble. There are people after you."

She tried to pull free. "How can you know that?"

"The same way I know you were sent here. I feel it." He let go of her hands. "You're in grave danger."

Tears welled again in her eyes. She glanced toward the door to Lexi's bedroom. "I have to protect my daughter."

"I know. I'm not sure how, but I want to help you." He didn't tell her that he had a plan, and if it worked, they would be together—one way or another. Because he could never let her go now. They were meant to be together. Even if she would have to die to stay here with him.

The phone rang, startling Jenna. She'd completely forgotten about Charlene. She got up and went to answer it, her back to Harry.

"Hey, it's me," Charlene said. "I'm starting up the mountain to the hotel. Everything okay at your end?"

"Yes."

"You sure? You sound like someone has a gun to your head," Charlene stated, as if she might be only half joking.

"No, I'm fine. Just nervous. I want this over with," Jenna said.

"Hang in there. It will be over before you know it." Charlene disconnected.

Jenna wished she could believe that as she hung up the phone and turned.

Harry was gone.

She hadn't heard the door open. Nor close. She checked the rest of the suite. Gone. As she came back into the living area, she glanced quickly to the coffee table, where she'd put the taped-up cardboard box that she'd filled with money.

It was still there.

But part of her had expected it to be gone.

Chapter 13

Lorenzo couldn't believe this gas-hog of a car he'd rented. He pulled into a fuel station at the edge of some Podunk town and happened to glance in his rearview mirror.

A dark-colored sedan swung to the side of the road in front of an abandoned store. Jolly. The son of a bitch was tailing him!

Lorenzo jumped as someone tapped on his side window. A kid in a grimy green uniform looked down at him. Lorenzo turned the key back on and hit the button that lowered his window a few inches.

"Fill 'er up," he said to the attendant as he realized he'd pulled into a full-service pump instead of a self-service. He hated to think what gas cost in a town this far from anything. A ghost town. Most of the storefronts were boarded up and there was no one on the street.

He looked into his mirror again. Jolly was still sitting in his car, waiting.

Lorenzo opened his door, got out and stretched, his back to Jolly. "Where's your restroom?" he asked the attendant as he walked around the front of the car.

The kid pointed to the back. "Key's just inside the door."

The key was attached to a carved piece of log that had to weigh two pounds. Lorenzo took it from the hook and carried the stupid thing around the side of the building, discarding it the moment he was out of sight.

He ran around back, sprinting across a side street and skirting the rear of the abandoned store, then up its side to the corner. He stopped to screw the silencer onto his gun, then keeping low, came up behind the dark sedan. Jolly was facing forward, watching the station, waiting for him to come out of the john.

The attendant at the gas station finished filling up Lorenzo's car, then sauntered back inside the station without even bothering to wash his windshield.

Lorenzo moved quickly forward, the gun against his leg. Once he was alongside, he raised the weapon and pumped three shots into the window.

The first shot shattered the glass. Nothing stopped the second and third ones from reaching their mark. Jolly slumped in the seat, eyes wide, mouth open.

Lorenzo went back the way he'd come, picked up the bathroom key and returned it to the office, hanging it on the nail where he'd found it. He paid cash for his gas, thanked the attendant, who hadn't even bothered to wash his damn windshield, and walked in a leisurely way to his car, all the time watching the street.

No movement of any kind. Especially from the dark car parked in front of the abandoned grocery store.

* * *

At the helicopter pad, Raymond Valencia tried Rico's number one more time before boarding. He hadn't been able to reach him. Either cell phones didn't work high in the Cascades, or something had happened to him.

"Where's Erik?" Raymond asked in surprise as he slid up into the seat of the small chopper. With some alarm, he saw that this man wasn't his usual pilot. The guy couldn't have been over thirty, with startling blue eyes and blondish hair that was too long and curled at the collar of his leather bomber jacket. He looked as if he belonged on a surfboard at the beach, not at the controls of a chopper.

"Flu bug. Your service called for a pilot." The guy gave him a look as if to say, "So here I am." He stuck out a big suntanned hand. "John James Harrison."

Raymond shook his hand, a little less uneasy when he felt the strength of the man's grip. There was also a confidence about the young man. It eased Raymond's mind some as he watched him ready the chopper.

"How long will it take to get there?" Raymond asked.

"Half an hour once we're off the ground."

"You been flying long?"

Harrison gave him an amused smile, showing a lot of white teeth as he cranked up the engine. "Since I was a kid. My father was a pilot," he said over the whoop-whoop of the blades.

Raymond nodded and tried to relax. Half an hour. He glanced at his watch, wondering what he was doing. This was a mistake. He should never have gotten involved in Jenna Dante's life to begin with. More to the point, Lorenzo Dante's life. Raymond hoped he was wrong, but couldn't help thinking he was somehow responsible for Jenna running. For her taking his money, if indeed she had. For what was bound to be a show-down at some remote hotel in the Cascades.

He'd always been so careful to stay in the shadows. Others before him had ended up in prison or dead because they got their hands dirty. They'd become public figures, with their photographs in the paper all the time depicted as crime bosses. He'd seen enough of those shots on the evening news to swear he wouldn't be one of them. He lived a secluded, quiet life and was very careful.

Now he'd broken his cardinal rule. He was getting involved. And for what? Five hundred grand? He knew it had little to do with the money, although half a million dollars wasn't anything to sneeze at.

He had to know who he could trust. That was much more important than money. He had to know who was behind this—and see that they were taken care of.

He felt his gun, where it was tucked in against his ribs. He hadn't killed anyone in years. Not that he hadn't kept up his marksmanship abilities at the shooting range he'd installed in the lower level of his home.

Some nights he shot round after round. He knew that to truly be safe, he needed to be able to protect himself. Then he would bowl in the single alley he'd had built next to the shooting range. No one knew about the bowling because he didn't want anyone to know just how lonely he was. Just how alone.

And that, he knew, was why he was doing this. Not because of the money or the trust issue. He wanted Jenna. He'd wanted her from the first time he'd laid eyes on her and he'd found out that Lorenzo had married the girl.

Raymond had been sick with desire for Lorenzo Dante's wife. And now he could have her. She would be grateful for his help. She would owe him. Especially if she'd taken his money. Even if she didn't want him, he knew he could convince her that she belonged with him. He would protect her. And her daughter. From Lorenzo.

The helicopter lifted off. The sinking sun glinted on the high-rises in downtown Seattle. The Space Needle stood alone, a soaring landmark, glowing in the sun.

The chopper headed east, crossing over miles of traffic-filled highways, clusters of small communities, until finally the landscape below them turned green.

Raymond breathed a sigh of relief, leaned back and closed his eyes. He thought about Jenna and prayed that she wasn't involved in trying to rip him off. Especially that she wasn't in this with Lorenzo. Raymond knew he couldn't forgive that.

Heavy at heart, he hated to think what he would have to do if he found out that Jenna had betrayed him.

Charlene came up over the rise and there it was. Fernhaven Hotel.

Even through the rain and fog, the place looked amazing.

"Wow." Charlene had dreamed about living a life like this. Fancy hotels, breakfast in bed, people to wait on her...

But how had Jenna Dante gone from that fleabag apartment where she'd lived to this? Last Charlene knew, Jenna had less money than Charlene herself.

Blackmail? Was she selling these so-called papers to her ex?

Charlene smiled at the thought. Would be nice to see Jenna get some backbone, that was for sure. The woman was more beaten down than Charlene had been even during the worse part of her marriage. Her husband used to kick her butt, but Charlene had always come back fighting.

She pulled into a spot in the parking lot near the trees, where she figured her car wouldn't be that noticeable, and turned off the engine.

The rain seemed to fall harder, with gusts of wind blowing it sideways across the windshield. She debated waiting to see if it was going to let up. Yeah, right. She wished she'd thought to grab an umbrella. Or at least a rain jacket. But she'd been thinking of sunny beaches, because she had no intention of ever going back to Seattle unless it was to catch a plane to a warmer clime.

She sat for a minute just gawking at the hotel. Never in her life had she ever stayed at anything more than a cheap motel, let alone a place this fancy. Maybe after she got the package from Jenna, she'd stay the night. What would it hurt to make Lorenzo Dante wait?

She knew the answer to that one. But there was little that scared Charlene anymore. She'd seen the worst of it in other men like him. Nothing could scare her now. Not even Lorenzo. He could hurt her physically, kill her, make the last few minutes of her life pretty miserable, but in the end, he couldn't take anything else from her because she had nothing worth taking. Death would be a welcome relief.

Not that Charlene had any intention of dying anytime soon. Nope, she'd put away any money she came across. Hidden it. She had added to her nest egg with the money Lorenzo had been giving her to spy on Jenna.

And now she had a car and was about to add twenty grand to what she called her "freedom fund."

She was a lucky woman, she thought, as she waited for the rain to let up. She had overcome obstacles that would have killed most men. And with no education or a husband or many prospects, she'd found ways to take care of herself.

Not that she was proud of spying on Jenna. She liked the woman, related to her. But this was about survival. And Charlene Palmer was determined to survive—no matter what she had to do.

It was a lesson that Jenna Dante still had to learn.

"Picking up some wind," the pilot said as Raymond Valencia's helicopter neared the hotel. The chopper began to shake, buffeted by the gale. Fog rushed by, and suddenly rain splatted off the helicopter like bullets off bulletproof glass.

Through the rain and fog, Raymond Valencia caught a glimpse of Fernhaven and was instantly filled with an unexplainable dread. He'd read about the hotel being rebuilt on the same spot where *fifty-seven people* had died in 1936, after a fire had swept through the original hotel. This place was said to be identical.

A fierce cold seemed to envelop the helicopter. He shivered and looked over at the young pilot, wondering if it was only his imagination or if Harrison felt it, too.

Harrison was frowning, seemingly intent on flying the chopper, and having some difficulty.

"You should be able to put it down in the parking lot," Raymond said. Thunder cracked, so close he felt the hair stand up on the back of his neck. Right behind it came a loud boom.

The pilot had to yell to be heard over it. "No way are we putting this baby down up there. The chopper's too light for the kind of wind coming down off that mountain. It would be suicide to try to land up there."

"What do you think you're doing?" Raymond demanded when Harrison started to turn the chopper around and head back the way they'd come. Raymond could see the clearing. They were too close to turn back.

He pulled his gun from the holster and pointed it at Harrison. "Fly this chopper as if your life depended on it and take me to the hotel."

Harrison looked from Raymond to the gun in his hand and smiled, while still fighting to keep the chopper in the air. "I knew when I woke up this morning this wasn't going to be my day."

Raymond looked out. He couldn't see the lights of Fernhaven through the pouring rain. "You think I won't shoot you?"

There was a loud thunk and the engine sputtered. "Shooting me might be the kindest thing you can do right now," Harrison said as he fought the controls.

You're going to die. The thought seemed to come from outside Raymond as the chopper suddenly began to buck. Then the engine died and the craft rolled to the side, dropping toward the dense green forest below.

The trees came up fast through the rain and fog.

Raymond could hear the pilot on the radio. "Mayday, Mayday."

Raymond thought his life might pass before him. Instead his last thought before the chopper crashed was of his mother. At least she would mourn his death.

Dark clouds hung over the hotel by the time Jenna saw a red car come up the mountainside and park at the back of the lot. It was raining so hard it was difficult to tell if it was Charlene. No one got out of the car.

Jenna waited, afraid. The wind groaned and raindrops ricocheted against the glass, obscuring her view.

What if it was Lorenzo?

Jenna held her breath as she stared down at the car,

waiting to see who got out. Part of her was screaming, "Run! You can't trust anyone." Especially Harry Ballantine.

You can't trust anyone.

Especially your own instincts.

Or even your own eyes.

It was Harry's voice again in her head. She shivered, convinced she was losing her mind.

Even when she saw the figure finally emerge from the red car, for a split second her brain saw Lorenzo. She recoiled, then blinked. It was only Charlene. No one else got out.

Weak with relief, Jenna clutched the window frame and finally allowed herself to breathe. No one else was in sight as Charlene started through the rain toward the hotel entrance.

As a bolt of lightning split the dark sky, Charlene looked up at the hotel and almost died.

She barely heard the boom of thunder, followed in a heartbeat by an explosion that lit the sky.

While Charlene had always been a little bit psychic, it wasn't like being a little bit pregnant. You had to work at the craft, hone your skills. Charlene had never liked work.

At an early age she'd accepted her so-called "gift," but also knew she didn't want to foresee her future.

"I don't have to be psychic to know it's going to be bad," she'd often said. "I'd rather be surprised than to see how bad it's going to be before I get there." So she'd pretty much learned to block it out.

That is, until the moment she looked up at Fernhaven, saw all the faces in the windows and knew that only one of the those looking down at her wasn't dead yet.

Her blood turned to slush. She no longer felt the rain pelting her. All she felt was fear gripping her by her throat.

Being a little clairvoyant, she should have known that a tragedy such as the one that had struck the original Fernhaven did more than scar the land. The horror stayed, trapped there often for eternity. Or until something or someone released the poor souls. But she now felt that truth to her very bones.

This place was haunted with the fifty-seven dead. Not only could she see and feel them, she knew enough to fear them. Fernhaven was a graveyard of lost souls and, she realized with a shudder, they'd been expecting her.

Chapter 14

Harry sent a warning to Jenna, but knew he had to stop Charlene. She couldn't be trusted. He sensed it on some level he couldn't explain.

As Charlene started toward the steps of Fernhaven, he moved in front of her.

To his astonishment and regret, she walked right through him. He saw her shudder as if she felt something, but clearly she couldn't see him. Or feel him. Only Jenna and her daughter were aware of him.

Which meant he had no way to stop what was going to happen.

Then, to his surprise, Charlene turned and looked back. Not at him, but at the headlights coming up the road. She quickly stepped into the shadows and waited.

The car stopped at the edge of the trees. The lights went out, the engine suddenly silent.

Charlene moved through the cover of darkness toward the car.

Something shone for a moment in her hand as she neared the vehicle and the man sitting in it, trying to get his cell phone to work.

"Mr. Dante, if you get this message, it's Alfredo. I'm at that place, Fernhaven, waiting like you told me to." He snapped off the phone, grumbling under his breath.

The man didn't see Charlene coming, didn't hear her steal alongside the car. Not until it was too late.

After Jenna saw Charlene disappear from view, she hurriedly packed up and put her suitcase by the front door.

She checked on Lexi, only to find her glued to the television. Jenna didn't allow her daughter to watch much TV, so this was a treat for her. She felt she had failed Lexi in so many ways.

A mother protected her child. Even against the child's father. Jenna hadn't done that. Worse, she wasn't sure she could in the future.

She closed the door to the sound of Lexi's childish laughter and Fred's irritated meow. Lexi hadn't said any more about her father. Only that she wanted a "new" daddy, a nice daddy.

Hurry, Charlene, hurry.

When Jenna heard a soft knock, she ran to the door of the suite and threw it open, belatedly realizing she should have asked who it was first.

Charlene stood in the doorway, soaking wet and looking as if she'd aged. She was panting, her face ashen, as she burst into the room, motioning wildly for Jenna to close the door.

"Did someone follow you?" Jenna asked as she

quickly closed and locked the door. "Lorenzo? Is he after you?"

Charlene seemed surprised by the question. She shook her head and, putting a hand to her breast, said between breaths, "It's not Lorenzo." She glanced around the suite, eyes widening.

"Are you all right?" Jenna had to ask. Her neighbor didn't look all right. For a moment Jenna wondered if Charlene was having a heart attack.

"I'm fine. Just…winded. Where's Lexi?"

"In the other room watching cartoons," Jenna said. "Thank you so much for driving up here. I really appreciate it."

Charlene nodded, her gaze going to the taped-up box sitting on the table. "That it?"

"Yes. I just need you to leave it in my apartment. I'll call Lorenzo and tell him where to pick it up once I know you made it home safely."

"Yeah. This place…" She waved a hand through the air and met Jenna's gaze. "It doesn't bother you?"

Bother her? Jenna wanted to laugh. This place made her crazy. "I'm anxious to leave, if that's what you mean. I'm all packed. I was hoping you could give me a ride to the nearest town."

Charlene was starting to breathe a little freer and didn't look quite so pale. She dragged a sleeve over her face and Jenna saw her shiver.

"I'm already packed," she repeated, motioning to her suitcase by the door. "I just need to get Lexi."

Charlene nodded.

"Are you sure you're all right?" Jenna asked her. "Would you like a glass of water?"

"No," she answered. "I'm fine. It's just the altitude up here. I'm not used to it."

Jenna smiled at her. "Thank you again for doing this. I owe you." She stepped to her daughter's door and opened it. "Time to go, baby."

"Go?" Lexi said from the bed. "No, Mommy."

Jenna turned off the TV. Lexi protested, burrowing down under the covers. Jenna picked up Fred. He began to protest, too.

She carried the cat and Lexi's suitcase into the living room and put the suitcase by the door next to her own. Charlene was standing at the window, looking out through the rain-streaked glass.

Jenna went back into the bedroom. "Lexi, please don't fight me. Not now. Baby, we have to leave. Don't you want to go on a big plane?"

Lexi peeked out from under the covers. She'd been crying, her face tearstained. It broke Jenna's heart. The child had been uprooted so much, and now Jenna was taking her away from the one place Lexi truly seemed happy.

"A really big plane," Jenna said, hearing the pain in her voice. She smiled, hoping to hide it from her daughter.

"Is Daddy going with us on the big plane?" Lexi asked.

Jenna could hear the fear in her daughter's voice. "No. He's not going with us."

Lexi pushed back the covers, scooped up Clarice and reached out to her mother. Jenna grasped her in her arms and headed for the living room. Reaching the bedroom doorway, she halted.

Charlene was standing near the front door. She had the box of Lorenzo's money under one arm. She held a gun in her free hand. The barrel was pointed at Jenna, and it had a silencer on the end.

"Give me Lexi," Charlene said in a voice Jenna scarcely recognized. "Give me the child. Don't make me force you."

"Charlene—"

"Now!" the woman snapped.

Lexi started crying. Jenna stepped back, thinking that if she could get into the bedroom and close and lock the door...

Charlene dropped the box and grabbed Lexi's arm before Jenna could carry out her plan. Struggling to hang on to her child, Jenna didn't see Charlene swing the gun in a deadly arc.

She felt the stunning blow, though, felt Charlene pry Lexi from her arms. And then Jenna was falling, screaming out her daughter's name as she pitched toward the darkness.

Lorenzo couldn't believe it. A hotel at the end of the road?

He stopped, furious at Jenna for bringing him to this backwoodsy place. He liked cities. Dark woods made him uncomfortable. Add one hell of a rainstorm and he wanted to ring her neck. And Charlene's, and even Alfredo's...

He took out his cell phone and called Alfredo. No service. Lorenzo had told the man to stay put, but as he drove by Alfredo's car, even in the dark he could see that Alfredo wasn't sitting inside, waiting. What was wrong with him?

A chill crept along the back of Lorenzo's neck. He rubbed at it with his hand as he realized Alfredo always did what he was told. He was too dumb to do anything else.

Something had happened.

Lorenzo looked out through the driving rain, considering what might be waiting for him at the hotel. Alfredo had killed Rico at the roadblock. Lorenzo had seen Rico's car pushed off to the side of the accident site.

And with Jolly out of the picture, who did that leave?

Jenna? Lorenzo scoffed at the idea. Sure, she'd taken the gun he had hidden in the bedroom, but did she even know how to use it? Unless she'd learned since divorcing him.

He ground his teeth at the thought of what his dear ex-wife had been up to since the divorce. But one thing he knew for certain: Jenna didn't have what it took to pull a trigger. Not to mention he was the father of her only child. No matter how she felt about him, Jenna couldn't kill him.

So that only left... Charlene. Lorenzo groaned as he shifted the car into Drive and parked at the edge of the lot—where, through the pouring rain, he could see the vehicle he'd bought Charlene. She would have his money by now. She would think she was going to live to spend it. Charlene didn't scare him. He'd kill her before she had a chance to do to him what she must have done to poor dumb Alfredo.

Thunder cracked overhead, a boom that shook the Jeep.

"Well, I'll be damned," Mike said, and pointed through the rain.

Rose saw the lights, dim in the pouring rain. "That's got to be it." Fernhaven. She felt herself tense, afraid what they would find once they reached the hotel.

Maybe they should have waited for the road to open. It might have been faster. For all she knew Lorenzo could already be down there.

She checked her weapon in the shoulder holster beneath her jacket. Fully loaded. She had an extra clip in her pocket and a knife in her boot, a little trick she'd learned from Luke.

Glancing over, she saw the truth in Mike's gaze. He knew she hadn't come all this way just to warn Jenna. Ever since Jenna had confided in her about the horrible things Lorenzo had done, Rose had been determined to take the man down. She'd hoped that she could do it legally—by getting Jenna to turn state's evidence against Lorenzo.

That had failed. Then Rose had been injured on another case.

Now she had a chance to make sure that Lorenzo Dante never hurt another person.

Mike reached over and squeezed her knee. Their eyes met in silent understanding. He understood her need to right wrongs—even if he didn't agree with it. But they both knew that things could go very wrong once they reached the hotel. "Be careful," he said.

She nodded. "You, too."

He smiled and shifted the Jeep as they dropped off the mountain, down what had once been a logging road but was now little more than a trail. With luck it would come out fairly close to the hotel.

Rose could see the lavish building through the rain and fog. She felt a chill, remembering the ad she'd seen announcing the opening of Fernhaven. The owners had touted the hotel's former elegance, its hot pools, its ornate, detailed decor and the big draw: its ghosts.

"Mommy! I want my mommy," Lexi cried as Charlene half carried, half dragged her down the hallway toward the elevators.

"Shut up!" Charlene snapped, stopping to shake the little girl. "Listen to me. You ever want to see your mommy again, you have to shut up. You understand?"

"I don't like you," Lexi said, choking on her sobs.

"Well, I'm wild about you, kid," Charlene said sarcastically. "I'll tell you what. If you quit crying and come with me without any more trouble, I'll give you some candy. Chocolate. You like chocolate, don't you?"

Lexi turned to look back down the hall. "You hurt my mommy."

"No, she just fell down. She'll be fine once she rests a little. We'll get some chocolate out of my car and then we'll see if she's ready to go with us, how would that be?"

The kid was giving her a suspicious look. Lexi had always been too bright for her own good.

Lexi had to run to keep up as Charlene half dragged her down the hall. The box under her arm was a lot heavier than it looked. *Papers, my behind.* There was something good in this box, something Lorenzo Dante would pay anything for. Charlene would bet on that.

But just to even the odds, there was always dear little Alexandria as a bargaining chip if Lorenzo tried to cheat Charlene out of what she had coming. She was no fool. She liked having all the odds on her side.

They reached the elevator and she pushed the button. She could feel the spirits. She jabbed at the elevator button. *Come on.*

Lexi was waving at someone down the opposite hall from where they'd just come—an odd bat in a purple hat with feathers. No one better try to help Lexi or stop Charlene.

The elevator doors opened and Charlene lurched in, jerking Lexi after her. She punched the close button three times before the doors shut. Then she leaned against the wall, breathing hard. Nervous sweat poured into her eyes. She wiped it with her sleeve.

Just a few more minutes and she would be out of this place. She looked across the elevator. She couldn't see them now, but she knew they were there watching her. The arm holding the heavy box began to tremble. She wanted to put it down but she couldn't. She leaned against the elevator wall, chilled and sweating, fighting for her next breath.

The elevator stopped. The doors opened. Charlene practically dived out, dragging Lexi with her.

The lobby was just yards away. She could see the door that opened onto the wide porch. Once she was through it...

Lorenzo looked around, surprised to realize the hotel didn't even look open for business. There was only one old pickup parked across the lot, other than Charlene's red car and Alfredo's vehicle back in the trees.

Odd. Was it possible Jenna wasn't even here?

No. Charlene had gotten a call from her. Charlene wouldn't try to double-cross him until she got her twenty grand. The woman was a lot of things, but she wasn't that stupid.

But what could Jenna be doing here?

He knew the smartest thing would be to wait in his car for Charlene. She'd eventually come back out with the money, and when she did, he'd be waiting.

But not only did he hate waiting, he couldn't stand the thought that Jenna had to be close by. What if she somehow got away?

During the whole trip up here he'd been imagining the look on her face when she saw him. He smiled to himself, enjoying the terror he would see there. Killing her was going to make all this worthwhile.

Then he would take Alexandria. The thought didn't please him as much as he'd imagined it would. Before, he'd known that Jenna would suffer, knowing he had their daughter. But if she was dead...

He realized he was having second thoughts about taking Alexandria with him when he left the country. If she'd been a boy, a male heir, it would be different. But he had a feeling she would be more trouble than she was worth.

And she was a strange child. He'd seen her studying him sometimes, and there were moments when he thought she could see beyond his veneer, see things he didn't want anyone seeing.

Yes, the more he thought about it, the more he didn't think he would take her. After all, she'd probably grow up to give him as much grief as her mother had. Maybe he'd just leave her here. She was cute enough that someone might want her.

He glanced toward the hotel.

Where the hell was Charlene?

He couldn't wait any longer. He'd just started to open his door when a Jeep came roaring up to the front door.

Lorenzo couldn't believe his eyes as Rose Garcia jumped out and ran toward the lobby of the hotel, followed by the man who'd been driving.

What the hell was she doing here? And who was the guy? Hell, they both looked like cops, now that he thought about it.

He quietly closed his car door and slid down in the seat. This wasn't going anything like he'd planned, and it was starting to make him very angry.

* * *

"Lexi?"

The child jerked free as a woman Charlene had never seen came running in the front door.

Charlene tried to grab the little brat, but realized it was futile. Lexi ran to the woman, crying again, saying, "She hurt my mommy."

Charlene shifted the box to get to her gun as she continued to run for the front door. Out of the corner of her eye she saw Lexi launch herself into the woman's arms. Who the hell was that?

As she reached the front door she saw a man coming in. She fired at him when she saw him going for a weapon. He dived to his right, but she saw him clutch his side, grimacing in pain. She'd shot him!

She was hit with a blast of cold, wet air, then was out the door, across the porch and heading down the steps.

She didn't look back, couldn't. She ran as if she was running for her life. She was.

Once she reached the pavement of the parking lot, she looked over her shoulder. She saw the man limp inside, the front door of Fernhaven closing behind him. No one chased after her. She'd gotten away.

Charlene slowed, breathing so hard she couldn't hear over her gasps. She'd never moved that fast in her life. She laughed. She didn't even notice the rain.

Because of the storm, an odd darkness had settled over the landscape, creeping her out almost as much as the hotel had. She half ran, half walked toward her car. The box was so heavy, and she was still having trouble catching her breath, especially at this altitude. She was used to sea level. She was also in terrible shape.

She wasn't even sure who she was running from anymore. She'd seen things back there in that hotel that she never wanted to see again. Felt things that would haunt her until the day she died.

But at least she would have money. More than twenty grand.

She'd parked near the edge of the lot, thinking to hide her car beside the dense vegetation. Now she wished she'd parked right at the front door.

A damp, cold breeze stirred the trees and bushes, with a rustle like a hoarse whisper. Dark shadows moved in and out, in sync with her frightened breaths. As Charlene moved away from the lights of the hotel, she felt as if she were falling into blackness.

She slowed to rest for an instant. The air felt heavy. The dark clouds low. She labored to breathe, straining to hear over the clamor of her pulse.

Through the pouring rain she thought she glimpsed another vehicle parked near Alfredo's in the trees. She was almost to her own car when she heard it.

The scrape of a shoe sole on the parking lot pavement.

She didn't turn—just ran, lumbering toward the little red car, the nicest thing she'd ever owned.

She never reached the car.

He hit her from behind.

She fell forward, unable to break her fall because of the box in her hands. She went down hard, landing on the box, which knocked the air out of her.

Charlene rolled over on her back and looked up. At first he was only a large black shadow. No features. No real shape. Just a faceless monster in the dark.

"You stupid bitch."

Still gasping for breath, she pushed herself up into a sitting position as he began to take shape before her eyes. Lorenzo. She'd know that voice and that attitude anywhere.

"I tried to call you," she said.

It was the wrong thing to say, and she knew it the instant the words were out of her mouth.

He kicked her in the thigh, the pain excruciating. Charlene let out a howl and bent over her leg.

He was on her then, grabbing a handful of her hair and snapping her head back so she was forced to look into his face. The face of the devil.

"Shut up or I'll cut your throat," he growled between gritted teeth as he knelt beside her.

The knife glittered in his hand, and she didn't doubt for a moment that he meant every word. She endured the pain, biting down on her lip.

He wanted something, needed something from her, or he would have already killed her.

"Where is Jenna?" he asked, tightening his hold on her hair, making her gasp back another cry of pain.

"Room 318. I got your package for you." Charlene tried to look at the box on the pavement, but he jerked her head up so she had to gaze at him.

He raised the knife blade so she could see it.

As he held her down, he reached over and drew the box to him. Carefully he slipped the blade beneath the tape and sliced. The top flapped open and he reached inside.

"What the hell?" He waved something in front of her face. "What is *this?*"

She could only stare as he dumped the contents of the box on her chest—brochures advertising the new Fernhaven Hotel. These were the papers that were so important to Lorenzo that Jenna had gotten Charlene to come all the way up here?

"Where is my money?" Lorenzo demanded from between clenched teeth. *"Where?"* He slapped the brochures away in a wild gesture, then put the knife to her throat.

"I don't know. I swear. She told me there were important papers in the box."

Lorenzo's gaze seemed to harden to stone. "The two of you were in on this, weren't you? You are going to regret it till your last breath."

An odd icy calm washed over Charlene. She looked at Lorenzo, seeing all the men who had used and abused her, men she'd allowed to hurt her in ways she couldn't bear to remember. Or forget.

And now another man wanted to take pleasure in her pain.

"You're too late," she said, and smiled up at him. "Jenna's gone, and so is your kid *and* your money."

Lorenzo reacted to her words just as she knew he would, and for the first time in her rotten existence Charlene Palmer really was free.

Chapter 15

Jenna. Jenna. He's coming!

She stirred, head aching. "Harry?"

Thank God you're okay.

She blinked and looked around the room, her blood running cold. "Lexi! Where's Lexi?"

She's all right. She's with a cop and a private investigator downstairs. She's safe.

Jenna slumped against the wall in relief. "The police are here?"

Who is Lorenzo Dante?

"My ex-husband," she said, fear turning her stomach.

He's here. Get the gun I put on top of the TV cabinet.

"Where are you?" she asked, looking around the room. "I want to see you."

"I'm here."

She watched him materialize just a few feet away

from her, and felt such a surge of emotion to see him again.

"I'm powerless against him, Jenna. You're the only one who can see me. Feel me."

She nodded, feeling just as powerless against Lorenzo.

"There is something else I need to tell you."

She pushed herself to her feet and had to stop for a moment as her vision dimmed and her head swam.

"It's about the money that was in the duffel bag."

"Charlene took it," she said, and couldn't believe that she'd trusted that woman. It just showed how bad her instincts were. Like now. She looked at Harry. She saw the expression on his face. "No."

"I switched the boxes."

She let out a laugh and shook her head in astonishment. What part of "he's a thief" didn't she get?

"You have to understand. I thought I would spend the rest of eternity here, feeling nothing, being nothing. But then you came and changed everything. I want to be with you, Jenna. I can't stand the thought that when you leave here, I will go back to being nothing again."

"What did you think you were going to do with the money?" Out of the corner of her eye she saw that the suite door stood open. She took a couple of steps toward it.

He grabbed her arm. "It was just an old reflex and this crazy hope that I could buy my way out of here. That I could be with you. I thought with something this strong between us, maybe..."

She looked into his eyes again and realized what he was saying. She felt tears fill her own eyes as he pulled her to him. In his arms, she had believed anything was possible, but now she realized only one of them would be able to leave here. No amount of money could buy Harry Ballantine's way out of Fernhaven.

"He's just outside, Jenna." Harry released her and went to the TV cabinet. He picked up her gun and handed it to her.

She took it, her fingers trembling. She still felt light-headed, and her heart was so filled with regret that the gun felt extra heavy in her hands.

Can you kill him? He'd asked the words in her head.

She met Harry's gaze. He must have seen that instant of hesitation. She heard him groan.

"We're going to need another plan. Quick, come with me."

Fog drifted past on a light breeze as Lorenzo cautiously approached the hotel.

Jenna couldn't have gotten away. Charlene had to be lying. He wiped a smear of her blood from his knuckles onto his pants, wondering what she'd done with his money.

What nagged at him was that Charlene had looked as surprised as he'd been when the money hadn't been in the box.

He slowed. The afternoon was dark, the clouds low and heavy with moisture. Mist moved through the air like floating cobwebs, and a strange cold feeling seemed to settle in his bones.

A light glowed in the lobby, and in front of it he saw figures in the lobby—Rose Garcia and the man she'd arrived with.

Apparently the man had been shot, because Rose was helping him. Alexandria was with her.

Lorenzo swore as he watched them disappear from

view. He didn't need any more trouble. All he wanted was his money. And Jenna.

Staying in the shadows, he moved up the steps and across the wide porch. No sign of Rose and the man. Where had they gone? He drew his gun and eased open the front door. The place was eerily empty. The lush, thick carpet muffled his footfalls as he moved quickly to the registration desk and quietly checked the book.

The first guest since 1936 was a Jenna Johnson. Johnson? Yeah, right. According to the book, she was in room 318. So Charlene at least hadn't lied about that. All the cubbyholes behind the desk contained two keys, except for the slot marked 318. It had only one in it.

He pocketed the key with a smile and turned toward the elevator.

As he did he heard a sound coming from behind the door marked Manager. He heard Rose Garcia calling the police. Too late to stop her. He'd just have to move quickly and finish his business here before the cops arrived.

At the elevator, he pushed the button and waited. He was considering taking the stairs instead when the elevator doors opened and he saw an elderly, gray-haired man. The man's surprised gaze went from Lorenzo's face to the gun in his hand.

Lorenzo stepped in, the elevator doors closing behind him as he reached over and hit the third-floor button.

"Who the—" That's all the old man got out before Lorenzo backhanded him with the gun. The old man slid slowly to the floor as the elevator hummed upward.

Locked inside the manager's office, Rose worked to stop Mike's bleeding. She'd pulled off her jacket and folded the soft fabric, pressing it against the gunshot wound. Mike was pale, his skin clammy.

"A lot of help *I* was to you," he said.

She smiled at him. "You're just a high-priced private eye. You're not used to women shooting at you. Or are you?"

His smile was feeble. "I didn't see the gun in her hand until it was too late. I was looking at you and Lexi."

That's what she'd feared.

Lexi was crying softly. Rose pulled her closer. "It's all right." She met Mike's gaze. "I've called for backup and an ambulance."

He nodded and covered her hand with his. Their eyes met and she felt her heart drop like a stone. "Don't dare think about taking off on me," she murmured. They both knew what she meant.

"Not a chance," he whispered. "Not after I finally got you to admit you wanted to date me."

She looked at Lexi. Where was the little girl's mother? Was Jenna still alive?

"Go on," he said. "Find Jenna. I'll be all right. I'll take care of Lexi."

He looked as if he might pass out at any moment. Rose knew if she left him he might die. She glanced from Mike to the little girl. Lexi had curled up beside Mike, hugging her rag doll and looking terrified.

"I know what you came up here to do," Mike said quietly.

Kill Lorenzo, Rose thought.

"Go ahead. I wasn't going to try to stop you," Mike said.

She felt the pull. She was a cop. A cop on medical leave. Out of her jurisdiction. On a mission. She *had* come up here to make sure Lorenzo Dante was stopped for good, and Mike knew it.

"Several of the highway patrol are close by because of more flooding on the road," she said.

She could hear sirens in the distance. They would be here soon.

"I'll be all right," he whispered.

She shook her head. She couldn't leave this scared little girl alone with a man who might bleed to death while she was gone. "The highway patrol will find Jenna and help her." If Jenna was still alive.

Rose looked into Mike's eyes. She had thought she would do anything to stop Lorenzo Dante. But she was wrong. "I'm not leaving you," she whispered. "Or Lexi. Come here, sweetheart," she said to the little girl. Rose might not be able to help Jenna right now, but she could protect her daughter. "Everything is going to be all right."

Lexi moved into the circle of Rose's arm as the three huddled in the dim office, the sirens growing louder and louder.

Harry drew her down the hallway. Jenna heard the elevator begin to rise three floors below. She looked up at the dial over the closed doors. Someone was coming up. Lorenzo?

The stairs. Take the stairs!

She looked around for the door to the stairway. Harry grabbed her hand and they ran down the hallway as the elevator dinged behind them. They were still yards away when the elevator opened.

Harry pulled Jenna into one of the rooms that wasn't quite finished yet.

She tried to hold her breath as she heard the heavy

tread of footfalls on the hall carpet. The elevator doors closed. Silence. Then she heard the door to suite 318 bang open. She looked over at Harry. He motioned for her to wait.

She looked into his eyes—bottomless blue eyes. She tried to imagine living in the same time he had, being with him then, and her heart ached. She thought about opening night at Fernhaven, June 12, 1936.

Closing her eyes, she imagined being in the big ballroom with Harry, dancing to the music of the orchestra. She could almost smell all the flowers she'd seen on the tables, their scents mixing with the expensive perfumes the women were wearing.

Jenna would be dressed in a gown the color of Harry's eyes. He would hold her close and they would sway to the music. She could almost feel his heart beating next to hers to the old-fashioned strains... Then she heard the sound of breaking glass, and Lorenzo swearing.

Lorenzo stared down at the broken lamp on the floor, then looked around for something else he could destroy. If Jenna was hiding in here, he'd find her.

He still had the gun in his hand, but he wasn't going to shoot her. He thought he might choke the life out of her so he could watch her die. He wanted to be the last thing she saw when she left this earth.

He couldn't believe this was where she'd been staying. A suite? The bitch had been staying in this elegant place on his money?

He moved deeper into the suite to check in the closets, under the bed. He'd seen her suitcases by the door. If she'd left, she'd left everything behind. Just taken the money, he thought with fury.

That's when he heard the creak of door hinges down

the hallway, and swung around. The stairs. He could hear her footfalls on the steps.

Jenna ran down the stairs, practically throwing herself down the stairwell. It was cold and gray in here, and her footfalls echoed loudly.

She couldn't hear if Lorenzo was behind her, if he was gaining on her. Nor could she hear or see Harry. Was he still with her?

Then she heard the door bang open above her, heard Lorenzo's lumbering steps, as if he was half falling down the stairs in his rush to catch her.

Breathe.

Her heart thundered in her ears, louder than the horrible sound of Lorenzo gaining on her. And she felt an overwhelming sense of relief that Harry was still with her.

Then, suddenly, there was the exit door. Ground floor.

Take that door.

She shoved it open and stumbled out into the stormy darkness, met by a wave of cold dampness. It took her a moment to realize where she was. The courtyard. The only light was around the fountain. Everywhere else held pockets of shadow and mist.

Run to the path up the mountain.

"Harry?"

Run. You have to trust me.

Trust him? She could hear Lorenzo coming down the stairs.

Wait.

She had reached the edge of the courtyard, where the dense forest began.

Wait for him.

She stopped. "Harry, you're scaring me."

I'm going to help you. But you have to trust me. Can you do that, Jenna?

She took a deep breath and let it out.

Mist rose from the hot pools as Jenna waited at the edge of the courtyard for Lorenzo, wondering what she was doing. More to the point, what Harry was planning.

Let him see you, then take the path behind you. Trust me.

She let out a small laugh, half-hysterical, at the sound of Harry's voice in her head. She'd more than lost her mind. She was about to lose her life. At least Lexi was safe. She did trust that Harry had told her the truth about her daughter. She could hear the sound of sirens growing closer.

There he is.

She could feel the gun tucked at the small of her back. Through the steam rising off the hot pools she saw Lorenzo come out the door into the courtyard. He spotted her and smiled as he began walking toward her.

This was crazy. But Harry was right about one thing. It had to end on this mountain. Jenna couldn't live in fear the rest of her life. She had to protect her daughter.

She turned and started up the path, through the dense woods, as Harry had instructed. As she climbed, following the narrow track, the trees like a wall on each side of her, the clouds grew darker, the fog thicker. She could barely see two feet in front of her.

She didn't look back, just kept climbing. Lorenzo wasn't worried about catching her. His arrogance wouldn't allow him to hurry. He thought he had her right where he wanted her. Maybe he did. Maybe this voice inside her head was of her own making. If so, then Lorenzo had driven her to this.

We're almost there.

The sound of Harry's voice sent a stab of yearning through her. She hadn't lost her mind. Instead, she'd found something else here at Fernhaven. Something she couldn't bear to lose.

She slowed as the path reached a small clearing. Mist swirled around large boulders and wind-twisted trunks of cedar trees.

Walk just ahead and wait for him. Stop.

Jenna stared back the way they'd come. A breeze stirred the tops of the trees, swirling the fog and mist, making a low groaning sound. The air was cold and damp and seemed to cut through her clothing. She hugged herself to still her trembling as she caught a glimpse of something moving through the fog toward her. Lorenzo?

She drew the gun and started to take a step back, but Harry stopped her.

There's a cliff behind you.

Jenna swung around. She could see nothing but fog. She kicked a small rock and heard it drop over the side, hit way below her, then again, the sound echoing up until she heard nothing. She could feel Harry with her.

Jenna...

She turned back around, hearing something in Harry's voice that scared her more than standing on the edge of a cliff.

"What is it?"

We're not alone. I don't know who it is.

She heard a strange sound in his voice and began to shake harder as a figure slowly took shape out of the mist.

Raymond Valencia stopped just yards from her. He

looked odd, his clothing almost too neat after the climb up the mountain.

"Raymond?" Why did she get the feeling it wasn't really him? "What are you doing here?"

"He can't save you, Jenna," Raymond said. "He was never interested in saving you—only himself. He's a con man, Jenna. A thief. Haven't you realized that?"

Who was Raymond talking about? Lorenzo?

"He tricked you, Jenna. Made you fall in love with him. You think it's a coincidence you ended up at Fernhaven?" He shook his head. "He willed you here, knowing you were in trouble."

She shook her own head. "I don't know what you're talking about."

"Harry Ballantine, Jenna. He's the one who got you here so you could save *his* life."

She stared at Raymond, her heart in her throat. Raymond Valencia knew about Harry?

"Tell her, Harry. You stole Bobby John Chamberlain's identity so you could attend the Fernhaven grand opening to steal the jewelry you knew would be here. But you got caught in the fire. Except Bobby John Chamberlain was supposed to die. Not you. Not Harry Ballantine. Come on out, Harry. Show yourself. Don't be shy."

"How do you know all this?" Jenna cried.

"Because Raymond Valencia's dead, Jenna," Harry said, materializing beside her. "His helicopter crashed not far from here in the storm."

"That's right, Jenna," Raymond said. "I can't help you, either. But I can warn you. Harry wins either way. If he fails, he's trapped here for eternity. But then so are you."

She felt her knees go weak. None of this was happening. She was still inside the hotel on the floor, suffering from a concussion after Charlene had hit her. Maybe she was dead. Or maybe just dreaming.

"There is no redemption for Harry Ballantine because of the life he led before his untimely death," Raymond said. "No matter what he does, he isn't leaving this place. Save yourself, Jenna, before it's too late."

Redemption? Is that what this was about? The mist seemed to engulf Raymond. Jenna stared at the spot where he'd been standing, but he was gone.

She looked over at Harry. Their eyes met. Was it true? Was he nothing but a thief and a con man? Had he lured her here for his own reasons? "Tell me what he said isn't true."

His image seemed to fade. He said nothing.

She heard the snap of a twig, the scuff of a shoe on stone. Lorenzo came lumbering up over the rise. He looked winded and his pants were muddy, as if he'd fallen.

He leaned against one of the large rocks, obviously trying to catch his breath, but his eyes were on her. His lips turned up in a smile. "Looks like it's just you and me, Jenna. You shouldn't have taken my money."

Jenna took a step toward him, remembering the cliff behind her. Lorenzo had strength and size on his side, not to mention a weapon under his jacket. Lorenzo always had a weapon close by.

He pushed himself off the huge rock he'd been leaning on and sauntered toward her. "You didn't really think you could get away from me, did you?"

"No," she said, realizing she never had. "I guess I always knew this moment would come."

He was close enough that she could smell him, the

sweat, the blood, the stale, leftover fear. "This is some freaky place you picked to hide in, you know?"

If he only knew. She drew the gun from behind her and pointed it at his heart.

He froze in midstep. "What do you think you're doing?" He let out a coarse laugh. "You don't even know how to use a gun."

She fired off a shot that ricocheted off the rocks behind him.

He swallowed, his face going slack, a flicker of fear showing in his eyes. "So you learned how to fire a gun. You ever see a bullet rip through flesh? Ever see someone die right before your eyes? It's an ugly sight, Jenna, one you would never get out of your head." His smile broadened. "Firing a shot into the air is one thing. But put a bullet into a man? The man who fathered your daughter? The man who you once loved?"

He started to step closer.

"Don't!" Jenna cried, her finger tensing on the trigger. He was right about one thing. She couldn't shoot him.

She lowered the gun, dropping it to her feet as she braced herself.

She'd already decided there was only one thing she could do: grab him and take him with her over the edge of the cliff. She tried not to think about leaving Lexi behind, because that would make her weak, and right now Jenna had to be strong. Dying herself was one thing, but she couldn't leave Lorenzo free. Couldn't leave knowing he could get her baby girl.

Lorenzo smiled. "I knew you couldn't shoot me."

She thought about what Raymond had said—that Harry had brought her here. That if he couldn't find a way to leave, then he would make sure she didn't, either. Was that why he'd brought her up here? He wanted her to die and be trapped here with him?

After you grab him, drop down and let the momentum of his motion propel him over your head and out.

At first she wasn't even sure she'd heard Harry, let alone heard him correctly.

Raymond's right, I can't save you. All I can do is try to help you. If you should fall, try to stay close to the edge of the cliff. There's a ledge about ten feet below you.

A ledge ten feet down. Right. "Always a con man, huh?"

Lorenzo frowned at her words. *"What?"* He quickly glanced behind him. "Who are you talking to?"

Jenna, Raymond was wrong, though, about us. If it makes any difference, I didn't bring you here. You were sent to me. I thought it was because we were supposed to be together. I guess I was wrong about that. Something is happening to me. Hurry. I feel as if I don't have much time.

"I asked you who you were talking to," Lorenzo snapped, and stuck his face into hers.

She grabbed him by the jacket and did as Harry told her, jerking him hard and at the same time ducking down. Her shoulder caught him in the groin. He let out a howl. His larger, heavier body went airborne over the top of her.

She'd done it!

Then she felt his fingers clutch the back of her jacket and find purchase. She was jerked backward. She grabbed at the ground, but the weight of his body pulled her over the edge of the cliff.

She turned in the air, throwing herself into the movement, breaking Lorenzo's hold on her as she shoved him away, propelling him outward and her toward the cliff.

But now she was falling, and below there was nothing but fog and the sound of Lorenzo's screams.

Jenna saw the ledge coming up at the very last moment. She closed her eyes, bracing herself for the inevitable. She hit, but something—someone—broke her fall.

She lay stone still for a moment, trying to catch her breath. Below her, Lorenzo's screams stopped with a sickening thud.

She closed her eyes and told herself it was over. She was alive. Lexi was safe. They would never have to fear Lorenzo again. "Harry?"

No answer.

Tears welled behind her closed lids. A sob escaped her lips and she choked on her tears. She had won. But her loss was overwhelming.

"Will I ever see you again?" she asked in a whisper.

She tried to feel his presence, but could sense him slipping away. She choked back more tears. "Do you have to stay here?"

Still no answer.

In the distance she could hear sirens and voices calling out for her.

But inside her head there was nothing but silence.

Chapter 16

Jenna remembered little of the rest of that afternoon and night. Fernhaven had been crawling with police. There were dozens of questions, statements to be made, bodies to identify.

Only one memory would remain from the moment Jenna was lifted off the rock ledge and taken back to the hotel.

That image was the sight of her daughter running out of the back of the hotel and across the courtyard to meet her.

Jenna had fallen to her knees, throwing open her arms as Lexi ran into them. She'd crushed her daughter to her breast, crying tears of joy. They were alive. They had survived.

Lorenzo Dante was dead, his body broken at the bottom of the cliff. Raymond Valencia's body had been found along with the ruins of his helicopter, which had gone down in the storm not a half mile from Fernhaven.

Detective Rose Garcia had ridden down the mountain in the ambulance with P.I. Mike Flannigan. He was listed in stable condition. Word was he would recover. Security guard Elmer Thompson had suffered a slight concussion, but would recuperate.

Four other bodies had been found. Rico Santos was discovered dead in his car back down the highway. Rico, a known criminal, had been murdered in what looked like a professional hit.

Farther down the road, Gene "Jolly" Barker was also found murdered in his car. Same MO.

Charlene Palmer, sister of criminal Stan Palmer, had been stabbed to death in the hotel parking lot.

Alfredo Jones was also found dead in his car—shot at close range.

If she could have, Jenna would have left as soon as the police were through questioning her. But she had to wait until a rental car arrived from the nearest town.

The hotel provided everyone with rooms. Jenna asked for one on ground level. She couldn't bear to stay in room 318, knowing that was where Harry Ballantine, aka Bobby John Chamberlain, had died.

She put an exhausted Lexi down to sleep. "Can we go to the ocean now?" Lexi asked before she drifted off.

"Yes."

"Is Daddy gone?" Lexi asked quietly.

Jenna had told her that Lorenzo had an accident and was killed. "Yes, honey, he's gone."

Lexi looked sad. "Is he gone because I wanted a new daddy?"

Jenna hugged her daughter to her. "No, baby. He's gone because he couldn't love us enough. You and me, we deserve someone who loves us…bigger than the sky."

Lexi laughed and looked up into her mother's face. "Bigger than the sky?"

Jenna nodded, fighting tears.

The events of the past few days didn't seem to have scarred her daughter in the least. But Lexi had youth on her side, and what to her was a happy ending. All the bad guys were dead or in jail. Jenna and Lexi were both safe.

Jenna was just glad her daughter realized they had to leave.

As Jenna curled up on the bed, she prayed Harry would come to her in her sleep.

He didn't.

The next morning the hotel was still buzzing with police and crime-scene investigators.

Jenna loaded the suitcases into the rental SUV, checked to make sure Lexi had buckled herself in to the car seat, and put Fred next to her.

Then she slid behind the wheel. As she started the car, she glanced at Fernhaven. In the morning sun, mist bathed the rooftops, the mountain behind the hotel shimmered a verdant green and Fernhaven looked like a fairy princess's castle.

She hurriedly looked away, turning the SUV around and heading off the mountainside. She didn't look back. She couldn't.

"Hey!"

Jenna glanced in her side mirror and saw a man who'd been talking to one of the policemen. He waved to her to stop. She braked and lowered her window as he ran up to her side of the car.

"Hi," he said, and smiled.

He wore jeans, boots and a leather bomber jacket, and he had a knapsack thrown over his shoulder.

Jenna stared up at him. There was something familiar about the man. The smooth, self-confident way he moved. The set of his broad shoulders. Something so familiar, and yet she knew she had never seen the man before in her life.

"Any chance of hitching a ride out of here?" he asked.

"Sure."

His hair was a tawny blond, long at the neck, curling up over his collar. His smile broadened as he crouched next to the car so she didn't have to look up. His eyes were a clear deep blue.

"I kind of got stranded up here," he said. He glanced in the back seat and gave Lexi a wink. "It's the strangest thing. If I told you how I got here, you wouldn't believe it."

She looked into his eyes and saw something that lifted her heart like helium. Was it possible? "Where are you headed?" she asked. If Fernhaven had taught her anything, it was that there were things beyond earthly understanding.

"Don't really have a destination in mind, to tell you the truth." He laughed, the sound making Jenna's pulse quicken with a familiar excitement.

She glanced back at her daughter. Lexi was smiling at the man in a way that made her heart jump.

"We're going to the ocean," Lexi said excitedly. "Aren't we, Mommy?"

"Yes, we are," Jenna said. That was exactly where they were going.

"No kiddin'? I grew up on the California coast. You headed that far south?"

"Quite possibly," she said, surprising herself, scaring herself, and yet having never felt so right about anything.

He laughed again, wiped his right hand on his jeans and stuck it in the window. "John James Harrison. My friends call me Harrison."

Jenna's hand trembled a little as she shook his hand. It was large and warm and fit hers perfectly. "Jenna... McDonald. This is my daughter, Lexi, and the cat is Fred."

"Glad to meet you and I appreciate the ride," he said as he ran around to open the door and slide in. He smelled of the outdoors, a mixture of fresh air and green trees. "I'm planning to keep both feet on the ground for a while."

"Oh?" Jenna asked as she got the car moving again.

"I'm a helicopter pilot," he said as he settled in, putting the knapsack on the floor between the bucket seats. "My last job just about killed me."

"Really?" Jenna said, thinking about the chopper crash that had killed Raymond Valencia. This man had been the pilot? And he'd walked away without a scratch?

"Someone must have been watching out for me up there," he said, looking out the windshield to the blue sky overhead. "I thought for sure I was a goner. That was one close call. Something like that changes you. I know it sounds corny, but I feel as if I've been given a second chance. Silly, huh?"

Jenna shook her head, thinking of Harry Ballantine and second chances. "No, that's a feeling I'm pretty familiar with," she said and smiled over at the man beside her.

* * * * *

We hope you enjoyed reading

The Presence

by *New York Times* bestselling author

HEATHER GRAHAM

and

When Twilight Comes

by *New York Times* bestselling author

B.J. DANIELS

Originally MIRA Books and
Harlequin® Intrigue stories!

From passionate, suspenseful and dramatic
love stories to inspirational or historical,
Harlequin offers different lines to
satisfy every romance reader.

New books in each line
are available every month.

"Bad luck always comes in threes."

Standing in the large kitchen of the Sterling Montana Guest
Ranch, Will Sterling shot the woman an impatient look. "I don't
have time for this right now, Dorothea."

"Just sayin'," Dorothea Brand muttered under her breath. The
fifty-year-old housekeeper was short and stout with a helmet of
dark hair and piercing dark eyes. She'd been a fixture on the ranch
since Will and his brothers were kids, which made her invaluable,
but also as bossy as an old mother hen.

After the Sterling boys had lost their mother, Dorothea had
stepped in. Their father, Wyatt, had continued to run the guest
ranch alone and then with the help of his sons until his death last
year. For the first time, Will would finally be running the guest
ranch without his father calling all the shots. He'd been looking
forward to the challenge and to carrying on the family business.

But now his cook was laid up with a broken leg? He definitely
didn't like the way the season was starting, Will thought as the
housekeeper leaned against the counter, giving him one of her
you're-going-to-regret-this looks as he considered who he could
call.

As his brother Garrett brought in a box of supplies from town,
Will asked, "Do you know anyone who can cook?"

"What about Poppy Carmichael?" Garrett suggested as he
pulled a bottle of water from the refrigerator, opened it and took a
long drink. "She's a caterer now."

Will frowned. "Poppy?" An image appeared of a girl with freckles, braces, skinned knees and reddish-brown hair in pigtails. "I haven't thought of Poppy in years. I thought she moved away."

"She did, but she came back about six months ago and started a catering business in Whitefish," Garrett said. "I only know because I ran into her at a party recently. The food was really good, if that helps."

"Wait, I remember her. Cute kid. Didn't her father work for the forest service?" their younger brother Shade asked as he also came into the kitchen with a box of supplies. He deposited the box inside the large pantry just off the kitchen. "Last box," he announced, dusting off his hands.

"You remember, Will. Poppy and her dad lived in the old forest service cabin a mile or so from here," Garrett said, grinning at him. "She used to ride her bike over here and help us with our chores. At least, that was her excuse."

Will avoided his brother's gaze. It wasn't like he'd ever forgotten.

"I just remember the day she decided to ride Lightning," Shade said. "She climbed up on the corral, and as the horse ran by, she jumped on it!" He shook his head, clearly filled with admiration. "I can't imagine what she thought she was going to do, riding him bareback." He laughed. "She stayed on a lot longer than I thought she would. But it's a wonder she didn't kill herself. The girl had grit. But I always wondered what possessed her to do that."

Garrett laughed and shot another look at Will. "She was trying to impress our brother."

"That poor little girl was smitten," Dorothea agreed as she narrowed her dark gaze at Will. "And you, being fifteen and full of yourself, often didn't give her the time of day. So what could possibly go wrong hiring her to cook for you?"

Don't miss
Stroke of Luck *by B.J. Daniels, available March 2019*
wherever HQN Books and ebooks are sold.

www.Harlequin.com

PHBJDEXP0319

HARLEQUIN®

INTRIGUE

EDGE-OF-YOUR-SEAT INTRIGUE, FEARLESS ROMANCE.

Save $1.00

on the purchase of

ANY Harlequin Intrigue® book.

Available wherever books are sold, including most bookstores, supermarkets, drugstores and discount stores.

Save $1.00

on the purchase of any Harlequin Intrigue® book.

Coupon valid until March 1, 2019.
Redeemable at participating outlets in the U.S. and Canada only.
Not redeemable at Barnes & Noble stores. Limit one coupon per customer.

52616219

5 65373 00076 2 (8100)0 12407